SERWA BOATENG'S
GUIDE TO
VAMPIRE HUNTING

SERWA BOATENG'S
GUIDE TO
VAMPIRE HUNTING

by Roseanne A. Brown

RICK RIORDAN PRESENTS

DISNEP • HYPERION   LOS ANGELES   NEW YORK

All rights reserved. Published by Disney • Hyperion, an imprint of Buena
Vista Books, Inc. No part of this book may be reproduced or transmitted in
any form or by any means, electronic or mechanical, including photocopying,
recording, or by any information storage and retrieval system, without written
permission from the publisher. For information address Disney • Hyperion,
77 West 66th Street, New York, New York 10023.

First Edition, September 2022
1 3 5 7 9 10 8 6 4 2
FAC-004510-22203
Printed in the United States of America

This book is set in Meridien LT Std/Adobe Systems
Designed by Zareen Johnson

Library of Congress Cataloging-in-Publication Data

Names: Brown, Roseanne A., author.
Title: Serwa Boateng's guide to vampire hunting / by Roseanne A. Brown.
Description: First edition. • Los Angeles ; New York : Disney/Hyperion,
    2022. • Audience: Ages 10–14. • Audience: Grades 5–9 • Summary: After
    her home is attacked by shapeshifting vampires, twelve-year-old Serwa
    Boateng is sent to live with her aunt and cousin in Maryland, but the
    aspiring vampire hunter discovers that middle school is harder than it
    appears on television, especially when she has to avoid detention and
    turn her classmates into warriors before they become vampire food.
Identifiers: LCCN 2021052031 • ISBN 9781368066365 (hardcover) •
    ISBN 9781368066402 (ebook)
Subjects: CYAC: Vampires—Fiction. • Magic—Fiction. • Mythology,
    African—Fiction. • Ghanaians—United States—Fiction. • Good and
    evil—Fiction. • Middle schools—Fiction. • Schools—Fiction. •
    Supernatural—Fiction. • LCGFT: Novels. • Paranormal fiction.
Classification: LCC PZ7.1.B7967 Se 2022 • DDC [Fic]—dc23
LC record available at https://lccn.loc.gov/2021052031

Reinforced binding
Follow @ReadRiordan
Visit www.DisneyBooks.com

To my grandparents—Akwei Bonso, Nteshi Odametey, Kwame Akuamoah, Afua Amoakoa, and Akosua Afi.

And to every person carving a space for themselves where the world refuses to make one.

This one's for us.

CONTENTS

Grab Your Sword and Your Spaghetti.
We're Going to War.

YOU CAN ONLY CHOOSE one. Would you rather:

A) Live with your parents as they travel the world, hunting vampiric monsters called adze, learning to handle a battle-ax and sword, and drawing magical Adinkra symbols, knowing you could die any minute?

Or:

B) Go to middle school?

If you chose B, what are you thinking? B is clearly the more dangerous option.

Serwa Boateng has lived the good life. She's full-on option A. She has spent most of her twelve years learning how to slay vampires, accompanying her parents on dangerous missions wherever the ruling council of Okomfo sends them, and just waiting for the day when she will get her own Adinkra tattoo that marks her as a full member of the Abomofuo—the ancient and powerful Ghanaian order of Slayers.

Then everything goes wrong. After an unthinkable attack, Serwa's parents send her to a cousin's house in the middle of nowhere to live like a normal kid and—THE HORROR—attend school for the first time. That's right, vampire slayers. You think you're tough? Wait until you meet Rocky Gorge Middle School. There will be cliques. There will be detention. There will be spaghetti fights.

Just when Serwa starts to think she might be able to handle seventh grade, her old problems come back to haunt her, too. There may actually be an adze in Rocky Gorge—but now Serwa is cut off from her parents and any possibility of magical assistance. She's on her own against bloodsucking fiends of both the monstrous and middle school variety.

Humor. Heart. Mythology. Action. Tragedy. Triumph. Lovable characters. And a conclusion that will leave you screaming, "Where is the sequel?!" With this book, you *don't* have to choose only one option, because *Serwa Boateng's Guide to Vampire Hunting* has all of the above!

I have always loved the folklore of Ghana. Adinkra symbols are a beautiful, powerful way of thinking about the world. The monsters are terrifying. The gods are magnificent. (Sometimes the gods are terrifying, and the monsters are magnificent.) The magic makes so much sense yet is absolutely revelatory. And the Abomofuo are top-notch, world-class vampire slayers that put Van Helsing to shame.

This is a book I have been craving for at least thirty years, when I first learned about Ghanaian mythology and wished I had more adventure stories about it to share with my middle school students. Thank goodness Roseanne A. Brown has stepped up to the plate and delivered us this home run of a novel!

She writes about living between worlds—Ghana and America, childhood and adulthood, the magical and the mundane—and about navigating the liminal spaces to find one's own identity when one feels like they belong partly everywhere but completely nowhere. This is something many readers will relate to. Rosie writes her characters with such lyrical power, wit, and empathy that you can't help falling in love with Serwa Boateng, her family, and her friends. You will want to *be* Serwa Boateng. I know I do. I would even agree to chill with the family mmoatia and watch reruns of *The Bachelor* if it meant I could learn to draw Adinkra symbols and borrow Mom's battle-ax every once in a while.

So grab your sword. Grab a bowl of spaghetti. Grab whatever weapon you can find and gird yourself for battle, readers. We have some vampires to hunt.

Rick Riordan

I

How to Be Attacked by a Vampire

*"A Slayer must be combat-ready at all hours of the day.
The forces of black magic never falter. Neither do we."*

—From the *Nwoma*, a collection of
Abomofuo teachings and histories passed
down through the generations

TAKE IT FROM ME: A mom lecture is 1,000 percent more terrifying when she's holding an ax.

"Again, this is a one-time thing," says Mom as she dangles the throwing ax in front of my face. The weapon is nearly as long as my arm, with three razor-sharp points designed to inflict some serious damage when thrown correctly. "One. Time. As in, never happening again, *ever*."

I nod along, too focused on the ax's curved blades to really hear her. I still can't believe she's letting me train with it. I've had my eye on this baby ever since we picked it up during a raid on some adze down in Memphis a few months ago, but every time I asked my parents if I could even touch it, all I got was a *no* or a *no but with hysterical laughter* in response.

But it's my birthday this week, and it's a family tradition that the birthday person can have whatever they want for seven days straight. (Within reason. Dad's still salty that his request for all of us to binge *The Crown* last year got shot down.) That's why for the first—and probably last—time in my admittedly short life, my request to use the ax was actually accepted, and now here we are.

Mom continues, "If I ever see you near this without me or your father present, I will suspend your training indefinitely and confiscate your crossbows—*all* your crossbows. Do you hear me, Serwa?"

"Yes, ma'am!" I say, giving her a mock salute. I reach for the ax, but Mom suddenly swings it over her shoulder, not even flinching as one of the sharpened points comes dangerously close to leaving her earless and hacking off several inches of her shoulder-length twist bob.

"Actually, the ax is too dangerous." A line forms between her eyebrows, and I fight back a groan. I know that face. That's her *Will doing this make me the worst parent of the century?* face. "Maybe we should start you off with something safer. Like a throwing knife. Or a mace."

"Mom, you promised!" I cry. My parents will have these random moments of overprotectiveness, as if our family's lifestyle wasn't dangerous with a capital *D* generations before any of us came along. Why did they spend all this time training me if they're going to act like I can't handle myself when it really counts?

A loud chuckle cuts into our argument. Dad is knee-deep in his flower garden, his comically large sun hat pulled low over his brow. Bright pink begonia petals litter his dark brown skin as he digs up the tubers so he can store them before autumn starts. "Just let her take one swing, Delilah, or we're never going to hear the end of it."

I give Dad a mental high five as Mom narrows her eyes at him.

The water of the lake laps gently near our feet, and I imagine how hilarious this whole situation would look to an outsider—a grown man and woman debating over letting their daughter handle a magically enhanced weapon while they all stand beside a lake so blue it looks ripped from a postcard.

The line in Mom's brow deepens. "Akwadaa boni," she mutters with a kiss of her teeth. That means *troublesome child* in Twi, our native language. We mostly speak English around one another ever since we moved from Ghana when I was five, but she'll slip into Twi whenever she feels any strong emotion, good or bad.

Just when I'm sure Mom is going to say no again, she tosses the ax to me, handle first. I grab it at the last second. Carved into the side of the blade is a square filled with crisscrossing lines almost like a checkerboard—nkyimu, the Adinkra of precision. The magic imbued in the symbol hums through the weapon, making it steadier and more likely to hit its target.

"Keep both hands on the handle and the top point straight," says Mom, and I readjust accordingly. "Nkyimu will help you hit your target, but not if you aren't actually facing it. Adze move fast, so you always have to calculate your throw for where it's going to be, not where it is."

As Mom kicks my feet apart to fix my stance, I close my eyes and imagine an adze—first as a firefly, floating through the air like any other harmless bug, then as a hulking insect-like monster with razor-sharp wings and blood dripping down its fangs. The vampire in my mind screams at me, and I mentally lop its head off with one swing, feeling a lot like Thor must have when he showed up in Wakanda to save all the other Avengers' butts. Oh yeah, this is *definitely* an upgrade from my janky old training ax.

Out of the corner of my eye, I see Dad shaking his head.

"Girls and their weapons," he chuckles as he pulls out another begonia tuber and places it in a little bag. I stick out my tongue at him, and he sticks his out at me. My dad's been involved with the Abomofuo, the organization that hunts adze and other creatures of black magic, even longer than my mom. But though he knows his way around a battlefield, he's not a big fan of combat. He often jokes that if he had his way, he'd trade all his swords for knitting needles. Whenever he says that, Mom pretends to barf.

It's been so long since the three of us hung out at home like this. Only last night we got back from a three-month mission in Georgia, tracking down an adze that had sucked the blood out of the entire city government of Savannah and turned the mayor into a zoned-out husk. The whole time we were there, we stayed in this motel off Interstate 16 and survived almost entirely on Chinese takeout and Dunkin' Donuts.

I love a good hunt, I really do. There's nothing better than weeks of planning coming together as you rush into battle to free someone from the vampire that's taken over their mind. But being on the road all the time can get tough. We move safe houses every year or so, but this little blue one on the lake is my favorite yet. I've missed sleeping in my own bed and using my own bathroom. I've even missed that one floorboard on the stairs that cracks like a firework when you step on it. The only house I love more than this one is my grandma's compound back in Kumasi, where we lived until I was five. But we haven't been back to Ghana in years, and we probably won't be seeing it anytime soon.

Mom twists my shoulders so I'm facing away from Dad and toward the lake. Even without the ax, she's still armed to the teeth with daggers at each wrist, stakes in a utility belt across her chest, and her trusty akrafena, Nokware—*truth* in Twi—in its bead-bracelet form on her wrist. My mother wears her sword more often than most people do underwear. With Nokware at her side, Mom's become one of—no, *the* best adze slayer in the world.

Which means if I'm ever going to be the best adze slayer *of all time*, I should start by being at least as good as her.

"Hey, Mom, heads up!" That's all the warning I give before I launch at her, ax swinging. Dad yells in surprise, but Mom doesn't even flinch. She whips out one of her daggers from its wrist sheath faster than I can see, and our weapons crash together with a *clang* that ripples across the lake.

"Is that all you've got?" she taunts as she dances out of range of my weapon, black twists trailing behind her. "You're going to need more than that if you're coming for the best." I grunt and pull back, pivoting on my left foot to put more power into my next swing. But Mom counters with a swipe to my right, followed by an elbow thrust to my gut, sending us both tumbling back into the garden.

Dad jumps to his feet with a shriek as we roll by. "My begonias!"

"Sorry!" Mom and I both call out, but the destruction of Dad's flower garden isn't enough to get us to stop. Mom taught me everything I know about battle, from the best way to dive into a roll to how to get adze gunk out of your armor. I'm good, but she's better, and before long it starts to show. She matches me blow for blow, at one point switching her dagger to her left hand as if to prove that even fighting with a disadvantage she's still better than me.

Sweat is pouring into my eyes and I'm panting like a dog, while she has this huge smile on her face like she could take on ten more of me before getting tired. Sometimes I swear my mom is some kind of demon, because that's the only way she can fight as well as she does.

Mom ducks down, and I see an opening for me to dive for her neck, pin her down, and end this. But as soon as I commit to the maneuver, she feints behind me. In less than a heartbeat she knocks me off-balance and wrenches the ax from my grip. She tosses the weapon to the side, then begins to tickle me mercilessly.

"Surrender!" she demands.

"Never!" At that, she tickles me harder, and there are actual tears in my eyes now, but the good kind. Finally, it becomes too much, and I yell, "Okay, okay! I give up!"

Mom lets me go, and we both collapse onto our backs. My chest is heaving, Mom is cracking up, and Dad is shaking his head at both of us, but the huge grin on his face makes it clear he's not mad.

As far as birthday weeks go, this has been a pretty great one. Now that the Savannah hunt is done and our mmoatia have sent the official debrief to the Compound, we have nothing on our roster for at least the next several weeks. Today's lunch is jollof rice with a huge serving of powdered bofrot and ice cream on the side, and in two days, for my actual birthday, we're going to go camping up in the Adirondacks. Thanks to the protective Adinkra wards my dad draws, the safe house is completely safeguarded from adze.

Soon enough, the Okomfo who run the Abomofuo will send us another mission. Slayers don't get any say in where they're assigned—if the priests tell you that you're needed in Budapest, then you'd better practice your Hungarian, because you're going to Budapest. That's part of the Okomfo's job—keeping their wrinkly, old thumbs on the pulse of supernatural happenings all over the globe. Eventually, they'll dispatch us to whatever corner of the country needs our vampire-slaying expertise, but until then, we're free to do whatever we want.

After she finally finishes laughing at my expense, Mom rolls onto her side, facing me, and props her head on her fist. Everyone says we look alike, but I honestly don't see it. She's got these high cheekbones and one of those smiles that always make her seem like she knows something you don't, but whenever I try to replicate it, I just look like a serial killer. We do have the same skin tone, though—dark cherry brown—and the same kinky, coily curls, though right now mine are in box braids I usually wear in a high ponytail.

"You've got a couple more days left in Birthday Week," says Mom. "Do you want anything else besides the camping trip?"

My eyes fall to the blue-black lines of the tattoo peeking over the top of her shirt near her collarbone.

What I truly want—what I've wanted as long as I've been old enough to want things—is that tattoo. Or more specifically, what that tattoo represents: status as a full member of the Abomofuo.

The tattoo itself is abode santann, the All-Seeing Eye Adinkra. It's one of the most powerful Adinkra of all, as it's the one that represents the Abomofuo. Our organization has gone by many names over the years, but Abomofuo—*hunters* in Twi—is the truest one. The abode santann marks you as someone who has dedicated their life to protecting people from the adze and other creatures of black magic. Dad has the same exact tattoo in the same exact spot, though I can't see it now beneath his gardening gear.

Once I have my own abode santann, I'll no longer be just Serwa Boateng, daughter of the two strongest prodigies the Abomofuo have seen in generations. I'll be Serwa the Slayer, someone who has her own story outside of her parents'.

But my mom can't simply give me the tattoo. No one can. I have to earn it, and the only way to do that is to pass the Initiation Test.

We've had this conversation so many times I already know what Mom is going to say, but that doesn't stop me from blurting out, "Instead of the camping trip, what I'd really love is to take the test this year."

Mom's smile flattens into a thin line, just like I predicted it would. "We've already discussed this, Serwa."

She says *discussed* when the reality is that she and Dad made a decision, and I have no choice but to go along with it. Potential Slayers can take the Initiation Test at any age, though anyone under eighteen needs their guardian's permission. But you can only take the test once—if you fail, that's it. No retakes or second chances. Your dreams of being a full-time vampire hunter? Poof, gone, bye-bye forever.

But I wouldn't fail. I know it.

"Dad took the test when he was younger than I am!" I don't say what we both already know, which is that my father was also the youngest person ever to pass the Initiation, when he was only nine years old. As if I didn't have enough pressure already. "And you're always saying I'm just as good as he was when he was my age. Unless you're lying about that."

"I'm not. You've taken to training better than we ever could have hoped. But this isn't about your skills."

"Then what is it about?" *What do I have to do to prove myself to you?* The words burn in my throat, but I don't dare let them out.

"It's about . . ." I wait for her to continue, but Mom trails off with a strange look on her face. She gets like this sometimes. One second she'll be here, the next she'll be staring into the distance at something only she can see. She usually acts this way when I ask about her childhood, which, from the little I know, wasn't great. I try not to bring it up too often, because it clearly pains her. But we're not talking about her life right now. We're talking about mine.

"I believe what your mother is trying to say is that we'd feel more comfortable if you took the test after you turned eighteen." Dad's come over now, probably having sensed that the fake tension from our sparring match has shifted into the real deal. He squeezes my shoulder but sits beside Mom, making it clear that this is a two-on-one conversation, and I am not in the majority. "You have the whole rest of your life to be a Slayer and only a handful more to be a regular kid. We don't want you to look back one day and regret rushing through this period."

No offense to Dad, but I'm pretty sure the Regular Kid Train passed me by around the time they taught me to tie a garrote when I was six. Sure, our way of life isn't always easy, but I don't know what I'd do without my training or magic. I *am* a Slayer, like my parents before me, and their parents before them. All I need is to pass the Initiation Test so I can prove it to everyone else, too.

"Let me take the test, and I'll never ask for anything ever again," I beg.

"The answer is no, Serwa." Mom is back from whatever corner of her mind she wandered into. "You can take the test once you're an adult, and not a moment before."

It's clear from the hard edge in her voice that I've pushed up to the limit of her patience. I say nothing else, just nod with my own mouth in a tight line to keep myself from blurting something I will most definitely regret. Mom and I stare at each other, and a hot, syrupy feeling swirls through my stomach. I scratch behind my ear, and the sensation immediately goes away.

Mom breaks our staring contest first, closing her eyes with a sigh. "You can't take the test. But surely there must be something else you'd like for your birthday?"

Not to further annihilate a dead horse, or however that saying goes, but there really is nothing else I want. I mean, yeah, a phone might be nice, although what do I need one for when the only two people I talk to regularly are with me basically twenty-four seven? And maybe for the briefest moment yesterday, when I blew out the candles on my third birthday cake of the week, I wished I had someone my own age to share it with. . . . But those are small desires in the grand scheme of things. If your biggest complaint in life is that you've never had a party at Chuck E. Cheese, things are going pretty great for you.

I shake my head, and suddenly Mom's face gets so sad it makes me forget my own disappointment for a second. I reach up to hug her, but she jumps to her feet before I can and plasters on a smile. "Come on, go inside and wash up before lunch. I know you didn't think you could walk into my house covered in all that outside mess."

She offers me a hand, and I'm seriously considering another sneak attack on her when something catches my eye. It's the smallest movement—not a flash of light, but a steady yellow pulse, like a glowing heartbeat. It's so subtle that most people would have missed it, but I've been trained to spot things most people would miss.

It's a firefly. Fear freezes me in place.

"Mom, behind you," I whisper as loudly as I dare.

She scoffs. "You can't really think I'd fall for—"

"Look out!"

My warning doesn't come fast enough, because before the words are out of my mouth, the firefly screams.

2

How to Weaponize a Ceiling Fan

"There is no good witch."

—From the *Nwoma*

THE FIREFLY'S SCREECH IS worse than the sound of a thousand nails running down a chalkboard amplified through a megaphone. The shrillness of it rattles my teeth as I clap my hands over my ears.

Piercing bright light, like an earthbound star, flashes across the lakeside as the firefly doubles in size, then grows five times bigger than that, then ten times bigger than *that* until it stands before us eight feet tall, head bigger than a basketball and thorax as round and thick as an oil drum. Its six spindly limbs end in wickedly sharp talons that it clicks together with menace, and when it lifts the shiny black elytra on its back, the iridescent wings beneath whir like the blades of a helicopter. We all cough from the clouds of dust the creature's wings blow up around us, hardly processing what we're seeing.

An adze, here at our safe house. But that's not possible! No creature of black magic should be able to get past the protective Adinkra surrounding our home.

But somehow, this one did. And if we don't hurry, it's going to kill us all.

The creature is closest to Mom, and the predatory grin it gives as it lunges for her is more akin to a lion's than a bug's.

"Mom!" I scream just as she yells to Dad, "Get her inside!"

Mom squeezes the largest bead on her bracelet as she dives to the ground to avoid the adze. Golden light from the akofena Adinkra on the bead swirls in the palm of her hands, and by the time she's back on her feet, the bracelet has transformed into a sword with a midnight-black blade and shining gold hilt. An Adinkra has been cut out of the dark metal—nokore, the symbol of truth. With a stake in one hand and Nokware in the other, Mom collides with the vampire. I pick up my ax and try to run to her, but Dad grabs me by the waist before I can.

"We have to help her!" I struggle in his grasp, but I'm no match for my dad's strength. He throws me over his shoulder like a sack of rice and jogs for the house, forcing me to watch Mom get smaller and smaller in the distance. We're almost to the porch when another screech fills the air, followed by echoing calls. Two more adze drop from the sky, quickly transforming from firefly mode into a wall of fangs and claws blocking our only hope of escape. Their cries rattle my bones, and it's only my years of training that keeps tears from running down my face at how much the sound hurts.

Dad yells out a word I'm not allowed to say and quickly draws in the dirt with his foot. The symbol he makes looks like a curvy diamond made of four smaller diamonds—eban, the fence Adinkra.

My parents taught me that our ancestors, the Akan people of Ghana, used Adinkra to convey complex messages with simple symbols. Each Adinkra has its own meaning, and to this day people in Ghana and the African diaspora all over the world still use them in art and clothing and all kinds of other stuff. But in the hands of a Slayer, one of those blessed with divine wisdom from the gods, the Adinkra aren't just symbols.

They're magic.

Dad stomps his foot on eban, and several stone pillars rise from the ground, enclosing the adze in a rocky cage. The creatures hiss and scream as we finally reach the house and slam the door shut behind us.

Dad practically tosses me off his shoulder as he goes for his crossbow, which is lying on the kitchen table next to his abandoned Sudoku puzzle from this morning. "Get the mmoatia!"

I nod and race up the stairs two at a time. What the heck is even happening right now? Creatures of black magic like the adze are supposed to be vulnerable to the divine wisdom that powers the Adinkra. *We* hunt *them*, not the other way around. And not here. Never here.

When I burst into my parents' bedroom, I find the mmoatia attempting to scrabble up the dresser to see out the window. It's quite the struggle, seeing as they're both barely a foot tall. *The Bachelor* is paused on the TV, another part of our house's daily routine interrupted by the adze.

"Serwa! Where's your father? Is he injured? What happened?" Boulder demands at the sight of me. All Slayers have a psychic bond that connects them to their partner mmoatia; the one between him and my dad is probably going haywire right now.

If it weren't for the fact their feet point backward, the mmoatia would basically be indistinguishable from hairy gnomes. It doesn't help that all the hair in Boulder's beard and in the little puff on his head is bone-white, making him look like a tiny Black Santa Claus.

"Adze!" I gasp, way too out of breath from that run up the stairs. "They broke past the Adinkra around the lake, and we have to go fight, now!"

Normally, Boulder would make a stink about me ordering him around since he's, like, several centuries my elder, but thanks to the psychic bond letting both him and Avalanche feel my parents' terror, they know I'm not joking. I grab a backpack from the corner of the room and the mmoatia hop inside without complaint. A smell like rotting leaves mixed with Axe Body Spray hits my nose, and I struggle not to gag. The mmoatia's abilities to heal and communicate with the gods make them indispensable partners for any Slayer, but that doesn't change the fact that they stink. It's going to be weeks before any of us can use this backpack again, if we aren't all murdered by vampires in the next ten minutes.

My instincts scream at me to get back to the lake, but instead I pivot to my mom's closet and knock over several piles of shoes and weapons as I scramble to grab the leather case on the top shelf. I shove the black-and-gold case into the backpack, ignoring the mmoatia's squeals of discomfort. If we end up having to run away, we absolutely cannot leave this behind.

The window in the closet faces the lake, and from here I can see the edge of the flower garden and the remains of the eban cage, now empty. There's no sign of either of my parents or any of the adze, and that realization makes my heart start beating triple time. Did Mom chase them off the property? Did we win?

A scuffling noise followed by a *thud* comes from downstairs. I freeze in place, knuckles in a death grip around my ax's handle as panic blooms in my chest. Horrible images of all that could be going on down there flash across my mind—my parents being overpowered by the adze and having all the blood drained from their bodies, one or both of them becoming possessed by the monsters. What if they're hurt, what if they're dead, what if—

No, now's not the time to freak out! I fish for the necklace under my shirt and squeeze the familiar crystal charm on it until all the fear in my chest morphs into calm focus.

I'm a Slayer. This is what I was born to do.

I creep out of the bedroom and down the upstairs hallway, following the heavy footsteps below. At the landing to the stairs, I drop onto my stomach and army-crawl for the banister, which is a lot harder than it sounds when your hands are full of ax and your backpack is full of smelly forest spirits. The landing curves in such a way that it overlooks our kitchen, and it's there I position myself so that I can see what's going on.

Our kitchen is a war zone. All the furniture is smashed—the table we were just about to eat at now nothing more than a pile of splinters, and the only framed photo we have of my grandma shattered to bits. Dad is lying on his back, hands pressed to his abdomen. Even though I've seen Boulder heal far worse wounds, my stomach still flips at the sight of the blood running between my father's fingers. The mmoatia lets out a muffled cry from the pack at his partner's distress.

Mom stands protectively over Dad. She has Nokware in both hands now, a nasty cut going down her temple, and a look on her face that would probably make me pee my pants if she ever turned it on me.

On the other side of the room are three adze, more vampires than I've ever seen in one place. Unlike Western vampires, adze only have human forms when they're possessing a mortal. Adze's eyes turn gold when they're sharing a body. These ones' eyes are black, meaning they're host-less. From the way they're gnashing their teeth at my parents, they're itching to claim Mom's and Dad's minds for their own.

Standing in front of the adze is the most beautiful woman I have ever seen. Her skin is a warm brown, and her arms, ears, and throat are adorned with enough gold to outfit a jewelry store. She has a brightly patterned yellow-and-blue dhuku around her head to match. Her sleek fitted blouse and high heels couldn't be more different from my mom's worn T-shirt and jeans.

But it's her eyes that stand out most—they burn a bright crimson. The color of blood.

The shiny lady tilts her head to the side, her bangles tinkling as she inspects Mom like a lioness staring down her prey. "After all these years apart, Akosua, this is the greeting you give me?"

"Get out of my house before I make you get out," growls Mom.

Why is this woman talking like she knows my mom? Akosua is my mom's day name, the one only family and very close friends use. Everyone else calls her Delilah, her English name. Is this lady from my mother's past? I don't think she's an adze, because a possessed person doesn't usually have that much control over their own body. But why, then, is she with so many of them?

Whoever she is, she's going down. Nobody attacks my family in our own home and gets away with it. I shift into a crouch as quietly as I can and aim my throwing ax at the woman, pushing all the divine wisdom I can from my hands through nkyimu. If I time this just right, the weapon shouldn't kill her, but it sure will slow her down.

The shiny lady shakes her head with a sigh. "You're as quick to fight now as you were back then. Just tell me where the Midnight Drum is, and we can all get on with our day."

Midnight Drum? What is that—some sacred object I've never heard of?

At Mom's silence, the shiny lady waves a ring-covered hand toward her adze buddies, who screech ominously. "I'd prefer if you handed over the information willingly, for, despite what you believe, I do not enjoy violence for the sake of it. But I will force it out of you if I must."

On the ground, Dad lets out a groan of pain. Mom's grip on Nokware tightens. "I don't know where the drum is."

"Don't lie to me, Akosua. You were never any good at it."

I tighten my hands around the ax handle, then pause. Even if I make this throw and impair the shiny lady, there are still the three adze to deal with. There's gotta be some way I can incapacitate all four at once. My eyes search the remains of the kitchen until they land on the ceiling fan, which is whirling on high since Mom forgot to turn it off after breakfast like she usually does.

That'll work.

But as I'm prepping for the throw, Boulder wiggles out of the backpack and crawls up near my ear. "That shot is too risky!" he hisses as his eyes follow mine. Still, I have to try. I can't stand by and do nothing.

Downstairs, the shiny lady is still talking like they're all chatting over tea and aren't about ten seconds from ripping one another to bits. "Haven't you grown tired of this farce of domesticity? You can run all you want, but the past always catches up. The day you can no longer keep the drum hidden is coming sooner than you think."

The woman looks around, and I shrink back just in case she can see past the upstairs railing. "I saw your daughter run into the house earlier. How about a deal? You give me the Midnight

Drum, and I won't hunt her down to see if she's as breakable as her grandmother was."

A shiver runs down my spine, and a flash of terror crosses Mom's face before she lets out a roar. She leaps toward the shiny lady, sword first. In the same moment, I mutter a quick prayer to Nyame and let my ax fly.

My weapon hits its target, slicing straight through the rod that attaches the fan to the ceiling. With a groan, the fan smashes down on the shiny lady, two of the adze, and Dad's favorite fern. While the adze who wasn't hit scrambles to help its friends, I charge down the stairs.

"Mom! Dad!" I yell.

Relief washes over both their faces when they see me. Mom hauls Dad to his feet, throws his arm over her shoulders, and together we all run out of the house. A voice inside me screams to turn back and fight because this is our home. It was the place that made all those months on the road bearable because we knew it was here waiting for us. But it's swarming with adze now, and there's no saving it if we can't save ourselves.

When we finally reach our car, Mom jumps behind the wheel, Dad limps into the passenger seat, dripping blood the whole way, and I dive into the back with the mmoatia. As Mom revs the engine, I take one last look at the lake house. Adze crawl up and down its blue sides like ants on a sugar cube, and my throat starts to hurt as I watch them take apart our safe house—our home—board by board.

Just as we start to pull away, the shiny lady comes to the front doorway. She's covered in some nasty cuts and bruises from my ceiling fan assault but is otherwise very much alive. Our eyes meet through the car's back window, and her mouth curls into a smile that would be pretty if her bloodred gaze wasn't full of murder.

"No matter how far you run . . ." she yells, her voice somehow getting louder the farther away we get. "No matter how many Adinkra you draw, I will find you. And when I do—"

I can barely see her now, but her voice booms as if she's in the car with us.

"—you're going to wish I never had."

3

How to Not Eat Pancakes

*"The Middle Men are a Slayer's eyes and ears within
a community. Utilize them well, for without them
our fight would've been lost long ago."*

—From the *Nwoma*

MOM HITS THE GAS, and we go careening out of our
secluded country road onto the highway. I'm 99 percent
sure my parents used some Adinkra on the car at some
point, because not a single police officer stops us, even
though we're going at least a million miles above the
speed limit.

None of us says anything, not that there's anything
to say. It still doesn't feel real, like any second now
someone is gonna yell "SIKE!" and we're gonna go
home and everything will be the way it should be. The
backpack shifts, and I let out the mmoatia. Boulder
immediately scrambles over me onto the passenger
seat. He's clearly spooked, but he keeps his voice low
and soothing, like a grandparent comforting a scared
child, as he begins to heal Dad's wounds. Avalanche is
a lot newer to being a Slayer's partner mmoatia than
Boulder—think only a couple decades of experience

versus Boulder's millennia of it. I have to rub soothing circles on her back to calm her whimpering.

My throat is super dry, so I reach for my water bottle, but— Oh. Right. My water bottle was in my travel bag, the one I didn't have time to grab because I was too busy running for my life.

It's not like my bottle was super special or anything. We bought it for three dollars at a Walmart when we were doing a reconnaissance mission on some adze activity at a daycare in Seattle. The bottle was covered in purple flowers and the cheesy phrase DRINK IN THE DAY! in curly script, and now all I'm thinking about is how I'm never going to see those ugly flowers or tacky font ever again, and how I had to leave my new ax behind, and how much I want to sleep in my own bed, and I can't stop the tears from rolling down my face.

My house is really just . . . gone. No more sparring in the garden with Mom. No more slipping Oreos from the pantry when everyone else is asleep, or swimming with Dad in the lake.

No more home.

The hot, syrupy feeling I had earlier when Mom told me I couldn't take the Initiation Test—gods, that wasn't even an hour ago, but it feels like a different lifetime—returns. The sensation isn't new to me. The "Big Feeling," as I call it now, used to come in the middle of the night, during those moments between sleeping and waking—when I wasn't dreaming, exactly, but I wasn't in full control of my thoughts, either.

I tried asking my dad about it once, since he's always been the more emotional of my parents. All he said was that everyone feels weird sometimes, even him. I haven't brought it up again since, even now that it's happening for the second time in one day, which it's never done before.

My parents must be just as upset as I am because they don't say anything when I take off my seat belt and lie across the backseat. Avalanche grunts when I place her atop my hip, while Boulder remains silent in his perch on Dad's shoulder. I used to be able to lie completely flat back here, but sometime between last summer and this one I grew so much that now I have to curl up to fit. I wipe my tears with a grimy hoodie sleeve until they stop. If my parents aren't going to cry, then I won't, either.

At some point I must have fallen asleep, because one second Mom is driving and the sun is annoyingly high in the sky, and the next, Dad is behind the wheel and there are stars everywhere. Instead of the tall pine trees that grow near the lake house, there are now patches of dark, open spaces rolling by the car windows. I'm guessing we're passing through fields, which means we've come pretty far south. (For obvious reasons, I can't tell you the exact location of our safe house. Imagine as far north as you can go in the US without hitting Canada, and you'd be pretty close.) I begin to sit up but stop when I hear Mom and Dad talking in the low voices they only use when they think I'm not listening.

"Perhaps I didn't draw the wards correctly?"

"Kwabena, in all the years I've known you, you've never drawn a single Adinkra incorrectly."

It takes me a second to understand what they're saying, since they're talking in Twi. Even though I grew up speaking it, my parents focused on English when we came to America so it would be easier for me to blend in. Even now, my brain struggles to translate the Twi words, like they're friends whose faces I know but whose names I just can't remember.

"The problem wasn't you—it's them. Somehow, they've figured out how to get past the Adinkra."

I clutch Avalanche to my chest, ignoring the mmoatia's squeals of protest. No Slayer alive is better at using Adinkra than my dad, not even my mom. If his Adinkra can't stop the adze, no one's can.

"So what do we do?" asks Dad.

"Boulder's already sent a message to the Okomfo. Hopefully they'll get back to us soon and give us the official go-ahead to track her down." Mom sighs. "After all these years . . . I can't believe she comes back into our lives like this."

"She didn't get any information out of us." Dad's voice is firm. "We're safe. The Midnight Drum is safe. That's all that matters."

All right, now I'm really confused. It was weird enough when the shiny lady was talking like she knew my parents, but now they're talking like they know *her*, too. And what is this Midnight Drum everyone keeps mentioning? The closest thing we had to a drum was this old laundry detergent bucket Dad used to beat to scare animals away from his garden. I highly doubt a flock of adze attacked us over *that*.

Even though my foot has fallen asleep and there is a strong possibility I've cut off all circulation to my head in this position, I don't move a muscle. Maybe if I pretend to be asleep for long enough, I'll eavesdrop my way into some answers.

But my stomach decides to be a little snitch and rumbles loud enough to make my eyes fly open.

Dad glances at me in the rearview mirror. "Sorry, did we wake you?" he asks, switching back to English.

"No," I lie. "Where are we going?"

"Somewhere with good food. I thought we could all use a little pick-me-up after the day we've had."

Dad's tone is light, but there's a strain in his voice, like you sometimes get when you try to lift something heavy and speak at the same time. However, he seems a lot better than when we left—Boulder did his job, and the mmoatia is now resting in Mom's lap, glancing up at her with a worried look. She doesn't say a word, just keeps on staring straight ahead, absentmindedly twisting Nokware around her wrist.

A few minutes later, Dad pulls into the parking lot of a large diner with a bright blue roof and white sign, and I almost cheer. Never in my life have I been so glad to see an IHOP.

All diners are liminal spaces—areas where the boundary between our world and the magical one is at its thinnest. The same is true of things like highway rest stops, train stations, and airports—all the places where people gather but don't linger. Travelers have pushed against the veil so often that doing magic in a liminal space is easier than in other spots. With all of us as weak as we are, this will be the best place for the Abomofuo to reach us. Also, it's been almost a full day since I last ate, and if I don't get some food into me within the next ten seconds, I will very much stab someone and it won't be pretty.

Once inside, we slide into a booth, Mom and Dad on one side, the mmoatia (concealed in the backpack) and me on the other. We all order our usual: strawberry crepes, scrambled eggs, and a hot chocolate for me; a steak omelet and coffee, no cream, four sugars for Mom; and a stack of buttermilk pancakes with bacon on the side for Dad. The poofy-haired waitress doesn't bat an eye at the fact that we're sweaty, grimy, and a little bit bloody, which says a lot about the kind of people who must frequent this IHOP. She just asks us in a bored drawl if we'd like extra butter with our food, then drifts off when we say no.

I subtly check around, wondering why my parents chose this restaurant out of all the ones on the East Coast. Then I lock eyes with one of the cooks—a burly Black man—through the window where the servers pick up the food. He nods at me and fishes out a gold chain from under his shirt to flash an abode santann charm. I smile back at him, some of the tension that's been weighing me down all day finally relaxing.

We're in the presence of a Middle Man, a noncombat operative of the Abomofuo. There are Middle Men spread all over the globe to help fund, shelter, and support Slayers in everything from securing them regular jobs as cover to reporting signs of black magic within their communities. (They're not all men, but the Okomfo refuse to change the title, even though people have been pointing out how sexist it is for years.)

If there's a Middle Man here, then this IHOP is part of the Abomofuo network. It's covered with protective wards out the wazoo, so no creature of black magic would dare step foot in here.

But if the adze broke through the spells on our house, what's to say they can't do the same here? Are we safe anywhere anymore? Mom must sense my sudden paranoia because she reaches across the table to squeeze my hand. Seeing her so collected calms me down, too. We might not be safe, but we're together, and that's more important.

As soon as the waitress turns away, Dad pulls out a marker— he always keeps extras in the car, thank Nyame—and draws three Adinkra onto each of the four sides of our table: eban again; dwennimmen, the ram's horn, which can mean concealment; and mframadan, fortitude. When combined, these Adinkra create a wall of silence around anything enclosed within. The bleary-eyed diners in the other booths can still see us, but to them, our conversation will sound like whatever they consider too boring to pay any attention to.

The questions explode out of me as soon as Dad finishes

drawing. "Who was that woman? How did she get past our Adinkra? What did she mean about Grandma?"

Dad sighs, then flinches, his hand flying to his newly treated wound. We all keep a change of clothes in the car, so his current polo isn't stained with blood like the old shirt was, but he still doesn't look great. "You can't even wait until my pancakes come before you start asking the hard questions?"

The smile drops from his face, and he looks at Mom, who has on a faraway expression again. When she finally speaks, her voice is surprisingly soft. "That woman you saw today—Boahinmaa—is an obayifo."

At the last word, my whole body goes numb. "An obayifo, like a witch?" I whisper.

Mom nods, a hint of anger creeping into her gaze. "Adze are creatures. All they want is to live and feed, and they attack mostly out of survival instinct. But obayifo are fully thinking beings with their own wills and agendas, with just as much access to black magic."

A shiver runs down my spine, and I suddenly remember how Boahinmaa spoke to her using her day name. "How do you know each other?"

The anger dies in Mom's eyes, replaced by a sadness so big it could swallow us all whole. Though I asked her the question, it's Dad who leans forward and says, "Do you remember the stories I told you about my mother?"

I nod, and my hand instinctively goes to the charm on my necklace. It's a flat, golden circle with a pointed pink crystal hanging inside. My dad's mother, Grandma Awurama, was a goldsmith. This necklace is one of the few pieces of hers we have left.

"She died during the war," I say.

Not long before I was born, there was a big war between the Abomofuo and the forces of black magic we fight against. I don't like to ask my parents about it, because they get so sad when I do, but I know they lost a lot of people they loved.

Dad's voice is so small I nearly miss what he says next. "Boahinmaa was the one who killed your grandmother."

A million words come to my mouth. I don't say any of them. Instead, I think about my grandma's name—Awurama Oseiwa Boateng. That's where my own name comes from—Serwa is an alternate form of Oseiwa. My name is an homage to a woman I never got to meet because she was murdered by a witch before I was born.

Without thinking, I pick up my napkin and begin shredding it into teeny-tiny bits.

Boahinmaa is the reason I have no house. She's the reason that all I have of my grandmother are a single necklace and other people's memories.

I twist the remains of my napkin tight.

"Your grandmother was the best person I've ever known," Mom says, her voice scratchy. "She taught me how to be a better mother—a better person—when nobody else believed I'd be any good at either of those things. And I promised myself that if I ever saw Boahinmaa again, I'd make sure she faced justice for what she did."

Dad places his hand on top of Mom's. "*We're* going to make sure she faces justice."

My parents like to tease, and sometimes they give each other such a hard time I wonder why they even got married in the first place. But they've known each other almost their whole lives and have fought side by side since they were almost as young as me. My mom and dad are a perfect team. Sometimes it feels like they're the sun and the moon, and I'm stuck on Earth watching them both share the sky.

"Yeah, we're going to make her pay," I repeat. I'm not sad anymore—I'm angry. I'm so angry there's no room in me for anything else. Besides, sadness will only slow you down on a hunt. But anger? It keeps you going.

Anger helps you win.

Both my parents look at me, then back at each other. They know each other so well they can have a conversation without words, like they're doing now. The only sign something is wrong is the small line between Dad's eyebrows.

Before anyone can say anything more, Avalanche begins to squeak. She hops out of my backpack and onto the table, coughing and wheezing. Then, like a cat hacking up a hairball, she spits out a small piece of paper with two Adinkra on it. The first is abode santann, which marks this as official Abomofuo correspondence. The second looks like a sideways crescent moon on a vertical line crossed with four horizontal ones. Akoben, the war horn Adinkra, which represents a call to action. We're being summoned to speak to the Okomfo directly about what happened with Boahinmaa.

Based on my parents' surprised looks, they weren't expecting this—normally our orders are delegated via the mmoatia communication network. Things must be worse than we thought if they want to speak to us face-to-face.

Dad nods at the Middle Man cook, who quickly draws the server's attention to himself so we can sneak out of the main dining area. Unfortunately, it's right before the waitress was finally going to bring over our food—just our luck. We crowd into the one-stall bathroom, getting the first full look at ourselves since the fight. The bags under our eyes are deep enough to hold groceries. Both my ponytail and my sanity are seconds away from falling apart, and Mom tries half-heartedly to smooth her twists into place, but there's no time to pretty ourselves up with an active summons over our heads.

Dad takes a handkerchief from his back pocket, stuffs it into the sink drain, then lets the faucet run until the bowl is full. With the marker he draws abode santann onto the mirror, and then he drops the two pieces of paper into the water.

Nothing happens. With a frustrated sigh, Dad begins to hit the sink with his palm. "Not today, you stupid—"

Golden light pours out from the Adinkra, its rays extending across the smooth surface of the mirror. The rays spiral all around us, looking for a second like galaxies before they coalesce and envelop us in an entirely new environment. I can't help but grin as the familiar scents of earth and metal hit my nose and the IHOP bathroom transforms into the Compound, the ancestral headquarters of dozens of generations of Abomofuo.

Yeah, magic never gets old.

4

How to Argue with a God

"To be in the presence of a god is one of the greatest honors any mortal may receive. Speak to them only with the deference they deserve."

—From the *Nwoma*

I SHOULD MAKE IT clear right now that we have not actually traveled to the Compound. First of all, our headquarters exists at the border between the human realm and the magical one. There are so many Adinkra protecting it that I'm pretty sure anyone who tried to portal in directly would be immediately vaporized. I don't know about you, but I like all my atoms where they are, thank you very much.

Second, even if portalling—is that a word?—into the Compound were possible, we wouldn't do it, because portal spells are some of the most advanced and regulated types. The Okomfo say casting too many of them would destabilize time and space as we know it, throwing all of existence into chaos, yadda, yadda, blah, blah. Besides, if my family and I could portal wherever we wanted all willy-nilly, we wouldn't have to worry about stupid things like "immigration laws" and "visas" and "international customs regulations."

So yeah, we're not physically in the Compound, but the magic of the summons makes it *feel* like we are, similar to virtual reality. Through the windows of the stool room, I can see a fraction of the Compound's sprawling exterior. Like most traditional Ghanaian residences, the Compound is a built around a long central courtyard surrounded by dozens of structures built in the old style, using mudbrick, stone, and wood. The tan walls are painted with various patterns and symbols in sepia, and some of the buildings still have their original thatched roofs.

But don't let the Compound's appearance fool you—its humble exterior hides one of the most state-of-the-art and well-defended fortresses in history. The buildings extend at least twenty stories belowground, and my dad says when he was a kid growing up here, he once counted twenty-six training rooms, dozens of dining halls, even more dormitories, record rooms detailing every single Adinkra and all the known spells/enchantments/wards they could possibly make, and several groves filled with sacred badie trees before he gave up.

The unmistakable sound of Slayers training fills the air—the ring of blade against blade, golden flashes whenever someone unleashes divine wisdom, shouts from the trainers in Twi and other languages. Though the majority of the Abomofuo are Ghanaian, there's no requirement that you have to be in order to join. Mom says that's because when our people started leaving the region that would one day become Ghana—some by choice but most because of colonialism and the slave trade—the ancestors quickly realized we'd be overwhelmed by the forces of black magic if we limited our ranks to only those who remained on the continent. Anyone who passes the Initiation Test can join, but you do have to respect that our practices are steeped in Ghanaian cultures and traditions.

My parents and I "stand" within the stool room, one of the largest chambers inside the Compound. The walls are laced with gold filigree, making the room feel like it's glowing, and hanging from the ceiling are dozens of Adinkra cloths in every color of the rainbow. But the real focal point of the hall is the two golden stools on a dais at the front.

I say *stool*, but don't imagine something you'd find at a bar. They're both wider than they are tall, and each has a thick column of gold sandwiched between the curved seat and rectangular base. Among my people, a stool is essentially a throne, a seat so sacred that only someone royal or divine can sit on it. The ones here are bigger than a pickup truck, and just an inch of the enchanted gold they're made from could probably buy an entire nation. The stool on the left has been engraved with images of raging storms and flashing lightning. At its base is an Adinkra that is meant to look like a swirling galaxy. That's gye nyame, marking the stool as belonging to Nyame, the most powerful of all the gods.

The stool on the right is slightly smaller but no less beautiful. It has all kinds of flowers and fruit carved into it, along with an Adinkra that looks like an upside-down heart on top of a right-side-up one—asaase ye duru. That stool is for Asaase Yaa, the earth goddess and wife of Nyame. Neither god is here right now, but the power buzzing from their stools is enough to make goose bumps rush up my arms even through the illusion.

Though Asaase Yaa and Nyame aren't present, the stool room is far from empty. Seven Okomfo dressed in traditional black-and-white Adinkra cloth robes stand at the front, and there's a woman with a mmoatia in the corner. Three unnaturally tall figures stand in front of the stools, and when they turn to look at us, my parents and I immediately drop to our knees.

"Nana Tegare, Nana Tano, Nana Bia," says Dad, referring to the gods with the term for a respected elder in Twi. "I didn't realize you would be attending this meeting."

Despite the fact we're all gathered here because my family kind of almost died, I can barely hold back my excitement. Holy mmoatia poop, this isn't just a meeting with the Okomfo. It's a meeting with the *gods.*

The tallest of the three is Tegare, god of hunters. He's the deity who blessed the original Seven Founders of the Abomofuo with divine wisdom, so he's the reason all Slayers are stronger and faster than regular mortals. Like the Okomfo, he's dressed in the traditional style, with a bright orange-and-green kente cloth thrown over one shoulder and wrapped around his body. A thick red fabric embedded with gold ornaments wraps around his bald head, and the tip of the spear in his hand looks sharp enough to cut someone before they can even blink.

The two gods flanking Tegare are dressed far more casually. Tano and Bia are twins, though you wouldn't know that by looking at them. Tano is huge enough to carry two quarterbacks under each arm without breaking a sweat, and when he speaks, the ground rumbles. He totally fits the image of a god of war with his bomber jacket and combat boots. Bia, on the other hand, is thin and willowy, and his clothes are always littered with fur or feathers or, unfortunately, droppings from the animals he oversees as god of the bush. He's dressed more like a zookeeper. Right now, the only twin-like thing about them is the identical grimaces on both their faces.

The Tano and the Bia are two of the longest rivers in Ghana, and if you were to visit them, you'd find lots of fishing and boating and all sorts of other river-related activities going on. Stories of the rivers as gods who have protected the people since ancient times are well-known there, though most folks don't believe them anymore.

Then again, most don't believe that adze are real, either, yet here we are.

"Are you being watched?" asks Tegare, his voice booming through the hall even though he didn't yell. Unlike the other two, Tegare isn't tied to a singular river, but he has existed for centuries, smiting evildoers and hunting witches. His magic, more than any other god's, is what makes the Abomofuo possible.

"I don't believe so, my lord," says Dad, still on his knees. My parents have met Tegare, Tano, and Bia before, but I never have. I shift from knee to knee, wondering what the deities have heard of or think of me, the daughter of two of the most famous Slayers of all time.

Tegare nods. "You may stand."

We do. Tegare gestures at one of the Okomfo, who steps forward. Now I can make out the lion mask covering his face. This is Okomfohene Nsiah, the leader of all the priests.

"We received the report from your mmoatia that you had an altercation with Boahinmaa this morning. Tell us about it," says the man.

Dad recounts what went down, and with each word the air grows heavier and heavier. The only movement is from the mmoatia standing on the shoulder of the woman in the corner of the room. The woman is a griot, and her job is to memorialize everything that happens today through stories and songs for future generations. Her mmoatia partner furiously scribbles notes on a pad bigger than itself, something I'd find hilarious on any other day.

When Dad finally finishes his story, Bia wipes a glob of bird poop from his shoulder and says, "If the Adinkra no longer work on Boahinmaa, then all our Slayers around the world are in danger. Have the mmoatia send out a notice that everyone should be on high alert. And perhaps we should call Anansi?"

"Why does everyone always want to call Anansi?" Tano huffs. "Just because he's the only child of Nyame anyone ever remembers? No, no Anansi! We are just as good as he is—better, even! Besides, I'm pretty sure he's still busy with that kid from Chicago." Tano cracks his knuckles, the sound like a crash of thunder. "If it's another war Boahinmaa wants, then we'll give it to her."

"That seems unwise, seeing as the last one almost ended the world," Bia points out. "Bashing in skulls isn't the answer to every problem, even if it is what you do best."

Tano scoffs. "Jealousy isn't attractive, brother."

"Neither is cheating, brother."

It takes all my self-control not to laugh. According to the old stories, back when Nyame was deciding which of the gods would rule over what parts of the world, he originally wanted to give Tano's river to Bia and Bia's river to Tano. But with the help of the folkloric being Goat, Tano stole Bia's gift for himself, and the twins have been bickering over it ever since.

Tegare breaks up his brothers' fighting by interjecting, "No, Bia is right—we need to keep this as low-profile as possible. Have our best Slayers neutralize Boahinmaa before she can locate the Midnight Drum."

Again with this drum. When we get back to the real world, I'm going to need a long explanation from my parents about what this instrument is and why everyone cares about it so much. But not here, because I know better than to start yapping in the presence of the gods.

"I'll send a squad right away, my lords," says the Okomfohene. During official proceedings like this one, each of the thirteen priests who run the Abomofuo wears a mask representing a different animal. Right now, Okomfohene Nsiah's lion mask looks like it's snarling.

At his words, a line appears between Mom's eyebrows. "Nana Nsiah," she says to the Okomfohene. "Let my husband and I go after her. We've faced Boahinmaa before. We know all her tricks."

"It's precisely because you've faced her before that I worry about sending you on this mission," says Nana Nsiah. Though it's impossible to tell what expression he's making behind the lion mask, I can practically feel the way he's scrutinizing my mom.

Tegare adds, "I agree. Given your personal history with Boahinmaa, I'm not certain you are the best choice for this hunt."

Hold up. I don't care if he's a god—no one talks to my mom like that. I pull myself up to my full not-that-tall height and look straight at Tegare.

"My mom is the best Slayer in the world," I say, ignoring my parents' *If you don't shut your mouth right now . . .* looks. "There's no one better for this mission than her."

For the first time since we arrived, the gods give me their full attention, and I suddenly wish I had escaped our collapsing house in something a little fancier than my usual striped T-shirt, hoodie, and pink sweatpants with LATER, GATOR! printed on the side.

"Is this your daughter speaking to an elder with such rudeness?" asks Tegare, his voice a dangerously low rumble.

Dad quickly yanks me behind him. "So sorry, my lords. She is young and impulsive and *knows better than to speak out of turn.*" He hisses that last part my way.

"Come here," the god of hunters orders me, and Dad reluctantly lets my arm go. My parents watch nervously as Tegare and his brothers peer down at me. I'm pretty sure it would be rude to look away, so instead I stare straight back as all three examine me up and down. They could almost pass for mortals, except for their eyes, which are too wild and bright, like stars stuffed into human faces. Tegare and Tano just seem offended, but Bia wears a thoughtful expression.

To Mom, he says, "There is a lot of you in her."

You'd think that would be a compliment, but Mom grimaces. "She is young. Her training is not yet complete."

She is standing right here and getting sick of everyone speaking like she doesn't exist. But the gods aren't exactly known for being sweet and friendly, and something tells me that if I backtalk them again, somebody is going to get a fistful of divine wisdom to the face. So I keep my lips shut.

Tegare rubs his chin thoughtfully as he regards me again. "Your daughter has a big mouth, but she also has a point," he says. "Though this attack just occurred, it feels like the culmination of something that has been brewing for years. Despite your unfortunate history, you are correct that no one is more entitled to apprehend Boahinmaa than you."

Unfortunate history? Are they referring to the childhood Mom refuses to talk about?

Without explaining further, the divine brothers look at one another and some kind of understanding passes between them. The air seems to grow more alive with magic as Tegare continues. "Let the words that I say reach up to my father, Nyame, in the heavens, and my mother, Asaase Yaa, deep inside the earth. On this, the twenty-sixth day of the eighth month, I bestow upon you a quest. You are to seek out Boahinmaa, she who calls herself leader of the forces of black magic, and defeat her by any means necessary. Under no circumstances is she to get anywhere near the Midnight Drum. Do you accept this mission?"

"We accept," I say before anyone else can speak.

"*We* accept," says Mom with a fiery look that dares me to challenge her. "*You're* not coming."

What?! "But I always go with you!"

Tano whistles, looking between me and my parents. "Awwwkward."

"Not this time," says Mom. "It's too dangerous."

"Your mother is right," says Dad. "Boahinmaa's ability to break through an Adinkra ward is unlike anything we've ever seen before. It wouldn't be safe for you to come with us when we're not certain what we're dealing with."

What he actually means is I'd get in the way of the *real* Slayers. But I'm just as good as anyone who's passed the Initiation. I literally just saved my parents' lives today! Besides, Boahinmaa has hurt me just as much as she's hurt them. There's no way they can leave me behind when they finally take her down.

"Where would I even go?" I argue. "Would I stay here at the Compound?"

Actually, that doesn't sound half bad. Living and training at the Compound would be the literal dream, and surely if I was there—er, here?—I could impress the Okomfo so much that they'd practically beg my parents to let me take the test.

But Mom shoots down that plan quickly. "No, not here. You're not old enough to live here on your own yet."

An Okomfo wearing a rhino mask chimes in, "Richard Amankwah is our head of the Mid-Atlantic region. Your daughter should be safe in his care."

I consider that possibility for a minute. On the one hand,

the Amankwahs live in this mansion down in Washington, DC, with its own pool and movie theater. They come from super-old money, and they're not afraid to flaunt it. On the other hand, their son, Declan Amankwah, is my Eternal Nemesis and the bane of my entire existence. We're nearly the same age, but his parents let him take his Initiation Test at eleven and he just *loves* rubbing that fact in my face. If we live together, there's a not-zero chance one of us would strangle the other within a week.

However, Dad shakes his head "If Boahinmaa comes looking for Serwa, the house of the most renowned Slayer on the East Coast is the first place she'll look. Serwa's not going to stay with Richard, either."

The rhino-masked Okomfo bristles at my father's swift rejection, but Dad just stares him down. My father is so friendly that sometimes I almost forget he's been in the monster-hunting game even longer than my mother. When push comes to shove, he'll never back down from a challenge.

And wanna know a tiny detail people always seem to forget?

My dad's ancestor was one of the Seven Founders of the Abomofuo, making our family one of the highest-ranking within the organization, though we don't act all high-and-mighty about it.

The Okomfo cracks first, rolling his neck like it doesn't bother him that Dad just undermined him in front of several gods. "I completely understand. Nothing matters more than your child's safety," he says coolly.

Tano looks crestfallen that the conversation didn't devolve into full-on fisticuffs—something tells me he himself would have jumped in if it had—but Tegare speaks before his brother can. "Our business today is complete. Go swiftly and quickly, my Slayers. The fate of the world is in your hands."

"Yes, Nana Tegare," we all say as we put our fists over our hearts in a customary Slayer salute. My eyes land on the dozens of Adinkra cloths fluttering above the stool room; each one of them is all that remains of a Slayer who fell in the line of duty. More cloths will join the rows if Boahinmaa isn't caught soon.

The image is still in my mind long after the magic fades and we're standing once more in the IHOP bathroom. As soon as we're sure we're alone, Dad lets out a groan as he checks his stomach wound.

"So, what's the plan? Where are we going first?" I ask. It feels good to be plotting and strategizing again. It's almost like my entire life hasn't been flipped upside down.

But Mom frowns. "We meant what we said earlier. You're not coming with us."

My face falls. "Then where can I possibly go that's safer than the Compound *or* the Amankwahs?"

This stumps both my parents for all of a second before Mom asks Dad, "Is your cousin Patrick's wife still out in Maryland?"

"Latricia! Yes, she is."

Latricia? The name sounds vaguely familiar in a way I can't quite place. Dad's smile widens in realization.

"Her daughter is Serwa's age, too. Yes, I can call her right away."

Oh Nyame, they're really going to leave me. They can't do this! I won't let them. "But you can't—"

"Serwa." Mom's voice is low, and if her tone wasn't enough to stop my arguing, the look in her eyes would be. "This is done."

From the hard steel in her voice, I can tell it is. The hunt for my grandmother's killer is on.

And I have no part in it.

5

How to Say Goodbye

"To live the life of the Slayer is to forsake the comforts granted to regular mortals. Mourn not that which you have lost, but instead rejoice for all that your sacrifices protect."

—From the *Nwoma*

HERE ARE A FEW fun facts about Rocky Gorge, Maryland, courtesy of the free guidebook my dad picked up at the Pennsylvania/Maryland State Line rest area off Interstate 95:

1. Rocky Gorge was once named Harristown and has twice been voted the most pumpkin-friendly city on the East Coast by *Porch Swing* magazine, though Paddlesburg, North Carolina, is a close second.

2. The town's mayor, Elena Morrison, was elected in a landslide victory just last year on a platform of eliminating noise pollution from the local turkey farm that has been plaguing the residents of Rocky Gorge for thirteen years and counting.

3. The gorge the town is named after is exactly two hundred fifty-six feet deep and five hundred ninety wide, and home to sixty-three varieties of birds found only in the greater Chesapeake Bay region.

4. Literally nothing interesting has ever happened in this town and likely never will.

(Okay, the guidebook didn't *technically* say that last part, but it was heavily implied.)

The reason I'm researching this town no one's ever heard of is because it's supposedly where my aunt Latricia and cousin Roxanne live. This is where I'm going to be trapped while my parents hunt down the vampire witch who broke our family.

From the moment we left the IHOP, I did everything I could to convince my parents to take me with them. I tried logical arguments. (*Everyone knows all the most effective stealth formations work better with at least three people!*) I tried guilt trips. (*As my parents, what example are you setting by depriving me of this once-in-a-lifetime learning opportunity?*) I even tried full-out begging. (*Please, please, please, please,* please *take me with you!*)

Nothing worked. According to my parents, I'm safer with Auntie Latricia than I would be anywhere else in the world, because both she and Rocky Gorge are completely off the grid. There hasn't been any recorded magical activity in the area in more than a century. Wherever the action is, it's happening far, far away from this town.

"Look, Serwa, isn't it pretty?" says Dad, his voice unnaturally cheerful as we cross the city limits. "The leaves are already changing here!"

I force myself out of my cramped sprawl across the backseat and take my first peek at my new prison—I mean my new home. Rocky Gorge looks like what would happen if Disneyland and a Hallmark greeting card had the world's most autumn-y baby. Even though it's only the last week of August, a lot of the trees are already turning red, and their leaves blur together like embers as we pass. Hand-painted signs hang from storefronts, advertising sales of pumpkin-related items or reminding people to submit their gourds for the town's annual Harvest Festival. All the buildings are either redbrick or painted with bright, cheery Crayola colors. Main Street has a bank, a multicultural community center, and a candy shop all on the same block, and everyone stops to talk to one another on the street.

A woman in a red hijab who is walking an overweight beagle waves to us when we pull up at a red light. Instead of waving back, I slink back down in my seat.

"This town is too perfect," I say. "Are you sure it isn't a movie set?"

"I've always liked it. It's very folksy," says Dad.

Mom says nothing, which doesn't help me feel any better. She's been unusually quiet ever since Tegare gave them their mission, and both Dad and I know better than to bother her when she gets like this. A hundred questions about the Midnight Drum and why everyone is so worked up about it crowd my tongue, but something tells me she won't answer any of them right now.

The only one surlier than me is Boulder. After Auntie Latricia agreed to let me live with her (*agreed* is putting it mildly—when Dad made the request, my aunt squealed so loud I'm pretty sure they heard it up in the International Space Station), my parents decided that Boulder would stay with me to make sure I don't step out of line. I can tell from his constant huffing in the front seat that he's as unhappy about his new babysitting gig as I am. Mmoatia hate being separated from their partners, but there's no one else my parents can trust to keep an eye on me while they're gone. No one who knows the truth about magic, at least.

We leave Main Street and enter a neighborhood on the outskirts of town with a bright silver sign that says IVY RIDGE ESTATES.

The homes here are huge—any one of them could eat our former house whole and still have room left for dessert. All the lawns are at least the size of a football field. I sit up a bit straighter to get a better look at the boats and basketball hoops in the driveways we're passing.

If Auntie Latricia's place is this fancy, maybe living with her won't be so bad after all.

"And here we are!"

Dad turns onto the street behind Ivy Ridge Estates and into the parking lot of a large gray-and-white apartment complex with more broken windows in it than whole ones. The sign out front is supposed to read SUNNY OAK TOWERS, but someone crossed out the *unn* part of *sunny* and added a few new letters to turn it into another word I'm not supposed to say. There has to be some kind of mistake. Aunt Latricia can't live here.

Dad clicks his tongue as we park. "This place could certainly use a fresh coat of paint."

I snort. A bulldozer would probably help a lot more.

Knee-length weeds poke up from the cracks in the sidewalk leading to the building's front door, and we have to wade through them to reach the intercom. I'm doing my best not to trip and crack my skull open as Dad slips into lecture mode.

"Latricia's husband, Patrick, is my old teacher's nephew and my friend from primary school. We grew up together," he says, and my mind mentally maps out how we actually know these people. It's pretty common among Ghanaians to throw around terms like *cousin*, *uncle*, and *aunt* so easily that it becomes a headache trying to parse who is actually blood-related to who. At this point, my parents could call the pope my cousin and I'd just go with it.

"But most importantly, Latricia and her daughter, Roxanne,

are regular mortals," Dad continues, somehow managing not to trip without even looking down. "You probably don't remember this, but when we first moved to America, Uncle Patrick and Aunt Latricia let us stay with them for a bit while we got our affairs in order."

Now that makes me pause. I was only five when we left Ghana, so I don't really remember the move itself. My memories of it are more sensations, the feeling of being uprooted from one world and thrown into another with no explanation. If Aunt Latricia knew us back then, that means she's not a complete stranger, but I'd still prefer living with a Slayer.

Dad continues, "Any and all Slayer-related topics are off-limits while you're here. Don't draw any Adinkra, and don't let any classified knowledge slip."

I'm still not sure how I feel about my parents' hiding-me-in-plain-sight strategy, but considering that Boahinmaa already broke through the Adinkra, there's no guarantee I'd be any safer with the Abomofuo than I would here. But, putting safety aside, the thought of not being able to talk about *anything* related to my true life makes me want to gag. What do non-Slayers even *do* all day? Go on walks? Pay taxes?

"No talking about the mind-controlling vampires that plague us all," I say. "Got it."

Mom gives me her patented side-eye, the one that dares me to see what will happen if I show any more attitude, so I keep my mouth shut as Dad punches 6-1-4 into the intercom. The device crackles and hisses for almost a whole minute before an excited voice cries from it, "Edmund! I'll be right down! ROXY, THEY'RE HERE!"

Auntie Latricia speaks so fast that Dad doesn't have a chance to get a word in before the intercom goes dead. I crane my neck and count exactly twenty-three possible exits and not nearly enough footholds if one needed to scale the building in the event of an emergency adze attack. Very concerning.

The door to the complex bangs open and two people burst through. The taller one flings her arms wide and screams with excitement.

"Edmund! Delilah! And look at you, Serwa. You were so tiny the last time I saw you!"

Auntie Latricia is almost half a foot shorter than I am, but that doesn't stop her from lifting me in a bone-crushing hug that squeezes all the air from my lungs. She's wearing five different multicolored scarves even though it's at least eighty-five degrees today, enough bangles to start her own mall jewelry booth, and a faded white T-shirt that has I LIKE BIG BEES AND I CANNOT LIE written on it in bright green letters.

Compared to her mother, Roxy is dressed like an extra out of *The Nightmare Before Christmas*. She's wearing a dark red skirt with a black leather jacket, a T-shirt with an alien throwing a peace sign, and a silk scarf patterned with skulls is wrapped around the Afro puff on her head. Despite her macabre appearance, she has one of the most chipper smiles I've ever seen.

"It's so nice to finally meet you! Well, meet you again!" Roxy exclaims. She pulls me into a hug, too, as our parents exchange their greetings. I stiffen and awkwardly pat her back, because hugs from people who aren't my parents aren't exactly a regular thing for me. But Roxy doesn't seem to mind, and soon she's dragging me to the elevators, talking all the way.

"I wanted to go down an hour ago so we'd be here when you arrived," explains Roxy, "but Mom was all like, *Traffic is sooooo bad, they probably won't get in until three*, and look, it's not

46

even two and here you are! I was going to make you a sign and everything, but there was just no time."

"Um, thank you?" I reply, because what else are you supposed to say when someone is this excited about making you a sign? But my response must be perfect because Roxy beams.

Luckily, the inside of Auntie Latricia's apartment turns out to be much, much nicer than the outside. Almost every surface is covered with little knickknacks and doodads, like the bread box shaped like a wiener dog and the tapestry of quilt scraps that is serving double duty as both wall art and a cover for the fire extinguisher. A quick scan for exits reveals three—two windows in the living room plus the door we entered through. Not ideal, but I could make it work in a pinch.

"Latricia, I can't thank you enough for taking in Serwa on such short notice," says Dad as he pulls out a chair at the cluttered table.

Auntie Latricia scoffs. "Don't even mention it. It's the least I can do after all the help y'all have given me with Patrick's immigration case. Besides, you can't take a child with you to Antarctica."

It's hard to restrain my laughter at that one. My parents' cover story for all the traveling they do for the Abomofuo is that they're a pair of reporters who explore local cultures and traditions across the globe. They've told some pretty far-fetched lies to cover their butts before, but Antarctica? Really?

Mom stomps on my foot beneath the table to stifle my laugh, keeping the sweetest smile on her face the whole time. "Roxy, why don't you show Serwa around? She's so excited to see where she's going to be staying."

Roxy jumps up and drags me to the bedroom to the right of

the living room. Her room is just as packed as the living room/
kitchen was, and on instinct, I begin to scrutinize the space to
glean as much information as I can about my cousin. There's
a sewing machine and dress mannequin crammed in one corner, skeins of dark fabric hanging from both—Roxy likes to
design clothes, and probably made the outfit she's wearing.
Candles, crystals, and more skulls line the shelves—an interest
in the occult? The posters and photos lining the wall are just
like her shirt, featuring either aliens or black-and-white animals too blurry to make out. Only one photo actually has Roxy
in it. She's with her mom and a man I've never seen before.
They're standing on a boat surrounded by fishing gear, and
Roxy is half the height she is now, so it must have been taken
years ago.

"Is that your dad?" I ask, and she nods. "Is he here right now?"

The smile drops from Roxy's face. "Oh, um, my dad had
some problems getting his citizenship stuff figured out, so he's
living in Ghana while they try to fix it."

Well, aren't I just the biggest jerk in the world? We haven't
even been here ten minutes and I've already made everything
awkward.

"That . . . really sucks," I say, shifting from foot to foot.

Roxy's shoulders droop, then perk back up. "Look at what
my mom found in an old box!"

She dives into her closet, tosses aside a comforter embroi-
dered with a picture of Bigfoot, and pulls out a dusty plastic
photo album. I didn't even know people still had those. She
pulls out a picture of two kindergarteners, and I recognize the
one on the left as me from the little mole under my right eye.
The other one must be Roxy, and in the photo we're both sitting
in a red plastic booth at some kind of '50s-themed diner with

checkered floors and a jukebox in the corner. We have both cake and huge grins on our faces.

Some of Roxy's excitement dims at the surprise on my face. "You don't remember this?"

"Not really. Do you?"

"Yes! Well, no. I mean, kind of. I remember another kid living with us, and that can't be anyone but you. But it's okay that we don't have those memories, because we're going to make so many new ones!" Roxy puts down the photo album and picks up a scrapbook that already has ROXY AND SERWA written on the front in sparkly black gel.

Roxy explains, "I thought this could be a fun way for you to keep track of your visit. My mom's family has lived in Rocky Gorge since, like, forever, so I can show you all the cool places in town while you're here. We can also fill it with pictures of us at school or home or wherever. And I thought we could practice Twi by writing in it together, since I don't have anyone to speak it with right now with my dad gone."

I run my fingers over the gel letters, suddenly feeling like an even bigger jerk than before. This was all really sweet of Roxy to do, but this isn't my home. The lake house was the closest thing I've ever had to one, and I'll never be able to return to it again.

I drop the scrapbook on the desk and ask, "What was that about school?"

"The first day is Monday."

I stare at Roxy, and she cocks her head to the side. "You . . . You know you have to go to school, right? Your parents didn't tell you that?"

No, they most certainly did not tell me that. My hands are clenched in fists at my sides when I return to the kitchen, where my parents and Auntie Latricia are crowded around the table, several Costco sandwiches and a large jug of iced tea on the table between them.

"Just when you think you have it all together, there's another form you need to sign or another person who needs to approve your case. It's demoralizing." Auntie Latricia grips her glass of tea tighter. "I hate seeing them treat him like some sort of criminal, but I don't know what else I can do. The immigration process in this country is just that convoluted."

"Nobody told me I had to go to school," I say, cutting off my aunt.

All three of the adults' heads snap up. Mom narrows her eyes. "Serwa, come with me. I left something in the car."

She exits the apartment without even checking to see if I'm following. When we get to the sidewalk outside the building, I say again, "No one said anything about school."

"I thought it went without saying," replies Mom. "You're twelve years old—of course you have to go to school."

"But I've never had to go before! Why can't I keep doing what I've been doing?" Thanks to our unusual life situation, I've been homeschooled for as long as I can remember. Dad usually handles science and English while Mom does my social studies and math courses. And there's no textbook anywhere that can teach me what I need to know to survive the adze.

"Latricia works full-time. And even if she didn't, we can't ask her to teach you on top of taking you in."

There are about a million things you should never fight my mom about, and education is definitely in the top three. One of the few things I know about her past is that she had to drop out of school at a young age so she could support her family. She wants me to get the opportunities she never did, which is why no matter how wild our hunts get, she always makes sure I keep up with my studies. This is a fight I'm not going to win, but that doesn't stop me from trying.

"But how am I supposed to protect the apartment from adze if I'm stuck behind a desk all day?"

"Like we mentioned earlier, there hasn't been any magic sighting in this area for more than a hundred years. You aren't at risk of an adze attack here. Besides, don't think of this as a punishment. Think of it as . . . a mission. One only you can do."

"What about—"

"Don't make me repeat myself."

"But I—"

"*Enough*, Serwa."

"*But what if you don't come back?*"

Mom and I both freeze, and I have to wipe my eyes with the back of my hand. So much for convincing her I'm not afraid. Even though she's right in front of me, all I see are the Adinkra cloths hanging in the stool room back in the Compound. If this hunt goes wrong, if Boahinmaa outmaneuvers them again, then my parents' own Adinkra cloths will go from the leather case I saved back at the lake house to hanging beside my grandmother's.

And I'll be all alone.

"I don't want to be separated from you." My voice cracks, and I have to cough to keep talking. "Everything is changing really fast, and nothing makes sense. What is the Midnight Drum? Why does Boahinmaa want it so bad? Why have I trained so hard for so long if I can't come with you when it really counts?"

Several emotions cross over Mom's face—sadness, fear, and

a third one that I can't name but makes my chest go tight. She kneels in front of me, putting her hands on my shoulders.

"Boahinmaa wants the Midnight Drum because it's the key to freeing Nana Bekoe, the obayifo who led the forces of black magic during the Third Great War," she says slowly. "Nana Bekoe has been sealed inside it for more than twenty years. If she got out, there is no telling what damage she'd cause as vengeance for her banishment."

Mom's voice is small and thin, and it feels like if I breathe too hard she'll shatter completely. This is the most I've heard her speak about the war ever. Her mouth tightens as if there's more she wants to add, but she can't quite get the words out.

"Where is the drum?" I ask.

A small smile plays at her lips. "Nice try, but you know I can't tell you that. Rest assured the drum is in a place where no one can get to it. Not even Boahinmaa."

It makes me nervous to think a single instrument is the only thing keeping such a powerful witch at bay, but if Mom thinks it's safe, then it's safe. If I can trust anyone in this world, it's her.

"Can I let you in on a little secret?" Mom asks.

My throat hurts too much to speak, so I just nod.

"Every time we leave for a mission, I ask myself the same question: What if we don't come back? But that isn't a good enough reason not to do the thing that scares me."

I force myself to look at her. "I don't want you to go."

"And I don't want to. But, sometimes, being a warrior means doing the things you don't want to do so the people you love don't have to."

I look down at the battered tops of my Nikes. Mom and Dad are about to leave for what might be the most dangerous mission any Slayer has ever done, and all I can think about is how much I don't want to be left behind. The fate of the world matters way more than my feelings.

Mom opens her mouth, then closes it quickly. "Actually, I have something for you."

She slides Nokware off her wrist and hands it to me. My eyes practically bug out of my head. "You're giving me your sword? But won't you need it for the hunt?"

"Eh, I have others. Besides, I'd feel a lot better leaving it with a Slayer I trust."

Mom slips the bracelet onto my right wrist. It's so big I have to slide it all the way up to my forearm to get it to fit. The multi-colored wooden beads are warm to the touch, and they hum when I press my finger to them. When I look up at Mom, her eyes are bright and shiny.

"Promise me you'll take good care of it?" she whispers.

"I promise."

Mom wraps her arms around me and I hold on as tight as I can, inhaling her coconut-oil-and-shea-butter scent. Her breath is warm against my ear as she whispers, "You're my warrior, Serwa. Be a good one."

If I could stop time, I would freeze it right here and stay in this hug forever. My parents wouldn't have to risk their lives, and I wouldn't have to stay behind wondering if I was ever going to see them again.

We break apart when Dad comes down and pulls me into a bone-crushing hug of his own. Then we do our special hand-shake, complete with an under-the-leg knuckle touch. His eyes fall to Nokware, and he grins. "Nice bracelet."

I grin back. "It's all right."

Sensing we're alone, Boulder pops his head out of my backpack, only for him to yell in protest when Dad pulls him into a hug.

"Kwabena, you know how I feel about hugs!" he barks, and Dad laughs.

"I know. I'm just going to miss you."

"You'll be fine. Remember to eat three square meals a day," the mmoatia instructs him. "And don't forget your inhaler, just in case."

"I haven't had an asthma attack since I was fourteen," Dad replies with affectionate exasperation. "I'm not a child anymore."

"You will always be a child to me." Despite his grumpy frown, Boulder gently pats Dad's cheek. It feels more like I'm witnessing an uncle say goodbye to a favorite nephew than a monster hunter and his partner separating. "Take care. Avalanche will watch over you both. I'll protect Serwa."

Footsteps approach, and Boulder quickly slides into my backpack before Auntie Latricia and Roxy can see him. Now that my cousin and aunt are here, my parents slip back into being the no-nonsense Slayers I've known all my life.

"The day isn't getting any longer," says Mom. "If we leave now, we can beat the traffic on 95."

Auntie Latricia sighs while fanning herself. "I still wish you two would post about your travels. Some of us back home would like to know what y'all are getting up to out there."

Mom and Dad share a small smile.

"It's really not that interesting," says Mom.

"Work is work, no matter the job," Dad adds.

I tap my knuckles against the trunk of the car as a goodbye to Avalanche, who is hiding inside. She taps back, gently enough that no one else can hear. My parents and Auntie Latricia exchange a few more words, they both hug Roxy good-bye, and then they pile into our car.

Without me.

Suddenly my chest feels tight, like all the air in in the world has sunk into my lungs. Mom is driving, so Dad waves with both hands as she backs out of the parking lot and turns into the street. I wave and I wave and I wave, until the traffic light goes green and the car vanishes around the bend.

My hand is still in the air long after they're gone.

As I awkwardly lower it, Auntie Latricia looks at me and then says, "Roxy, come help me pick out what to order for our wel-come dinner tonight. I'm torn between Indian or Chinese."

Auntie Latricia and Roxy vanish up the stairs, leaving me alone on the curb. I sit down on the cement and double-check that no one else is around. Then I press the biggest bead on Nokware. It immediately shifts into its sword form, the black edge of the akrafena gleaming wickedly in the sunlight.

All I've wanted my entire life is the chance to wield this sword.

And now that I have it, all I want is my mom and dad back.

I take a deep breath, and then another. I rub the spot behind my right ear until the Big Feeling—that hot, swirling ickiness—goes away. I don't know whether it's just a placebo, but massag-ing that area often helps in times like this.

I might be sad, but I'm not cry-on-the-curb-outside-Sunny-Oak-Towers sad. I've got some dignity left. My parents are out there doing their best, and now they need me to do mine.

Besides, I've seen *High School Musical*, like, nineteen times. I fight vampires on a daily basis. Compared to beings made of unspeakably evil magic, how hard can middle school really be?

6

How to Start a Food Fight

"The world of mortals is often a confusing, contradictory place. Though our work is in service to their safety, it is advised that all Slayers limit their interactions with those outside our network as much as possible."

—From the *Nwoma*

IF I'VE LEARNED ANYTHING from Disney Channel Original Movies, it's that the first day of school makes or breaks the entire experience. That's why, by the time the school bus dumps me and Roxy outside the entrance to Rocky Gorge Middle School on Monday morning, all my sadness from Friday has been replaced by resolve. I don't even care that my actual birthday—August 28—passed by on Saturday with no recognition from my aunt and cousin since I couldn't bring myself to tell them about it. As far as I'm concerned, my pre-birthday celebration with my parents was the real one.

RGMS is one of the most expensive buildings in town, and the wealth is on full display from the moment we cross through the wrought-iron gates. It's three floors of shiny glass walls and chrome beams, with a giant LED sign out front that is currently welcoming everyone back to school. The crown jewel of the structure is the clock tower that keeps a watchful eye over the kids running around willy-nilly, saying hi to friends they haven't seen all summer, or trying to figure out where their lockers are.

I stop to stare at some parents who are peppering their sixth-grader with kisses. My face flushes when they catch me watching, and I hurry along before I can do anything else to embarrass myself. But Roxy saw, and she gives me a pitying glance, which only embarrasses me more.

"Don't be worried. Most of the people here are really nice," she says. The multicolored baubles Auntie Latricia twisted through Roxy's hair this morning clack together as she walks, and today's T-shirt features a faded picture of Bigfoot reclining on a tropical beach. "Did you sleep well?"

"Yeah," I lie as I silently count all the windows and doors in the front of the building. (Seventeen and six, respectively.)

Truth is, I barely slept all weekend, and not just because the air mattress on Roxy's floor is super lumpy. Every time I closed my eyes, all I could see was Dad with blood dripping down his stomach and Boahinmaa with her claws around Mom's throat. Too many questions ran through my head to let me sleep: Where are my parents now? Have they caught Boahinmaa's trail yet? What'll happen if Boahinmaa gets her hands on the Midnight Drum and lets out Nana Bekoe?

There's only one person—er, spirit—I can pose these questions to, but he's not here right now. Boulder is currently living it up back at the apartment, probably catching up on those trashy reality TV shows he loves while Auntie Latricia is at work.

The last time I attended school was when Socrates was running them, he'd said when I asked if he wanted to come with me this morning. Apparently, the mmoatia has lived long enough to personally know every major historical figure, and he has an opinion on all of them. *You shouldn't be in any danger surrounded by so many people. Try not to cause any trouble.*

So much for "protecting Serwa" and all that jazz. It's probably for the best. It'll be hard enough being the new kid—I don't need to make it harder by being the new kid who carries a hairy baby doll around.

Roxy must take my curt answer as worry because she gives me a sympathetic smile. "I always get nervous before the first day of school, too."

Nervous? I'm not nervous. Only people without plans get nervous, and I have a great plan. An incredible plan. Quite possibly the best plan of all time, if I do say so myself (and I do).

In my backpack is a full blueprint of the school, courtesy of my old friend Google, with every potential escape route highlighted in different colors to indicate efficiency. I also have a file containing headshots and all the important information I could find on every teacher via their social media profiles, and an ongoing list of where one might find power tools on the grounds (just in case). All this I compiled last night, because keeping busy feels better than sitting around freaking out over a hunt I have no part in.

My plan today is simple: keep my head down and learn enough about this school to blend in unnoticed. After all, this is just another mission—a super-boring mission, but a mission, nonetheless. And I don't screw up my missions.

"Oh hey, do you want to bike around town after school today?" Roxy asks. "You can borrow my mom's. I could show you all the best spots to hang out."

"I'm feeling pretty tired," I lie again. Exploring Rocky Gorge is exactly what I had planned after school ended, but without Roxy. She'd only slow me down. "Maybe another day."

Her smile falters. "Yeah, of course . . . Another day."

Roxy escorts me to the main office—which she didn't have to do, since I've already memorized the school layout, but I appreciate the gesture—and she stays with me until I get my schedule and student ID sorted out. She's crestfallen to realize we only have sixth period, Home Economics, together.

"I gotta go now, but let's eat together at lunch!" she yells over the bell. Our homerooms are on different sides of the school, so she frantically waves goodbye as she charges in the opposite direction to make it to her class on time.

I get to my homeroom with several minutes to spare and find that the desks are arranged in clusters of four. The seat next to mine is empty, while across from me is a blond white girl dressed in all pink. She's whispering to the kid beside her, an East Asian girl with her hair pulled back in a single braid and her nose glued to her phone. I check their name tags—Ashley Stevens, and Eunju Kim, respectively. Neither of them says hi to me, so I don't say hi to them.

Two people stand at the front of the room. The taller of the two must be Mrs. Dean, our homeroom teacher. She's a short white woman with tightly coiled gray hair and those glasses with strings on them that librarians in old movies wear. She's tapping a finger against a glass paperweight shaped like a bird on her desk. The other one is a light-brown-skinned boy with dark, curly hair, comically large glasses, and an oversize green sweater despite the fact it's hotter than the sun today. His gaze is planted firmly on the ground, as if making eye contact with any of us might actually kill him.

When the final bell rings, Mrs. Dean narrows her eyes at our cluster and purses her lips. I smile at her, and she looks away. After clearing her throat, she says, "It is time for roll call. When I call your name, say *present* and nothing else."

Whoa, what's up with her? Her voice is so chilly, you could build a snowman with it.

Mrs. Dean begins to read off the list of names. "Mateo Alvarez . . ."

The boy next to her raises his hand. "P-p-present."

"Lesley Baker . . . Evelyn Bennett . . ." She pauses and scrunches up her brow. "Sa—Se—Sarah Boating?"

Snickers flood the room, and it takes me a second to realize she is trying to say *my* name. I jump to my feet and clear my throat. "Actually, it's Serwa Boateng," I say, clearly enunciating the way the *bo* and *ah* in my last name almost blend to make something closer to a *bwah* sound.

Mrs. Dean's lips pull into a thin frown. "In my classroom, we do not stand unless called upon," she says. I sit down, heat rushing to my face as more snickers erupt. "This is your first warning, Sarah."

"But that's not my—"

However, Mrs. Dean has already moved on to the next student. No one was looking my way before, but now several curious eyes peer at me. I force myself not to slink down in my seat.

Is my name really that hard to pronounce? Then again, I only really hang out with my parents, who obviously know how to say it right. But *Boateng* really isn't that difficult, and *Serwa* is said exactly as it's spelled. First period hasn't even truly started, and I've already drawn more attention to myself than I'd planned to all day.

Mrs. Dean finishes roll call and then orders Mateo, who apparently is our homeroom class leader, to pass out the school guidelines and our worksheets for the day. He does so and then sits down in the seat next to mine, managing not to look at me or anyone else in our cluster the entire time. Then Mrs. Dean begins a long lecture on the updated rules, which now include a campus-wide ukulele ban after an unfortunate incident at last year's end-of-school pool party.

As she starts to explain that, yes, selfie sticks will be prohibited at Back-to-School Night, both for their original purpose and as a weapon, Ashley Stevens leans toward me and says, "I think it's so messed up that she won't even, like, try to say your name right."

My chest fills with the sweet feeling of vindication. "I know! I thought she was supposed to be a teacher."

"Plus, no other exchange students will ever come to this school if they hear we're being rude to them."

. . . Wait a minute. "I'm not an exchange student."

Ashley blinks in surprise. "Oh, I thought because of the accent . . . Where are you from?"

That is a question with no easy answer when you spend at least eight months of every year on the road fighting vampires. "Up north," I say and wave my hand in a vague circle that will hopefully get her to stop asking questions.

"But your accent. Where are you *really* from?"

The heat returns to my face. I have a little bit of an accent, but I've worked hard not to let it affect the way I talk. "I was born in Ghana."

Ashley nods, as if someone has just handed her the key to solving the Rubik's Cube that is my birthplace. "I've heard of that! Isn't that where *The Lion King* takes place?"

I stare it her, unsure of what to say. Should I start with the fact that I've spent almost my entire life in America and don't even really remember Ghana? Or that *The Lion King* is about as accurate to Africa as *Beauty and the Beast* is to France?

But luckily, Mateo answers for me. "*The Lion King* is set in K-K-Kenya, which is in East Africa. G-G-G . . ." He stops and takes a deep breath. "G-Ghana is in *West* Africa, near Nigeria."

I turn toward Mateo, who quickly looks away. I'm just about

to thank him for standing up for me when Mrs. Dean barks, "Mr. Alvarez! Sarah! I would appreciate it if you'd keep your attention to the front!"

Mateo gets redder than a strawberry and stammers out an apology as I sit up straighter. Ashley is the perfect picture of innocence, and it makes no sense that she didn't get called out when she started the conversation.

After that little snafu, nothing else happens for the rest of homeroom, and in first period (Math, taught by Mrs. Dean), it turns out I'm ahead of where everyone else is. I finish the review packet with almost twenty minutes to spare and spend the rest of the time scoping out my classmates. They are almost painfully normal—in fact, I'm pretty sure if you googled the word *normal*, all these kids' faces would pop up at the top of the results.

Perhaps because it is as bored as I am, Nokware buzzes against my skin, and I have to actively restrain myself from switching it into weapon form. Here I am with one of the best swords in the world, and I can't even use it.

It turns out I have second period—Earth Science—with Ashley and Eunju as well, and Ashley insists all three of us walk there together. The whole way, she peppers me with questions about Ghana: *What's it like there? Do you really eat everything with your hands, and doesn't that make a big mess? You speak English so well— how long did it take you to learn?* I try to answer her the best I can, but the questions give me a weird feeling. There's nothing wrong with them, but . . . I don't know. Eunju is mostly silent, only talking when Ashley speaks to her first.

The work in the next two periods is just as easy as in the first. Part of me wishes I could tell my parents: *See? School's a waste of time—come back for me!* But deep cover means deep cover, and they won't be sending or receiving messages anytime soon.

After that comes lunch, where I meet up with Roxy in front of the salad bar line. The vegetables here look sad. Asaase Yaa didn't bless the earth with bountiful vegetation for the lunch ladies of Rocky Gorge Middle School to call a slice of tomato and a handful of shredded lettuce a "salad."

"How's your first day going?" my cousin asks.

"It's been fine," I say, because it mostly has been. I don't mention Mrs. Dean refusing to say my name or Ashley's weird fascination with me being foreign. Neither really matters. Plus, even if they did, there's nothing Roxy could do about it. "And you?"

"Math is the worst, but I'll live. Where are you sitting?"

Since my hand is full of school lunch, I gesture with my shoulder toward the table where Ashley has saved me a seat with her hot-pink Vera Bradley bag. Roxy looks over and her smile falls a bit. "Oh . . . Are you sure it's okay if I join you?"

"Yeah, why not?" I ask, but Roxy doesn't reply.

Ashley and Eunju both look up from their phones when we approach, and Ashley gets this weird expression, then quickly replaces it with a big smile. Eunju just seems uncomfortable.

"Oh, hey, Roxy."

"Hey." Roxy's tray trembles in her hands. "Is it cool if I sit with you?"

"Yeah, it is. It's just . . ." Ashley's mouth scrunches up. "I'm so, so sorry, this is so embarrassing, but I thought it was going to be just the three of us, so I only saved one more seat—for Serwa—and it might be a tight fit. But let me move some stuff around." She half-heartedly pulls her bag closer to her, which opens up only three more inches.

Roxy gives a fake laugh. "Actually, I totally forgot I promised to help the media center ladies during lunch today. Let's eat together next time!" She scurries off as I take the free seat Ashley left open for me.

As soon as Roxy is gone, Ashley lets out a big sigh and rolls her eyes. "Oh my God, she is so annoying. How were we ever friends with her?" she says to Eunju, who silently picks at her nasty salad.

My fork freezes in midair. Ashley, Eunju, and Roxy used to be friends? Roxy never mentioned that.

Ashley continues, "And can you believe she's still into all that Bigfoot and ghost nonsense? Who does she think she is, the Ghostbusters?"

"Hey, it's not like her hobby is hurting anyone," I say, though secretly I do agree that Roxy's fascination with the supernatural is a little weird. But it's not like I have any right to talk when I spend the majority of my day thinking about vampires.

Ashley sniffs as she double-checks her mascara via her phone's front camera. "I know she's your cousin, but be careful. She's got a bit of a reputation, and you don't want it dragging you down, too. It's part of the reason we don't talk anymore."

Before I can ask what happened to make them end their friendship, Ashley switches topics. "Hey, what's your FaceSplap handle? Let's add each other!"

"What's FaceSplap?"

Ashley begins to laugh, then stops at my confused look. "How have you not heard of FaceSplap? It's only the best app in the world! Do you not have internet in Ghana?"

I take a bite of my sloppy joe to stop myself from grimacing. "We do. But I don't have a phone." And I didn't move here straight from Ghana, but something tells me reminding her of that isn't worth the trouble.

Ashley looks at me like I just told her my parents make me spend every holiday scrubbing the floor with a toothbrush. "But how do you *live* without one?"

Like a caveman banging rocks together to make fire, is what I want to say, but I bite back the snarky response. It's really not as hard not having a phone as people would think. Slayers are advised to limit the number of trackable devices they own for safety reasons, so I use my Adinkra-sealed iPad when I need to go online. Besides, who would I even call besides my parents if I had a phone? Declan Amankwah? No way.

"What's FaceSplap?" I ask again.

"It's this meme-sharing app where you upload photos and videos, and people in your area can rank them." She nudges Eunju with her elbow. "Eunju's parents made it."

"Yeah, it's pretty cool," says Eunju in a flat voice. She immediately goes back to her food, which leaves me to spend the rest of the time talking with Ashley about nothing. But no matter how hard I try, I can't stop thinking about how sad Roxy looked when she walked away, and I now wish I had fought harder for her to stay. Something went down between her, Ashley, and Eunju, but what?

Fifth period—Language Arts—is so boring I almost pass out in my seat, but finally it's time for sixth period, the last class of the day. For me, it's Home Economics, the only class I share with Roxy. The teacher is Mr. Johnson, a wrinkly old white man with the bushiest eyebrows I've ever seen. After a quick safety lesson about not setting ourselves on fire with the gas stoves, he has us separated into groups and cooking spaghetti and meatballs.

I'm a bit relieved he didn't let us pick our own groups, because then I would've had to choose between Roxy and Ashley. Instead, I end up with Eunju and a Black boy named Gavin, who makes it clear from the jump that he's not interested in taking this assignment seriously.

"I don't do knives," is all he says when I try to get him to mince our garlic, and more than once Eunju snaps at him for using the spatulas like drumsticks and for putting the colander over his blue-dyed twists and pretending it's a space helmet.

Compared to our lively-if-chaotic station, the one across from us is practically a graveyard. It's clear from the way Ashley and Roxy dance around each other that their beef runs deep. The third member of their group, Mateo, has taken over the cooking. He chops their tomatoes and onions, stirs the sauce, and measures the water with surprising efficiency. Once again, he doesn't talk to or look at anyone.

Aside from the fact that one of my group members might be about to murder the other, I think this first day of school has been a success overall. A part of me still feels weird without my weapons belt, and I don't think I'm ever going to fully stop looking over my shoulder, but I think I've got the hang of this normal-girl thing already. I turn to Gavin to ask him to pass me the pasta strainer, and—

There's a yellow light coming from Eunju's backpack.

I freeze for one heartbeat.

Two.

The light's still there, pulsing slowly. All the sound seems to drain from the room as my focus narrows in on the yellow dot. I grab the closest utensil—a ladle—and creep slowly toward the backpack with my heart pounding in my throat. I have to be careful. Even the slightest wrong movement might startle the adze into attacking.

"Uh, hey, Eunju, nice backpack. Do you mind if I take a look at it?" I say in my best *Don't panic, there's most definitely not a vampire in our midst* voice. If I'm smart about this, I should be able to give everyone enough time to run while I trap the adze. There might even be a pen or something in the bag I can draw an Adinkra with.

Eunju tenses, her hands full of parmesan cheese. "Why?"

"No reason. I just . . . uh, always wanted one like that. If I could—" I reach for the backpack as Eunju drops the cheese and pulls her bag toward her chest. Soon we're in a tug-of-war over the stupid thing, and the adze is still inside, blinking like crazy.

"What are you doing? Get off!" she cries. Girl's got some serious grip, I'll give her that.

"I'm! So! Sorry!" I say between tugs. Everyone's staring at us now, but I don't even care. I'm okay with looking stupid if it means I can save everyone's lives.

Eunju pushes forward with the backpack like a battering ram, and I skid into the counter. The bowl of spaghetti sauce takes what can only be described as a swan dive off the table and lands straight on me and Ashley, who has come over to see what all the fuss is about.

The class goes absolutely silent as Ashley stares down at her $200 outfit, ruined forever by a fragrant mixture of marinara and mushrooms. Then Michael Smith lets out this loud guffaw that echoes through the classroom. With a screech that would put any adze to shame, Ashley wipes a handful of sauce off her shirt and lobs it at him. Michael ducks just in time, and the sauce hits Anthony Chen square in the face. He grabs a hunk of garlic bread and chucks it back at Ashley.

"FOOD FIGHT!" someone screams. With those two words, complete anarchy breaks loose.

Pasta and sauce and bread fly through the air at speeds never before seen on this earth. I dive to the floor to avoid an onion to the face. Melissa Bukowski isn't so lucky, and she goes down hard when the bulb whacks the back of her head. I army crawl on my stomach for Eunju's backpack, avoiding pasta the entire way. All this commotion is surely going to trigger the adze into going monster on all of us. I've got to catch and seal it before it does. I swipe for the bag, but Eunju, with Gavin close behind, is faster and grabs it back.

"What is wrong with you?!" screams Eunju as I try to pull the backpack to me.

"Leave her alone!" cries Roxy, coming to help me. Soon it's me and Roxy on one side, Gavin and Eunju on the other, and now Mateo is here trying to calm us all down, and any second the adze is going to attack and it's going to be my fault if anyone gets hurt, because I'm the Slayer. I have to stop this, because I'm the only one who can, and—

"WHAT IS GOING ON HERE?"

Everyone freezes as Principal Hashimoto enters the room. Her face is nearly purple with anger, and I swear steam comes out of her ears when she shouts, "Who is responsible for this?"

Two dozen fingers immediately point toward Roxy, Gavin, Mateo, Eunju, and me.

Principal Hashimoto's face gets even more purple. "Detention! All five of you! Gather your things and report to Room Two-Five now!"

We all do as we're told, since there's really no way to argue when we're covered in pasta sauce. But on our way out, Eunju slips something from her backpack.

It's her cell phone, with a bright yellow notification light blinking at the top. She catches me looking at it, glares, and then presses the Home button. The light immediately goes off.

Too embarrassed to meet anyone's eyes, I hang my head and shuffle out of Home Economics, my shoes leaving tomato-y prints down the length of the hall.

Some Slayer I am.

1

How to Plot an Escape

"Retreat should only ever be considered when all
other options have been exhausted.
Better to die with honor than to live without it."

—From the *Nwoma*

IT'S OFFICIAL. I HAVE to leave the country and change my name.

I mean, who mistakes a cell phone light for an adze? For the first time since my parents left, I'm glad they're not here, because if they saw what happened in the Home Ec room, they'd never let me go on a hunt ever again.

Principal Hashimoto ordered us to detention, but we have to make a quick stop at the locker rooms first, since they can't have us tracking pasta sauce all over the halls. By the time we're all done showering and changing into gym uniforms (mine hasn't arrived yet, so I'm wearing an extra one the gym teacher, Mrs. Lucas, gave me; it smells like basketballs and children's tears), school is over for the day. Our classmates stream out of the halls ecstatic that the first day is done, leaving the building eerily quiet as the five of us trudge to Room 2-5 to face our punishment.

Waiting for us there is a youngish-looking teacher

with light brown skin, wavy black hair, and a much-too-pleased look on his face considering it's the first day of school and he's stuck on detention duty. As soon as we're all seated, he claps his hands together and breaks out in a grin.

"I've gotta say, I'm almost impressed. A food fight on the first day of school? That's *pasta-tively* incredible."

Dead silence.

The teacher coughs awkwardly. "I thought a joke might lighten the mood. . . . You know what? Never mind. Forget I said any of that. It didn't happen. Moving on." He clears his throat. "My name is Mr. Riley, and I'll be supervising your detention and the cleaning of the Home Ec room while the principal and Mr. Johnson decide whether further disciplinary action is required. Now, in the past, similar events have usually led to suspension, sometimes even expulsion."

Wait, did he just say *expulsion*? My parents will kill me if they hear I got expelled!

Mr. Riley must see the panicked looks on all our faces, because he quickly adds, "Don't worry—no one here is getting expelled! At least, I highly doubt you will. This is the first major offense for all of you, so it's unlikely to be added to your permanent record. But first, we need to take care of the Home Ec room."

Mr. Riley leads us back to the scene of the crime, which looks and smells like the inside of a Hot Pocket. There he points us all to a bunch of mops, rags, and buckets full of soapy water. Judging from the amount of parmesan cheese we somehow wedged into the light fixtures, it's going to take hours to get this place clean again. If I could use my Adinkra, we'd be done in five minutes, but nooooo, nothing can be easy in the mortal world.

Gavin's hand immediately shoots up. "Excuse me, sir, but I have a livestream planned for this evening that I absolutely cannot miss. Plus, I'm pretty sure you can't keep us here without our parents' or guardians' permission."

Mr. Riley cheerfully slaps a mop into Gavin's outstretched hand. "You're right about that, which is why we've already alerted them. They've been instructed to come and get you *after* you're done cleaning."

If looks could kill, the ones the other four kids give me would send me six feet under the ground. I don't blame them, not when I'm the reason they're going to waste a beautiful August afternoon doing manual labor. All this because I've been in vampire-hunting mode for so long I literally forgot how the normal world works.

Mr. Riley takes one look at our glum faces and sighs. "Look, I know this situation isn't ideal. Personally, I don't think it's fair that you five were singled out when the whole class participated in the fight. But rules are rules, and, unfortunately, people like us often have to work twice as hard to deal with others' judgments."

Though he doesn't say it outright, we all know exactly what he means—the five of us were easy to blame because we aren't white. In a school and town where almost everyone is, we'll always be the first ones people point fingers at. The unfairness of it burns through my chest hotter than magic, but there's nothing I can do.

"I know we just met, but I'm on your side," Mr. Riley continues. "I've been in your shoes before, which is why I volunteered to look after you today. I don't want any of you to have to go through what I did when I was in middle school. But if I'm going to help you, I need you all to meet me halfway. Come on, let's get started."

He rolls up the sleeves of his red plaid button-down shirt, revealing impressive tattoos climbing up both forearms. They're mostly nature-based, with lots of flowers and birds. He pulls out a tote bag covered in paint splatters, rummages through it, then frowns. "Erm, it seems I've forgotten the sponges. Forgive me, I've been in such a brain fog lately. You all can get started while I go fetch those. . . . And keep your phones in your pockets!"

Mr. Riley bolts from the room, and the silence after he leaves is thicker than an overfed house cat. It's not even four p.m., but I wish this day were over already. I wish I could go home—my *real* home.

I wish Mom and Dad were here.

Roxy is the first to break the silence. "At least we're probably not getting suspended?" she says hopefully as she grabs a rag and begins wiping down a tomato-covered oven.

"I've never had a mark on my p-p-permanent record b-b-before," mutters Mateo, more to himself than any of us. Across from him, Gavin scoffs.

"Please. Permanent records are a scam used to scare kids into following the rules. My older brother was in detention, like, every other week when he went here, and not a single college asked about it when he applied to them." Gavin pointedly ignores the bucket Mateo tries to hand him in favor of pulling his blue twists into a half ponytail. "I've been posting about this livestream all week. If I lose any followers because I have to cancel it . . ."

He gives me another glare, as if I personally hacked into his channel and deleted his entire follower list. I turn my back to him, my knuckles tightening around the handle of my own mop. Luckily, Eunju cuts off Gavin's rant when she snarkily asks him if he ever shuts up, and the two devolve into some back-and-forth name-calling.

"Can you pass the bleach, please?" I ask Eunju through gritted teeth, since she's closer to it than I am. There are so many things I want to say, but something tells me letting any of them out will only make a sucky situation even worse. I wonder if Boulder is worried about where I am. Nyame help me, explaining to him what happened today is one conversation I'm not looking forward to.

Eunju stops bickering with Gavin, gives me a mean side-eye, then pulls her phone out of her pocket and immediately starts scrolling through it. "I still don't get why we all have to do this when *most* of us didn't do anything wrong."

"Leave her alone. It was an accident," says Roxy.

Suddenly I'm so grateful she's here with me. Then I remember what happened at lunch, how I let Ashley turn her away, and wow, I really am the worst.

Eunju's laugh pulls me out of my thoughts. She looks at her phone, then at me, then back to her phone. My hand flies to my hair. Do I still have pasta sauce in it?

"What?" I snap.

"Nothing. It's . . ." She barely hides her giggle. "It's nothing."

Gavin peeks over her shoulder, and his eyes widen. He covers his mouth with his hand to fight back his own laugh.

All right, that's it. I march over. "Show me what you're laughing at."

Eunju turns the phone to me and I see a bright yellow FaceSplap logo before she switches the video to full screen. Apparently someone recorded our food fight, because there I am virtually falling into the spaghetti sauce. The uploader put the video on rapid loop and added some warping filters and epic music to the video. I check the timestamps. "#PastaPants Epic Fail" has only been up for an hour and it already has sixteen thousand views and climbing.

Pasta Pants. I've been at this school for one day, and I'm already Pasta Pants. I go back to my little corner of mess and scratch behind my ear until the burning in my eyes goes away.

Roxy looks down at her own phone, then up at me in horror. "I'm so sorry, Serwa."

I don't say anything back.

Mr. Riley says he's been in my shoes, but he hasn't. I don't belong here—not in this school, not in this town. I'm not cut out for lockers and classrooms and book bags. I'm meant for scheming and hunting and battling, not trying to make small talk with four people who hate my guts.

I shouldn't have to put up with this.

You know what? I *don't* have to put up with this. I can leave. Just go somewhere else, lie low until Mom and Dad come back from their hunt. Sure, they'll be furious at first, but they'll get over it. I've lived on the road before, for months at a time. I know I can pull it off. I'll even let Boulder come along, if he promises not to be a huge grump the whole time, which, honestly, is unlikely.

Detention becomes a lot less boring when you use it to plan your grand escape. As I'm mentally running through a list of supplies I'm going to need—Gatorade, definitely, the blue kind, not the red—Mr. Riley returns carrying several sponges and a ceramic mug. He looks weaker than he did when he left the room, and by the time he makes it back to the teacher's desk, he's swaying.

"I'm so sorry, y'all. There must've been something weird in my coffee." Mr. Riley glares at his mug like it's personally wronged him. He opens his mouth to say something, takes a step forward, and immediately collapses on the floor. His mug goes down with him, smashing into bits when it hits the ground.

For several seconds, none of us moves, too shocked to know what to do. I'm the first to react, running over to Mr. Riley and propping him up into a sitting position as the others quickly follow.

"Oh my God, is he dead?" whispers Eunju, while Gavin looks ready to faint. I press two fingers against Mr. Riley's neck, just like Mom taught me to do during my basic wound training. The knot in my stomach loosens at the fluttering pulse I feel.

"Not dead, just unconscious," I declare, and everyone sighs in relief. Something tells me the administration would change their minds about not expelling us if Mr. Riley died in our arms.

"We should g-g-get the nurse," argues Mateo.

"She's already gone for the day," Roxy shoots back. "We need to call 9-1-1!"

As the others squabble over what to do, I check Mr. Riley once again. That's when I see it—two small puncture holes, red and dripping, on the side of his right thumb.

The exact kind of marks an adze leaves after it has fed on its prey.

My heart pounds in my ears as I jump to my feet and run out the classroom door. The hallway is deathly cold, the kind of cold no August afternoon can make. The sun isn't even close to setting, but the corridor is evening dark. The only light comes from a single yellow orb floating in the air, illuminating rows upon rows of silver lockers.

Even though it's right in front of me, part of me doesn't believe it. How can there be an adze here? How did my parents miss it?

Shadows on either side of the hallway twist and hiss, edging toward the light instead of away from it like shadows are supposed to do. The glow from the orb becomes brighter and brighter, until I have to shield my eyes from the glare. Then it zips around the corner, gone so fast I might have imagined it.

But I didn't imagine it. Not this time.

There's an adze terrorizing this school, and I have no one but these four nincompoops to help me fight it.

Nyame help me, we're all gonna die.

8

How to Lose an Argument

*"Never allow magic to be witnessed by anyone
outside our society."*

—From the *Nwoma*

MY BODY MOVES BEFORE my mind. I summon
Nokware in an instant and sprint down the hallway,
only to turn a corner where the path branches into
three identical corridors. Right, left, or middle—which
way did the adze go? I crane my neck to check each
option, but there's no sign of the vampire's eerie golden
light. I can't afford to get this wrong, not when even a
second wasted gives the adze more chances to attack
innocent people.

"Serwa?" Roxy's alarmed voice calls from behind me.
"What are you doing?"

Nokware vanishes as I whirl around to see Roxy and
everyone else with their heads poking out of the classroom doorway. "Nothing. I— What are *you* doing?" I
ask, which has to be the worst comeback in the history
of comebacks.

"Mr. Riley woke up. Was that a sword?"

"Sword?" I give a laugh that I hope doesn't sound as

77

wooden to her as it does to me. "What is this, *Elden Ring*? All the panic has you seeing things. I was running to get help, but I guess we don't need it anymore."

Roxy's eyebrows furrow, but she nods. I run back to the classroom and shove past Eunju and Gavin, refusing to meet their suspicious stares, and join Mateo in helping Mr. Riley up off the ground. Not even a whole minute has passed since he collapsed, but the adze is definitely long gone by now. Going after it would be a waste of time, not to mention a threat to my cover.

Mr. Riley is surprisingly cheerful for someone who almost smashed his head open on the floor.

"I am so sorry you all had to see that," he says as Mateo and I ease him into the teacher's chair. He gives the remains of his coffee mug a mournful glance. "I haven't been feeling well for a little while now, but to think I'd faint at work . . . How long was I out?"

"B-b-barely a minute," says Mateo. "Are you in any p-p-pain? Should we c-c-call someone?"

"If you'd like anemia supplements, I know a guy on McGraw Road who—" starts Gavin.

Mr. Riley shakes his head. "No, don't call anyone. Teachers like me don't exactly have ambulance money lying around. Besides, I've always . . . recovered from injuries faster than most people. Let's just get this cleanup done so we can get you all home, and I'll pop by Urgent Care later."

The next hour passes by in awkward silence punctuated only by the sloshing of mops and swiping of sponges. Mr. Riley seems weak but stable. An adze can only possess one person at a time, and he's not showing any signs of being taken over by it. While being the vampire's afternoon meal can't have been fun, at least it's not rooting around inside his head. I'm literally bursting with questions for him: *Did you see anything weird when you left the room? Anything firefly-shaped, perhaps? Not to alarm you, but are you aware of the very strong possibility that your recent illness is the result of a vampire going to town on your blood like it's a tube of Go-Gurt?*

But I can't say anything in front of the other four. By the time we're finally done cleaning the Home Ec room, I feel like a kettle ready to burst from the pressure of everything I'm holding in. Searching the school for the adze isn't even an option, because Mr. Riley sends us to wait in the principal's office for our guardians while he goes to the nurse's office to "lie down for a spell."

None of us says anything, and I have no idea what the others would say if they even wanted to speak. *Hey, wasn't it freaky how our teacher just fainted out of nowhere, haha. Anyway, still hate your guts!* Eunju's suspicious glare hasn't lessened all evening. Did she see Nokware's true form? Nah, there's no way she'd be able to keep something like that to herself for this long. And even if she did, I've got bigger things to worry about now.

There's an adze here in Rocky Gorge Middle School, and I didn't sense it. Even worse, my *parents* didn't sense it. That freaks me out more than anything else. What if this adze is like Boahinmaa and somehow resistant to the Adinkra? Two fully trained Slayers at the top of their game barely managed to take her and her hench-bugs down. If a similar attack happened and I was all on my own . . .

A shiver runs down my spine.

I need to call my parents. *Now.*

Everyone else has someone pick them up within an hour, so by six p.m. it's only me and Roxy sitting in the front office with a sour-faced secretary, Miss Penny, who looks like she'd rather watch paint dry than spend another second baby-sitting us.

"Is there any other number I can call?" Miss Penny asks in a sickly-sweet voice as she raises an over-painted eyebrow.

Roxy squishes down in her seat. "There's no one else. Just my mom."

"Well, I can only release you to an authorized parent or guardian, so I guess we'll all just have to hang tight until she gets here." The woman sniffs. "Though I can't imagine anything that's more important than picking up your own child," she mutters.

The part of me that isn't thinking about hunting down the adze bristles with irritation. I haven't known her that long, but Auntie Latricia has been nothing but nice to me, and it's not her fault she can't just drop work at any second. This lady has no right to talk bad about her.

Fortunately, Auntie Latricia bursts through the door five minutes later. She's still wearing her scrubs, and there's a stain down the front that it looks like it might be from the Indian-food leftovers she had for lunch.

She narrows her eyes at Roxy and me. "Detention on the first day of school?" she asks. Though her voice is calm, her eyes have the patented *Oh, you better have a story, and it had better be good* look that I think all mothers are taught at Mom School. She signs us out wordlessly, and we pile into her Honda.

The second the seat belts are in place, Roxy breaks down. "I am so, so, *so* sorry, Mom," she says, her bottom lip trembling. I hope she doesn't cry. Seeing other people cry always makes me cry, and this day has been bad enough already. "I know how hard it is for you to get time off last minute."

Auntie Latricia doesn't say anything until we're pulled into the parking lot in front of Sunny Oak Towers. Then she turns in her seat and gives us that look again. "Explain."

Since Roxy is on the verge of tears, I jump in and say, "I thought I saw a bug on another girl's backpack, and I tried to kill it, but she thought I was stealing her bag instead. While we were arguing, I accidentally spilled spaghetti sauce on Ashley, and she started a food fight, but we got detention and she didn't!"

Okay, so nothing I said was *technically* a lie. I really did think Eunju's cell phone was an adze, and it really is messed up that Ashley didn't get in trouble for the fight when we did.

Auntie Latricia's anger slips a little, and she asks, "Ashley Stevens, as in that girl you played with all the time in elementary school, Roxy? I thought you two were best friends."

Best friends? I glance over at Roxy for confirmation of this surprising tidbit, but she is turned away from me, her face pressed against the window.

"Things change," she mumbles.

Auntie Latricia looks at me, but I shrug. I'm as clueless as she is about what went down between them—I just got here.

She sighs. "Go inside and do your homework. No phone or screen time for the rest of the day. I'll call you when dinner's ready."

I can't believe a woman I just met is grounding me, but my parents did leave her in charge while they were gone, so there's nothing I can say back. The real problem is how I'm going to get a message to my parents when I'm stuck with Roxy all night. I'm already breaking the rules by trying to contact them at all, so I will be in super trouble if my cousin catches me using magic at the same time.

Luckily, my chance comes a lot sooner than I expect, because not even two hours into our exile, Auntie Latricia pokes her head through the bedroom door and yells, "Roxy, Daddy's on the phone!"

I swear, there are Christmas trees that don't light up as quickly as Roxy does when she gets that news. She practically runs out the door, and seconds later I hear her talking excitedly to a deep male voice coming from the living room. I guess calls from her dad are rare, because Auntie Latricia forgot all about the grounding the second he phoned. It's gotta be almost midnight in Ghana since they're about four hours ahead of the East Coast (five when there's not Daylight Savings going on here). I keep meaning to ask exactly what happened to get him deported, but it never seems like the right time.

I tiptoe out of the bedroom to eavesdrop. For a second, all I can do is watch Roxy and Auntie Latricia crowd around my aunt's tablet, so far apart from the man on the screen but a laughing, happy family all the same. Even from here I can tell how much Roxy takes after Uncle Patrick—the two of them smile in the exact same way, like their entire face is crinkling with joy.

My chest tightens the longer I watch the three of them wrapped up in their own little world. Just a few days ago, that was what my parents and I were like. . . .

Wait, what am I standing here moping around for? This is my chance! I run back to the bedroom and dig through the closet until I pull Boulder out of the makeshift nest of blankets and T-shirts he's made for himself. He lets out a sleepy cry at the rough handling, clearly having been in the middle of a nap.

"What are you doing?" he mumbles through clenched teeth as I drop him into my backpack. Another one of my parents' rules is that I shouldn't interact with Boulder when there's anyone else in the vicinity unless it's an emergency. I can't think of anything more emergency than a vampire snacking on my teacher.

Ignoring Boulder's grunts of protest, I quickly unscrew the screen from Roxy's bedroom window, haul myself over the ledge, then climb up the bricks protruding from the side of the building. I estimate I'll probably have half an hour or so before Roxy or Auntie Latricia realizes I'm gone, but I still have to hurry. A few minutes later, the mmoatia and I are seated safely on the roof, nobody to bother us but the wind and an extremely fat pigeon who doesn't even blink at our arrival. It's not eight o'clock yet, but the first stars are already twinkling overhead. This high up, they feel close enough for me to grab one from the sky and keep it in my pocket.

Boulder rolls out of the backpack and growls while I search for a marker. "What is the meaning of this, Serwa?" he snaps. "I am not some common doll you can just—"

"I saw an adze at school today," I interrupt. His shocked look at this news would be hilarious on any other day. "I need you to call my mom and dad right now."

Boulder's surprise quickly switches to disbelief. He shakes his head with a scoff. "That's not possible. If there were an adze or any other source of black magic in this town, I would have sensed it by now."

"Like you sensed the adze who attacked us at the lake house?" I argue back. "Your radar must be off or something, because I saw it with my own eyes! The adze bit my teacher, and he fainted!"

Even though I'm physically with Boulder right now, my mind is still in the classroom, replaying the horrible moment when Mr. Riley passed out. Maybe it's for the best the adze got away, because I don't want to imagine what might've happened if it had turned its attention on me and the others.

Shame fills me for even thinking like that, and I squeeze my Grandma Awurama's pendant to remind myself of who I am and where I come from. I shouldn't be relieved that the adze got away, because a real Slayer is always ready for a fight.

I failed today. It won't happen again.

"I'm not making it up," I say. "There was an adze in my school. We need to get my parents and the Abomofuo involved before anyone else gets hurt."

My voice cracks on the last part, and that must be what convinces Boulder I'm truly freaked out, because he finally nods. "All right. I'll call them."

I uncap the marker and quickly get to work drawing the Adinkra we need on the concrete ledge of the rooftop. First is nkonsonkonson, the Adinkra of unity and human relations, to forge the connection. Next comes hwe mu dua, the measuring stick, which represents quality. This one ensures that the connection I make will be strong enough to reach my parents wherever they might be. Then akoben, the war horn, as a summons. I could just have Boulder eat a message so that Avalanche coughs it up, but I think it would be better to share this news with them face-to-face.

Plus . . . it would be nice to see them. Just to know they're okay.

When the Adinkra are done, Boulder and I sit across from each other with the three symbols between us. He presses his hands to the concrete, and light races from his fingertips to the Adinkra. At first they glow strong and bright, but soon they begin to flicker like burned-out lightbulbs.

Boulder grits his teeth. "They've put a ward around themselves to prevent communication," he explains as sweat drips down his wrinkled brow. "I can't get through."

I thought my parents might pull something like this when they said they'd be going into deep cover, but I didn't think they'd make it difficult for even Boulder to reach them. The sound of Mr. Riley's body hitting the ground echoes through my ears on a loop, and that's what makes me slam my own palms down beside Boulder's. I have to reach Mom and Dad, no matter what.

I've practiced the communication spell hundreds of times, but something is different tonight. My stomach twists like someone is trying to pull it out through my belly button, and the air in front of us shimmers in a way I've never seen before. I try to yank my hands back, but they won't budge. The Big Feeling returns, pushing up through my core, bright and demanding. It doesn't feel bad, exactly, but it doesn't feel like divine wisdom, either, and it just. Won't. *Stop.*

Until it does.

In half a heartbeat, the weirdness disappears and the Big Feeling goes with it. The shimmering in the air extends into a flat silver surface like a mirror before revealing my bewildered parents standing in what looks to be the screwdriver aisle of a Home Depot.

"Serwa? Is that you?" asks Dad, and even though it's only been a few days since I last saw him, I drink in every line and freckle of his face like I've never seen them before. Right now there's nothing inside me but relief and a homesickness big enough to drown me from the inside out. That weirdness I felt just now was probably nothing but stress.

"Daddy!" I cry, only to immediately wish I hadn't. I don't think I've called my father that since I was in diapers. I'm really not helping my whole *I am a confident and competent individual* case here.

"Are you outside?" he demands as Mom steers him toward the back of the aisle, where they'll be less likely to be overheard. "Why is it so dark? How did you even reach us? You shouldn't be able to—"

"Mom, Dad, I saw an adze," I say, and his shocked face is super similar to Boulder's. I guess the old wives' tale that Slayers and their mmoatia start to resemble each other after a while really is true.

"Where?" he asks sharply.

"Today after school. I was in detention and—"

"Detention!" Mom interrupts. "Serwa Acheampomaa Boateng, you got detention on your very first day of school?"

"It was all a big misunderstanding! I accidentally started a food fight and—"

"You started a food fight?" For the first time since they left, I'm glad my parents aren't here, because Mom's voice has risen so many octaves she'd shatter my eardrums if we were in the same place. "Explain *now.*"

Beside me, Boulder grimaces. Even from miles away, my mom's Scary Mode is *scary.* I tell them everything that happened today, from the weird feeling I got during Mrs. Dean's class to the fake adze during Home Ec to Mr. Riley's collapse and everything after. By the time I'm done, my parents' expressions have changed from alarm to . . . pity? What?

"Serwa," my dad says slowly. The fatigue in his voice is thick—he probably hasn't slept since the last time I saw him. He glances over his shoulder to double-check that the aisle is still empty. "If the first adze you saw today was fake, what makes you so sure the second one wasn't?"

"I know what I saw!" I protest.

"Boulder, did *you* see this supposed adze?" Mom asks.

The mmoatia squirms uncomfortably beside me. "I did not," he admits. *Traitor.* "I was not on the school premises today."

"Did you sense a flare-up of black magic today anywhere within Rocky Gorge?"

"No. In fact, I haven't sensed anything at all since we got here. This town is all but a magic dead zone."

"But Boulder didn't sense Boahinmaa arriving at the house either!" I cry.

"Boahinmaa is different," Mom says softly. "She always has been."

My eyes widen as the truth hits me: They don't believe me. My own parents don't believe me. "But I saw the adze bite mark on Mr. Riley's thumb!" I argue.

"You say you only saw it after he had left the room. How do you know he didn't have that mark before?" Dad asks, and my memories start to falter. If Mr. Riley had been bleeding when we met him, I would have noticed . . . right?

"But—"

"Did you actually *see* the second adze bite your teacher? Did you see it transform?"

I look down at my hands. "No."

Mom kisses her teeth, then sighs. "Look, Serwa, our concentration on this mission is crucial. We can't focus if you're bothering us with false alarms."

Heat rushes to my face. So now I'm a bother. "I wouldn't have to *bother* you at all if you'd just brought me with you! I could've taken the Initiation Test and—"

"We are done with this conversation."

Between my life flipping upside down, my buttcrack-awful first day of school, and now my parents thinking I'm crying wolf, the last thread holding my patience together snaps.

"No, *you're* done with this conversation! I still don't understand what's going on!" I yell. "No one's given me a single straight answer since Boahinmaa tried to kill us! So sorry for not being all cool and calm about being abandoned in the middle of freaking nowhere!"

The second the words are out, I know I've screwed up bigtime. It doesn't matter if you are the pope and a Kardashian mixed with Obama himself, you don't ever, *ever* yell at Ghanaian parents. Any sympathy or pity my parents may have had vanishes.

"We are apart for a few days, and you think that you can yell at us? You think you have it harder than we do when we are out here risking our lives?" Most of the time Mom's English is clear with the slightest hint of a British accent, like many people in Ghana have, thanks to colonialism. But sometimes, when she's really upset, like right now, her real accent slips through, and that's how I know I've really, *really* messed up. "No, Serwa, your ungratefulness is appalling. The things I would've given at your age to have a roof over my head and a safe place to sleep. A childhood—" Mom's voice cracks, and she looks away.

Dad steps forward, putting one hand on Mom's shoulder as if she might disappear if he doesn't hold on to her. When he speaks to me, his tone is stern. "I'm ashamed, Serwa. Your aunt and cousin are doing us a great favor by taking you in, yet it sounds like all you've done so far is cause them trouble. We raised you better than this."

I almost wish the adze that bit Mr. Riley would reappear,

because surely being attacked by a vampire would be less painful than dealing with your parents' disappointment. Tears burn at the back of my eyes.

Dad sighs. "I'm sorry to have to do this, Boulder, but it seems we have no choice."

Before I can even ask what *this* is, Dad presses a hand against his abode santann tattoo. Boulder lets out a strangled gasp, his tiny hand flying to the same spot on his own chest. The image of my parents in the Home Depot begins to ripple and fade.

"Wait!" I cry, but it's no use. In seconds, the magic shatters, leaving me, Boulder, and the fat pigeon alone on the roof.

The mmoatia's mouth opens and closes several times without anything coming out. When he looks up at me, his eyes are wide with fear. "It's gone," he says, and I don't think I've heard him sound so lost. "My connection to your father . . . It's gone. I—I can't feel him anymore. He's . . . It's gone."

The implication of Boulder's words hits me harder than any blow ever could.

My dad muted his connection to his own mmoatia to keep me from contacting him again.

We're on our own.

9

How to Pick Up Trash

"Divine wisdom is a gift from the gods, a higher connection to the world around us. There is no power that rivals it anywhere in the world."

—From the *Nwoma*

MY PARENTS CUT US off. They cut *me* off.

I'm still in shock about it the next morning. Roxy seemed to notice something was wrong at breakfast and tried several times to cheer me up, but I could barely hear her over the swirl of my own disbelief.

Boulder is taking it even harder than I am. A Slayer's psychic connection to their mmoatia is sacred. They feel pain when we feel pain, we feel joy when they feel joy. The link is only meant to be muted under the most extreme circumstances.

And, magic aside, Boulder's been a part of my dad's life since my father was nine. The little guy practically raised him. To go from feeling Dad's emotions every second of the day to nothing . . . No wonder Boulder spent the whole night curled up in the fetal position in his little nest in the back of Roxy's closet.

Gods, I've never seen my parents that worked up before. It feels like Boahinmaa showed up, smashed us all to bits, and now our pieces don't fit together like they used to. Maybe her real goal wasn't physically hurting my family but turning us all against each other. If that's her plan, it's working wonderfully.

All I want to do is stay in bed, blast some angsty pop, and wallow, but I can't, because I'm back in a school that may or may not be vampire-infested. By the time I reach my locker, I've had no less than five phones shoved into my face and overheard twice as many whispered conversations about me. I guess when you're the new girl at a small school where everyone has known each other since they were in diapers and the first thing you do is start a food fight that goes semi-viral, you gain a bit of a reputation.

And by *a bit of a reputation,* I mean everybody's gawking at me as if I've grown a second head that can only speak German.

"Ugh, I haven't been around this many children since I helped Mother Teresa open up her orphanage," Boulder murmurs as we make our way to homeroom. Even though he's bummed, he still insisted on coming with me today to avoid another pasta-scented fiasco, which is just stellar. Getting caught with a hairy, musty doll in my backpack is really going to convince everyone I'm not out of my mind.

"Just keep your senses on alert," I whisper out of the corner of my mouth. "Do you feel any black magic yet?"

"Not a whiff. Like I said last night, Rocky Gorge might be the least magically attuned town we've ever visited. But perhaps my senses are off? I just . . . I don't know anymore." I can practically feel the displeasure radiating off the mmoatia. I can't really blame him. I'd be mad, too, if my lifelong best friend suddenly stopped talking to me.

Then again, I've never had a best friend, so what do I know?

There are icebergs warmer than the glare Ashley gives me when I reach our cluster of desks, and Eunju's expression is even colder. So much for joining their little clique. Mateo makes eye contact with me once, goes red, and then pointedly looks away, probably overwhelmed by the *Do not talk to me* vibe I'm giving off right now. But halfway through Mrs. Dean's lecture on root radicals, he slips me a piece of notebook paper with a message scribbled on it.

Are you okay?

Those three small words make my eyes sting, and I accidentally-on-purpose knock the note to the ground so I don't have to reply. Even if I did want to talk to him, what would I say? I'm upset because my vampire hunter parents think I'm a liar who can't be separated from them for three days without freaking out?

Recalling the disappointment in their eyes makes me feel like someone's punched a hole straight through my chest, and the harder I try to fill it up, the wider it gets. I dig my nails into my palms to keep the sadness at bay, pointedly looking away from Mateo until he takes the hint and shifts his attention back to his work.

After class I sprint to the bathroom to check in with Boulder again—nothing. He doesn't feel a speck, not even a crumb, of black magic. At this point it's pretty clear that I was wrong about the adze—a weird light and a passed-out teacher alone do not a vampire make. All my parents asked was that I keep my head down and not cause any trouble until they got back, and I failed on the very first day.

Well, that's it. I'm done. No more checking over my shoulder everywhere I go. No more plotting escape routes from every building I enter.

If my parents want a normal, boring daughter, that's what I'm going to be.

Being normal and boring is pretty easy when school itself is just as uninteresting today as it was yesterday. *High School Musical* lied to me—I'm two days into the whole public education thing, and not a single person has burst into song yet.

Instead of singing and choreography, I get more stares. Each one feels like I'm being pricked with a needle, and by the time we get to lunch, my body hurts all over. I shouldn't care what these kids think about me or what they might be commenting on the #PastaPants video. A week ago, I didn't even know any of them existed, and when my parents come back for me, I'll never see anyone at Rocky Gorge Middle School ever again.

But judging from the way my heart races anytime someone whispers as I pass, I do care. I care a whole lot.

It totally sucks.

Lunch today is meat loaf (though I don't think they should legally be able to call whatever this gray substance on my tray is "meat") and after I grab my food, picking a place to sit becomes a challenge. Ashley makes it clear there's no room for me at her and Eunju's table by piling their backpacks into the empty seat the second I look over. Roxy must have left to go eat with the media center ladies again, and I can't pick out Gavin or Mateo among the masses, though I wouldn't want to eat with them even if I could. And honestly, just the thought of sitting down here for a whole hour as the entire seventh grade class waits for me to mess up in another super meme-able way makes my skin crawl.

With hundreds of eyes focused on me, I leave the cafeteria and head to the benches outside.

I'm halfway to the sweet freedom of the outdoors when a bright splash of color from one of the classrooms catches my eye.

It's a painting of a Black woman turned away from the viewer, and her head is wrapped in a beautiful red, yellow, and green Ankara print scarf made up of hundreds of tiny little dots and lines. It takes me a second to realize why she feels so familiar— this is Mama Africa, a personification of the legend that our continent is shaped like a woman's head. Mr. Riley is deep in concentration at the easel, adding more gold to Mama Africa's necklace, when I step into the art room.

"Oh, Serwa! What brings you here?" he asks when he finally notices me. The man seems weirdly chipper for someone who smacked his head against the floor less than a day ago.

I should give him your basic *Nothing, I'm fine* and keep heading toward my lunchtime exile. But even though I promised myself, like, an hour ago that I was giving up the Slayer stuff for good, I can't make myself walk away.

"I just wanted to check on you," I blurt out, and Boulder pokes me sharply through my backpack to make his disapproval clear. "Yesterday was really . . . um, not great. I wanted to make sure you're doing okay."

"Why, thank you. I'm so sorry I worried you all, but I stopped by Urgent Care last night, and I feel just fine today. Besides, like I said, I've always had a knack for recovering from injuries quicker than others."

Mr. Riley's eyes move from the tray in my hands to the clock on the wall. He nods at one of the long tables in the center of the room. "If you'd like, you can eat your lunch in here. I wouldn't mind the company."

A mix of relief and embarrassment fills my chest as I slide onto the bench. I don't know if eating lunch with your teacher is more or less pathetic than eating lunch all by yourself, but right now, it's all I've got.

"Did you make that?" I ask, gesturing toward the painting with my fork full of meat loaf.

"I wouldn't be much of an art teacher if I didn't make any art," he jokes. "You know Mama Africa?" I nod, and Mr. Riley's face breaks into a grin. "I've always found the concept of her so comforting—the idea that the land is sentient and that she's watching over everyone who is connected to her."

If he thinks the idea of Mama Africa is cool, I bet he'd pee his pants if he knew about Tegare, Tano, and the other gods. But I hold my tongue and instead study the rest of the room, which is filled with more artwork. Some of the subjects I recognize, like Anansi and Mama Africa, but there are others dressed in clothing from cultures I don't know and engaged in rituals I don't recognize. But every subject in Mr. Riley's art is Black. An energy ripples through his work, connecting each piece to the next. As my eyes scan each piece of art, Nokware hums against my wrist, and the feeling is warm and familiar.

Mr. Riley follows my gaze to the wall and his grin grows wider. "I teach art from all over the world, but my focus is on the artistic traditions of the African mainland and diaspora. You only get to design your first-ever classroom once, so I figured why not make it feel like home?"

He takes a bunch of brushes to the sink, which is beneath a giant painting of gye nyame surrounded by other Adinkra. The lines on his symbols are perfect. Dad would be impressed.

"I love studying the art of the diaspora. It's all as varied as we are, but if you dig deep enough, you can see the similarities and overlaps among the beliefs. Like, did you know there's a theory that the West Indian concept of the obeah is derived from the Akan belief in the obayifo?"

My head snaps up at the last word, heart racing. It has to be a coincidence that he mentioned obayifo of all things, right? Mr. Riley continues, "Our peoples were taken from the continent against their will, yet we managed to thrive and build something new everywhere we went. Across space and time, across centuries of joy and loss, triumph and defeat, that connection to where we're from was never lost. That's why I make art—to add my own small link to the chain that binds us all together."

He stops suddenly, rubbing his neck sheepishly. "Sorry, I'm rambling again! You eat your lunch—don't let me bother you."

I want to tell Mr. Riley he wasn't bothering me, but he's already returned to cleaning his brushes and humming a tuneless song to himself. His words bounce around in my head as I stare at my not-meat meat loaf. I've never thought of the diaspora like one big web. Where do I fall in it? I was born in Ghana but didn't grow up there, so calling myself Ghanaian doesn't fit the full picture. I'm Black and I live in America, but I'm not Black American like Mr. Riley, Gavin, and Roxy. I'm not even a full citizen yet. If I'm not really Ghanaian and I'm not really American, what am I?

I scarf down my lunch and let its nastiness distract me from hard questions with no answers. I scan Mr. Riley again as he washes his hands. I wish I could get close enough to see his thumb, where I thought the puncture wound was. . . .

"Mr. Riley," I ask before I can talk myself out of it, "do you often pass out like you did yesterday?"

"Hmm, not these days, no. But I used to when I was a kid. I had really bad anemia for a long time," he says, and my heart sinks. Another check added to the *There really was no adze and I'm just losing my marbles* theory.

"But you looked fine when you left the room," I argue. Without concrete proof it's hard to tell if someone's been the victim of the adze, because the effects of their bites look like so many other illnesses—fatigue, weakness, a general sense of unease, etc. He's recovered faster than I'd expected, though. . . .

I don't know what my problem is. Being wrong about the vampire would be a *good* thing. I guess the prospect that there is no adze in this town, no magic of any kind, nothing even close to my old life anywhere nearby is harder to accept than I thought it would be. "Did anything . . . unusual happen while you were gone?"

"Unusual? I don't think so. I just went to the custodian's closet to get the sponges, then I crossed through the media center on my way to the teacher's lounge to grab my coffee." Mr. Riley turns off the faucet then looks at me with a frown. "Is everything okay? You seem distressed."

"I'm all right. It's just . . ." *I miss my mom and dad, but they don't miss me* is the first thing that comes to mind, but instead of that I say, "My whole life changed overnight. I'm still getting used to it."

Mr. Riley smiles, and there's something so kind and understanding about it that I feel like crying again. "I know how that feels—like the world is just throwing you around and you're powerless to stop it. But something tells me you're going to land on your feet, Serwa. And when you do, even you will be surprised by how far you can go from there."

The lunch bell rings, bringing our impromptu meeting to an end. He reminds me to report back during sixth period to face my sentence for yesterday's food fight. As much as I'm dreading that, the feeling left over from our conversation makes the rest of the day roll by easier. I didn't tell Mr. Riley any details about myself or my life, but just talking to him made me feel better than I have since I got here. Maybe the rest of school today won't be as bad as yesterday was.

ALL THE WARM FUZZIES immediately die at sixth period. Mr. Riley is waiting for Roxy, Gavin, Mateo, Eunju, and me with a pile of gloves, garbage bags, and those long sticks with pointed ends that people use to pick up trash. His wavy brown hair is pulled back into a low ponytail.

He informs us that the Forces That Be have banned the five of us from Home Ec for the rest of eternity—or until the end of the semester, whichever comes first.

"What're we supposed to do instead?" asks Eunju, hands on her hips.

"That's where the good news comes in," says Mr. Riley. "I talked it over with Principal Hashimoto and Mr. Johnson, and they decided to go with my alternative form of disciplinary action. As of now, you five are officially members of the inaugural Rocky Gorge Middle School Good Citizens Committee!"

From the way Mr. Riley says this, it's clear he wants us to cheer or something, which is probably why his face falls when we all stare at him blankly. He sighs. "That means that for the rest of the semester, you'll be engaged in various community service projects. Today we'll start with cleaning up trash in the woods behind the school."

A chorus of groans rise from us, and Eunju physically recoils at the trash bag Mr. Riley hands her. He frowns.

"I know the GCC sounds like a lot of work, but please give it a try," he says. "There are people at this school—and in life—who will make assumptions about you based on where you're from and how you look. Let's prove them wrong."

So that's how the five of us find ourselves outside in

eighty-degree weather picking up candy wrappers and old beer cans while our classmates are probably whipping up delicious desserts inside. As if this situation weren't fun enough, nobody is speaking to anyone else. You'd think going through the shared trauma of our teacher almost dying in front of us would force some group bonding, but nope.

Mr. Riley looks completely recovered as he sits at a picnic table a few yards away, sketching something. He'd better not be drawing us. I'm sure we look like a chain gang on the side of the highway.

As I try to get a particularly stubborn soda bottle out from under a log, Eunju stomps past me in a huff. She's muttering under her breath and punctuating each word with a jab of her pointy trash-picker-upper thingy. (Seriously, what are those called?)

"Worst"—stab!—"first"—stab!—"week"—stab!—"of"—stab!—"school"—stab!—"*ever*!"

"I'm pretty sure this violates some kind of child labor law," Gavin grumbles as he struggles to tie his bag closed. He pulls the bag too hard and it bursts open, re-littering the area we just cleaned. Gavin jumps backward with a yelp, knocking into Eunju, who shoves him away.

"Stop goofing around and work!" she snaps.

"This is a vintage band tee—they don't make them anymore!" he yells back. "Or are you going to go back in time and get me another if this one gets ruined?!"

"Let's not fight," says Mateo, putting a hand on Gavin's shoulder to pull him back. "The faster we finish, the faster we c-c-c— the faster we're out of here."

Mateo hasn't mentioned how I ignored his note earlier. Maybe he's given up on being nice to me. I would.

Gavin yanks his shoulder from Mateo's grip. "Easy enough

for you to say, Mr. Teacher's Pet. Why are we even here when this is all *her* fault?" He points his trash stick at me.

"Get that thing out of my face," I snarl.

My backpack is piled in a heap at the base of a tree with the others, but I can just imagine Boulder inside warning me to keep my temper in check so I don't do or say anything that might give me away.

Gavin pokes me in the shoulder with his stick, and I'm about three seconds from breaking the stupid thing over his head when Roxy jumps between us.

"Mateo's right. Bickering isn't going to make this any better," she says. "Besides, we're out here in the sunshine while everyone else is cooped up inside. We may as well enjoy ourselves while we can."

Leave it to my cousin to find the bright side of an all-around awful situation. I get what Mr. Riley is trying to do here—create bonding via forced labor—but it isn't going to work. You could probably take five random people from human history, each from a different time and place in the world so they don't even speak the same language, and they'd *still* have more in common than the five of us do. In fact, the only reason *GCC* and *become friends* should be used in the same sentence is if the words *will never ever* are between them.

About a million years or so into this literal torture, Roxy begins to hum. It's not a song I know—which isn't surprising since I don't know most songs—but it's upbeat and peppy, which is basically the opposite of how we all feel right now.

Eunju throws back her head and screams, "Oh my God, will you please stop that!"

For a second, it looks like Roxy is about to cry, but instead she squares her shoulders and says, "Why? I'm not hurting anyone."

"You're hurting my ears!"

"You used to love the *Galaxy Dimension Turtle Warriors* opening!" says Roxy. "You're the one who posted, like, six videos of yourself covering the theme on YouTube."

Gavin snickers as Eunju's face goes red. "Yeah, when I was in third grade," she says. "Only little kids care about stupid stuff like that."

"*I* care about stuff like that," Roxy cries.

Eunju gives a mean laugh. "And that's exactly why we don't hang out anymore."

"Leave her alone," snaps Mateo, but the damage is already done.

With tears in her eyes, Roxy whirls around and storms deeper into the forest, far enough away that Mr. Riley can't see her. Eunju stands there shocked, and for a second it looks like she wants to apologize, but then she just stabs her trash picker viciously into the ground.

"Roxy, wait," I call as I go after her. Even though I have no idea what to do in a situation like this, I don't think it's good for her to be alone right now. Plus, Mr. Riley told us to stay in view at all times, so I have to bring her back. I really don't want to find out what they'll do if we break school rules two days in a row.

I catch up to Roxy in a gnarled clearing where the tree trunks stand far apart but the branches mesh like interlocking hands. A strange feeling skitters down my spine, and if I didn't know better, it almost feels like the trees are . . . breathing around us. A small stream trickles near our feet, reflecting the little sun with sparks of light. "Are you okay?"

She gives a fake laugh, rubbing her nose with the back of her hand. "Of course I'm okay. I don't *get* to not be okay."

Before I can ask her what that means, Eunju joins us, with Gavin and Mateo not far behind. "Hey, don't take everything so personally," she says. "I didn't mean it like that."

"Well, that's definitely going to win Apology of the Year— Ow!" says Gavin as Mateo oh-so-casually stomps on his foot.

Great. Now everyone's gone AWOL. I need to get this under control before this goes from a semester-long punishment to a yearlong one. I step in front of Roxy and face Eunju. "Say you're sorry for real," I demand.

"Or what, you're going to stab me with that sword you're not supposed to have?"

It feels as if ten adze have punched me in the gut at the same time. "Sword? What sword? Quit making stuff up and apologize."

Eunju fishes her phone from her pocket and pulls up a video. It's super blurry but very obviously me from yesterday, running through the hallway with Nokware in my hand. All I can do is stare.

This is bad. Really, really bad.

"Are you going to try to tell me that isn't a sword?" she presses, and now everyone else is looking at me like I'm going to pull a weapon on them at any second.

Which technically I *could* do, but they're not supposed to know that.

I've got to do something to fix this, fast, but I have no idea what. But before I can even say anything, something wet drops onto Eunju's phone.

And another drop.

And a third.

Eunju and I slowly look up at the same time to see an adze hanging in the trees directly above our heads, saliva dripping down the razor-sharp fangs angled straight for our throats.

10

How to Lasso Like a Pro

"Attack or be attacked."

—From the *Nwoma*

THREE PLANS IMMEDIATELY RUN through my mind:

1. Run . . . leaving the others to get eaten alive or worse.

2. Look for something to draw an Adinkra with . . . giving the adze enough time to vanish without a trace just like yesterday.

3. Launch myself at it, sword swinging, and hope for the best.

Option three might get me killed, but options one and two will definitely get other people killed, so three it is.

Eunju screams, and the adze's attention immediately zips to her.

The vampire is fast, but I'm faster. It dives for Eunju, and in the split second before its teeth rip into her neck, I shove her out of the way. We both go rolling across the forest ground, the adze biting only the open air where we once were. Ears ringing, I scramble for my fallen trash picker.

"What the heck *is* that thing?" Eunju cries, but I ignore her, keeping all my attention on the enemy in front of me. The adze looms over us, blocking the little sunlight that's filtering into the clearing. This creature is smaller than the ones that attacked my house—about six feet instead of eight—and there's a purple-pinkish iridescence to the shiny shell protecting its body. But its talons and fangs look just as sharp, and they click together ominously like knives against a sharpening block. Its antennae are curved and twisted like a bull's horns, and right now they're twitching violently as it takes stock of the world around it. Its golden eyes flash—we're dealing with an adze that's taken a human host. There's a person trapped somewhere inside that thing.

Panic blooms through my stomach, but then I hear my mother's voice whispering in my ear. *Fear has killed more good Slayers than any adze ever has.*

I shove the terror deep inside and let the cool calm of my training take over. But as my fingers reach to switch Nokware from bracelet to weapon form, I hesitate with a backward glance at Eunju. The absolute first rule that every Slayer learns is that you never, ever perform magic in front of regular mortals. She already has a video of me with the sword—is it really safe for me to pull it out again?

But in that single moment of hesitation, Bullseye (as I have now decided to nickname the adze) shifts its focus from me and Eunju toward Mateo, Roxy, and Gavin, who are just stand-ing there staring with eyes wide as planets. Bullseye lets out a screech before dropping onto its six spindly beetle legs and barreling straight for the other three.

"Run!" I scream. Mateo and Gavin wisely scatter, but Roxy

dashes straight back into the forest with the adze close behind. My heart jams in my throat, and without thinking I press the largest bead on Nokware. Shining light swirls through the air as the golden hilt and black blade of the akrafena appears in my hand. Eunju, still on the ground, openly gapes at the weapon, but I don't even care—saving my cousin is way more important than keeping my secret.

"Get to safety!" I yell to the others. Then I plunge into the forest after Roxy and the vampire.

It's easy enough to pick up their trail, as the adze left behind long tracks and broken branches in its haste. When I catch up with them, Roxy has her back against the chain-link fence that marks the edge of school property. Tears stream down her face, and she's swinging her trash picker uselessly in front of her. A *crunch* rings through the air as the vampire's teeth chomp down on the wooden stick, snapping it in two. It rips the pieces from her hands and hurls them aside.

"Help!" screams Roxy. As she lets out a whimper and drops to the ground, I shift Nokware to my left hand, then pick up a rock with my right and throw it at Bullseye's head.

"Hey, bug breath, over here!" I scream.

My rock hits its mark, and the adze finally turns back to me. In several bounds, I close the space between us, and I swing Nokware at the vampire's neck. But Bullseye ducks out of the way just in time, then extends one of its wings into my chest to knock me off-balance. As the earth becomes the sky and the sky becomes the earth, I catch a glimpse of Roxy running from the fence. Good. No matter what happens to me, at least she and the others will get away.

As I'm struggling back to my feet, the adze launches for me again. It wraps its jaws around Nokware, and we engage in a tug-of-war that the adze quickly wins. Pain shoots up my arms as the adze wrenches the sword from my grasp, and I fall. Okay, so now I'm facing an adze one-on-one without a weapon. This is . . . not great.

But I'll figure something out. I always do.

I toss a handful of dirt straight for the adze's eyes and take advantage of its disorientation to scramble backward. My hands brush against something smooth—one half of Roxy's broken trash picker. I pick it up, ignoring the pain throbbing through my arms, and hold it in front of me like a sword.

The adze's elytra, or shell, protects its vital organs—the best way to slow it down would be to take out one or more of its limbs. I can see the golden hilt of Nokware sticking out of the bush where it landed, but there's no way for me to grab the sword without getting within reach of the adze. Half a trash picker isn't much as far as weapons go, but it'll have to do.

I'm just about to slash for Bullseye's third set of legs, the pair that hold it upright, when a pencil case flies through the air and bounces harmlessly off the adze's shell. My stomach drops to my feet when Roxy busts through the trees with her backpack in hand as she hurls more school supplies at the vampire.

And it's not just Roxy. Mateo, Eunju, and Gavin all come running toward us, too, everyone throwing whatever they can at the adze instead of running for safety like I told them to. I bite back a scream of frustration. Can *anyone* in this stupid group follow orders?!

"You leave her alone!" cries Roxy, and as much as I appreciate her courage, all she and the others are doing is making the adze really, really mad. But at least it provides a momentary distraction. Bullseye swivels to them, and I put all my strength into a leap that lands me on its back.

SERWA BOATENG'S GUIDE TO VAMPIRE HUNTING

"Why don't you pick on someone as ugly as you are?" I yell. Okay, I really need to work on my battle taunts.

True to its nickname, Bullseye spins and tries to buck me off, but I wrap my legs around its thorax to hold on tight. Then I spit on the trash picker and draw two Adinkra on the wood with my finger—epa, the handcuffs, and denkyem, the crocodile, for adaptability. In a flash of light, the trash picker transforms into a wooden chain that I loop around the adze's neck. Bullseye thrashes and screams against the lasso as I hop from its back and pull it away from the other four as hard as I can.

But part of an Adinkra's strength comes from the permanency of what you use to draw it. My spit is already starting to dry, and I can feel the magic holding the chain together weakening. I yell once more for the others to run, but they're frozen in fear again, pressed together against a tree only a few feet from the vampire that's fighting hard to reach them. In seconds the chain will break, and Bullseye will rip us all apart.

And once the adze is done with us, there will be no one to stop it from devouring the rest of the school, then the whole town, and who knows what else.

All because I wasn't a good enough Slayer to stop it when I had a chance.

The same twisting, overwhelming feeling I felt while on the roof yesterday washes over me again. As the chain shatters in my hand and I go flying backward, the adze lets out a roar of triumph and swings around to face my classmates. Even though my ears are ringing and the world is spinning, I throw myself between the other four and the adze with the last of my strength.

"If you want them, you're going to have to go through me!" I yell.

Power roils deep inside me. It feels like if I open my mouth hot lava will come out and scorch everything. But that's not possible. Humans can't do magic without an Adinkra to channel it.

The adze's eyes lock on mine, and something flashes across its face. It's almost like . . . recognition? It opens and closes its mouth several times, and nothing but a gargling sound comes out. But then . . .

"*Grrrgglllel* . . . The drum . . . *grrrggglll* . . . Where is . . . *grrrgl grrrgl* . . . drum?"

My eyes bug out of my head. D-did that adze just . . . *talk*? To *me*? How is that even—

"Kids?" calls a voice from beyond the trees. "Are you back there?"

Mr. Riley. *Oh no. Oh no, no, no, no.* This just went from bad to amazingly, horrifyingly awful.

But Mr. Riley's call surprises the adze, too, and it whips its head toward the sound. In an instant, its shrinks down into firefly mode.

"CATCH THAT BUG!" I scream, but none of us are fast enough to stop it from zipping up into the sky, leaving me to deal with a teacher who is definitely not going to be happy about the mess we've made, and four kids who are staring at me with a whole lot of questions I'm not allowed to answer.

Panic rises in my chest as Mr. Riley's footsteps get closer. I dive for Nokware, yank it from the bush, and yell at the others, "You guys didn't see anything? Okay. You didn't see anything."

All four of them are wearing the exact same expression—mortal terror mixed with complete and utter confusion. The second after I switch Nokware into its bracelet form, Mr. Riley walks into the clearing. He takes one look at us all covered in dirt with trash lying everywhere and yells, "What the— What happened?!"

This is it. This is where it ends. The others are going to snitch, and then I'm going to be kicked out of school for bringing a weapon on campus, and then I'm going to be kicked out of the Abomofuo for exposing magic to civilians, and then my parents are going to disown me, and I'm going to have to live the rest of my life in exile with only dirt and bugs to keep me company.

For several tense, heavy seconds, no one speaks. Everyone is covered in scratches, and Eunju has a nasty bruise on her arm from where I shoved her to the ground. Gavin and Roxy just look stunned, but when Mateo looks at me, his confusion shifts into an expression I can't read. He steps forward and speaks in a voice so quiet it's almost lost on the wind.

"N-n-nothing happened here. . . . Nothing at all."

II

How to Get Some Answers

*"Never tamper with a human mind unless absolutely
necessary. Such acts are the domain of the adze, not us."*

—From the *Nwoma*

> Roxy tell your cousin I want answers.
>
> NOW >:(
> **EUNJU**

> Yeah wth????
> **GAVIN**

> This is Serwa.
>
> Don't have a phone. Using Roxy's.
> **ROXY**

> EXPLAIN!!!!!!!
> **EUNJU**

> Not over text. Meet @ Sunny
> Oaks playground tn. 8pm.
>
> I'll explain everything.
>
> Come by yourselves.
> **ROXY**

I HAVE TO ERASE their memories.

I have no other choice. They saw way too much that
can't be explained without delving into the whole *secret
war against the forces of black magic all around us* thing.
And if my parents ever find out I exposed the truth of

the Abomofuo to so many people, they will literally go back in time and make sure they never have me. Memory-altering magic is considered one of the most dangerous types, used in only the worst circumstances. This is definitely one of those.

Thank Nyame that Mr. Riley believed Mateo's lie about the wind blowing the trash everywhere, because he let us finish the period and go home without any more problems. We've barely stepped through the front door of the apartment when Roxy blocks my beeline for the bathroom.

"Serwa, what was that thing?" For a person obsessed with the occult, Roxy seems way less excited about discovering that vampires are real than I would have expected. Her eyes are wide and she seems a few seconds away from breaking down. I guess some people only like monsters when they stay in stories where they belong.

"I'll explain everything tonight," I promise, pushing past her. As much as I wish I could comfort her right now, the more I say, the more I'll have to erase later. Keeping my distance is the fairest thing for both of us. "Just . . . I need some me time."

Before Roxy can argue, I shut myself in the apartment's sole bathroom and lock the door behind me. Only when I'm truly alone does the rush of what happened finally hit me.

There's an adze here, in Rocky Gorge, Maryland, the place that supposedly hasn't had any magical activity in decades. The vampire's in my school, and the only reason the others and I survived today is because it was almost spotted. Had Mr. Riley not come to look for us when he did . . .

A shudder racks my whole body, and I wrap my arms tight around myself as I slide down to my knees on the cool tile. Images of the five of us bloody and broken on the forest floor flood my mind, and it takes me several minutes to calm my breathing and thoughts. We survived. We're okay. The worst hasn't happened.

Yet.

Once I've finally calmed down, I realize Boulder has been scratching to be let out of my backpack for a while now. I pull him out, and he stares up at me with an expression of astonishment that should feel a lot sweeter than it does.

"Do you believe me about the adze now?" I whisper so Roxy doesn't overhear us. As spooked as we both are, it'll be a cold day in the Sahara before I ever pass up an opportunity to gloat.

"I don't understand," the mmoatia says. "I just don't understand it. My black magic sense didn't go off, even when it was right in front of me. How does this keep happening?"

I shake my head at Boulder and gesture toward the door: *It's not safe to talk here*. After checking to make sure Roxy isn't eavesdropping, I stuff Boulder back into the pack and haul myself out the window toward the roof. This time the fat pigeon is gone, though there is a one-eyed orange cat who hisses at us when we arrive.

"We need to call Mom and Dad again. They'll have to believe me now that you've seen the adze, too."

The mmoatia shakes his head. "When your father dampened our connection yesterday, he cut off my ability to contact him *and* anyone else in the network. All I have left are my healing abilities."

I fight the urge to punch something. It's times like this that having a powerful magic user for a father really, *really* stinks. In his hasty rush to protect me, Dad basically dropped me into a steel cage with a monster and then stole the only key.

"Okay, so we can't use the magic network, but email is still a thing. And my parents aren't the only Slayers in the world. There's gotta be someone else we can contact." I snap my fingers in a nervous rush. "Mr. Amankwah! He lives in DC—he'll help us! Do you know his address?"

Boulder shakes his head. A quick Google search pulls up no results, not even a phone number. Members of the Abomofuo rely almost entirely on the mmoatia network for all communication. Once you're off it, there's basically no way to reach any Slayer whose location you don't already know. And even if I could reach anyone else in the Abomofuo, there's no telling they'd believe me and Boulder when all evidence claims there's no magic in Rocky Gorge.

As I stare at my useless screen, the realization of what I have to do hits me.

"We need to take down the adze," I tell Boulder. "Locate it and remove it from its host. That's the only way to protect the town."

Boulder lets out a strangled noise of disbelief. "All by ourselves?"

"What other choice do we have?"

We stare at each other for a long time, neither saying what we're both thinking—what good are one Slayer-in-training and one mmoatia against a whole adze? The silence grows heavy until Boulder breaks it by saying, "We also have to deal with the children who were with us in the forest. Was it wise to let them leave after what they witnessed?"

"They won't tell anyone what they saw," I say, remembering how they all went along with my lie in front of Mr. Riley. Them not snitching is the only thing I'm confident about right now. If they try to talk about Bullseye to anyone, they're going to sound just as nuts as I did to my parents yesterday. "Plus, I already have a plan to deal with them. We're meeting at the playground tonight, and when we do, I'm going to erase their memories."

"That's an extremely advanced spell, Serwa. Are you sure you can handle that?"

"I have to try."

Boulder mutters something in Twi too low for me to hear. His mention of magic reminds me of something I've been meaning to ask for a while now. "Two times now we've been attacked by an adze looking for the Midnight Drum. Where is it? Exactly what did Nana Bekoe do to get trapped inside it?"

Boulder grimaces. "That is classified information I am not allowed to share with you."

"So classified I deserve to die over it?"

The mmoatia opens his mouth then closes it. Even though I've known Boulder my whole life, we've never been close. But I think it hits us both at the same moment that we're really on our own out here. As long as our survival depends only on each other, keeping secrets isn't going to fly.

He begins, "Since the beginning of time, for as long as good has existed, so too has its counterpart—evil. While the beings aligned with divine wisdom found order, the beings of black magic were as chaotic as the power that fueled them. For centuries the latter fought and attacked with no real plan. That is, until Nana Bekoe came along.

"In all my centuries of working with the Abomofuo, I have never seen the forces of black magic as unified as they were under her leadership. Nana Bekoe's mastery of black magic was second to none, and she wrought devastating destruction upon the world. She singlehandedly turned the tide of the Third Great War, and over a few years she dealt more damage to our society and the humans caught in the cross fire than most armies could do in decades. Countless families were torn asunder because of her."

This Nana Bekoe lady sounds like a real piece of work. Though I've faced down many adze over the years, and even other creatures of black magic like bonsam, the only obayifo I ever met was Boahinmaa. She was bad enough.

"If Nana Bekoe was so powerful, how did the Midnight Drum defeat her?"

"It's not so much that the drum itself is special but rather that the circumstances that created it were. The turning point in the Third Great War happened about twenty years ago, when a member of Nana Bekoe's forces felt her destruction had gone too far and that the world would be reduced to ash if she wasn't stopped. So this young obayifo switched sides and joined forces with one of our Slayers. Together they combined divine wisdom and black magic in an ordinary djembe drum. The result was the Midnight Drum. They were able to lure Nana Bekoe into it and seal her inside, where she remains to this day."

No matter how hard I try, I can't imagine an obayifo turning against her leader to conspire with a member of the Abomofuo. It's like Tom cooperating with Jerry, or Superman working with Lex Luthor. Mortal enemies don't just come together like that. No wonder the one time it did happen, it created something so powerful.

"So where's the drum now?" I ask again.

"After the war ended, the Okomfo ruled that the Midnight Drum was far too dangerous to be left in any one place for long. Therefore, every few years a new pair of Slayers is tasked with hiding it and protecting its location to the death."

My eyes go wide as the puzzle pieces finally click together in my head. "And right now, those people are my parents."

Boulder nods. "Indeed, they are."

Keeping secrets is one of those things all parents do, like dancing badly at weddings and loving ABBA, but who knew Mom and Dad were hiding an object that could literally end the world? Wow. Now I understand why my mom was so freaked out by Boahinmaa. That lady is willing to kill for this thing, and there's no way she's going to stop just because her first attempt didn't work.

Boulder's given me more answers than anyone else has in a long time, but something still nags at me. I clutch my pendant, drawing strength from the way it feels in my palm. "And what about Boahinmaa? Where does she fit into the story of Nana Bekoe and the Midnight Drum?"

The mmoatia bites his lip, and I can tell he's wondering if he's already told me too much. "Boahinmaa was one of Nana Bekoe's most loyal disciples," he says reluctantly. "I believe she took Nana Bekoe's imprisonment harder than anyone else. Boahinmaa has devoted her life since to freeing her."

"But why did she go after my grandma specifically?" My mind keeps replaying the conversation Boahinmaa had with my parents before I cut the ceiling fan. It was too personal to be just a meeting between enemies from opposite sides of a war. "Was it because Grandma Awurama was a descendant of one of the Seven Founders?"

Boulder looks away from me, staring out at something I can't see. "No, I don't believe that was why."

His tone makes it clear I've reached the limit of how much he's going to share tonight, which is fine. Honestly, it doesn't really matter why Boahinmaa went after my grandmother. Grandma Awurama is gone, and no force on earth can bring her back. And because my dad's stepfather died of old age when I was a baby, and Mom won't talk about her own parents, there's a giant, gaping hole where my connection with my grandparents should be. It's a dull ache you carry with you everywhere you go—missing people you never knew.

I look down at my pendant. "I wish I could've met her."

Boulder's eyes soften. "I wish so, too."

I've never seen the Midnight Drum, but I suddenly feel the need to protect it with my life. The only good thing about all this is that I honestly have no clue where it is, so anyone who tries to beat that information out of me is straight outta luck.

"Those butt buckets took my grandmother. No way they're taking the drum, too," I say.

Boulder chuckles. "Though I can't condone the term 'butt buckets,' we are in agreement. We may not know the Midnight Drum's location, but we must do everything in our power to keep it safe. Even if that means protecting ourselves so we can't be used to blackmail that information out of your parents."

Just as Boulder finishes talking, my iPad alarm beeps—twenty minutes till eight. I should really get down to the playground before the other kids arrive, but there's one more thing I need to ask Boulder while we can still talk freely.

"Last question, I promise. Both yesterday and today, when I used my magic, something weird happened."

"Weird how?"

"Weird like"—I put my hand on my stomach, but the Big Feeling is long gone; I try to find a better word to describe it, but none of them really fit how . . . *vast* it is—"weird. Not like my normal magic. Have you ever heard of a Slayer's powers shifting before?"

Boulder looks up at me, and it's in moments like this, when his eyes go heavy, that I remember that though he might resemble an extremely hairy Cabbage Patch doll, he's been alive for thousands of years and has seen things I couldn't even imagine.

"Sometimes," he says, and it doesn't feel like he's lying, but it doesn't feel like he's telling the whole truth, either. "It's probably just your magic reacting to the stress of the last few days. It should settle down on its own soon."

I'm not sure about that, because I've been stressed before. For me, being stressed usually means extreme hangriness, not bursts of super magic. But I nod along because Boulder knows way more about this stuff than I do.

With that, we head down to the playground so I can prep it for the meeting. The first thing I do is set up the same silence ward my dad used in IHOP so no one can eavesdrop. The next step is the tricky one. For the memory erasing to work, I'm going to have to draw the Adinkra on each kid one by one, and something tells me that after the first person goes down, the other three aren't just going to wait around to have their minds zapped.

My solution is to set up a paralysis perimeter I can activate at any time during the conversation. Boulder scoffs at me kneeling in the weirdly sticky plastic gravel to draw the symbols needed for this spell: asawa, the Adinkra of pleasure, to dull their senses; and mpatapo, the Adinkra of pacification, to physically freeze them in place as I apply the mind wipe.

"This seems risky," says Boulder. He's already slipped into his frozen mode, half-buried in the sandbox, so he can monitor the conversation while blending in with the dolls and other toys left overnight.

"I'm sorry, but have you come up with a better plan to keep these kids from blabbing the truth about vampires to the entire world? Because if so, I'd love to hear it."

Boulder is about to snark back when the alarm rings at eight p.m. on the dot.

Showtime.

12

How to Assemble a
Vampire Hunting Team

*"Your team is your life's blood.
Choose them wisely and well."*

—From the *Nwoma*

I WAS KIND OF hoping this meeting would run on CP Time, but, unfortunately, by 8:02 the last bike pulls up to the playground and I have four faces staring at me.

Everyone's changed clothes since I last saw them, which is good, since we all looked pretty scruffy after our playdate with the adze. What hasn't changed is the paranoia in all their eyes. Mateo won't stop checking over his shoulder, as if the adze might pop out of the slide and attack us all at any second. He keeps fiddling with a thread trailing from his sweater, and I have to suppress the urge to ask why he keeps wearing them when it's not even that cold yet.

Eunju is trying to play it cool, but I can tell from the way her weight shifts as she leans against the jungle gym that her bruises still hurt. Roxy sits cross-legged in front of the elephant on a spring that toddlers are supposed to ride. Her fingers absentmindedly doodle in the gravel. Only Gavin seems unchanged. He's hanging upside down with his knees hooked around the monkey bars, his usual *Nothing ever bothers me ever* smile on his face.

"All right, where are the cameras?" he asks.

Okay, didn't expect him to lead with that. "Where are the what?"

"The cameras. You've hidden them somewhere to record the moment we all learn we've been Punk'd."

"There are no cameras. In fact, I put a silence spell on the playground so no one can hear or record our conversation."

No one will be able to hear or record when I steal their memories, either, but I don't mention that part.

Eunju barks out a dry laugh. "Silence spell? You can't be serious."

"Why would I lie about that?" I demand. I'd let Boulder tend to her injuries before I mind wipe her, except something tells me busting out a forest spirit with magic healing abilities would only freak everyone out even more.

Gavin flips from the monkey bars with a heavy *thud*, nearly landing on poor Mateo, and he begins digging through the gravel. "Seriously, where are the cameras? Are you filming us from above with a drone? Or was the person in that bug suit wearing a GoPro or something to capture our reactions in real time?"

His voice cracks a bit at the end, and that's when I realize he isn't calm at all—he's terrified. They all are. I can't help but pity them. Even in the face of literal, actual magic, the human brain will go to any lengths to deny the undeniable.

In his frantic search for cameras, Gavin gets a little gravel on Eunju, who snarls at him. She shoves her phone into her pocket, turns to me, and snaps, "Enough of this—spill. Who are you, and what was that thing that attacked us?"

Boulder grunts from the sandbox. The others swivel to look

at him, but in his frozen mode like this, all they think they see is a doll—one very close to blowing his cover if he speaks. His warning is a reminder that I shouldn't reveal any classified info if I can help it. Even now it's taking all my self-control not to activate the paralysis spell on these kids and begin the mind wipe. But there's something my dad always used to say to me, which he claims is something Grandma Awurama always used to say to him when he tried to rush things: "Akokono de betebete ne eri abe." *A bagworm slowly chews the palm fruit,* which is basically the Twi version of *Slow and steady wins the race.*

Of course, whenever Dad said that, Mom would hit him back with "Dua a enya wo a ebewo w'ani no, yetu asee; yensensene ano." *Before a tree pokes you in the eye, uproot it.* In other words, *Deal with your problems before they become a problem.*

I shouldn't rush through this conversation, as much as I want to. Though I could get in all kinds of trouble for breaking the Abomofuo's rule of secrecy, I'm going to have to give these four some answers if I want them calm enough for the spell to work.

And if everything goes according to plan, they won't remember anything I share tonight anyway.

I pull out my iPad. "What we saw today was an adze—a kind of vampire from Ghana that can turn into a firefly."

I hand them the tablet and let them swipe through the very few results that come up when you google *adze.* Most of the information is shrouded in folklore, and the illustrations are about as accurate to real adze as Mickey Mouse is to your average rodent, but it's something, at least.

Roxy stands up, her eyes wide. "My dad told me stories about this creature!" she exclaims. "They take over people's minds and make them do bad things."

Mateo gulps hard. "So, there *was* a p-p-person inside that th-thing?"

"Not literally *inside* the monster, but yes. An adze has the ability to switch between its true form—the one you saw today—a firefly, and the human body it stole," I say. "They don't always transform into a firefly, though. Someone hosting an adze can look identical to a regular human, like you or me, which is part of what makes them so hard to catch."

Silence falls over the playground once more, only to be broken seconds later by Gavin's hysterical laughter.

"Y-you're joking, right?" he says between guffaws as his blue twists fly with each shake of his head. "You really want us to believe we were attacked by Edward Cullen?"

"No, not Edward Cullen!" I cry. "Adze and Western vampires are completely different!"

Denial might be the first stage of acceptance, but that doesn't make it any less annoying when someone compares something that's tried to kill you on multiple occasions to a sparkling pretty boy from an honestly awesome movie franchise.

"So, you're saying these . . . 'ad-zee'? Am I pronouncing that right? Anyway, if these ad-zee are real, why have we never seen them before?" demands Eunju.

I suck in a deep breath. *Be calm, Serwa. You're the experienced Slayer here, Serwa. You will undermine all your authority if you start smacking people silly, Serwa.*

"It's pronounced 'ah-*djeh*,' and the reason you've never heard about them is because of a society full of people like me, the Abomofuo. We've been specially chosen by the gods to fight adze and all other creatures of black magic so that normal people like you can sleep safely at night. You're welcome, by the way."

Roxy's eyes brighten. "You said *gods*, plural. Like Nyame, Asaase Yaa, and the other Ghanaian ones?"

"The very same."

"Hang on a second, just . . . hang on," says Gavin. "Vampire fireflies? Gods? Black magic? This whole thing sounds like bad X-Men fan fiction. This isn't funny anymore. What's *really* going on?"

"I can't believe I'm saying this, but Gavin is right," adds Eunju. "I don't buy it."

Mateo bites at his lip, the thread from his sweater now twice as long as it was when this conversation began. "Vampire fireflies *are* p-p-pretty hard to believe."

"It's all true!" I argue. I don't want to share any of this with them, but now the fact they don't believe me is just making me annoyed. Another reason why coming to this town and trying to interact with non-magic mortals was a mistake.

Eunju gets up in my face. She's not that much taller than I am, but there's a fire in her eyes that makes me flinch. Honestly, if she had training like mine, she wouldn't make a half-bad Slayer with all that anger she's holding in.

"Prove it," she commands.

When I don't reply, Eunju shakes her head, turns to Roxy, and says, "This was a waste of time. Roxy, your cousin is completely nuts. I'm emailing the school right now and telling them what happened."

She slips her phone out of her pocket. My body moves faster than my mind does, stepping in front of Eunju before she can send the message that'll ruin things even more. "You want proof? Here's your proof." I press the biggest bead of Nokware, and golden light floods the playground as the weapon switches forms.

Now Eunju is the one flinching. They all saw the akrafena before, but it's still pretty jarring to have it suddenly appear in your face. "What the—?"

I angle Nokware away from her and toward the jungle gym. With the tip of its blade, I scratch into the metal the first Adinkra that comes to mind—eban—and channel my power through it. A creaking groan fills the air as the jungle gym expands and twists into a cage that traps us inside. The bars above our heads crisscross one another until it looks like we're gazing up at the stars through a giant metal basket.

"Magic is real. Adze are real," I say coldly.

"Oh . . . Oh my God," says Eunju as she makes the sign of the cross over her chest.

Gavin picks up a stick and nervously pokes at the bars. They hold.

"It's real," he squeaks out. Isn't that what I literally just said? "It's— It's real."

Mateo runs his hands over the bars, his eyes wide with wonder. He turns to me. "C-c-can you d-d-do it again?"

Normally I wouldn't perform tricks on command like some sort of birthday clown, but it's been so long since I used my magic in a noncombat situation. This time I draw nsoromma, the star Adinkra, into the side of the riding elephant. The contraption begins to glow with white light and rock wildly by itself.

Something new flickers in everyone's expressions—belief. I can practically sense Boulder having a conniption over on the baby swing, but right now I can only focus on the other members of the GCC. I return the jungle gym to its usual form so they aren't distracted by it.

After about thirty straight seconds of hyperventilating, Roxy finally speaks. "So, if you were telling the truth and the school really has an . . . adze . . ." She stumbles over the word but says it in a way that shows she has some familiarity with Ghanaian languages. "What do we do now?"

The others all turn to me, and it feels like they're seeing me—the real, true me, not the watered down, fake Serwa I have to be at school—for the first time. It feels . . . good. Like maybe Boahinmaa didn't destroy everything about who I thought I was when she tore my house apart.

Unfortunately, we won't be doing anything. With all of them finally calmed down, now is the perfect time to activate the paralysis spell. All I have to do is touch the Adinkra on the ground right behind me. I pretend to stretch, lifting my foot ever so slightly. It hovers right over the string of symbols . . .

And freezes.

I look again at the other kids, and a third proverb floats up in my mind like an air bubble bursting to the surface of a swirling river.

"Baanu so a emmia." *When two people carry something, it doesn't hurt.* In other words, more people is always better than one.

Even if I mind wipe them all, nothing about the current situation will change. There will still be an adze roaming the halls of Rocky Gorge Middle School, and I will still be on my own trying to fight it.

But right now, there are four other people who know the truth. Maybe not the four best people to know this secret, and definitely not the four I would have chosen, but it's four more than I had yesterday.

Mom always says that the best Slayers win their battles not by being the strongest or the fastest, but by knowing the odds and turning them to their favor. The odds in a one-on-one battle against an adze? Completely, 100 percent nightmare awful.

But the odds in a *five*-on-one battle against an adze . . . ?

Better. Much better.

I look slowly into each of their faces. Gavin the Smart Aleck, Eunju the Snob, Mateo the Teacher's Pet, and Roxy the Occult Enthusiast. And me, Serwa "Pasta Pants" Boateng at the front, leading them into battle against an enemy no one else could possibly hope to defeat. It's not the choice my mom would make, but she isn't here.

I am.

"What we do now," I say slowly, and something in the air feels like it's shifting, as if the gods themselves are holding their breaths to see what happens next, "is fight."

What should be a supercool, triumphant moment for me is completely ruined when Boulder hops out of his hiding place and waddles over to us.

"Uh-uh. No way. *No way.* I've put up with a lot of nonsense over the years, Serwa, but this? This is where I draw the line. *No.*"

Unsurprisingly, the others immediately commence freaking out.

"DID THAT BABY DOLL JUST TALK TO US?"

"It's walking! It's walking!"

"Someone kill it!"

Gavin chucks his stick at him, and Boulder barely dodges it before toddling as fast as his tiny legs will carry him to hide behind me. "A pox upon you, children!" he yells. "A pox upon your houses, and upon all your bounties and fields!"

I sigh. "Everyone, meet Boulder. He's my father's mmoatia. Boulder, meet everyone."

Roxy's eyes light up. "My dad used to talk about mmoatia all the time. They're kind of like Ghanaian forest fairies." She kneels before Boulder and wiggles her fingers at him like he's a dog. "Don't worry little guy, I'm not going to—OW, HE BIT ME!"

"Do not patronize me!" he spits at her. Thanks to Boulder's healing magic, the bite wound immediately closes without leaving a trace. To me, he says, "Serwa, you cannot be serious about enlisting these four in your fight against the adze. They wouldn't last five minutes in battle."

"As is, maybe. Which is why I'm going to train them. By the time I'm done, that adze won't even know what hit it." Boulder opens his mouth to argue once more, but I cut him off. "I don't like this, either, but there's nothing else we can do."

I gesture at the other four, who have gathered around Boulder again and are trying to poke him in the head. "Reinforcements from the Abomofuo aren't coming to help," I say. "No superhero is going to drop down from the sky to our rescue. There's just us. Boulder, you've helped train hundreds, maybe thousands of Slayers across the centuries. Let's do this. If we win, we can save all of Rocky Gorge. And if we lose . . . Well, at least we'll die knowing we did everything we possibly could. What do you say?"

Besides, I could always use these kids to help fight the adze and then mind wipe them once everyone is safe. Never let them tell you Serwa Boateng isn't a pragmatist.

Boulder still doesn't look convinced, so I give him my best puppy-dog eyes. "Please, Boulder? I can't do this without you."

It only takes ten seconds for him to give in. "Fine, fine, I'll help you! Just stop looking at me like that!" He mutters a prayer to Nyame under his breath and runs his hands down his face. "But if anyone calls me a fairy again, I reserve the right to poop in their backpack."

"Deal." I turn to the others. "If anyone wants out, now is the time. I will let you go right here, right now, and won't hold it against you." This is a lie—anyone who leaves here without swearing to keep the secret will have to be mind wiped. But I don't want them to know I have that ability just yet, in case I need to use it later.

Mateo raises his hand.

"We're not in school, you don't have to—" I sigh. "Yes?"

"How c-c-can you tell if someone is p-p-p—" He stops, face red, and takes several deep breaths before he speaks again. "How d-d-do you know if someone has an adze inside them?"

"You don't. Unless the vampire takes the insect form we saw earlier today, there is no physical difference between a normal person and an adze's host." I look each one of them in the eyes as I speak, hoping my words ring clear. I need their help, but I want to make sure they all understand the risk they're agreeing to. "The adze who attacked us—and who I think bit Mr. Riley and caused him to pass out yesterday—could be anyone. All we know is it's someone who has access to the school grounds during the day, making them most likely a student or a member of the faculty and staff. But that's the only lead we have right now."

"So, if Mr. Riley was bitten, is he possessed now?" asks Gavin. "He *did* make us do that dirty work while he just sat around. . . ."

"No!" I blurt out—maybe a little too quickly, but I like the man. I really don't want him to lose his mind to a bloodsucking monster. "Sometimes adze just . . . um, feed on people without taking over their bodies."

Welp, if they weren't freaked out enough before, that certainly did it. Everyone looks ready to throw up.

Roxy gulps. "Can an adze leave one host and enter someone else?"

"Yes," I confirm for her. "And if it did, you'd never know. Your parents, your siblings, even your best friends you've known your whole lives—if an adze possessed them, they'd act the same as always. But they'd be a prisoner inside their own mind, while the vampire controls their body and life. It's a fate worse than death for the host."

Right now, that same torture is happening to someone in our school. And we're the only ones who can stop it.

"It's not just the host who suffers when an adze enters a community," I continue. "As creatures of black magic, they trail chaos and destruction everywhere they go. They've been known to sicken entire towns, poison food supplies, and even cause accidents without laying a finger on anybody. Every single person in Rocky Gorge is in danger right now."

"But you said your parents have been trained to fight them?" argues Eunju. "Where are they now? Why didn't they deal with it when they came through?"

A lump forms in my throat at the mention of my mom and dad, but I've come too far to break down now. "They're currently busy on a different hunt, and I'm not sure how the adze avoided their detection. But it doesn't matter. They can't help us, and neither can anyone else from the Abomofuo. As far as they're concerned, this town is off the grid. They've cut off all communication between me and the network, for our mutual safety, so nothing that happens here will be getting out to anyone on our side."

Roxy gives me a pitying look, and Mateo says, "S-s-sorry, Serwa."

I quickly turn to Gavin and Eunju so I don't start crying. Both of them look shocked, no sign of a smirk or sneer on either face. Good. This isn't a game, and I don't want them treating it like it is.

I take a deep breath and blow it out. "If we want to protect ourselves, our friends, and our families, then we need to catch this thing, and fast. I can't give you magic, but if you join me, I will teach you everything I know about fighting not only adze, but every kind of black magic creature there is. You'll never again be defenseless like you were today."

I hold my arm straight in front of me, palm down. "Who's in?"

Nobody moves, and I suddenly feel more than a little stupid.

Roxy bites her lip. "There's really no one else who can fight this thing?" she whispers.

I shake my head. "The only ones who can save us are us."

Mateo is the first to step forward, and relief rushes through me when he places his hand over mine. "I'm in."

Gavin is next. "You know what? Sure, why not. This'll make great content for my channel one day."

Roxy puts her hand over his. She doesn't say anything, but when she looks up, her expression is nothing but determined. She nods at me, which only leaves Eunju.

"Come on, don't leave us hanging," I prod.

She scowls before throwing her hands in the air. "Fine, whatever! But as soon as this adze is dead, we are never speaking of this ever again!"

I grin in response, taking in my first true look at my new team.

Whoa. I have a team.

Now *that* is going to take some getting used to.

13

How to Be Blamed for Literally Everything

"An unguarded mind is as much a weakness as an unguarded body."

—From the *Nwoma*

I'M STANDING IN A pitch-black space. There is no light, yet somehow, I can see my arms and legs. Nokware is in my hands, but I don't remember summoning it. There's no sound in the air, no smell, nothing surrounding me—just an endless void. I try to scream, but my voice refuses to come out. A strange tugging in my stomach is pulling me *somewhere*, and it feels like I'm moving even though my legs are staying in place.

And then the nothingness is broken by windows, each one several feet wider and taller than me. I recognize the outline of my dad's back in the first one, and I race toward it, pounding on the glass and screaming his name . . . but still no sound comes out. Dad walks away without even looking at me, and tears form in my eyes.

Mom stands in the next window, her twists in a low ponytail and her arms and chest wreathed with weapons. I try to call to her, too, but she also leaves me without even a glance.

In the third window is the profile of someone I've never met before. She's shorter than my dad but has his stocky build, and wrapped around her body is a white-and-black Adinkra cloth people often wear to an ayie, a typical Akan funeral. The only thing I recognize about her is the pendant around her neck.

A perfect match to the one around my own.

"Grandma Awurama!" This time, my voice actually comes out. Unlike my parents, my grandmother pauses, and I reach for her. But just as she starts to turn toward me so I can make out her face, the sensation in my stomach pulls me backward. My family disappears, and the nothingness engulfs me, flooding my eyes, mouth, and ears. A horrible voice that I don't hear so much as feel reverberates through my body.

I'm waiting for you, little one.

That's when I wake up, sitting bolt upright on the air mattress with my body drenched in sweat.

Roxy is normally a deep sleeper, but she pushes herself to her elbows with a yawn and looks my way. "Everything all right?" she mumbles, her words slurring together as she sleepily readjusts her bonnet.

According to the iPad, it's four a.m. I grope around for my grandma's pendant, which I had taken off before bed. Relief floods me when my fingers close around the familiar gold disk. With my other hand, I rub behind my ear.

"Nothing. Just a nightmare."

The stress from the last few days must be getting to me. It's hard to believe not even a whole week has passed since Boahinmaa attacked our house. It hits me then that, for all the planning and scheming we've done since it happened, my parents and I never actually talked about what it meant to lose one of the few places on the planet where we felt safe.

I wonder if, wherever they are, they feel just as lost as I do.

Probably not. After all, they have each other to lean on. I only have me.

Roxy sits up so she can see me better in the dim light. "You're shaking."

I didn't even realize it until she pointed it out. "I'm fine."

Awkward silence. Then she says, "Did you know there's a Slavic cryptid called the kikimora that sits on people's chests and causes sleep paralysis?"

Yeah, that's a helpful image right now. "I didn't know that."

"Do you wanna talk about the nightmare?"

"No." If Roxy and the others are going to help me fight this adze, I need them to see me as competent and capable, not someone who falls apart over one bad dream. Who would accept help from a person who can't even help herself?

Once my stomach has settled, I lie down again with my back to Roxy, hoping she takes the hint not to talk to me.

I hear rustling behind me, and then Roxy softly whispers, "I'm always here if you need me."

Now I feel bad. I should talk to her—thank her at least, ask her to tell me more about that Kiki guy. But before I can think of the right thing to say, her soft breathing slips into gentle snoring.

As for me, I'm still lying there tense and wide-awake long after the sun begins to rise, my head too full of vampires and the people terrorized by them to let me sleep.

AT SCHOOL LATER THAT morning, the effects of my night of not-sleep on my body are obvious. My head feels like it's been stuffed with cotton, and everything around me seems sluggish. Plus, though Boulder healed my minor wounds after the fight with the adze, my muscles are sore. I try to subtly massage them during homeroom as Mrs. Dean blathers on about some new school policy regarding Heelys and reminding us that Back-to-School Night is coming up soon.

Mateo and Eunju are almost comically stiff at our table, the same paranoia they showed at the playground last night clear on their faces. I bet Roxy and Gavin look similar in their respective homerooms. There's no need for them to be quite so panicked. Both times Bullseye attacked, it was either after school or far from the main premises. The adze doesn't want to be caught any more than we want to be bitten, which is why I'm not worried about it making a move while classes are in session and everyone is indoors.

No, the real problem right now is that even though I talked a big game about turning them into an Adze-Fighting Dream Team, I actually have no idea where we're going to train. It's not like we can just roll up to the YMCA and ask if we can use their fitness rooms for activities of the vampire hunting variety. The playground is a central location between all our houses, but it isn't big enough, and it would take too much of my energy to shroud it every time like I did last night.

What we need is a wide-open but secluded area. One where I can show the others everything I know about combat and magic without having to worry about any prying eyes or streaming phones. But where in this town could I find a place like that? Everyone is quite literally in everyone else's business all the time here.

Just like in the past two days, I finish my worksheets long before everyone else. I'm sitting there zoning out as I try to solve our training ground issue when my eyes meet Ashley's.

She glares at me before thumping an arm over her paper. I just turn away, and you'd think that would be the end of it, except Mrs. Dean looks over at us and frowns. When class ends, she calls for me to stay behind.

"Don't worry, Sarah, I know you have your next class to get to, so this won't take long," she says as I approach her desk. This time, I don't even bother correcting her pronunciation of my name. It still grates to hear her say it wrong, but that's the least of my problems right now. "Please, have a seat. How are you adjusting to Rocky Gorge?"

"It's fine," I reply, because there's no way I am going to tell her I've almost died twice in the five days I've been here. She gives me a smile that somehow doesn't look like one.

"You're probably wondering why I detained you. I've noticed something rather odd about the assignments you've turned in this week."

She spreads a pile of papers across her desk, and I see all my worksheets from the past few days staring back at me. All of them have earned As, none below a 95 percent. "These are amazing marks. You haven't even been here a week, and you're already scoring higher than everyone else in class."

"Um, thank you?" I'm confused. That should be a compliment, so why does it feel like I'm in trouble?

The not-a-smile slips from Mrs. Dean's face. "However, I noticed during today's independent work time that you were glancing over at Ashley's desk. I want you to know that cheating will not be tolerated in any way, shape, or form in my classroom."

My eyes bug so far out of my head that I probably look like a praying mantis. This lady thinks I'm *cheating*? Off *Ashley*, of all people?! It's not my fault my parents' lessons were light-years ahead of where her class is now!

"I didn't cheat!" I cry, but she puts up a hand to silence me.

"What have I told you about speaking out of turn, Sarah?" she snaps, and my hands curl into fists inside my jacket sleeves. *My name is Serwa!* I want to scream. But yelling at her isn't going to make this any better. My eyes fall to the paperweight on her desk. The little glass bird glares at me, like it thinks I somehow deserve this.

This isn't the first time I've ever been in trouble, but normally when I'm being scolded, it's over something I actually did, like that time I pranked Dad by tinting his conditioner pink. Getting in trouble for something I didn't even do feels way, way worse. Like *about to burst into tears in front of a woman who hates me* worse.

Mrs. Dean continues, "Before I was transferred here, I spent thirty years teaching at the worst inner-city schools Baltimore had to offer. I know students like you, and I have dealt with all of them the same way. I am going to let you off with a warning this time, and a chance to redo your work for half-credit instead of zeroes, but I'll be keeping an eye on you. And know that one more sign of inappropriate behavior from you will result in disciplinary action. Do you understand me?"

The look on Mrs. Dean's face pins me in my seat better than any adze could. I have no idea what I'd say to her even if I wasn't too scared to say anything. I hate the way she said *students like you* like . . . like . . . like just me being here is somehow making the entire school worse. And I've never lived in the inner city, but the people I've met there have been nothing but wonderful and warm and kind. Being compared to them should be an honor, not an insult.

"Do you understand me, Sarah?" she repeats.

Dozens of words bubble up in my throat. I don't say any of them.

"Yes," I whisper.

"Yes, what?"

"Yes, Mrs. Dean."

She nods. "You are dismissed."

I practically have to sprint to make it to Earth Science just as the bell rings, but once I'm there, I can barely focus on the class. Mrs. Dean's voice circles through my head like a video stuck on repeat. Everyone in the Abomofuo thinks I'm a liar, and now my homeroom teacher thinks I'm a cheat. I know I'm not perfect, but what is it about me that makes people always assume the worst? Is there something wrong with me that everyone else can see but I can't?

As my teacher explains the difference between sedimentary and igneous rocks, I replay the conversation with Mrs. Dean, trying to figure out if there is anything I could have said or done differently to get myself off her hit list. . . .

Wait a minute.

Hold up.

What if . . . What if *she* is the adze?

Bullseye's host is someone with access to the school during both main and after hours, which all teachers have. And Mrs. Dean has had it out for me since even before the food fight. What if it's because she sensed I was her enemy from the jump? She couldn't risk getting rid of me in the obvious way, because that would mean her secret getting out, too, so she had to make up this whole cheating mess. . . .

The more I think about it, the more sense it makes. But it's just a theory—my parents' voices ring through my head, reminding me to gather more evidence before I act on it. However, having a direction to work with makes the rest of the day feel better, and even having to eat lunch with Mr. Riley again doesn't feel so lonely this time.

By the time sixth period rolls around, I'm feeling—dare I say it—excited. I have a lead on the adze. I have a team of people to help me fight it (even if I'll have to wipe their minds after). For the first time since I've arrived in this awful town, things are going my way.

"What are you so happy about?" asks Eunju as she and the others file into the art room for today's GCC meeting. She looks loads better since Boulder healed her bruises from the adze fight, but she's still walking a little stiffly.

"The thought of another afternoon full of community service and beautifying our lovely school," I say back. The sarcasm goes completely over Mr. Riley's head; in fact, he looks so happy he might actually pee himself.

"That's the spirit, Serwa!" he exclaims. "Like I said, I think you will find the GCC to be a transformative experience if you just give it a chance."

I have no idea what's so life-changing about picking up garbage, but maybe that's why I'm not in charge of the American public education system.

Instead of trash bags and gloves, today Mr. Riley hands us all notebook paper and pencils. "As you know, Back-to-School Night is coming up in two weeks," he explains. "Not only is this the first major event of the new school year, it's also a chance for students, parents, and teachers to connect with one another and for us to show off the strength and pride of the Rocky Gorge Middle School community."

"More like a chance to beg for donations from the rich folks over in Ivy Ridge," mutters Gavin.

Mr. Riley sighs. "Yes, there is a fundraising component as well. But showcasing our students' talents is the most important part. Right now, a portion of the east wall outside the second gymnasium needs some sprucing up. I've gotten permission from Principal Hashimoto for us to paint a mural on it in time for the big event."

He gestures at all his artwork lining the art room's walls. The eyes of the deities and figures of the African diaspora loom over us, like they're keeping guard over everything that happens in this space. If they are really watching us, it'd be nice if one of them could do quite literally anything about our little vampire problem.

"The theme of the mural is 'Where We're From.' I want each of you to incorporate elements of the theme into the final piece. And don't feel like you have to go with how you're supposed to answer that question. For some people, the answer is the city they were born in, or the country their parents came from. For others, it's not a place but a person or an experience."

"Where are you f-f-from, Mr. Riley?" asks Mateo.

Mr. Riley points to one of his paintings, a nighttime land-scape of a small farmhouse surrounded by wide, rolling fields beneath a sea of stars.

"I'm from summers spent down on my poppy's farm. I am from sweet tea and pecan pie and fighting with my cousins over Uno. I'm from mosquito bites and stories about Boo Hags told when the sun has just begun to set but the night hasn't fully arrived yet. That's where I'm from."

No wonder Mr. Riley is an art teacher. The image he paints in our minds is so vivid I feel like I'm the one spending a summer down South. He instructs us to take some time to figure out our own answers to his question before we start planning out the mural.

Roxy takes to the assignment instantly, and in five minutes she has a bulleted list that takes up a whole page. Eunju and Mateo are filling theirs out, too, while Gavin writes two things before leaning back on his stool and playing with his head-phones.

I'm the only person whose page is blank. Every time I try to write something, I freeze. The obvious answer to where I'm from is Ghana, but that isn't completely true. You could also say I'm from the lake house, but that isn't right, either. None of these options feels wrong, it's just . . . I don't know. I'd ask Boulder how he thinks I should answer, except he's currently at the bottom of my backpack being crushed beneath at least three different textbooks.

I tap my pencil on the table, looking around to see if every-one else is already done, when my eyes meet Gavin's.

He quirks an eyebrow. "By the way, what's the plan for after school today?" he asks.

Mr. Riley excitedly pops his head out from behind the stack of sixth-grade color-theory assignments he'd started grading. "You all are spending time together outside of school?" I can practically feel the *Yay, my plan to force these students to like one another is working!* energy coming off him.

I mentally hit Gavin with my shoe. How many times did I say last night that we were never, ever to talk about Slayer business in front of civilians?

"Um, yeah, we're meeting up later to . . . to . . . to bake cookies!"

As soon as the words are out of my mouth, I cringe. Come on, Serwa, *bake cookies*? I don't even know how to bake!

"That's so wonderful! Any particular reason, or just for fun?"

Luckily, Roxy jumps in before I can stammer out a worse lie. "We wanted to give them as an apology to Mr. Johnson for messing up the Home Ec room."

Mateo nods. "Nothing says 'We're sorry' like a warm p-p-plate of cookies."

Mr. Riley smiles so wide it's a wonder his cheeks don't hurt. I have to fight to keep my laughter down.

"Yeah, that's it!" I say. "But baking cookies is a lot harder than people realize. Things can go south really fast."

"Oh, I'm sure we can figure it out," says Gavin. "Serwa says she knows a super-secret recipe only she can teach us."

Eunju shifts toward me on her stool, favoring the side of her that wasn't injured yesterday. "But we still don't know where we're meeting yet to . . . bake these cookies."

My good mood deflates faster than a balloon dog in a cactus shop. Poop, I'd forgotten about that. "So, funny story, I, uh, actually haven't figured that out just yet. But I'm working on it!"

"Yeah," adds Roxy. "Our oven isn't working at the moment."

Oh gods, am I turning her into a liar? I'm a bad influence, aren't I?

Eunju ignores Roxy and scoffs at me. "This was all your idea, but you don't know where we're actually going to be doing it?"

"I literally moved here less than a week ago!" I snap. "I don't suppose you could—"

Mateo puts a hand up between Eunju and me, which is good, because there is a not-zero chance that fists might start flying if either of us says another word. "It's all right. There are lots of . . . ovens in this t-t-town. We'll figure something out."

Gavin strokes his chin, before snapping his fingers. "Actually, I think I know the perfect place! Let's meet up at the tot lot at four—I'll take you there."

I stare at him. "'Tot lot' . . . Do you mean the playground?"

"Yeah, everyone here calls it that," he says, and the others nod in agreement.

Well, add that to the list of reasons why Maryland makes absolutely no sense.

Mr. Riley puts a hand over his heart, and you can just tell that he's thinking about what a great teacher he is and that he has no idea what "bake cookies" actually means. We all manage to stifle ourselves for the rest of the period, but the second the final bell rings and Mr. Riley lets us go, we burst into laughter in the hallway. Other students look at us like we've lost our minds, but we don't care.

And you know what? Nothing about the adze or the Mrs. Dean situation has changed, but having other people to share the secret with does make me feel lighter.

Maybe this whole team thing wasn't such a bad idea after all.

FAST-FORWARD SEVERAL HOURS, AND that's how we all find ourselves traipsing through the forest behind Sunny Oak, our fates resting in Gavin's hands. The renovated part of Rocky Gorge has the sleek, just-out-of-the-box feeling of a still growing city, but the forest feels old, as if hundreds of years ago these same trees watched a group of kids walk beneath their shade, and they'll watch another group do the same thing a hundred years from now. About twenty minutes into our hike, we pass by a rusted barbed-wire fence with a tattered WARNING! sign hanging lopsidedly in front of it.

"That's the entrance to the gorge the town was named after," Roxy whispers at my obvious curiosity. "A couple years ago a toddler fell down and died over there, so now no one is allowed to go near it."

I only catch a glimpse of the chasm through the trees, but the little I can see makes a shiver run down my spine. It just . . . never ends, like a jagged black hole smile cut straight into the earth.

Luckily, Gavin takes us past the gorge. We go so deep in the forest that soon all the sounds from town fade away. At first, all we can see are the dark cluster of trees and greenish sunny spots in the few places where the light pierces through the canopy. But then, in the distance, flashes of bubblegum pink, royal blue, and other unnatural colors break through the gloom. They're so out of place that at first I wonder if I haven't stepped through the rabbit hole.

When we burst through the trees, a giant neon-purple-and-pink wonderland stretches in front of us. Gavin raises his hands with a triumphant grin.

"Everyone, I give you . . . Sweetieville!"

According to the Wikipedia article I skimmed when I first moved here, Sweetieville Amusement Park was once the crown jewel of Rocky Gorge. People used to travel from all over the country just to enjoy its many candy-themed attractions. But now, three decades after a gruesome accident on Marshmallow Mountain shut down the park forever, Sweetieville is nothing more than a pastel-colored ghost town. The rusted statue of Queen Peppermint in her taffy pink ball gown stares down at us with half her jaw missing, and I can't help but feel like she's glowering as Gavin leads us through a gap in the wafer cookie chain-link fencing.

"My older siblings and I found this place when we were out here hiking a couple years ago," he explains. "It's so far off the main trail that even the forest rangers don't bother to check it anymore. We can practice all the magic we want here, and no one will ever know."

We set up our base of operations in Candy Cane Commons, a flat open area surrounded by giant replicas of the red-and-white-striped confections, though they are more rust-and-gray-striped now. The space must have been used for shows or something back in the day, but today it's home to nothing but weeds and . . . Was that a raccoon just now? The others watch me closely as I unpack the items I nabbed from Roxy's place: a pack of markers, three dusty Barbie dolls that have definitely seen better days, a whole thermos of lemonade, and a box of stale Girl Scout cookies I found in the back of the pantry (gotta keep our energy up). Boulder climbs out of the backpack to perch on my shoulder, his face twisted in a tiny scowl.

Once I have the materials ready for our very first adze fighting lesson, I turn to face the others, open my mouth to speak . . . and suddenly forget every single thing I've ever known about anything.

Sweat pours down my neck. Nyame help me, this is really happening. I am really in charge of these kids. Who let this happen? Why did no one stop me?

Boulder, of all people, is the one who brings me back to my senses with a gentle poke to my cheek. "Start at the beginning," he suggests.

I nod, suddenly grateful he's here with me. I think of my parents standing up to Boahinmaa, ready to die before giving up the whereabouts of the Midnight Drum.

They're doing their part to keep the world safe. It's time for me to do mine.

I pick up a marker and begin drawing on the cracked concrete. "At the beginning of time, long before there were most things, there was Nyame, Sky God and Creator of All."

I press my finger against the gye nyame I drew, and an image of Nyame enshrouded by swirling galaxies appears. The others watch wide-eyed, and even I feel that same spark of wonder that magic is real and I get to see it.

"With the help of his wife, the earth goddess Asaase Yaa, Nyame created our world. To every human, he gave an okra—a soul—and he breathed into them sunsum, the breath of life, so we could live and gave them honam, a body. And then he retreated to his kingdom in the sky, leaving his children, the various deities of the rivers and forests and other natural landmarks, to rule over what he had created. They were the abosom.

"But though there was much good in the world, evil soon followed. Not long after Nyame left, creatures of black magic appeared to sully his great work. The absolute worst among them were the obayifo, followed by the sasabonsam, and of course, the adze. When the gods saw how the humans suffered, they chose the strongest among our kind and gave them a piece of their own power—divine wisdom. Those seven founders were the first Abomofuo, and it is through their work we continue the great fight against the forces of evil."

I look each kid in the eye, hoping my face is even half as scary as my mom's when she gets into serious business mode.

"Right now, there's an adze stalking the grounds of Rocky Gorge Middle School. I don't know how or why it got there, but if we don't stop it, no one else will. What I'm about to show you is never to be shared with a non-Slayer, do you understand me?" I don't mention that I'm not supposed to be sharing it with *them*, either.

They all nod solemnly.

I grab the first doll, Graduation Barbie, and draw three Adinkra on her torso: sesa wo suban—the Adinkra of transformation—for sentience and size; nkyinkyin—the symbol of twisting—for resilience and toughness; and hye wo nhye—the symbol of imperishability—for permanence.

Light swirls around the doll, and in seconds she goes from a plastic toy barely a foot tall to an automaton who towers above our heads at about six feet. Her arms and legs move of their own free will, though her face is still frozen in a creepily perfect painted smile.

Veterinarian Barbie and Pilot Barbie are next, and soon we have three full-size training dummies ready to go. Now all we need are weapons. For this I use various bits of junk I found lying around the apartment. (Then again, the stapler prooobably isn't junk, but they always say it's better to ask forgiveness than permission.)

A hop, skip, and a whole lotta Adinkra later, there is a pile of swords, bows, staffs, and spears on the ground before us. I sit back and drink at least half the thermos of lemonade in one gulp as the others inspect my handiwork. Eunju is immediately drawn to an akrafena similar to Nokware, while Mateo gingerly picks up a few arrows and Roxy takes a few messy swings with a spear. Gavin's the only one who hangs back, nervously eyeing the weapon pile.

"Hang on," he says. "I thought when you said 'training' you meant we'd be learning magic like you use."

I shake my head. "I could teach you all one hundred and ten of the basic Adinkra and it wouldn't help us capture Bullseye, because none of you have divine wisdom. No, my goal with these lessons is to get you combat-proficient enough so that next time you're face-to-face with an adze, you don't die within ten seconds. I can handle the magic on my own."

I toss Gavin a practice sword. He barely catches it, holding it at arm's length from his body.

"So now," I say with a grin, "it's time for lesson number one."

You know what? This might actually work.

14

How to Lose Friends and Demoralize People

"A good leader listens as often as they talk."

—From the *Nwoma*

THERE IS NO WAY in the name of Nyame's soggy shorts this is ever going to work.

For one thing, I don't think Mateo has it in him to hurt a teddy bear, much less an adze. I have him practice sparring with Veterinarian Barbie, and every time he has an opening, he hesitates. VB has knocked him flat on his back five matches straight now, and I don't see that streak getting broken anytime soon.

But if Mateo's not aggressive enough, Eunju is *too* aggressive. She throws her full power into everything she does, basically telegraphing her moves to her opponents and leaving herself open to attack on all sides. She is the most athletic of the whole group, but she loses just as often as everyone else. Every time she does, she gets more frustrated, her moves get sloppier, she loses again, and the whole cycle repeats.

As for Gavin, on the field he shows none of the obnoxious confidence he has in class. In fact, you'd think, from the way he barely manages to lift it, he's scared of his own weapon. I don't know how I'm ever going to get him to face down Bullseye when he's this uncomfortable with a blade.

And Roxy . . .

"Arms up, Roxy, *up*! As in the opposite of down!" I scream for the hundredth time as Roxy lowers her weapon yet again in the middle of a fight. Graduation Barbie takes advantage of the sudden opening to swing at Roxy's now completely undefended left side. Roxy goes down hard. She's super lucky I blunted all the weapons, because that blow from a normal sword would have left her head on one side of Sweetieville and her body on the other.

"Don't worry—just shake it off," I say weakly, fighting a grimace. "Next time, try to— No, Eunju, don't hold a staff like that!"

Eunju doesn't listen, and she charges for Pilot Barbie in a move so obvious I'm pretty sure astronauts could see it from the International Space Station. Pilot Barbie somersaults over Eunju's head, grabs her by the collar of her expensive-looking cream sweater, and tosses her straight into Mateo. Gavin tries to sneak up behind Pilot Barbie, but then Veterinarian Barbie kicks his legs out from under him, and just like that, my entire team is down.

I run my hands down my face and ask Nyame for the millionth time why this is happening to me. "Time. Boulder, how long was that round?"

Boulder pauses his episode of *90 Day Fiancé* to check his stopwatch app. "Twenty-five point sixty-seven seconds exactly."

Oh gods. If they can't last even half a minute against a few Barbie dolls, how are these kids going to survive a fight with an actual live adze?

"Have I mentioned yet what an awful idea I think this is?" Boulder asks.

"Once or twice, yes."

"I still don't understand how you thought you could hand a group of untrained twelve-year-olds a bunch of deadly weapons and expect them not to chop their own heads off."

"Yes, yes, this was a huge mistake, and we may as well hand ourselves over to the adze now to save it the trouble of hunting us down. I heard you the first thousand times." I grit my teeth, clap my hands, and yell to the group, "All right, that was . . . less completely awful than last time! Weapons up—let's go again!"

Everyone looks at me like I just told them all the soda in the school vending machines has been replaced with prune juice. "Serwa, we've been doing this for *two hours*," whines Gavin. "When do we get to take a break?"

I scoff. "I used to train a minimum of four hours a day with my parents—six on the weekends. And you can take a break when someone actually lands a blow on one of the dolls— which, I would like to add, I was able to do when I was five."

Eunju storms over and shoves the staff into my hands. "If you're so good at this, why don't you show us yourself, Miss Know-It-All?"

I want to snap back, but you know what? That actually isn't a bad idea. Before we began, I gave everyone a basic rundown on each weapon, but maybe watching me in action will give them a better idea of what I need them to do.

I flip the staff a couple times to test the weight, wrap my braids into a bun to keep them out of my face, then nod at Boulder. "Start the clock," I tell him before marching into the center of Candy Cane Commons.

All three Barbies circle me, the magic from the Adinkra I drew on them giving their bodies an otherworldly golden glow. Their movements are jerky and marionette-like, but despite the stiffness, fighting them is not all that far off from what facing an adze is like. My right leg slips back and my left arm comes up as I shift into a basic defensive stance with my hands at thirds on the staff, just like my parents taught me. Suddenly everything else melts away, and I'm no longer in the middle of a creepy candy forest with four people who probably hate my guts. This is just another fight. It's what I do.

"Go!" shouts Boulder, and Pilot Barbie leaps for me first, the tip of her spear flashing straight toward my head. I duck beneath the attempted strike and dance back to create more space, shifting my hold on the staff to allow me to block her next swipe, then her next.

Graduation Barbie tries to surprise me from behind, but I'm already spinning out of reach of her hammer, which ends up slamming into Pilot Barbie. PB's plastic arm goes spinning through the air, almost whacking Roxy in the face. I make a silent note to fix that later. Even one-armed, though, the Adinkra keep Pilot Barbie up and fighting, and her attacks remain quick and accurate.

I don't realize I've lost track of Veterinarian Barbie until she spins out from the cover of Pilot Barbie and gets me in the side with the blunted blade of one of the swords. Oof, that's going to hurt tomorrow. Graduation Barbie grabs my staff to try to yank me toward her, so I let it go and roll across the grass.

"One minute!" calls Boulder as I spit the dirt in my mouth onto the ground. This is admittedly not my best showing—normally, at the minute mark I would've taken out at least one of my opponents by now. My parents would want me to be better than this. I *am* better than this.

Graduation Barbie moves to pin me in place with my former staff, but I push myself up and knock her off-balance with a swipe to the legs. While she's disoriented, I jam my elbow into her chest, then pierce the staff through her flowing graduation robes so she can't move anymore.

One down, two to go.

Pilot Barbie and Veterinarian Barbie move in as one, clearly hoping to corner me with the candy canes at my back. On the ground near my feet is the bow and arrow set Mateo was eyeing. I grab the bow, strap the quiver to my back, and then allow Pilot Barbie to grab me by the front of the shirt.

Once she's within arm's length, I slam the heel of my free hand into her chin, then use my left leg to push off Veterinarian Barbie, who is trying to grab me by the waist. This gives me the momentum I need to break from Pilot Barbie's grasp, then, using her as a springboard, I jump from her toward one of the candy canes at the edge of the commons. Bow between my teeth, I climb to the top. From there, I fire two arrows in rapid procession. The first gets Veterinarian Barbie in the head, the second hits Pilot Barbie's chest. They both keel over, and once the last plastic limb stops twitching, I scurry down the candy cane and face the other members of the GCC, whose mouths are all open with shock.

"Time!" I yell out.

"Two minutes and thirty-eight seconds," calls Boulder, and I don't even bother hiding my grin. Lots of people, especially girls, feel like they can't be honest when they're good at something, because they think it'll make them seem like a huge jerk. But I am good at this. Very good. If anyone thinks I shouldn't be able to admit that, that's their problem, not mine.

"What did I tell you?" I say, unstrapping the quiver from my back. "Easy peasy. And I didn't use a drop of magic."

Eunju looks impressed for all of five seconds before she switches back to her usual *I hate you and want to make sure you know it* face. "You expect us to be able to do *that*, on our very first day?"

"Obviously not. What you just witnessed is twelve years' worth of training. But the general idea, yes."

She throws her hands into the air. "How are we— I don't even— Not all of us can do backflips, Serwa!"

"Technically, I didn't do a backflip—"

"Whatever! You're out of your mind if you really think you can just throw a bunch of weapons at us and expect us to do what you just did!"

"I've never been the best at sports," admits Roxy, and I shake my head.

"You don't have to be super athletic to know how to defend yourself. If you can locate your opponent's weak spots, you're already halfway to winning."

Mateo looks glumly over at the broken bodies of the Barbie dolls. "I d-d-don't want to hurt anyone," he says softly, and I bite back a groan.

I get their hesitation, I really do. I know better than anyone how grueling Slayer training can get. But if we don't do this, and do it right, the blood of everyone in this town is going to be on our hands.

"Adze might take on human hosts, but they're not people. Any damage we do to them while trying to extract the vampire is a small price to pay compared to the destruction being caused to the person possessed. And besides, part of the reason Slayers team up with mmoatia is so we have a way to heal the injuries we cause."

I look over at Gavin, already preparing a response to whatever sarcastic complaint he surely has ready, and see that he has his headphones over his ears. I try to channel my dad's steady patience, but it's my mom's fire that comes out when I spit, "Gavin, take those off! I want everyone back on sword drills. We can stop when you get it right."

"No. I'm on break!" he yells, likely over whatever he's listening to, and the last remaining thread of my patience snaps. I march over to him, yank the headphones away, and toss them on the ground. His eyes bug out of his head at the crack of them coming apart.

"What is wrong with you?!" he screams. He dives for the two halves, but I get there first and pull them into my chest.

"This isn't a game!" Deep down I know he's not the one I'm truly mad at. But the frustration inside me has been building for days, and there's nothing I can do to stop it from pouring out. "There are no extra lives or starting over if we mess this up! We're going to have *one chance* to try to catch this adze, and unlike the Barbies, it will fight to kill when cornered. So I need you to stop goofing off and actually take something seriously for once in your life!"

Gavin stares at me, his usual grin replaced by something tight and hard. Instead of responding, he lifts up the corner of his vintage band T-shirt.

Thin cuts and mottled burn scars litter the otherwise smooth brown skin of his stomach. They're all faded in a way that suggest he's had them for a long, long time, but there's no denying the wounds must have hurt whenever he received them. Suddenly his fear of the weapons pile earlier makes a lot more sense.

"You don't know anything about me." If I wasn't already frozen with shock at the sight of his scars, the coldness of his tone would keep me in place. "The rest of us might not be vampire hunters with magic powers or whatever, but stop acting like you're the only one who's ever survived a life-or-death situation."

Eunju's and Roxy's surprise mirrors my own, but there's recognition in Mateo's eyes. He knew about this. I open my mouth, but nothing comes out. Gavin looks at each one of us, drops his T-shirt, and shrugs. His emotions change so fast, like water twisting and turning through rapids, I can barely keep up.

"Fix my headphones," he orders. I slide the two separated parts together, and he snatches them back and wraps them around his neck.

Four pairs of defeated eyes stare at me, and it's only then I notice just how much dirt and scratches they're covered in after only two hours of practice. Everyone really tried their best today. Their best wasn't that good, but they tried.

I know how it feels to give everything you've got and still not be good enough. I know that feeling real well.

"Let's call it a day," I say weakly. An apology lies on the tip of my tongue, but Gavin's glare makes it clear he doesn't want to hear it.

I stay quiet while Boulder heals everyone's wounds. Soon we look like we weren't doing anything more strenuous than picking up more trash.

Earlier I thought I saw a spark of something real in this group when we all worked together to pull one over on Mr. Riley. But I was wrong. There's something broken between the five of us, and not even the strongest Adinkra can fix it.

I know this is the part where I'm supposed to give a rallying speech, but my mind remains blank as one by one, Gavin, Eunju, and Mateo walk away. Soon there's nobody left but Roxy and me, and we head home in silence, the weight of my failure hanging heavy around my shoulders.

15

How to Pull Off a Stealth Mission (and Look Good While Doing It)

"A good Slayer must learn to guard the mind as well as the body; it is in sleep they are the most vulnerable."

—From the *Nwoma*

I'M DREAMING ABOUT THE dark void again. Just like last night, all the people I love stand behind glass, and just like last night, they all move away when I try to reach them.

But this time, when I call for Grandma Awurama, the void doesn't carry me away. She turns around, and I see the face I've only known from pictures—the thick brows both me and my dad have, the slightly upturned nose that's all hers. The glass shatters as she opens her arms and beckons for me to come to her. I do, throwing myself into her embrace. She holds me tight, and I feel so safe in that moment, like nothing bad will ever happen to me again now that she's here.

"Oh, Serwa," she sighs, her voice reconstructed in my memory from all the videos of her Dad has shown me. I look up just as she removes her hands from my waist.

And squeezes them around my neck. I glance up to see Boahinmaa leering down at me.

"Got you," cackles the witch.

When I wake up, my throat feels like it's on fire. This time, Roxy sleeps through my distress, her snores bouncing around the room. Though it's only 11:20 p.m., I know there's no way I can go back to bed after what I just saw. I put my head in my hands and draw my knees to my chest, waiting for the roiling feeling inside to fade like it always does.

Is this what a panic attack feels like?

I don't know if it's the stress from the lingering adze attack or my guilt over today's disastrous training session, but these recurring nightmares are not it. I'm sick of sitting around feeling powerless when I was raised to be powerful. Maybe Roxy and the others aren't ready to go out into the field yet, but I am. Doing something, anything, has to be better than lying here and letting my mind rip me apart from the inside.

I change into a T-shirt, jeans, and hoodie as quietly as I can so I don't wake my cousin. Then I draw asawa and adwo, the serenity Adinkra, on the corner of her bedsheet, where she won't notice it. From the way she's snoring, I doubt she's waking up anytime soon even without the magic, but the Adinkra will make sure she sleeps even more soundly and that any dreams she has are pleasant.

I tiptoe out into the living room, intending to do the same to my aunt, and then freeze when I find her sitting at the kitchen table with a tall stack of papers and a glass of what smells like wine.

"Oh, Serwa. I hope I didn't wake you." Auntie Latricia quickly flips her phone over, but not before I catch a flash of the calculator app on her screen. Those papers in front of her must be bills, and judging from the amount of wine in her glass and the tightness around her eyes, this month's numbers aren't great. "Do you need something?"

"Just a glass of water. But don't worry, I can get it myself!" I add quickly as my aunt begins to rise from her seat. Gods, I can't believe I didn't listen at the door to make sure no one was awake before I came out here. Rookie mistake.

"Would you like some, too?" I ask, and when she says yes, I grab two glasses from the cabinet but turn away from her so she doesn't see me draw the sleep spell on the bottom of hers. Look, I don't *want* to knock out my aunt, but there's no way she's going to let me leave the apartment this late.

I begin to hand the glass to her, only to pause as I take in the stack of bills again. I've only been here a few days, so I don't think any of the expenses include me yet, but bringing another person into your home isn't cheap. And it hits me that between losing my house, losing my parents, and discovering the adze in town, I haven't thanked my aunt for giving me a place to stay when the entire world felt unsafe.

"Thank you, Auntie, for everything," I blurt out awkwardly. It feels like too little too late, but she gives me a tired smile and shakes her head.

"What's that thing Patrick always used to say . . . Ye . . . ? Yeni . . . ?"

"Yeni aseda?" I guess. It's an expression meaning *There are no thanks between us* in Twi.

She snaps her fingers. "I always loved that phrase. We may not be blood, but you're family. You have nothing to thank me for." She frowns. "If anything, I wish I could do more. Middle school is volatile enough—I can't imagine trying to get through it for the first time without your parents around.

"I'm sorry that my job means I can't always be there for you girls. But even though I'll never be one of the PTA moms who volunteers at every event or hosts every sleepover, know that I will always, *always* have your back. I'll never replace your parents, and I wouldn't want to, but while you're under my roof and even after, you're mine just as much as Roxy is."

The back of my eyes burn, but this time it's with gratitude instead of frustration. I cough awkwardly and say, "I'm glad my dad knew where to find you."

She scoffs. "As if I'd ever go anywhere else. My family has lived in Rocky George since it was known as Harristown."

"So you've lived here your whole life?"

She nods. "Just like my mama before me and her daddy before her and so on for decades. In fact, one of my ancestors participated in the slave uprising at Harristown Manor that shut down the entire plantation in the 1800s."

My eyes go wide. "That happened? I had no idea."

"Of course you didn't, because that school refuses to teach any history about this town that might tarnish its *nice* image." She shakes her head in disgust. "They can try to whitewash the truth all they want, but our roots here run deep. My granddaddy grew up here, too, and he swore his grandmother was so in tune with this land that she could predict the weather or tell if a person was pregnant just by talking to the trees. Old wives' tales, a lot like you'd hear in Ghana, but Roxy loved 'em. He's probably the source of her fascination with monsters and magic and all that."

Auntie Latricia shakes her head again, but this time with a small smile as she thinks of my cousin's antics. I finally hand her the glass of water, my mind whirling as I try to process all I've learned from this conversation. Lots of families have stories about relatives with unnatural quirks and skills, but something in my gut is telling me it isn't a coincidence there's a legend like that tied to one of the oldest families in this town. But what, if anything, does that have to do with the adze?

Auntie Latricia is halfway through her water when she

finally notices I'm not in my pajamas. "Why are you . . . ?" she begins, but the magic from the Adinkra kicks in, and in seconds she's out like a light. I nab a blanket from the couch, drape it over my aunt's shoulders, and pivot toward the front door . . . until a creak from behind pulls me up short.

A kitchen cabinet swings open, revealing Boulder's head poking out of a box of Cheez-Its. He takes one glance at Auntie Latricia drooling at the table and his frown deepens.

"Where do you think you're going?" he demands. With a pang of guilt I realize I've never thought about how the mmoatia would keep himself fed in a house where he has to hide. I've really been dropping every ball since I got here.

"I'm going to do some reconnaissance at the school," I whisper. "If I can get into the video surveillance system, I might be able to see the exact moment when Mr. Riley was bitten on Monday. That might give me some clues about who the adze's host is."

And learning that might help me figure out why the adze is hanging around the school of all places. The mysteries of the vampire's identity and why magic is so unpredictable in this town feel like threads in a giant tapestry. If I keep looking long enough, surely the threads are bound to weave into a picture.

Boulder shakes his head and crosses his crumb-covered arms over his chest. "You can't go now. It's too dangerous."

"I won't draw any attention to myself. The adze won't even know I'm there, if the host is even still on the premises this late."

"I wasn't referring to the adze. How do you think the police will react if they catch a twelve-year-old Black girl wandering around the school grounds by herself?"

The air grows heavy between us as we both think about all the kids who lost their lives for the "crime" of being Black in the wrong place at the wrong time. There are many threats lurking in the mortal world waiting for kids who look like me, and I've lived so long in my little bubble that I've never come into contact with any of them.

But I can't keep sitting here doing nothing. I don't know how to explain to Boulder that it feels like my mind will actually fall apart if I don't so something, and soon.

I take another step toward the door. "I won't get caught."

"Serwa, you are not to step foot outside this apartment tonight. That is an order."

Ugh, I'm so sick of everyone bossing me around all the time! I draw myself up to my full height, which admittedly isn't very tall by human standards but is a giant compared to a mmoatia. "Make me."

The last emotion I expect to see flashes across Boulder's face—hurt. "Does that make you feel good?" he asks softly. "Reminding me that you're big and I'm small? That for all my centuries of wisdom and experience, I can't physically force you or anyone else to do anything? Does putting me in my place make you feel strong?"

And, for the first time, I think about what life must be like for a mmoatia in a world not designed for their kind. Where everything is literally an uphill battle. It must feel a lot like how I've felt since coming to Rocky Gorge, and Boulder has had to live with it for millennia. The annoyance drains out of me, shame bubbling up in its place.

"I'm sorry—you didn't deserve that." I wrap my arms around myself even though the apartment is far from cold. "It's just . . . I can't stand the idea of the adze wreaking havoc all across town while we're no closer to catching it. There's no way I could ever access the camera system during school hours. And if I don't do this and someone else gets hurt, I don't know if I'll be able to live with that."

Boulder is quiet for a long time before he finally sighs. "Your father wouldn't want me to tell you this, but he used to pull similar stunts when he was your age. I could never talk *him* out of them, either." He shakes his head, but his tone is far from unkind. "Fine, I understand. You may go. But hurry—your aunt and cousin will only stay enchanted for so long. And I'm coming with you, too."

Boulder's not my mmoatia. He's not doing this out of any loyalty to me, but rather the promise he made to my dad, so I shouldn't feel glad he wants to come with me. But still I nod. I grab the mmoatia, Cheez-Its crumbs and all, drop him onto my shoulder, and run out of the apartment before he can change his mind.

DURING THE DAY, THE clock tower of Rocky Gorge Middle School feels like something out of a storybook with its warm red brick and swooping tiled roof. But tonight its face seems to watch with a disapproving glare as Boulder and I hop the fence and approach the main building.

Thanks to my study of the school blueprints—it's amazing what you can find on the Internet if you know where to look— I know where all the security cameras are mounted. I easily pick the lock of an unmonitored side door with a hairpin, and then, using a zigzagging pattern of movement, we sneak down the hall.

While Mom handled the majority of my combat training, Dad taught me everything I know about stealth work. His voice rings through my ears as I make my way forward.

Keep crouched and close to the ground, stepping from toe to heel. You make less sound that way.

Walk in cover as much as possible. Open areas are a death sentence. Trust what you feel more than what you see.

Surprisingly, there are no cameras near the main office, either inside or out. I guess Principal Hashimoto values her privacy. It makes me wonder what she's up to. . . . Turning into an adze, perhaps?

The security room is tucked inside the front office. After pressing an ear against the door to make sure it's empty, I make quick work of the lock and head inside. The space is little more than a glorified closet with a chair, a desk, and a computer. The monitor's screen shows a grid of multiple views from all the security cameras in the building.

Bingo.

You'd think the magic of the Adinkra wouldn't work on modern technology, but they make bypassing computer passwords a breeze. However, the first flaw in my plan is that the cameras are few and far between, only in the most used common areas of the building, like the front lobby, the media center, the cafeteria, etc. Private spaces like restrooms and locker rooms, plus most of the rooms in the older wing of the building, don't have any surveillance. Unfortunately, the teacher's lounge, where Mr. Riley said he stopped during our detention, is one of those rooms. If the adze bit him in there, there's no record of it.

Pushing down my frustration, I comb through all the footage from the first hour after school that day with the hope of finding something that'll make this whole risk worth it. It takes nearly forty-five minutes of zooming and reviewing until I finally see Mr. Riley, with his unmistakable mop of wavy hair, walk across the media center after leaving the teacher's lounge. He stops to talk to the media center lady, whose name I haven't yet learned, and that's when a bright glimmer flickers across the screen.

There's my vampire.

The whole thing takes less than ten seconds—the adze enters the media center, bites Mr. Riley on the thumb without him noticing, and flies from him to land on a bookshelf. Then it zips out of the media center, down the hallway, and outside, where I lose sight of it. So now I know where and when Mr. Riley was bitten, but I still have no idea who did it.

"Do you see anything I've missed?" I ask Boulder.

He shakes his head. "The adze was smart to transform outside. We can't even narrow it down to a teacher or a student with this."

I start to exit from the program, then pause. I replay the recording, this time focusing not on Mr. Riley but instead the book that Bullseye landed on after biting him. The title is too blurry to read on the video, but, judging from its worn spine, the book is clearly older than any of the other ones on the shelf. It could just be a coincidence the adze descended there, but if there's even a small chance it's not . . .

"I'm going to check the media center," I tell Boulder as I slip out of the chair. "You stay here and swap out any footage of us with an empty loop."

He nods once, and then I'm on my own.

The only light is coming from dim emergency bulbs, so I draw nsoromma on my palm to illuminate my way. The star Adinkra casts an eerie glow on the rows and rows of books lining the media center. It takes me a few circles around the room to find the book the adze landed on. It's both older and thinner than I expected, the worn brown leather binding cracked from decades of use. The title reads HARRISTOWN MANOR: A HISTORY.

That's the second time tonight the fact that Rocky Gorge was once called Harristown has come up. The book covers everything from the town's formation during the pre–Revolutionary War era to celebrations at the end of World War II. Near the middle of the book, there's a photo taken during the time of the Civil War. It shows a large three-story house with a wide wraparound porch surrounded by weeping willow trees. In the distance I can make out squat wooden dwellings at the edge of a field of crops bordering a forest. But the centerpiece of the picture is the large clock tower jutting from the back of the grounds.

The same clock tower that sits over the building I'm in right now.

Suddenly, the truth clicks into place. RGMS used to be Harristown Manor. They built this school on the site of a former slave plantation.

This shouldn't be as surprising to me as it is. Even though Maryland wasn't a part of the Confederacy, it was a slave state. Harriet Tubman and Frederick Douglass were both born here. The history of enslavement runs deep through this land, no matter how hard they try to cover it up with new paint and state-of-the-art tech.

But what does any of this have to do with the adze? The vampire could have landed on this book randomly, but my instincts tell me there's more to it. But what? And does it have anything to do with why neither Boulder nor my parents could detect any black magic in this town?

If I'd planned ahead, I would've brought the iPad with me to take pictures of the book. Instead, I put the tome back on the shelf, making a mental note to come back tomorrow during school hours.

Just as I'm about to head back to the security room to collect Boulder, something rustles behind me.

No, not something.

Some*one*.

16

How to Make a Friend

"The connections you make as a Slayer can either save your life or endanger it. For your own protection, know few and trust fewer."

—From the *Nwoma*

YEARS OF TRAINING KICK in. I whirl around, twist my potential attacker's arm behind their back, and slam them against the ground. Their cry of pain is familiar, and only then do I recognize the curly hair, large glasses, and oversize sweater of the person beneath me.

"Mateo? What are you doing here?"

I haul him to his feet. The boy is lucky I attacked only to disable, not harm. He stumbles, then fixes the glasses I knocked askew.

"I c-c-could ask you the same thing. What are you d-d-d—Why are you here?"

"I wanted to look for the adze while the grounds were empty." I narrow my eyes. "Hang on—you didn't answer my question. What are *you* doing here?"

Mateo gulps audibly as he glances over his shoulder. An awkward second passes. I step closer, and he steps back.

"I didn't see you when I checked the security monitors," I say. "Where were you?"

Could Mateo be an adze? I know he isn't the one who bit Mr. Riley, because he was with the rest of us the whole time, but there could be more than one vampire in the school. *Or* the original adze could have left its host and jumped into Mateo sometime after the first day of school. . . .

"Is this what that note was about?" I press. "Is this why you've been so nice to me since I arrived? You're trying to make me let down my guard so you can bite me in the back?"

"What are you even— N-no!"

His eyes go wide as my hand goes for Nokware at my wrist. He stammers out something, only to stop when footsteps echo toward the media center. The color drains from his face, and he quickly grabs me by the arm and pulls me behind the open door. I try to shove him off, but he's surprisingly stronger than he looks.

He puts a hand over my mouth. "Sorry! Sorry!" he hisses.

I'm this close to biting his palm when the source of the footsteps becomes clear. I look through the crack on the side of the door to see a middle-aged, light-brown-skinned man in a blue jumpsuit. When he walks by, I can just barely make out the name on his front pocket: ALVAREZ.

Mateo waits to let me go until we hear the man heading out of the lobby and outside.

I step back with a snarl. "If you ever do that again, I will bite your hand off."

He sighs. "That's f-f-fair."

I gesture toward the lobby. "That man—was he your father?"

Mateo nods. "I know we p-p-promised to stay away from the school. B-b-but my father's an electrician. I heard he g-g-got a late-night request to fix some wiring in one of the b-b-bathrooms. I couldn't let him b-b-be here alone when there might b-b-be a . . . you know what."

Mateo gives me a defiant grimace, as if daring me to scold him for doing something so reckless. And you know what? I can't. Because if the roles were reversed and I thought my parent was going into a building where a vampire might be lurking, nothing could stop me from trying to keep them safe.

Besides, electrical wires suddenly freaking out of nowhere sounds like an after-effect of black magic to me. Our vampire was on the premises sometime today, I just know it.

I simply nod, feeling bad for having doubted him. "I believe you. And I'm sorry I slammed you against the ground," I say sheepishly, and he gives a one-shoulder shrug in response. "Don't you have to hurry to catch up with your dad?"

Mateo shakes his head. "I rode my b-b-bike over here. He d-d-doesn't know I came. He's off to his next job."

"A valiant sneak," I say admiringly. "Didn't know you had it in you."

"I may not b-b-be the strongest or fastest, b-b-but I'll never let someone I care about go into d-d-danger by themselves."

I'll be honest, I kind of wrote Mateo off as a wimp the moment I met him. But since day one he's been calm and steady, his courage quieter than I'm used to but no less important. It's like the wind—you can't see it, but when it counts, you can feel it.

"Well, I'm impressed." I punch him lightly on the shoulder. "Keep that up and we might just make a true Slayer out of you after all."

Mateo beams with pride even as his face flushes pink.

We head back to the security room to grab Boulder, who throws his tiny hands in the air and groans.

"Are there any more children sneaking around this school I should know about?" he demands.

"I think there might be a couple orphans living in the air ducts, but I can't be sure," I say, and Mateo laughs while Boulder gives me the world's smallest glare.

"I'm going to tell you the same thing I once told Napoleon when he began that nonsense about invading Russia in winter: Arrogance will get you places fast, but it won't take you far," he warns, and I roll my eyes. "Did you find anything in the media center?"

When I tell Boulder about the book, a line appears between his eyebrows. "Building a school over a site that caused such pain and suffering . . ." he says. "The lengths some people in this country will go to deny its own history never cease to amaze me."

"But why would an adze care about that?" I ask as the three of us head outside. The night air is surprisingly cool, the first hint that autumn will be arriving soon and with a vengeance.

Mateo picks up his bike and walks it next to me. "We d-d-did a unit on the Civil War last year," he says slowly, as if mulling over something he doesn't want to say. "It focused a little b-bit on . . . on the p-people who worked on p-p-plantations."

I cringe inwardly. Non-Black people always get really weird when it comes to this subject. But just because it's a hard topic doesn't mean we can just ignore it.

"Enslaved people," I correct him.

He nods. "Right, I'm sorry. We learned that most enslaved p-people came from West Africa, including G-Ghana. Is there any chance some of them were p-p-part of the Abomofuo and they b-b-brought magic with them?"

As soon as he says it, it seems so obvious that I'm mad I didn't think of it myself.

I glance at Boulder, who is riding on my shoulder. "Is that true?" I ask. "Were members of the Abomofuo enslaved?"

Boulder nods solemnly. "Our society did all we could to fight the scourge of colonizers who came to our lands. But we couldn't save everyone."

A knot tightens in my stomach. It's terrible to know that even with all our magic and the gods on our side, there were some things even the Abomofuo couldn't stop. As someone born in Africa, I'm always aware that it was simply luck that someone else's family was stolen instead of mine. Even though no one in my direct line was enslaved—that we know of, anyway—my family could have been ten—no, twenty times bigger if others weren't taken. Even though the people responsible have been dead for centuries, I suddenly hate them so much it hurts to breathe.

"Okay," I say, "so there's a possibility that at some point people with divine wisdom lived at the plantation, which is now the school. But why, then, can't anyone detect black magic around here? You'd think it would be easier. . . ."

None of us has an answer for that. We walk down the path in silence, all three of us lost in our own thoughts. Suddenly Auntie Latricia's claim of a witch in their family line sounds a whole lot more credible, but things still aren't adding up here.

When I finally look up, I notice Mateo is staring at me. "What is it?" My hands fly to my braid bun. "Is there something in my hair?"

"No, your hair looks nice. I was wondering . . . D-d-did you really think I wrote that note the other day just to hurt you?"

I bite back a grimace. "In my family's line of work, almost everyone around us has an ulterior motive. You can never be too cautious."

Mateo tilts his head. "That sounds really lonely."

"Loneliness is a fair price to pay for safety." Now I'm the one staring at him. "But why *did* you write that note, then, if it wasn't part of some nefarious master plan to stab me in the back, especially when I was being such a . . ."

Mateo lifts an eyebrow "Such a b-b-butt to everyone?"

I grimace again. "Yeah, that."

He looks up toward the few stars we can see past the streetlights. "Three years ago, my family moved here from C-C-California to take care of my uncle after a c-car accident. I remember what it was like b-being the new kid, having people q-q-question where you're from or why you sound the way you do. So I guess I wanted to do for you what no one ever d-d-did for me— welcome you without asking anything."

I don't know what to say. And I don't know why it was easier for me to believe he was acting out of pity or plotting against me than to believe he was just being kind.

Wow. Maybe my life has been lonelier than I thought.

"I g-g-get why you need to be careful around most people," says Mateo. "But the GCC—we're not your enemies. At least, I'm not."

He smiles at me and heat rushes to my face. I stumble, even though there wasn't anything on the path.

Mateo catches me by the elbow. "You okay?"

"Huh, wha—? I mean yeah, I'm fine. Never better!" I say, my voice just a little too high-pitched. Boulder fights back a laugh, and I *really* don't like that smug look he's giving me right now. "And . . . I'm really sorry for what I said at training yesterday. I went way too far, and it wasn't right."

Mateo shakes his head. "You owe G-Gavin the apology, not me."

Images of Gavin's scars run through my mind, and I suppress a shudder. "Did you know about his secret?"

"Yeah. We had the same gym class last year, and I saw the

m-m-marks in the locker room a few times. But we weren't friends, and I always hate it when strangers question my stutter, so I d-d-didn't ask."

I bite the inside of my cheek to keep from shuddering. "I don't think he'll want to talk to me ever again," I say glumly.

Mateo shakes his head. "We're not close, b-b-but I don't think he's someone who would hold a grudge. G-g-give him a chance. He might surprise you."

The bright lights of Sunny Oak Towers appear in the distance, and I realize . . . I don't want this walk to end. I can't remember the last time I walked for this long without looking over my shoulder or checking for escape routes. For a little while, I even forgot the adze existed, and I was just a normal girl having a conversation with a normal boy (and a mmoatia, but he doesn't count).

It feels . . . nice. Really nice.

"Uh, don't you have to be getting home now?" I ask him when we get to Sunny Oak.

"I *am* home," says Mateo. "I live here t-t-too."

"That's awesome!" I blurt out. Then, "Uh, I mean, really convenient. For tonight." Wow, so smooth. Much confidence. Love this for me.

After Mateo locks his bike to the rack, we enter the lobby. He stuffs his hands in his pockets as we wait for our respective elevators.

"B-b-by the way, where do you go d-during lunch? I've looked for you, but you haven't been there."

Of all the ways Mateo has surprised me tonight, this is the biggest. I didn't think anyone had noticed I was gone. "I've been eating in the art room with Mr. Riley . . . which, now that I've said it out loud, is even sadder than I realized."

Mateo laughs. "Can I join you g-guys tomorrow? The cafeteria can g-get . . . overwhelming. Eating somewhere else sounds nice."

"Don't you have people you usually eat with?"

He chews his lip. "Yeah, b-b-but we're not friends. Yesterday one of them offered me a d-d-dollar if I'd attempt a t-t-tongue t-t-twister."

My mouth falls open in shock. "That's horrible!"

He shrugs, picking idly at his sweater sleeve. "I'm used t-t-to it. That's how people t-t-treat the t-t-teacher's p-p-pet," he mutters darkly.

Technically, I don't have the authority to approve his lunchtime request, but that doesn't stop me from saying, "Of course! The more the merrier."

We say goodbye when our elevators arrive, and it's a lot easier to go back to bed after knowing that at least one member of the GCC doesn't hate me. I'm glad both of us followed our instincts tonight. Even Boulder agrees it was a successful mission—we spotted the adze.

Though my original plan was not to get close to anyone in Rocky Gorge who I didn't have to, I'm actually looking forward to the thought of hanging out with Mateo at school . . . in just a few hours. Ugh.

Roxy is sleeping peacefully, so my Adinkra must still be working. As I watch her breathe slowly and steadily, I think about how she's always been there for me, too, even though I've been standoffish at times. I'll have to make up for that.

I settle onto my air mattress, but before I fall asleep, my mind slips back to what I saw in the book. I twist and pull the threads of this mystery over and over again to make them all fit. The tapestry is bigger than I ever could've imagined. I just have to figure out how to see the whole image at once.

I grab my pendant from the nightstand, but for once, squeezing it doesn't calm my thoughts. I look at my Nokware bracelet, studying the Adinkra carved into the beads. A particular one captures my eye. It looks like two hearts stacked one on top of the other. Asaase ye duru, *the earth is heavy*. The symbol of Asaase Yaa, the earth goddess.

The earth is heavy, and so are my problems. But at least I don't have to carry them alone.

And that's when an idea hits me.

Being a Slayer is about much more than weapons and cool battle spins. It's about our connection to the gods, the divine wisdom that sets us apart from regular mortals. Even if I had one hundred years to train the rest of the GCC, it would never be enough. I thought my magic was sufficient, but it's not. I need to get *them* magic, too.

If we want to take down this adze, we're going to have to get the gods involved.

17

How to Summon a Goddess

*"Feel the grass beneath your feet, the wind on your face,
the water flowing through your hands. That is the source
of divine wisdom. That is our power."*

—From the *Nwoma*

DURING LUNCH THE NEXT day at school, I don't
even give Gavin a chance to protest before I place my
tray at his table and sit across from him.

"I know you're mad at me, and you deserve to be, but
just hear me out, and I won't bother you again," I say.

I place my hands in my lap so he can't see how bad
they're shaking. I practiced this apology at least a dozen
times in the bathroom this morning, but I didn't factor
in how much harder it would be to get the words out
with Gavin staring at me. "I messed up real bad yesterday. You were right—I don't know any of you well
enough to act the way I did. I'm sorry. I can't promise I
won't mess up again, but I'll do whatever I can to make
it right every time."

I brace myself while Gavin appraises me, taking slow,
purposeful bites of his lasagna.

"Are you only doing this because you don't want to
lose another person for your little 'after-school project'?"

"That's definitely part of it," I admit. No reason to make this worse by lying. "But the biggest part is that I hurt you yesterday. And I don't want to be that kind of person."

I wait, feeling like a bug under a microscope while Gavin's eyes run over my face. I've never had to give an apology like this before, and it's much more nerve-racking than I expected. But nerves aren't as bad as knowing I crossed a line I might not be able to uncross.

"Thank you," he finally says, his face uncharacteristically soft. Then his normal smirk reappears. "And I guess I owe you an apology for dropping the whole tragic backstory on you out of nowhere."

"You don't have to talk about it," I say, but he shakes his head.

"Nah, I want to. Talking about it makes it feel less like something that was done to me and more like something I get to own. Besides, my therapist is always saying I should avoid using humor to hide how I'm really feeling." The hand that isn't full of lasagna drifts toward the bottom of his shirt in a motion so subtle I'm not sure he realizes he's doing it. "My birth parents weren't great. One day my kindergarten teacher noticed one of my wounds, called CPS, and I haven't seen or heard from my birth family since. I used to feel worse about it, but these days it's easier to laugh instead. No one ever gets weird around the kid who makes everyone laugh."

I think back over the last few days, taking note of every time Gavin cracked a joke when things got scary or tense. Even humor can be a form of defense if you know how to wield it. "That must've been hard for you."

"Oh, it was," he replies. "To this day I can't be around a kitchen knife without getting wigged out, which is why I'm glad we don't have Home Ec anymore. But if it hadn't happened, I never would've ended up with my foster dads. And they're the best. So I'm not glad about it, but I'm not sitting here broken up every day, either."

There's so many things I could say, but none of them feel big enough compared to what Gavin's shared. "So . . . we're cool?" I ask, my voice small.

He grins back, raising his fist for a bump. "Yeah. We're cool."

There are some people who, when they're mad at you, will say everything's all right when it's really not. But I can tell from his energy that Gavin isn't one of them. Mateo was right—Gavin won't hold back if you go too far, but it's not in his nature to stay angry for long. He reminds me of a river—fierce and forceful when it needs to be, like yesterday, but usually flowing and calm.

"Where ya headed?" he asks when I pick up my tray and angle for the doors.

"Upstairs. I usually eat in the art room with Mr. Riley." And today, Mateo. I don't see him at any of the long tables in the cafeteria, so he must already be up there. I pause for a moment, before adding, "You're welcome to join us. I highly doubt Mr. R would mind. And I understand if you don't want to come to the 'after-school project' anymore, but you're welcome there, too."

I don't mention my epiphany last night about trying to summon a god to help us. I don't want to pressure Gavin into doing anything he doesn't want to do, even though if he refuses to come I will have to mind wipe him. But . . . I hope he returns. It wouldn't feel the same without him.

"I'll think about it" is all he says, and with that I head back to the art room.

The rest of lunch goes by without incident. As classroom leader, one of Mateo's tasks is helping Mrs. Dean with her administrative work, so we spend most of the time stapling math packets together in comfortable silence while Mr. Riley grades a pile of eighth-grade sculpture projects.

I'm thinking about Mrs. Dean and how she must be the adze— why else would she torture us with these math worksheets?— when the art room door opens. Gavin walks in, drops into his usual stool, puts his headphones on, and starts rocking out to a song only he can hear. Mateo lifts an eyebrow at me, and I just shake my head, a grin as big as Gavin's spreading across my face.

"SO, CAN YOU PLEASE explain exactly how going to the grocery store is going to summon a god?" asks Eunju.

It's after school now, and all five of us in the GCC have just pulled our bikes into the parking lot of Walnut Tree Shopping Center. (If you ask me, Rocky Gorge leans a bit too hard into the whole plant aesthetic. Like, we get it, you're a town in the middle of a forest! Get some new material!)

"We're going to use the power of ice cream to bribe Asaase Yaa into visiting us, obviously," says Gavin, jumping into the shopping cart just as Mateo pulls it out of the row. Eunju rolls her eyes at his immaturity, while Roxy looks as if she wishes she'd gotten there first.

"Close, but not quite," I say. "Also, gods don't eat . . . I think? They take offerings, but it's not literal."

"Imagine being a god and you've still gotta deal with diarrhea!" Roxy says, her voice bright with excitement. She's been that way since I told her about my plan to summon Asaase Yaa.

I'm relieved that she and Eunju are still with me after yesterday. Gavin is the one I hurt the most, but I wouldn't have been surprised if the others had given up on training because of my outburst.

But during today's GCC meeting, when we started sketching out ideas for the mural, Gavin was all smiles and jokes like usual. Roxy was intent on the drawing, and Mateo had already started logging what equipment we'd need to get started. Even Eunju seemed into it, though she hid it behind her insults. (Speaking of the mural, I still have no idea what's going in my section, but anyway . . .) Maybe everyone just came back because they want to learn how to protect themselves and their families. Whatever the reason, I'm not going to squander this second chance.

"Summoning a god is a lot easier than you'd expect," I explain. "If you know the right words and have the right materials, you're good to go."

The real problem is location. Gods like Tano and Bia are strongest near their rivers, but flying all the way to Ghana isn't exactly an option for us right now. Plus, I personally am in no rush to see them again after our last meeting.

However, there are a few gods who have global jurisdiction, Nyame being the obvious one. But Nyame is . . . well, Nyame is Nyame. The OG. The Big Guy. I think I'd have better odds convincing Barack Obama to come teach lacrosse at our school than I would reaching Nyame. Which leaves Asaase Yaa, Mother Earth herself.

Asaase Yaa is not tied to any location on earth, because Asaase Yaa *is* the earth. Asaase Yaa exists in the first leaf that sprouts after winter, in the bend of every river, and the stone of every mountain. If any god is likely to respond to a plea from a few nobody kids who are in way over their heads, it's her.

"But I thought the whole reason you were training us is because you couldn't reach your secret society," says Eunju, lowering her voice as we cross the parking lot. "If you can just summon a god directly, why can't one of them handle the adze for us?"

Boulder's muffled voice rises from my backpack, "The gods see you humans the same way humans see ants—valuable to the overall functioning of the world but operating on a level so minuscule that there is little they can do to affect the day-to-day minutiae of your life."

"Besides, the Abomofuo were created so that we Slayers could handle all the things too small for the gods to bother with," I add. "Asaase Yaa can't defeat the adze for us, but that doesn't mean she won't help."

I can feel Boulder nodding along from beneath all my notebooks. "By the way, Serwa, I've been craving chocolate malt lately. Buy me some Milo when you get inside."

"What's the magic word?"

"Buy me some Milo or I will pee in your closet."

Mmoatia are jerks.

The first thing that hits me when we walk inside the Ghanaian grocery store is the smell—the thick scent of cocoa butter, plantains, dried spices, smoked fish, and something else I can't put into words but I know deep in my heart. The second thing is the cheerful highlife music blaring from the speakers. Then there's a cracked flat-screen TV at the front showing some Gollywood movie that was probably old even when my parents were born.

The store is barely bigger than Roxy's apartment, and I honestly couldn't tell you what the majority of the items on the shelves are actually for. But for the first time since I sighted the adze, I feel truly calm. For a few minutes, I just wander through the aisles, taking in the familiar bags of chicken feet and jars of shito from my childhood. I wonder if Ghanaian grocery stores, like diners, are liminal spaces, too, because they all feel the same no matter where you are in the world—a little too small, a little too crowded, a whole lot like home.

Mateo, Gavin, and Eunju make a beeline straight for the candy aisle. Not that I'm biased or anything, but Ghana has the best chocolate in the entire world, and the dozens of candy bars on display here are only a fraction of what we have to offer. While they begin stuffing the cart with as much chocolate as it can hold, Roxy and I look for the materials we're actually going to need for the summoning: a few boiled yams, some eggs, a mortar and pestle, palm oil, and a wooden figurine. The first three are easy, but the last two are nowhere to be found. As I'm pushing aside dusty cans of garden eggs, I notice Roxy is staring off at nothing.

"Everything okay?" I ask. She nods, though her expression doesn't match the gesture.

"I'm fine. It's just . . . I used to come here all the time with my dad."

Oh. *Oh.*

"How is he doing?" Gods help me, I know five different ways to break a man's arm. I know how to assemble a crossbow with my eyes closed. But I have no idea how to comfort someone who needs it.

"He's good. Got a job as a driver for a family in Cape Coast. We should be getting an update from his lawyer soon on what else we can do to appeal his deportation, but until then it's just wait and see."

I really want to know exactly what happened with Uncle Patrick, but this isn't the place for a conversation that heavy. And Roxy clearly doesn't want to talk about it, because she switches topics fast. "Did you know I was born on a Thursday?"

"I didn't. So your day name is Yaa?"

She shakes her head. "No, my dad's from the Fante tribe, so it's Aba. My parents made it one of my middle names. Roxanne

Aba Darlene James, that's me." She looks wistfully at the summoning materials in my arms. "Dad always told me Thursday was Asaase Yaa's day, and in ancient times it was so sacred people weren't even allowed to work the fields on it. I can't wait to meet her. I hope she likes me."

"I'm sure she will."

"But what if . . . What if she thinks I'm not Ghanaian enough? Because I can't speak Twi, and I've never actually been to Ghana?"

I stop in the aisle to look at Roxy, but she turns her head away. I shift my goods awkwardly so I can put a hand on her shoulder.

"Asaase Yaa is the kindest of all the gods," I tell her. "She's going to love you. I just know it."

Roxy smiles at me. We reconvene at the front of the shop, where the others have already bought their stuff. I lift an eyebrow at the five bags of chocolate between them. "How did y'all pay for all that?"

Mateo and Gavin both point at Eunju, who goes red. "Thank you," they both say in singsong unison, and she gets even redder.

"It's not a big deal! My parents are used to seeing junk food purchases on their bill. They don't care what I use the credit card for!" she snaps, which only makes the boys smile at her harder.

Aww, Eunju has a sweet tooth. Who knew?

I take my things to the counter, which is run by an elderly Black woman in a purple-and-gold-patterned caftan, thick square glasses, and large hoop earrings. "Good afternoon, Auntie," I say, because it doesn't matter if you've known a Ghanaian woman for ten seconds or ten years—if she's older than you, she's your auntie. "I'm looking for palm oil and a figure of Asaase Yaa."

"Unfortunately, we're all out of palm oil," she says.

If Dad were here, he'd pass out from shock. An African grocery store out of *palm oil*? That's like the Louvre running out of art!

"Someone has been coming in and buying out my palm oil stock every few weeks for the last year," she continues. "They were just in a few days ago. My next shipment won't be in for another week."

That catches my attention. Adze love palm oil—it's one of the only non-blood foods they consume, and legends say a single vampire can deplete a village's entire supply. It might be a coincidence that the only Ghanaian grocery store in town started running out of palm oil around the same time an adze was spotted here for the first time in decades, but my gut tells me otherwise. If my timeline is correct, the adze has been in Rocky Gorge for a year now.

I ask in my most nonchalant *I'm definitely not trying to interrogate you right now* voice, "Did you get a good look at the person who bought out your stock?" I ask, but my tone must be way too eager, because she gives me a suspicious glare.

"Why do you want to know?"

Roxy saves my butt by jumping in. "Hi, Auntie Francesca! Mom asked us to grab the palm oil so she could make okra stew tonight."

The suspicion melts from Auntie Francesca's face when she turns from me to Roxy. The pity in her eyes makes my cousin squirm. "Ah, Roxanne, me huu wo akyɛ." *Roxanne, I haven't seen you in so long.* "How is your father?"

Roxy lowers her head. "He's, um, good."

Auntie Francesca gives her a sad smile. "I'm truly sorry that I have no oil left to give you. You and your mother have suffered enough. And to answer your friend's question, the customer wore a low hood and gloves, so I didn't get a good look at them."

Ooh, the hood is one thing, but wearing gloves is extra smart, because skin color would narrow down the list of adze suspects. Whoever Bullseye's host is, they know to cover their tracks. We're going to have to be on our toes with this one.

Auntie Francesca shifts, and I can see the shelf behind her. It's full of figurines of all different shapes and sizes—some of them animals, some of them people doing various tasks in a village, like fetching water or weaving cloth. She picks up a shiny reddish-brown wooden figure that's about a foot tall. It's a naked woman standing with her arms upraised, holding a globe that's meant to be the earth, and it hums with an energy the others lack.

Auntie Francesca hands the Asaase Yaa figure to Roxy but refuses to take her money. "It's yours. A gift to your family after all you've been through."

Roxy looks equal parts touched and embarrassed. "Medaase paa, Auntie," she says, and though the American accent in her Twi is heavy, her gratitude comes through clearly.

After I buy my items—including Boulder's drink powder—we ride back to the school, where we stash our bikes before heading over to Sweetieville. There's no way we can ride through that treacherous terrain. In fact, I'm pretty sure Candy Cane Commons has grown more vines and gotten more raccoon residents since yesterday. Under Boulder's guidance, I grind the yam and boiled egg together with the mortar and pestle, then place it on the ground in front of the Asaase Yaa figure. The other four hang back as I work, recognizing that this is something only I can do. It's a shame we don't have the palm oil, but by the time I'm done, my makeshift shrine doesn't look half bad.

Still, even though this is something my people have done for centuries, I feel embarrassed as I begin pouring the libation— actually a pouch of Capri Sun I found in the back of Auntie Latricia's pantry—onto the dry earth. I can't stop recalling Ashley's comments about how weird everything about Ghana is, and I know some people look down on practices from so-called third-world countries as being primitive and backward. It makes me want to curl up into a ball and shove the shrine under a blanket, which then makes me want to shove myself under a blanket, because why do I even care what she thinks anyway?

I push away the embarrassment and draw into the soft dirt the most important part of the prayer: an Adinkra that looks like an upside-down heart on top of another heart, asaase ye duru. The symbol of the earth itself. As soon as it's drawn, I press my palms to the dry ground and begin the prayer.

"Asaase Yaa nsa ni, Asaase Yaa nsa ni." I sing out to let the goddess know I am offering food and drink in her honor. Divine wisdom flows up from deep inside me, through my arms, and into the Adinkra. It's warm and familiar, like a lullaby whose words I learned in the womb. For a single moment, everything in the forest, from the tallest trees to the absolute tiniest grass shoots, is connected, and I'm at the very center of it. Today is the best day to be doing this, too, as Thursday is Asaase Yaa's day.

"Tumi nyina ne asaase," I sing. *All power emanates from the earth.* At this point I'm so into the magic I no longer care if I look stupid. Even more than the weapons, even more than the cool battle armor and training, this is what I love most about being a Slayer—the feeling that I'm a part of something bigger than myself, and that just by being part of it, I become bigger, too.

I sing and sing until my throat dries up and my arms start to shake. When I finally look up, the other four are staring at me, but not in a mocking way, which I appreciate. Just like me they hold their breaths as we sit and wait for a goddess to appear.

A minute passes . . . and then another . . . and then ten more. I hope and hope and hope, but after thirty minutes of nothing, the truth becomes impossible to ignore.

Asaase Yaa isn't coming.

"Maybe you forgot a line?" Roxy asks.

Boulder shakes his head. His voice is kind, but full of disappointment. "Serwa said and did everything correctly. Unfortunately, just because you can call a god doesn't mean you're guaranteed a response."

I suddenly feel like a toddler again, and all I want to do is throw myself on the ground and scream and kick like I used to when things didn't work out. But I can't do that anymore. I'm the leader here. I've got to keep it together, for the others if not for myself.

I give myself five more seconds to feel awful, and then I put on my game face and say, "All right, enough standing around. We can always try again later. Right now, it's back to training. This adze isn't going to catch itself."

Since Eunju seemed to take to the sword pretty well yesterday, I give her one to use against the Barbies, while I teach Mateo and Roxy some general hand-to-hand practice drills that also double as strength training. I keep Gavin away from anything sharp and instead have him focus on wielding a staff. I don't know if everyone is just bummed because our plea to Asaase Yaa failed, but even though the energy is less tense than it was yesterday, everyone somehow performs worse today. Their moves are clumsier, their reflexes are slower, and more than once I have to jump in to save someone from losing an ear.

I do my best to keep up the cheerful *We got this!* attitude a leader should have, but honestly, at the rate they're going, it'll be a thousand years before any of them are ready to face an adze. That's a thousand years we very much do not have, but I have no other choice. The gods are silent, my parents are gone, and no one else can help.

Just like yesterday, today's practice ends with everyone grouchy and tired, and just like yesterday, we trudge our way through the forest and back into town in complete silence. However, unlike yesterday, when we reach the school parking lot, there's a teenage girl standing near our bikes who grins and waves when she sees us.

Mateo's eyes brighten in recognition. "Alicia! Why are you here?"

"Mom told me to come get you. Temi called in sick, so we need your help at the café. Where were you? I've been calling you for, like, twenty minutes."

Now that they're next to each other, the resemblance is impossible to miss. She has the same curly dark brown hair and light brown skin that he does, though there's a chipperness in her voice that I don't think Mateo would have even if he guzzled eight energy drinks. "Oh, are these your friends from that club your school forced you to join? They look hungry. Are you guys hungry? Come by the café and grab something to eat before you head home."

We all begin to protest that we're fine, really, but Alicia will not take no for an answer, which is how, not even five minutes later, we're all sitting at a table while Mateo's mom—who insists we call her Miss Gloria—hands out menus.

"Everything is on the house, you understand?" Miss Gloria says. "No friends of Mateo's pay a cent in my restaurant."

We all look at one another awkwardly. Are we . . . Are we friends? Everything I know about friendship I learned from Disney Channel Original Movies, where they mark camaraderie by singing and dancing. We hate each other slightly less than before, so that's something, right?

Once we've all ordered, Mateo runs off to help his sister wait tables, and suddenly it's just Gavin, Eunju, Roxy, and me cramped in a leather booth. The café itself is cozy, like a homey little diner my parents might stop at during a long drive to our next hunt. Cheerful Latin pop wafts through the air, and the smell coming from the kitchen is literally heavenly. But none of that changes the fact we are four near strangers being forced to make small talk with one another for at least the next twenty minutes, which is both a cruel and unusual punishment, if you ask me.

"Um, good job today?" I blurt awkwardly, because there isn't much else I can say. I'm way too pooped to draw the silence barrier, so we can't talk freely in here. And even if we could, I don't think any of us want to rehash today's failures.

Gavin shakes his head. "We stink."

Yeah, they do. "No, you don't!"

"Yes, we do. I know how it feels to be good at something. All this running around and physical training? I'm not good at it."

Roxy glumly nods along while Eunju icily picks at her manicure. I gotta change the subject before they talk themselves out of helping me. "So, the, uh, weather here. It's very . . . autumn," I say before mentally kicking myself. *Very autumn?* That's not even a thing.

"Yeah. Lots of trees," Eunju says, and the conversation dies again. I don't get why this is so hard. I've gone head-to-head with vampires and witches. I could break into the White House to save the president with one hand tied behind my back. But somehow, trying to hold a conversation about normal-people things with actual normal people is the hardest thing I've ever done. Whoever invented small talk probably hated me personally.

Miss Gloria finally returns with our food, saving me from continuing the world's most awkward dinner conversation. "Here you go, kids. I'm so sorry it's late. The woman at table eight has been making demands all evening. Just now she asked me to triple-check that all the lettuce we use is locally sourced and free of fifty-four different kinds of growth hormones. I didn't even know there *were* fifty-four different kinds of growth hormones."

Miss Gloria shakes her head and mutters something in Spanish while I take a peek over at the woman who has been causing her so much trouble. Her back is to us, so all I can make out is long locs piled on top of her head in one of those messy-on-purpose buns. She seems to be taking pictures of her food. But the most notable thing about her is the scent—lilacs.

Asaase Yaa's flower.

"Be right back. Bathroom," I lie to the others before sliding out of the booth and heading her way. As I pass her table, it's impossible to miss the symbol on the back of her rhinestone-studded phone case—mirrored hearts stacked one on top of the other in the same shape as asaase ye duru.

"Asaase Yaa?" I breathe out.

The woman lifts her head and gazes at me with eyes that hold the same too-bright, starlike quality I'd only ever seen in Tegare, Tano, and Bia.

"Ah, so you must be the one who summoned me. What can I help you with, my dear?"

18

How to Make a Goddess Cry

"Regard the gods with nothing but respect and humility and respect. It is thanks to their gifts that we do what we do."

—From the *Nwoma*

AT FIRST, ALL I can do is stare, because it WORKED. My summons worked and I am currently, right now at this moment talking to an actual live goddess.

Omg, omg, omg, omg, omg.

Asaase Yaa lifts a perfectly threaded eyebrow as I continue to stare openmouthed like a fish at her. "Am I wrong? Was it not you who called me here?"

The goddess's voice is smooth and rich, like the feeling of running fresh leaves between your fingers. Part of me wants to jog around the café whooping and cheering. But I am nothing if not a professional, so I slide into the booth across from her as if I talk to earth goddesses literally every day. Roxy lifts a *What the heck are you doing?* eyebrow at me, but I just mouth *Give me a minute.*

"You came. You . . . You really came," I say. "I don't mean to be rude, but I summoned you over in the woods hours ago. What are you doing in here?"

"Oh yes, that quaint little shrine in the forest. I heard

189

your call, and I was on my way there when— Oh, wait, look at this perfect lighting! One second, dear." She stops in mid-sentence to take several more pictures of her food, including a few selfies of her making a duck face over her salad. "Yes, thank you. What was I saying?"

"Um, the quaint little shrine?"

"Yes, the one with the Capri Sun! Right. I was on my way, but then I saw this adorable little hole-in-the-wall place, and I just knew I had to come in and snap a few pics for my followers."

I fight to hide my confusion. "The followers of your religion back in Ghana?"

"What? No, my followers online! You have to upload new content every day if you want to stay on top of these algorithms. I don't have anything scheduled for tomorrow, so the timing of this meeting could not be better."

The more Asaase Yaa speaks, the farther she gets from the image of the all-loving divine being I had in my head. At the very least, she must have used some magic to mask our conversation, because nobody in the cafe is even looking at us. "Are you a blogger?"

"I prefer the term *eco-influencer*."

"But your whole thing is nature! Leaves and flora and the connection between life and death. Shouldn't you be above all that fake social media stuff?"

Asaase Yaa laughs and shakes her head, flooding my nose with even more of her lilac scent. "Darling, you are about fifty years too late for my bra-burning hippie phase. If there is one thing to know about the earth, it's that it changes. I change along with it, even if people's expectations of me don't."

Okay, so maybe Asaase Yaa isn't what I expected, but a goddess is still a goddess. I don't care if she spends every waking minute live-streaming nonsense as long as she helps us.

"Well, anyway, thank you for coming all this way—"

"I truly didn't. I am literally everywhere."

Would it be rude to rub my temples in front of a deity? I breathe out slowly. "Fine. Thank you for manifesting here, because I do have a request for you. There is an adze in this town, and my classmates and I are trying to capture it before it can hurt any more people. But to do so, they need divine wisdom, which I have but they don't. I was hoping you might be able to bless them with it."

Asaase Yaa doesn't stop looking at herself in her selfie camera, but her hands tighten around her phone. "Then you should contact the Abomofuo. They exist to deal with situations just like this."

"I've tried, but they've cut off all communication with me. Who knows how much damage the adze could cause by the time they come around? Unless you want to send them a message for me?"

The goddess purses her lips. "Do I look like some common mmoatia messenger to you?"

"N-no, that's not what I meant!" Welp, guess I can add annoying a god to the list of ways I've screwed up this week. Way to go, Serwa. "Please, I know you're way too important to be dealing with stuff like this, which is why I'm not asking you to handle it for us. All we want are the tools to deal with it ourselves."

I can practically see the wheels turning in Asaase Yaa's head as she processes my request. Eunju, Gavin, and Roxy, no longer even pretending they aren't eavesdropping, are inching closer and closer to hear her verdict. Even Mateo has paused wiping down the counter to listen in.

The mother of gods opens her mouth, closes it, then shakes her head as she stuffs her phone into her all-organic hemp-woven purse. "I'm sorry, little one, but no. There was once a time when I might have honored such a request, but those days are long gone. If you want this adze dealt with, you must do so via the appropriate human channels."

Wait, what? Did she actually turn us down? "But the adze—" I begin, only for her to cut me off.

"I hate to eat and run, but there's a famous rock structure in your local park that would be perfect for my next Instagram carousel. Ta-ta, and don't forget to follow and subscribe!"

The others have been pretty good about letting me handle this up to now, but Eunju can't hold back any longer. "Hang on. You do realize that without this divine wisdom, the adze is literally going to eat us all? What kind of earth goddess doesn't even care about the people who live on her planet?"

The smile drops from Asaase Yaa's face. For the first time I truly understand how she is considered a goddess of both life *and* death, because it looks like all she'd have to do is blink to vaporize us into flower petals.

"How *dare* you accuse me of not caring!" she growls. Now her voice is all dark rumbles, the warning tremors that come before an earthquake. "*Me.* Nyame might have created the world, but it was *I* who nurtured it into the beautiful realm you see now. It was *I* who gave humans chance after chance to live and thrive among the bounty I gifted you. And how has your kind repaid me? With greenhouse gasses and oil spills. With thousands of species extinct and thousands more on their way out. No more. You mortals had your chance, and you squandered it. Your problems are yours to deal with now, not mine."

Grief laces Asaase Yaa's every word, like she's felt each attack against the earth as a wound to her own body. The goddess picks up her purse and turns away.

That's it. If Asaase Yaa, the kindest and most generous of the gods, won't help us, no one will. I know I should say something to the others, because I'm the leader and leaders are supposed fix everything, but I don't know how to fix this.

But before I speak, Roxy does. "You know, my dad told me all about you," she says to Asaase Yaa's back.

When the goddess doesn't respond, my cousin continues. "Because I was born on a Thursday, he made sure I knew everything about you, even more than the more famous gods like Nyame and Anansi. He taught me that every good thing that exists on earth is because of you, and the best way to honor you is to care for the gift you gave us."

This seems like the most I've heard Roxy talk about her dad . . . ever. It's also the most determined I've seen her, with hands in fists at her sides.

"I know to you gods humans are just a bunch of ants," Roxy says, "but even ants care about their anthills. I'm sorry we have betrayed your trust over the centuries. I'd be bitter and angry, too. But just because some people hurt you doesn't mean you get to ignore everyone who needs you."

Asaase Yaa still has her back turned to us, so there's no way to tell how mad she is. I run over to Roxy and throw my arm over her shoulder.

"Okay, Roxy, that's quite enough yelling at the divine being who could kill us all," I whisper out of the corner of my mouth. I try to pull her back, but she yanks herself out of my grip.

"Walk away if you want!" Roxy shouts. "Pretend this isn't your problem! But just remember that there are people who love you who are going to be hurt by this. People who never did anything wrong. If you're okay with that, then leave!"

Asaase Yaa is silent for a long, long time, and now I'm trying to calculate how fast we'd have to run to make it out of here before she smites us. My estimating stops when she turns around. Are those . . . tears running down her face?

Holy poop, we made a goddess cry.

"We're so sorry. She didn't mean it, she's just upset—" I begin, but Asaase Yaa ignores me and faces Roxy. In her human form, she's the size of an adult woman, not even as tall as my mom, but it feels like she's towering over us all when she locks eyes with my cousin.

"Meba wo atwɛn me akyɛ?" she says softly, and Roxy hangs her head.

"I don't know what that means. My Twi isn't that good."

Asaase Yaa gently lifts Roxy's chin with her finger. "I said, you've been waiting for me for a long time, haven't you, my child?"

Roxy nods. "I have."

Asaase Yaa pulls away from my cousin. "I— It's been so long since I've interacted with humans face-to-face that I forgot that the wisest words often tumble from the mouths of babes." She dabs the corners of her eyes with her handkerchief. "I'm— Fine. I cannot give you children divine wisdom, but I can give you the chance to earn it. I take it you know the story of my sword?"

"You used to have a magic sword that could cut down any enemy, but after a mishap with Anansi, you lost control of it," Roxy says. "No one has been able to use it since."

"Exactly. I loved that sword and have always wanted it back. So here is a task for you, little ones: If you can fetch my sword for me, I'll bless you with the divine wisdom you need to defeat your enemy."

She waves her hand. Two seeds and a shiny green badie leaf appear in her palm.

"The green seed will take you down to Asamando, which is the last place where my sword was seen. The yellow seed will bring you back." She hands the first one to Roxy, the second one to me. "Now, who among you is the least likely to do something rash?"

We all look at Mateo, who sheepishly raises his hand. Asaase Yaa hands him the leaf, which twitches like a compass before pointing downward in his palm. "This will guide you in the direction of my sword."

She makes a point to look each one of us in the eyes. "I have not offered any human a chance like this in hundreds of years. Do not squander it."

With that, the goddess vanishes, leaving nothing but a few flower petals and the scent of lilacs behind her. As soon as she's gone, a wave of exhaustion washes over me.

"New team rule," I say, staring down at the innocent-looking seed in my hand. "No more insulting goddesses who could grind our bones into dust without consulting the group first."

19

How to Line Up in a Safe and Orderly Manner

"The mere presence of black magic puts everyone in the vicinity in danger. Any area where an adze has been encountered should be treated as an active war zone."

—From the *Nwoma*

OKAY, SO QUICK RUNDOWN on Asaase Yaa's magic sword.

A long, long, couple-dozen-more long times ago, Asaase Yaa had this magic sword that was strong enough to defeat anyone. It was so powerful it didn't even need a wielder—when Asaase Yaa told the sword to fight, it fought, and when she told it to stop, it stopped. One day Anansi stole the sword, because that's what Anansi does, and used it to show off for Nyame in battle. But after the fighting was done, Anansi forgot the command to make it stop, and so it turned around and whooped his butt, too, before sticking itself in the ground all sword-in-the-stone style. Legend has it that, to this day, because no one ever commanded the sword to stop, anyone who tries to get near it will be immediately cut to ribbons.

All this to say I have no idea why Asaase Yaa thinks a bunch of middle schoolers can capture a weapon no one else has been able to for hundreds of years, but, hey, a quest is a quest.

Luckily, fighting a flying magic sword is way easier than fighting an adze, and by the next day, I have a plan.

It's sixth period on Friday, and today we're outside priming the wall where we're going to paint the mural. I still haven't finalized my section of the design, but Mr. Riley doesn't seem bothered by how behind I am.

When the time comes, you'll know your answer, he assured me when he checked my blank list of things that mark where I'm from. I seriously doubt that, because all the important facts that make me who I am are things I can't draw on the side of a public school building. If you take away the Abomofuo, take away my magic and my training, what am I?

Who am I?

Well, my existential crisis aside, we're outside priming the wall. Mr. Riley is helping us, but he has his earbuds in as he mixes paint, so we have a slim window to talk freely in.

Standing here covered in flecks of paint reminds me of all the DIY projects I used to do with my dad back at the lake house. If I close my eyes, I can see him standing next to me with a paint roller in his hands, his floppy hat falling over his ears as he explains how the new fertilizer he switched to has done wonders for his rutabagas.

My chest squeezes tight at the memory, but then I look up to find Gavin and Roxy racing each other to finish their sections of the wall, Mateo wrestling with a particularly stubborn paint can lid, and Eunju rolling her section literally inch by inch so she doesn't get any drops on her nice blouse. Seeing them reminds me I'm not alone, and that makes thinking about Mom and Dad easier.

Not easy, not yet, but . . . easier.

"We'll go for the sword this weekend," I declare when Mr. Riley turns away from us.

Roxy's eyes go wide at my declaration. "We're going to Ghana?"

Gavin leans back on his heels with a groan, having lost the contest. "My dads banned me from traveling on school nights after I snuck out to a debate competition in DC last year."

Eunju coughs *Nerd* into her arm, earning a glob of paint flicked her way. She ducks and it hits Mateo instead, knocking off his glasses. Gavin is very lucky it didn't hit me because he wouldn't have a hand left if it had.

After he gets his glasses back on (and makes a covert rude gesture at Gavin behind Mr. Riley's back), Mateo says, "Same. Training is one th-thing, b-b-but if I leave, who's going to help my mom at the c-c-café?"

"No one is breaking any travel rules, because Asaase Yaa's sword isn't in another country." I point at the ground beneath our feet. "It's down in Asamando."

I pause for dramatic effect and get nothing but blank stares in response. Ugh, sometimes it is very annoying being the only person who actually knows your language.

"'Asaman'" is Twi for *ghost*. "'Do'" is a suffix for *places*. So literally it's *the ghost place*, aka the afterlife. Home of the Nsamanfo, the ancestors. A few decades ago, a bunch of Abomofuo got together to send the sword there, because it was causing too much trouble back in Ghana. That's where we have to go to get it back. And we have to do it soon, because the adze—"

"Wait, so if this afterlife is underground, does that mean it's, like"—Roxy looks over both shoulders before whispering—"the bad place?"

I shake my head. "Asamando isn't a place of judgment—everyone ends up there, good or bad. The only reason it's underground is because Asaase Yaa is the goddess of death as well as the earth, so the realm of ghosts is part of her body, too."

The others nod slowly, though Mateo looks troubled. "What's wrong?" I ask him. After everything we've seen the last few days, the fact that ghosts are real shouldn't be all that surprising.

"It's just that . . ." Mateo pauses before speaking again, like he's weighing every word very carefully. "You've b-b-been telling us about your g-gods from the start. But it d-d-didn't feel real until we met Asaase Yaa yesterday. Now we're g-g-going to the underworld." He turns his trowel over in his hands. "I've g-g-gone to Sunday school all my life, and they taught us all these things about how the world works. B-b-but everything you've showed us recently g-g-goes against that. D-d-does this mean everything I was taught to believe is wrong?"

This is a lot for Mateo to say at once, which is how I can tell this is really bothering him. I open my mouth only to close it, with no clue about how to respond. The word *god* means so many different things to so many different people. Because I always knew what it meant for me and my family, I never stopped to think what it might mean for the other members of the GCC. I should have, though. A good leader would have.

The silence is getting awkward now, so I say, "That's fair. Here's how it was explained to me: The earth exists. The sky exists. These are undeniable facts, and this is why you see different variations of earth and sky gods cropping up in so many places around the world. Each culture is different, with its own history and stories and all that, but the basic core is the same. Asaase Yaa is just like that. Her existence doesn't take anything away from all the other beliefs about the earth that are out there, it just adds to them. Does that help?"

I have no idea if what I said made any sense, but when Mateo looks up he seems calmer. "Yeah. Th-thanks."

I'm hoping that might be the end of any doubts, but Gavin jumps in, "Okay, so the seed Asaase Yaa gave us will get us into Asamando. But how do we know we won't, like, immediately die the moment we step foot there? Because I for one am very much in the business of not dying."

All of Mateo's calm vanishes. He lets out a distressed moan while Gavin and Roxy pat him on the back. Eunju narrows her eyes at me. "Why are you so chill about this? Have you been there before?"

"No, but I know just being in Asamando won't kill us because of the story of Kwasi Benefo," I reply. "It's an old folktale about a man who went to Asamando, made it past Amokye, the old woman who guards the border between life and death, and returned to the human world unharmed. If he could do it, so can we. Besides, Asaase Yaa gave us a way to return." I take the Ziploc bag holding the yellow seed out of my hoodie pocket and hold it up. "If we're ever in mortal danger, we'll just use this to get home."

Of course, failing her task will also mean I lose my only chance of getting divine wisdom for the others. No pressure.

"Tell us more about this Amokye," Gavin demands. "What's she like? Does she have any deadly superpowers or claws we need to worry about?"

"Not that I know of . . ." I admit. Boulder would be way more useful on this front, but as usual, he is in backpack purgatory during school hours. "Honestly, I don't really know much about her. For most humans, a visit to Asamando is a one-way trip. Those who've seen Amokye for themselves don't usually come back to talk about it. But the legend of Kwasi Benefo proves she isn't invincible. We can get past her."

I quickly glance over at Mr. Riley, to make sure he's still deep in his music. "Use tonight to make any preparations you need to. We'll leave tomorrow morning, which will give us all of Saturday and Sunday to get the sword. If we do this right, we should be back before school on Monday."

"Well, you have fun with your little trip to ghost city," says Eunju.

"What do you mean?" I ask.

"There's no reason we all need to go," she says. "Mother Earth didn't give me a magic plant. In fact, I think it should just be you, Serwa, since you have the divine *whatever* and we don't. And anyway, I have plans with Ashley this weekend."

"Divine *wisdom,* and cancel them!" I say. "We're in this together, no backing out now."

"Yeah," says Gavin. "Where's your sense of camaraderie? Swashbuckling adventure?"

"Yeah Eunju, come swash your buckles with us!" Roxy adds, causing Eunju to pull a face.

"You're our b-b-best fighter," says Mateo. "After Serwa, I mean." He shoots me an apologetic look, which I appreciate. Finally, someone around here recognizes my expertise.

Eunju groans, but I can see that she's giving in to peer pressure. "Ashley's going to be so mad. We've been planning this sleepover for weeks."

"She won't die just because she misses one sleepover," says Roxy, her voice tight.

"Lay off her," Eunju says with a frown. "You know she's been having a hard time with her brother and everything—"

A loud trilling noise from the school cuts her off. My muscles

201

immediately tense with battle-ready hardness. I scan the area for any sign of threat, but the others only startle, then relax.

"Fire d-d-drill," explains Mateo.

Wow, those alarms are way louder in person than on TV.

But Mr. Riley frowns, pulling out his earbuds. "There's no drill scheduled for today. . . ."

Almost in unison, our heads turn toward the south part of the school, where thick plumes of black smoke are pouring out of several windows. Now I'm the one shaking.

This is no drill.

Mr. Riley immediately springs to action, hustling us into a single-file line and to our assigned emergency meet-up location on the blacktop as students, faculty, and staff start pouring out of every available exit. The Home Ec room isn't far from where we were painting, so Mr. Johnson and the rest of our former sixth-period classmates line up near us. We all watch in awe as several fire trucks screech into the parking lot and orange-suited firefighters race into the school. The teachers try to keep us all quiet, but they can't stop the whispers that are going around.

"I was in that part of the building. There was this large *boom*, and then suddenly fire everywhere!"

"It got so big so fast!"

"How did it just explode out of nowhere like that?"

The question wasn't directed at me, but still a shiver runs down my spine.

Black magic is how.

AN HOUR LATER, THE smoke has dwindled, but we're still standing there. Now that the teachers have confirmed who is accounted for and who needs medical attention, our fear is giving way to restless boredom. The hair on the back of my neck rises, and I look up to see Ashley and some of her goons from Home Ec staring at me and the rest of the GCC. They make a big show of gawking at us, then pretending they weren't, then whispering and laughing.

"I think I'd die if I was forced to do manual labor at my own school," says Ashley in a voice that is too loud for a whisper. "I don't know how Eunju puts up with it. Or *them* "

Eunju blushes. Though she's not allowed to leave our assigned spot until we get the all-clear, she takes several big steps away from us, clearly trying to make it look like we're not a group. Roxy's and Mateo's faces fall, while Gavin rolls his eyes. I'm just angry. I swear, it's one step forward, ten steps back with this girl.

I'm about to let Eunju know that the constant hot-and-cold act is getting real old when Ashley continues, "Then again, she probably just feels bad for them. That's why I hung out with Roxy as long as I did. But I never would've started if I'd known her dad was, you know, a criminal and all."

The words are barely out of Ashley's mouth when my cousin lunges for her. Roxy's expression is full of pure rage, and it's only Gavin and Mateo grabbing her that keeps her from clawing the smirk off the other girl's face.

"Easy, Rox, easy! She's not worth it." Gavin levels another one of those ice glares Ashley's way. "She's never been worth it."

He doesn't elaborate, and he doesn't have to, because we all know what *it* means. It doesn't matter we all witnessed Ashley provoke her—the second my cousin lays a finger on the other girl, Roxy is the one who's going to be in trouble. I'm getting used to some things about this school, but the unfair double standard will never feel right.

I turn to Eunju, my voice steely with anger. "You're just going to let her talk to us like that?" I demand. Eunju has the decency to look ashamed, but she doesn't say anything in defense of either her current best friend or her former one. I'm about to snap at her when Principal Hashimoto approaches the assembly with several of the firefighters in tow. She looks frazzled.

"Good news, everyone! The fire marshal has given us the all-clear to go back inside. It seems one of our generators over-heated and caught fire, but the few injuries were minor, and there should be no structural damage to the building. Since we're less than thirty minutes from the end of the school day, you'll all be led inside to retrieve your belongings and start heading home."

A chorus of cheers rises up from the blacktop, because the only thing better than a weekend is a weekend that starts slightly earlier than expected.

Mr. Riley frowns, rubbing his chin as we begin heading back toward the art room. "I'm glad there weren't any injuries, but it's odd . . ." he says, mostly to himself. "All the generators were replaced just last year."

The four kids and I exchange glances, and I can tell we're all thinking the same thing: A new generator doesn't overheat by itself. This was the adze's doing. It might not have bitten anyone since Mr. Riley (that we know of, anyway . . .), but just by being on the school grounds, its black magic is making the whole place more dangerous for everyone. Today it's a generator—next week it might be a crumbling foundation, or a falling stage light, or even a mysterious illness that wipes us all out.

And, interestingly enough, Mrs. Dean was nowhere to be seen during the evacuation. I know because I looked for her and saw a substitute teacher standing with her sixth-grade class. She's absent during a freak accident? That's mighty suspicious if you ask me.

The adze is her—I just know it. And as soon as we get the divine wisdom from Asaase Yaa, we'll have everything we need to take her down once and for all.

20

How to Survive Your First Human Sleepover

"Whenever you find yourself in the company of regular mortals, try to blend in. Learn their customs and rituals, always understanding that we stand apart from them for their own protection."

—From the *Nwoma*

THE COVER STORY FOR our quest to Asamando is that we're finalizing the mural design this weekend. Thanks to some well-timed magicked phone calls, Auntie Latricia thinks Roxy and I are spending the weekend at Eunju's place, Eunju's parents think she's spending the weekend at ours, and Gavin's and Mateo's families think they're at each other's houses. It's a huge headache trying to trick four different families, but at least we now have forty-eight hours to complete Asaase Yaa's task before anyone notices we're gone.

Eunju offered her house as our base of operations for this mission since her parents are going to be away at a tech conference this weekend. When I arrive at her place, at first all I do is stare. Just like every other house in Ivy Ridge Estates, Eunju's is a literal mansion. Four stories of white wood and sandy stone rise in front of me, and there's a guest house just at the edge of the lawn. It looks like something from a movie about rich people having rich people problems, and you'd never guess that Sunny Oak Towers is less than five minutes away.

"It's huge," I say aloud. Boulder pops his head out of the backpack, takes one glance at the mansion, then scoffs.

"You only think this is big because you never saw the Library of Alexandria in all its—OW, OW!" he yells as I shove him back into my bag.

"Get back in there before someone sees you," I hiss as I ring the doorbell. He hisses back a swear in Twi before he ducks to the bottom of the backpack.

"Oh hey, you're early. Where's Roxy?" Eunju asks as she lets me in and shows me where to put my shoes. The inside of her house is even nicer than the outside—there's an honest-to-Nyame chandelier hanging above the foyer, and it's making the hardwood floors and long bay windows sparkle.

But as pretty as Eunju's house is, there's a cold feeling to it. Everything here looks good but not lived-in, like a photoshoot from a magazine.

"She's at her math tutor. She should be here in thirty." I considered waiting for Roxy to finish her lesson before coming over, but being alone in the apartment makes me nervous. So far, we've only seen the adze at school, but there's nothing stopping it from following any of us home.

I can tell Eunju realizes the same moment I do that this is the first time the two of us have been alone together. Awkward silence fills the air. Roxy, Mateo, Gavin—I have a pretty good handle on what makes each of them tick. But Eunju is still a mystery to me. And honestly, if it weren't for the adze, I don't think we'd even have a reason to talk to each other. Especially after the way she threw us under the bus when Ashley showed up yesterday.

I'm about to ask if she has an ETA on Gavin or Mateo, when a fluffy white meteor crashes into me. I fall on my back as a dog nearly as big as I am starts slobbering all over my face.

"Down, Dubu, down! No, bad!" Eunju cries, and it takes her almost a full minute of wrestling to pull the thing off me. "Sorry. He really likes meeting new people. I must have forgotten to close the gate upstairs." She quirks an eyebrow at the shocked look on my face. "Serwa, don't tell me you can fight a vampire but you're scared of Samoyeds?"

"Regular dogs are fine. That *thing* is practically a bear!" I yell, and for the first time since we met, Eunju lets out a not-mean laugh. It must be a rare occurrence because she herself looks surprised it happened.

"Eunju, have your friends arrived to pick you up?" calls a voice, and her smile immediately vanishes. Two people I assume to be Eunju's parents come into the foyer, and now I get why the house is so nice. They look exactly how I expected rich app developers to look. Her mom has on a crisp three-piece gray suit with her black hair pulled back in a bun, while her dad is wearing a sweater over a button-down shirt and has a tablet tucked under his arm. Each of them carries a matching designer weekend suitcase. Honestly, the whole family looks like they belong out in Beverly Hills, not the suburbs of Maryland.

"Appa, Eomma, this is Serwa, one of the people I'm working on the mural with," says Eunju. "Serwa, these are my parents."

"It's so nice to meet you, Mr. and Mrs. Kim," I say. "You have a lovely home."

Mrs. Kim smiles, but it doesn't reach her eyes. "That's so sweet of you to say. Of course, it would be lovelier if there wasn't that crack in the driveway I keep asking Mr. Kim to fix."

Mr. Kim lets out a laugh with no joy. "And as I keep

reminding Mrs. Kim, I would have had time to fix it already if I wasn't doing all her extra reports on top of my own."

Eunju's face has gone tomato red, but she doesn't say anything. I shift awkwardly from foot to foot. Vampires are one thing, but nobody ever prepared me for what you're supposed to do when someone's parents argue in front of you.

"Eunju, what are you and your friends doing for dinner tonight?" Mrs. Kim asks. She pulls a fifty-dollar bill out of her purse and hands it to her daughter "Order some pizza for all of you—I know it's your favorite."

"Nonsense. Thai food is your favorite. Isn't that right?" asks her dad.

Something about the panicked way Eunju looks between her parents makes me step forward and say, "Actually, my aunt is making us dinner tonight. Thank you so much, though!"

That seems to please them, and after a couple reminders to Eunju about staying safe this weekend, they head off to whatever function they're going to.

As soon as her parents are gone, Eunju drops her head in her hands and screams. "They always do that! Why do they always do that?" she yells as Dubu nudges her leg sadly.

All parents argue, but at least mine have never forced me to choose between them, and they certainly wouldn't do it when someone else was watching. Suddenly the house seems way less beautiful than before—not even the prettiest paint job can turn a cold home into a warm one.

I have no idea what to say right now, but I can't leave her like this. "On the bright side, think of all the training Barbies we can buy with fifty bucks!" I cringe at my bad attempt at comfort, but Eunju laughs before wiping her eyes with the back of her hand.

"Thanks," she says softly. "For not being weird about what just happened."

I lift a shoulder in a half shrug. "Parents make mistakes. We shouldn't have to pay for them."

Eunju nods, and then, like a light switch has been flipped, she's back to her normal self. "Okay, so what do you want to do until everyone else gets here?"

I'm honestly not sure. Usually, when I'm in someone else's house, I'm rifling through their belongings for reconnaissance or we're fighting an adze. This is my first time just "chilling" with someone. Everything I know about hanging out I learned from TV shows, but I'm 99 percent sure no one actually has pillow fights or makes prank calls anymore.

"Roxy mentioned you're into Battlestar Dimensions?" I say, because it's the only thing I can think of.

Eunju's eyes light up, and she quickly drags me to her basement, which has a full movie theater setup going on, complete with reclining chairs and a wheeled popcorn maker. There I get the complete rundown on all things Battlestar Dimensions, which, from what I can gather, is less a sci-fi movie franchise and more a way of life for its fans. Now that Eunju's parents are gone, Boulder is free to shuffle through Eunju's extensive Blu-ray collection, visibly disappointed by the lack of reality TV options available.

". . . and a lot of people think you need to watch the movies in order of release, but if you do that, you completely miss the full impact of Lothrax's redemption arc. The best way to watch them is actually the way me, Roxy, and Ashley did it back in fifth grade—"

"Ashley is into Battlestar Dimensions?" I ask, because a retro space opera series from the 1980s really doesn't fit her whole Suburban Princess vibe.

"Ashley was the one who got me and Roxy into it." Eunju frowns, turning her TV remote awkwardly in her hands. "She was the biggest fan I knew, and she always said that as soon as one of us could drive, we would all go to DimensionCon together."

"Why aren't you two friends with Roxy anymore?" It's none of my business, but I have to know how the trio went from best friends to almost trading blows on the blacktop.

For a second it looks like she might not answer, but then she says, "Me, Ashley, and Roxy were best friends since kindergarten and did everything together. You know the gym teacher, Mrs. Lucas, is her stepmother? I'm pretty sure she still has pictures of the three of us in cosplay hanging up in the gym office. But about a year ago, Ashley's stepbrother got really sick. Leukemia. For a long time things were looking really bad, and her family was preparing for what would happen if he didn't make it. Ashley was always a bit oblivious, but she was never mean before his diagnosis.

"Suddenly, everything and everyone annoyed her. All she wanted to do was talk about how stupid so-and-so's new outfit looked or how annoying that kid was. And for a while, neither me or Roxy said anything, because Ashley was going through so much. But one day Roxy put her foot down and she told Ashley it wasn't cool to be mean to everyone else just because she was having a hard time. Ashley accused her of being a bad friend and not supporting her, and then she deleted her from all our group chats and everything. They've barely talked since."

Wow, I can barely imagine Roxy standing up to Ashley . . . but then again, she did dress down Asaase Yaa the other day. Maybe I've been underestimating my cousin.

Eunju continues, "I tried to talk to Ashley about it a couple of times, but she made it clear that I was either on her side or on Roxy's. And I guess . . . I was scared. I didn't want to lose both of my best friends. But her brother has been doing a lot better these past few months and she's still not her old self yet. I have no idea what happens now."

I try to imagine the sweet version of Ashley that Eunju hopes will come back, but it's impossible. If this is what all friend groups are like, maybe it's for the best I've never had one.

"It sounds to me like you're a better friend to her than she is to you," I say.

"She's going through a rough time."

"Everyone goes through rough times. That doesn't mean we get to treat everyone around us like garbage because of it."

There's one more question I want to ask—about what Ashley meant by Roxy's father being a criminal—but I don't say it. I think that story should come from my cousin directly. Eunju's mouth goes tight, like she wants to say something else, but the doorbell rings before she can. We were almost friendly for a second there, but now that the others are here, her usual *I'm better than all this and all of you* mask slips back into place. We go get the door, where Gavin and Mateo both stand carrying literal piles of supplies. I scoot backward so the boys can drag their stuff in, Roxy close behind them now that her tutoring session is over.

"What is all this?" I ask.

"*Someone* got a little overzealous with the packing," gasps Gavin.

"Excuse me for wanting to be p-p-prepared for a literal trip to the underworld!" replies Mateo.

Five minutes later, Gavin is dramatically folded on the couch to "catch his delicate breath" while the rest of us sort through the supplies in the living room. There are several first aid kits, some rope, flashlights, and a couple gallon jugs of water, and that's all just in bag one.

Roxy picks up a giant bone like you'd buy for a Great Dane or some other dog that's far bigger than it needs to be. "And how is this going to help us in Asamando?"

"To d-d-distract any three-headed d-d-dogs."

"Wrong underworld, but your head's in the right place," I say as Roxy tosses the bone aside. From his exile beyond the doggy gate, Dubu stares at it with drool coming out of his mouth. "Amokye is the only threshold guardian in Asamando, and I don't think she'll take a bone bribe."

"Ooooh, 'threshold guardian.' Sounds like something out of a video game," remarks Gavin. He reaches for one of the glasses of tea Eunju poured for everyone, but she yanks it out of his reach.

"Oh no, you're not getting any stains on my mom's good couch."

"Oh, come on, Eunju, didn't you see how much I carried?" he whines. "I'm going to keel over from dehydration if I don't get something to drink soon!"

She pushes the glass farther away from his hand. "Then get off the couch or die."

"We're all going to d-d-die if this d-d-doesn't go well," Mateo mutters darkly.

I throw my hands in the air. "Nobody is going to die! It's just the underworld, not Mordor! Roxy, stop petting the dog and get over here so I can explain the plan before Mateo has a panic attack."

"I'm not having a p-p-p-p—I'm fine!"

"You do look kind of green," says Gavin, finally getting off the couch. Eunju nods in agreement.

My cousin reluctantly stops scratching Dubu to join the rest of us in the circle. "What's your plan to get past Amokye?" she asks me.

"We'll sneak in. Around one hundred and fifty thousand people die a day, so there is no way she'll notice five extra people slipping through. Then, once we're inside, we follow the leaf until we find the Sword of Asaase Yaa."

"Can we give it a nickname?" asks Gavin. "'The Sword of Asaase Yaa' is such a mouthful. . . . How about Pointy? All in favor of Pointy, raise your hand."

Nobody but Gavin raises their hand. He lets out a scoff. "None of you have any joy in your hearts."

I grab my backpack and pull out the things I prepared for the journey: an old net, a faded Tupperware container, and five scarves.

From his perch on my shoulder, Boulder scoffs. "This is a foolhardy mission. Few have entered Asamando and returned to tell the tale."

"Heard you the first hundred times," I mutter.

Dubu notices Boulder sitting on my shoulder and begins to bark until Eunju shushes him. The mmoatia curls up against me with a shiver.

"A pox on you, canine! May your fields always be ugly and barren!" Boulder yells, and I pat the mmoatia's head mockingly.

"Asaase Yaa never told us to stop the sw—Okay, fine, she never told us to stop *Pointy*," I add at Gavin's glare. "She just told us to capture it. I've enchanted the net so that it shrinks anything caught inside it and the Tupperware to be extra durable. Once we cover Pointy with the net, we'll put it inside the container and—*boom!*—one magic sword ready to transport. The scarves have spells on them to cover our energy when we're down there so we don't attract any unwanted attention." I nod at Mateo, who is visibly shaking now. "I'm not going to let anything happen to any of you. I promise."

He gives me a small smile before nodding back.

"I've got the green seed," says Roxy, holding up her Ziploc bag. "What do we do with it?"

I'm stumped for a second, but then Boulder says, "Plant it, of course. Is there a container and some dirt we could borrow?"

Eunju fetches a ceramic flowerpot full of topsoil from her family's garden shed. Roxy buries the green seed, and we all sit in a circle watching the pot with bated breath.

"Is now a bad time to mention every plant I've ever taken care of has died?" asks Gavin after minutes of nothing.

"D-d-do we need to water it?" asks Mateo.

But before he even finishes the question, thin shafts of emerald light start poking up through the dirt. They're followed by vines about as thick as my pinky. As we watch, amazed, the vines continue to grow and grow, curling and twisting into each other until they form a rectangular shape. . . .

It's an elevator! Two doors slide open to welcome us, and I step inside to find a button with a downward-pointing arrow. The others' eyes fill with equal parts disbelief and awe at the magic before us.

"Oh, there is no way this thing is up to safety code!" Gavin says excitedly as he runs his hands over the thick vines.

"Is th-there a phone, or someone we can c-c-call if it gets stuck halfway down?" asks Mateo.

"Pretty sure the fire department doesn't do rescues from magic elevators," Roxy points out.

Eunju lets out a groan. "My parents are going to kill me when they see this!"

"I'll make sure it's gone before they come back!" I promise.

Boulder yanks one of my braids to snap me back to attention. "Get in before our transport disappears."

Magic buzzes in my ears as everyone else crowds into the elevator, and it truly hits me that we're about to see something most living humans never will. Just as I'm about to press the Close button, an object falls from Mateo's overstuffed pack with a clatter—the ridiculous bone he insisted on bringing.

He bends to pick it up, and in that same moment a certain fluffy white monstrosity leaps over the gate. Dubu runs straight for the bone, slipping through the doors just a second before they close and the elevator plunges us into the underworld.

21

How to Enter the Underworld

"Death comes for all. Make it your ally, not your enemy."

—From the *Nwoma*

AS SOON AS WE step through the doors, the scent of roasting onions, fresh grass, and the musky cologne Dad always buys hits my nose. I freeze, my nerves all melting away in the presence of the familiar scent.

Home. Asamando smells like home.

The others must be feeling it, too, because their eyes have glazed over, like they're remembering something they hadn't realized they'd forgotten. "Do you all smell baby powder, coffee, and fresh laundry, too?" asks Gavin.

Mateo shakes his head. "S-salt water, cinnamon, and incense."

"Fresh ink, powdered sugar, and honeysuckle for me," adds Roxy.

Eunju doesn't share what she's smelling, but from the dreamy look on her face, it's clear she finds this place just as comforting as the rest of us do.

"What you're smelling is the magic of Asamando,"

explains Boulder from his perch on my shoulder. "Souls are more likely to pass on to the next stage of their journey if they're calm, and nothing calms people more than home."

Calm is one way to put it. I sway a little from side to side, completely enveloped by the warm memories of days in the garden with Dad and nights cooking jollof rice with Mom. This is so nice. . . . Why would anyone . . . ever want . . . to leave . . . this place . . . ?

Something hits the side of my face. "Snap out of it!" Boulder yells at us, slapping me once more for good measure. The others start blinking out of their stupors. "I will tell you the same thing I told George Washington when he was crossing the Delaware—keep moving. It won't get any easier if you stay in the same place."

"J-j-just how old *are* you?" asks Mateo.

"Old. Now march, all of you."

I rub my cheek—mmoatia are stronger than they look!—and turn my attention to the furry problem lying at our feet. Dubu grins up at us, pleased as punch, already halfway through Matco's bone.

"I am so, so sorry," says Eunju, but I just shake my head, taking a deep breath. I'm not about to start this mission on the wrong foot by getting angry.

"It's all right, let's just send him back to—"

I turn around, but the elevator's gone. Now there's only the yellow seed left. Asaase Yaa made it very clear that if we return to the human world without Pointy, she won't give us another chance.

For better or worse, we're stuck with Dubu until we get the sword.

"Okay, so the elevator's gone, but that's fine. We'll make it work." I pull a shoelace out of one of my sneakers and quickly magic it into a leash for Eunju to loop through Dubu's collar. "Eunju, make sure you keep an eye on him. Everyone else, stick to the plan."

Dubu being here is a complication, but complications are part of being a Slayer. This mission is way too important to let a dog ruin it.

While Eunju gets her pet under control using a silver dog whistle hanging around her neck, I join the others in checking out exactly what we've gotten ourselves into. Asamando sits in a state of perpetual twilight—the sky (ceiling?) above us purple, pink, and blue, as if the nonexistent sun can't decide if it's rising or setting. In the distance is a sparkling river, its water swirling with points of light like a liquid version of the night sky. I can't see the far bank from here. If it weren't for the old stories, I'd think it was an ocean with nothing on the other side but stars and more stars.

Dozens—no, hundreds—of shadowy figures are lined up along the bank. Their bodies are wisps of smoke in the form of human beings, in every size and shape imaginable. A shiver runs down my spine. Those must be the souls of the recently departed—their okra, the individual essence each person holds inside them. My ancestors believed that when a person dies, their okra goes to Nyame while their honam goes to Asaase Yaa. I guess Amokye processes both down here. The ghosts' voices are soft—there's no sound here really, except the gurgling of the river and the rustling of the trees around us, even though there's no wind.

At the front of the line is a set of wooden stairs leading to a dock where a great, long canoe with dozens of floating oars awaits. And standing on the dock is the head of this entire operation,

Amokye herself. She has dark brown skin, and the shining white afro blooming out of her black-and-white-patterned headscarf is like a halo almost enveloping her entire body.

Her lips are moving, but we're too far away to hear what she's saying. One by one the ghosts pass her and go sit in the boat. Once it's full, the oars start dipping into the water on their own and gently swaying into the horizon as a new canoe pulls up and the cycle starts all over again. Somewhere deep in my gut, I feel a tug in the same direction the boats are going, as if part of me knows that, someday, I'll be the one making that journey.

We spend several minutes just watching. It's so . . . peaceful. I know from my training that Asamando is just one of hundreds of possible afterlives among the world's cultures, but knowing a place like this is waiting makes death seem a little less scary.

Hardly daring to breathe for fear of making a sound, I put a scarf over my head (and Boulder's) and gesture for the others to do the same. Last night I drew the mpatapo on each one to suppress our energy from Amokye. The old lady has so many souls to process that there's no way she's going to notice five extra people and a mmoatia hitching a ride in one of her boats.

Once our scarves are in place, we slip into the middle of the line, out of Amokye's field of vision. None of the spirits seem upset about us cutting in front of them—I guess when you're dead, things like lines and time don't mean what they used to. We shuffle forward slowly with our heads down. Once we're closer to Amokye, we can finally hear what she's saying: the name, age, and cause of death of each and every person crossing the river to go beyond.

"Patience Barima, forty-six, cancer. Jennifer Bailey, seventy-eight, old age. Kodwo Osei Frempong, nineteen, car accident."

Amokye's voice is deep and raspy, and she goes through her list with practiced efficiency. I try not to think about how each one of these smoky wisps is a person whose body is lying cold somewhere back on earth. How many thousands of people up there are grieving for the hundreds of spirits surrounding us now?

My heart pounds louder and louder in my chest as we get closer to the front of the line.

"Adwoa Simmons . . ."

Ten feet away now. Eunju squirms awkwardly beside me but keeps on walking, as Roxy tries to stifle a small whimper.

"Lucas Garcia . . ."

Five feet. Gavin's grinning like always, but his eyes betray his nervousness.

"Noah Carter . . ."

Two. Mateo grabs on to my arm, his hand shaking so hard I feel it through my body.

"Emily . . ."

Suddenly, Amokye's muttering stops. For the first time since we arrived, she lifts her head.

And looks straight at us with pupil-less, pure white eyes.

"Someone is here who should not be."

She lifts a single finger and then curls it toward herself. All five of us rise in the air and zoom toward Amokye, halting in suspended animation just a few feet from her leathery face. Her eyes sweep over us, and I can practically see her reading our pasts like she's flipping through the books of our lives.

"Not your time. Not yet."

She waves her hand, and as we all go crashing to the dock in front of her, a chorus of low growls resounds through the air. I turn to see a small rapid begin to swirl through the river behind us. Three lions formed of the star-flecked water emerge onto the bank. Amokye lazily points our way, and the lions charge.

"Run!" I yell, not caring if it disturbs the ghosts. I grab the nearest person to me—Gavin—and haul him to his feet as I race back the way we came. The ground shudders beneath the lions' huge paws, and I can hear the other kids panting as they struggle to keep up with my frantic pace. Out of the corner of my eye, I see one of the lions swipe for Roxy, who veers away but stumbles and falls. Luckily, Eunju and Mateo are close enough to pull her up by the arms, and the three of them pound after Gavin and me. Dubu runs alongside them, his tongue lolling out like this is a great game of chase.

When we finally reach the grassy area at the edge of the forest where Asaase Yaa's elevator dropped us off, the lions suddenly skid to a halt. We stop and stare at them, gasping and clutching our knees. Dubu barks at them as they pace back and forth among the trees, as though there's some kind of magical border between us. Eventually the lions lose interest and dissolve into three streams that run quietly into the river.

In the distance, Amokye has gone back to reading off her list, as if we were never there.

"Well, that went well," says Eunju when we finally catch our breath. Boulder hops off my shoulder to attend to the scrape on Roxy's knee.

"What's plan B?" my cousin asks, and everyone turns to me expectantly.

How do I tell them there *is* no plan B? I put everything I know about magic into those scarves. If that wasn't enough to get us past Amokye, I have no idea what will be.

"I—I don't know." I look down, heat rushing through my face. Our first true mission and I've already messed it up.

Mateo shivers. "We d-d-don't stand a chance against those lions."

He's not wrong. How do you fight something that's made of water?

"How come you never mentioned that Amokye has deadly pets?" I ask Boulder with a glare.

The mmoatia glares back. "When I have come to Asamando, it has been on official Slayer business, not an unauthorized mission. Therefore, I have never run afoul of her before."

Before I can strangle the little guy or wallow in despair, Gavin pats me on the back. "Okay, your first idea didn't work. Don't sweat it! Almost every first idea I've ever had has been horrible, and I haven't died yet!" He makes a rectangle with the thumb and index finger of both hands, then looks through it like he's peering through a camera lens. "So, the boats are the only way across the river, and the only way onto the boats is past Amokye. She can sense whether a person is living or dead and also has a bunch of watery kittens at her disposal. What do we got?"

"We can pretend to die?" suggests Roxy.

"We could *actually* d-d-die?" moans Mateo.

"Let's save that one for a last resort," says Eunju.

Gavin's eyes sweep over the riverbank until they land on another boat that's bobbing on the water. It's covered in crates and boxes and has the words KWASI BENEFO DELIVERY painted on the side. "Serwa, you said Kwasi Benefo was the only human who made it into Asamando and returned? How did he do it?"

I'm touched that Gavin actually remembered something I said. "According to the old stories, his wives kept dying, and he grew so distraught that he attempted to cross into Asamando to be with them rather than live all alone. Amokye felt so sorry for him she let him in. But once he arrived, his wives told him to go back, because it's not good to be so obsessed with the dead that you forget about the living." I shake my head. "I haven't heard of Amokye letting in anyone else, though."

"Maybe not, but the fact that she *can* be persuaded gives me an idea," says Gavin. "Are there any Adinkra that can change a person's clothes?"

22

How to (Actually) Enter the Underworld

"Do not trifle with a god. You will not win."

—From the *Nwoma*

TEN MINUTES LATER, I'VE got all five of us dressed in blue KB Delivery jumpsuits. Boulder is in my backpack, and Dubu, complete with a KB Delivery bandana around his neck, is behind Eunju on his leash. This time Gavin leads the way, pushing a delivery cart piled with some boxes, and we skip the line completely to walk right up to Amokye.

"Lindsay Morris . . . Melissa Zhao . . . Johnny Borovich—"

"Excuse me!" calls Gavin. "You must be Amokye, guardian of the river between the human world and Asamando, yes?"

Amokye doesn't even look up from her list. "I am."

"I'm so sorry to bother you, but I'm with the union. I'd love it if you could answer a few questions about your employment here."

Now Amokye lifts her head. I brace myself for the moment she realizes we're not dead and sends her lions after us again, but it never comes. "What union?"

"Why, the Union of Supernatural Employees, of course!" Gavin's expression is completely sincere—from the way he talks, you'd think he practically founded this organization.

Which I guess he did because he's making the whole thing up.

Amokye's milky eyes narrow. "You look a little young to be a union employee."

"That's exactly why we created the union to begin with! What kind of ethical organization relies on child labor?" Gavin really wasn't lying about all those debate lessons his dads made him take—I know this is all a sham, and I'm still convinced by his tone. "That's why I want to talk to you. Everything about your situation sounds like a workers' rights nightmare. I mean, one person working twenty-four seven without breaks? Where is your bathroom? When was the last time you took any paid time off or got a raise?"

Amokye bites her lip. "They give me this little employee of the month plaque each month," she says weakly, and Gavin puts his hand to his chest, like what she just said has personally offended him.

"Amokye . . . you're their ONLY employee."

Several of the ghosts rustle impatiently behind us, but we wave at them to wait their turn. Somehow, Gavin's plan is actually working. We can't risk anything drawing Amokye's attention away from him right now.

Tears brim in the corners of the immortal's eyes. "I've asked several times for them to bring in another person, but they always say there isn't any room in the budget. I used to be able to hold each person's hand when they crossed over and listen to their life's story. Now, I'm so overwhelmed, the best I can offer is their name, age, and cause of death."

Gavin shakes his head. "That ain't right. You're undervalued!"

"I *am* undervalued!"

"You're underpaid!"

"I *am* underpaid!"

"You know what I would do if I were you? I'd march to the office right now and give them a piece of my mind! What are they going to do, fire you?"

Amokye slams her list down on the podium with so much force the whole dock shakes. "I think I will!"

And just like that, the guardian of the threshold between the living and the dead vanishes. All the boats except the KB Delivery one vanish, too. The ghosts start mumbling among themselves, and in the middle of the confusion, we push our way forward.

"Excuse us, coming through, very important delivery here!" I yell, and without Amokye there to detect that we're not actually Kwasi Benefo or his delivery team, no one stops us from piling into the boat and pushing it away from the dock. My guess is we have only a few minutes until Amokye realizes there is no Union of Supernatural Employees, but hopefully by then we'll already be on the other side.

Luckily for us, the boat knows where to go, and the moment we have it untied, the oars start rowing in the same direction the earlier vessels went. As soon as it becomes clear that neither Amokye nor her lions are following us, we settle into the benches.

Roxy gives Gavin a high five. "That was amazing!"

He grins and rubs the back of his neck. "It was nothing."

I shake my head. "I couldn't have pulled that off even if I'd had a script and time to memorize it, and you did it on the spot. That's not nothing."

Gavin might be hopeless with a sword, but clearly he has

other skills I didn't even realize could be useful in this line of work. I make a mental note to myself to fold this into our training when we get back home.

At first the ride is almost peaceful, and we spend the next few minutes just sailing through the water, taking turns giving Dubu belly rubs. I let Boulder out of the backpack so he can enjoy the view from my shoulder.

But then something in the air shifts. It gets . . . not colder or warmer, but *tighter*, like it's grown weight. And then I hear it.

Oseiwa.

I sit up. "Yeah?" I say to Boulder, but he shakes his head. He hadn't said anything. And none of the others know that Oseiwa is the traditional form of the name Serwa.

Oseiwa.

The voice is coming from a cluster of trees our boat is gliding past. But unlike the rest of the forest bordering the underworld, which was calm and beautiful if eerily still, this place has been torn apart. Dead branches and slashed trunks line the river, and the ground is black and charred. This corner of Asamando is more than just quiet—it's like a black hole, sucking in any noise and refusing to let it back out.

The pull I felt in my gut earlier beckons me toward this broken place. I push up against the boat's railing, trying to pinpoint why this spot feels so familiar. The others come over, too. Beside me, Roxy gulps.

"That place looks like a battlefield," she whispers.

I startle as Boulder shifts on my shoulder—I was so absorbed in staring at the dead trees that I forgot he was there. "That's because it was," he replies, his voice solemn. "This portion of Asamando was the site of one of the worst battles against Nana Bekoe and her forces during the Third Great War."

"The war extended all the way to the magical side of the veil?" I ask.

He nods. "The gods and the Abomofuo chose to leave this area untouched as a reminder of what the forces of black magic are capable of if we do not remain vigilant."

My eyes rove over the gray sand and twisted roots. In the land of the dead, this is the scariest thing we've seen yet. "I didn't realize Nana Bekoe was that powerful."

"Wait, who is Nana Bekoe? What was the Third Great War?" asks Eunju.

Shoot, I'd told the group about the Abomofuo but not the specific circumstances that led to me being dumped in Rocky Gorge. Since it looks like we'll have some time before we reach the other side of the river, I launch into the full story of everything that happened between Boahinmaa arriving at my house and the first day of school.

It's so weird to talk about it like it was the distant past when it was really only a little over a week ago. It already feels like all that happened to a different Serwa.

When I'm done, Mateo's eyebrows furrow like they do when he's working his way through a complicated math problem in Mrs. Dean's class. "Nana B-B-Bekoe led the forces of b-b-black magic d-d-during the war? What made her so strong?"

We all look at Boulder, the only one who was actually there. A cloud falls over his eyes. I sense he knows the answer but isn't sure he should share it.

"Nana Bekoe was one of the most powerful obayifo who ever lived," he says reluctantly. "But what made her such a singularly devastating threat was that she had two children who rivaled her in strength. On their own, any of the three had enough black magic to flatten an entire contingent of Slayers. As a trio, they were nearly unstoppable."

Just like that, something clicks together in my mind. "Boahinmaa was one of those children, wasn't she?"

Boulder nods. "She was."

Wow. I will never forgive Boahinmaa for what she did to me and my family, but her desperation to find the Midnight Drum suddenly makes a lot more sense. If someone took my mother from me, I wouldn't care what their reason was—I would tear the whole world apart if it meant getting her back.

Gods. Am I . . . Am I like her?

I wrap my arms around myself at the chilling thought of any similarity between me and the woman who murdered my grandmother. "And what about Nana Bekoe's other child?" I ask. "What happened to them?"

"That is classified information" is all he says, and no amount of needling or bribing him with the promise of uninterrupted TV time can get him to spill more.

By this time we've passed the dead battleground, and ahead of us, a tropical paradise looms into view. The palm trees sway gently, their branches bright with rainbow-colored flowers and huge fruit. Dozens of cabanas dot the beach, some of them sitting on stilts over the river itself so the water swirls harmlessly beneath the dwellings. It all reminds me of those ads you see on TV for all-inclusive trips to tropical vacations where even a bottle of water costs, like, six hundred dollars.

Dubu wags his tail and barks excitedly, eager to climb out of the boat, while Gavin whistles. "The place where people's eternal souls go to rest forevermore . . . is an old people's resort?"

"Just a corner of it," Boulder says, clearly relieved to switch topics. "What you're seeing now is the tiniest section of every-thing Asamando has to offer. The locales here are as varied—perhaps even more so—as the ones you have in the human world."

I guess that makes sense. There's no way you could keep billions of ghosts from every corner of the world happy by dumping them all in some random suburb and calling it a day.

The boat anchors itself, and we each take one of the KB Delivery carts from the back and hurry down the dock, where a tall spirit wearing an ASAMANDO, SWEET ASAMANDO! T-shirt awaits. Now that we're on the other side of the river, the wispy spirits from before have solidified. But their vibes are weird. Even though they're happily dancing or playing volleyball on the beach or just chilling all around us, they look just a little off, their motions too fluid and graceful to be human.

The tall female spirit is holding a clipboard and yelling into a pair of wireless headphones. "Look, I don't care how mad they are, the new ghosts cannot throw an all-night rave—" Then she addresses us. "Hey, are you all the ones bringing the extra routers for tonight's concert?"

"Uh—I mean yes, yes, we are!" I lie.

"Thank Nyame. You know how cranky the millennial ghosts get when their Wi-Fi goes down." The spirit points her pen to the left. "Follow the blue arrows, and for the love of all the abosom, hurry!"

We scuttle away and she goes back to yelling about the ghost rave, completely unaware we are neither dead nor delivery people.

Asamando unfurls in front of us like a quilt. Little huts are sprinkled all around, some simple with tiny windows and thatched roofs, others multistory complexes with their own pools and everything. Cheerful tropical music filters through the air, and everywhere we turn there are flyers for things like SPECTRAL BINGO! and SALSA FOR THE ETHEREALLY CHALLENGED! as well as ghosts zipping around on golf carts labeled with the symbol of Asaase Yaa.

Mateo pulls out Asaase Yaa's leaf. It now points straight ahead in his palm, in the same direction as the blue painted arrows on the ground. We ditch the packages—sorry, cranky millennial ghosts—and follow the foliage.

The path gets more and more crowded by the minute, until we're surrounded by a crush of ghosts. I'm amazed that I can actually feel them around me. The ground rumbles beneath our feet—not caused by the throng, but by . . . a pounding bass. It reverberates through our bodies, and when we reach the end of the path, the source reveals itself.

The blue arrows led us to the rim of a valley. Down below is an arena holding tens of thousands of ghosts. And on the stage in the center, a single person is currently ripping out a wicked bass solo. Dozens of Jumbotrons float around the venue, illuminating the figure for everyone to see.

In the glow I see something else, too, and I have to hold back a scream of triumph. Pointy is buried up to its hilt in the grass near the middle of the arena, right in front of the stage.

I'm about to make my way down, figuring the ghosts are too wrapped up in the concert to care about us, when I take a closer look at tonight's entertainer up on the screens. She's a Black girl about college age and dressed like a vacationing goth's dream—everything from her bikini top to her lipstick to the wrap skirt around her waist is midnight black. Even her bass guitar is darker than obsidian. But unlike the ghosts, she's almost too alive, and her eyes have that same bright, starlike quality that Tano's and Bia's did. She's one of the most beautiful people I've ever seen.

This is no ghost.

This is a goddess.

The solo ends, and a tsunami of cheers rises up as, through the speakers, the MC booms, "Specters and gentleghosts, please give it up for Antoa Nyamaa!"

At this point, both Boulder and I are trembling. Gavin nudges me. "Who is that?" he yells, fighting to be heard over the noise.

"Goddess of curses and revenge!" I yell back, heart in my throat.

According to my parents, Antoa is one of the most power-ful goddesses in the entire pantheon. *Antoa is the one people turn to when they need something done,* Dad told me once. *If someone robbed you and the police are refusing to do anything, or there's been some other wrong that needs righting, Antoa is who you go to . . . but always for a price.*

Apparently, there was a scandal in Ghana back in the 2010s when a politician invoked the name of Antoa to strike down his political opponents like flies. So yeah, Antoa isn't a being of black magic, but she is not to be messed with. Of course we'd choose to come down here the same day she does, because nothing can ever be easy, can it?

But maybe, just maybe, if we hoot and clap like every-one else, we can pull this off without her noticing. As Antoa launches into her next song, this one a rock ballad accompanied by spirit musicians on keyboard and drums, I explain my plan to the others, and then we follow the leaf deep into the heart of the crowd.

All the ghosts jumping and cheering at Antoa's performance keep a respectful distance from the sword—it's like there's an energy wafting off it warning souls to stay away. Boulder checks for traps and spells, but he finds none, though I have no idea how he can sense anything with the concert raging around us.

The sword itself is an akrafena, just like Nokware, but this one has razor-sharp emerald leaves wrapped around the golden hilt. I really do not want to touch this thing, but I don't know how else to pull it out without drawing too much attention to ourselves. Antoa finishes her song, and the ghosts start screaming, "Encore! Encore! Encore!"

I pass the net to Gavin and Roxy, then hand the Tupperware container to Mateo. Eunju stands off to the side, trying to make Dubu sit.

"Everyone ready?" I call, and they nod. The others get into position as I slowly approach the sword. One wrong move and that thing will slice me like a Christmas ham.

"That's it. . . . Good Pointy," I say as I creep toward the weapon, hoping against hope that something will go right on this mission.

But when my hands are less than an inch from the hilt, Antoa's voice booms across the speakers, "Before I start my next set, I'd like to introduce some very special guests here with us tonight!"

She snaps her fingers, and a single spotlight shines on the five of us, our shocked faces magnified a thousandfold on the Jumbotrons. On the stage, Antoa's black-lipsticked mouth slashes into a smile even sharper than the sword.

"Specters and gentleghosts, let's give it up for the living humans!"

23

How to Win a Rock Battle
Against a God

"Trust your teammates as if they were your own limbs.
Move as one, fight as one."

—From the *Nwoma*

ROXY, MATEO, EUNJU, GAVIN, and I all freeze as a
hundred thousand ghostly eyes fly our way.

Antoa struts across the stage, lazily strumming her
bass. "Isn't this a treat?" she yells, her voice holding all
the command and power her divine mother and siblings
have. "Real, living kids down here in Asamando! Are
we excited or what?"

"YES!" the ghosts all scream, their combined voices
sending a tremor through the entire underworld. A
bead of sweat rolls down my neck as I glance helplessly
at Pointy. The sword is literally within my grasp, but I
don't dare turn my back on Antoa.

The goddess of retribution taps her chin in an exag-
gerated thinking motion. "The proper thing to do would
be to contact Amokye and get them escorted out of here,
wouldn't it?"

"YEAH!" chant the ghosts, and the five of us

huddle together nervously as the specters near us start to close in.

"Then agaaaaaain, a couple of human kids sneaking past Amokye is the most interesting thing to happen down here since that group of ghost vegans staged a protest over the lack of non-dairy milk options at the smoothie bar." Antoa flips her head forward and gathers her waist-length braids into a high bun. "Why don't we keep the fun going with a deal? I won't turn you in . . . if one of you joins me up here onstage."

I cannot have heard that right. One of us? Singing onstage? With a *goddess*?

Antoa swings an index finger back and forth like a metronome. "Ticktock, kiddies. What's it gonna be? Sing up here with me, or face down Amokye?"

"Serwa, I strongly advise you not to bargain with a goddess," Boulder warns.

"What other choice do we have?" I shoot back.

The other four GCC-ers all look at me, but I shake my head frantically. "No way. If these ghosts hear how tone-deaf I am, they might actually kill us."

"Well, I can't sing either!" argues Gavin.

"If you p-p-put me onstage, I will vomit," swears Mateo, who looks even greener than he did back at Eunju's house.

Roxy bites her lip, her eyes flying around nervously. Eunju glances at her, then blurts out, "Roxy used to be in chorus!"

My cousin's eyes go wide, and she tries to step away as the spotlight focuses in on her. "Eunju! I mean yeah, I was, but that was in elementary school, and I wasn't that good—Ahh!"

Roxy's protests cut off as Antoa lifts her in the air with a single nod, sends her flying over the heads of the ghosts, and deposits her on the stage. Then the goddess snaps her fingers, and a microphone appears in Roxy's shaking hands. "Attagirl, let's go!"

Antoa plays the opening chords of a pop song I've heard Roxy sing to herself in the shower. But now my cousin just stands frozen onstage, her brown fingers clutching the mic in a death grip. All around us, the ghosts start to boo and hiss. Nyame help us, if they don't get some entertainment soon, we're going to have a full-blown spectral riot on our hands.

I cup my hands around my mouth and bellow, "SING, ROXY!"

"SING, ROXY! SING, ROXY! SING, ROXY!" the other kids start chanting, and the ghosts quickly join in. Soon the entire underworld is screaming her name.

Roxy's eyes find mine in the crowd and I give her a thumbs-up.

She nods, swallows thickly, and takes a tiny step forward.

She clears her throat, brings the mic to her mouth . . .

And she begins to sing.

I knew Roxy had a good voice, but this? This is next-level. From the moment the first note leaves her lips, my cousin owns that stage. Her voice winds through the air, growing with power and confidence by the second.

And the ghosts?

They. Love. It.

They scream twice as hard as they did for Antoa, and they all rush forward to be as close to Roxy as possible. It's like she has them in some sort of trance. Antoa lets out a wicked laugh, hopping around the stage with energy to match the song, her fingers flying over her instrument with superhuman speed.

Mateo, Gavin, and I all cheer as Eunju stands beside us with her arms crossed over her chest and a knowing smile on her face. Even Boulder is whooping from his perch on my shoulder, which I've never seen him do before. For a few minutes, we're just a bunch of normal kids (and a mmoatia) hyping up our friend because she is *killing it.*

But then one of the ghosts knocks into Mateo, who knocks into Eunju, who knocks into me. I go stumbling into Pointy, my fingers brushing against the razor-sharp leaves wrapped around its hilt.

Oh, poop balls. I forgot all about that.

I barely have time to duck out of the way as the Sword of Asaase Yaa rips out of the ground and swoops straight for my heart. Boulder and the three others dive into the grass, just missing being sawed in half. Dubu rushes the sword, barking furiously.

Antoa watches Pointy twirl through the air, readying for its next swing, and she lets out an excited yell. "Oh yeah, now it's a party!"

Some of the ghosts cheer along with her. Roxy's visibly frightened, but she keeps on singing like the boss she is, trying to keep the ghosts' attention on her while we deal with our little problem.

The music begins to rise again, and Pointy swivels around for another pass at us. But this time I see it coming. I hop onto a ghost's cooler, Nokware in my hand to meet the sword in midair. The *clang* that ensues when the two swords make contact rings through my ears in time to the beat. I fly backward, crashing through a ghost family's barbecue setup. Pointy darts toward Eunju, who manages to pull Dubu away from its lunge at the last second.

"Now!" I scream as I struggle to get back to my feet amid the hot dog and hamburger bun packages I landed on. Gavin and Mateo rush forward to cover the sword with the net, but at the last second, Gavin's fear of sharp objects takes over, and he skids to a halt. The sudden force of his stop sends Mateo crashing to the ground, and they're both now sitting ducks for Pointy. With adrenaline and panic mixing in my veins, I yank my foot free of the barbecue grill and rush forward with Nokware to intercept Asaase Yaa's sword before it can skewer my companions.

Even without a wielder, Pointy moves faster than any weapon I've ever faced before. I put all my years of training to good use as I dodge, weave, roll, and parry with a speed that would put an Olympic fencer to shame. To everyone else, we're just a blur of slashing iron, grass flying up everywhere we go. I lose track of my comrades, the only thing on my mind not being skewered alive.

Eunju runs toward me, Boulder in her arms and Dubu at her side. "Serwa, we've got company!" she screams.

She points to the top of the arena, where the three river lions race down the slope toward us, ghosts fleeing their thundering paws on all sides. Giant festering mmoatia dookie! Amokye knows we're here, and she's clearly unhappy about it.

"Scatter!" I scream, and for once, Mateo, Eunju, and Gavin actually obey. They run in different directions, and the lions split off from their triangle formation to follow each one. At least Roxy is safe on the stage—for now. I crane my head to see where they went, and Pointy takes advantage of my moment of distraction to slam its broadside into my gut.

Stars dance across my vision as all the air leaves my lungs. Nokware flies from my grip at the impact. Dazed and disoriented, I run to reclaim it.

But then my shoe—the same shoe that's missing a shoelace because of Eunju's stupid dog—slips off and I stumble, falling into a tent belonging to a few hippie ghosts. Now it's only Eunju left standing, Nokware not far from her feet as Pointy swoops back toward us with a vengeance.

"Eunju!" I scream, trying and failing to disentangle myself from the mess of poles and ropes and nylon. The world seems to slow to a crawl as Eunju bends to pick up my mother's sword, confusion and fear plain on her face. Her eyes meet mine, and the choice becomes clear: Fight or die.

"STRIKE, EUNJU!" I bellow.

Without another moment's hesitation, she does. Her arm shoots out in a clumsy arc with Nokware that manages to deflect Pointy's slice. She looks just as surprised as I am that her maneuver worked, but there's no time for her to revel in it, because the sword is already gearing up for its next move. I'm still too trapped to help, but from where I am I can see the whole fight playing out.

"High block!" I yell, and Eunju twists her arm up to push off Pointy again. "Side right! Middle! Cross-body!"

Eunju follows each of my commands, keeping Asaase Yaa's sword at bay by using the moves I taught her in Sweetieville. Her perfect facade cracks and the fire she hides from everyone—from Ashley, from her parents—rises to the surface, lending extra strength to her movements. Boulder calls out moves as well, and together we're able to guide her through the battle. In this moment, I get a glimpse of the girl she could be if she stopped being what everyone wants her to be. It's someone powerful and fierce who I definitely hope I never have to fight in battle.

But though Eunju has Pointy preoccupied for now, there are still the lions to deal with. The one that was chasing Eunju switches his focus to me, and I yank uselessly at my still-entangled leg as he prowls closer, watery jaws open in a snarl.

"Help!" I'm not even sure anyone can hear me over the sound of Roxy and Antoa still jamming onstage. "Someone, anyone, HELP!"

"Make way! Coming through!"

I only just register Gavin's voice when something large and white barrels into the water lion. It's a golf cart, and upon impact the feline bursts into millions of tiny water droplets.

The cart skids to a screeching halt in front of me. "G-get in!" screams Mateo. He and Gavin yank me out of the tent mess, and then we're on our way, Mateo behind the wheel as Gavin and I hold on for dear life.

"You know how to drive?" I yell over the racing wind.

"Yeah—in Mario K-Kart!"

Behind us the last two lions are in hot pursuit, and Mateo pushes the cart as fast as it can go to avoid their clutches. He drives with a reckless glee that would 1,000 percent get someone arrested back on earth (remind me to never let him give me a ride anywhere ever). The lions split up to flank us on each side, clearly trying to corral us into a collision. We're getting dangerously close to the stage now, seconds away from smashing straight against the foundation.

"Mateo, look out!" I scream. Just before the golf cart careens into the stage, Mateo takes a hard right. We go sailing straight through the second lion as the third one crashes into the platform, giving the front row of ghosts a lovely water display. Then, with all of us soaked to the bone and all three kitty-cats disposed of, Mateo swings the wheel around again to head back to help Eunju.

She's fought well for a beginner, but it's clear her energy is running low. Pointy, on the other hand, was quite literally designed to fight forever. Dubu growls and barks at the weapon, but it stays just out of reach of the dog's jaws as it continues to wear Eunju down.

"Bring us in as close as possible!" I order Mateo. He floors the gas, and the golf cart hurtles toward her. I grab the net, while Gavin takes the Tupperware. We exchange glances, nod at each other once, and then brace ourselves.

The cart comes parallel with Eunju and Pointy just as the latter disarms the former of Nokware. With a war cry, I leap from the cart and toss myself and the net over Pointy.

The sword struggles, dragging me into the air as it tries to disentangle itself, but I hold on with all my strength. Pointy pulls me up and up, but the Adinkra I drew on the net's ropes begin to glow. The weapon shrinks until it is small enough to fit in the palm of my hand, and at that size it's no longer strong enough to keep me airborne. I plummet to the ground, landing in Mateo's and Eunju's outstretched arms. Before Pointy can slice through its bindings, Gavin rushes forward and slams the Tupperware over the sword, his knuckles tight around the plastic.

The container rattles once, twice, three times.

Then it stops.

For several seconds, Gavin, Mateo, Eunju, and I just stare at one another. Then a cheer erupts from the stage.

"Now that's what I call a show!" calls Antoa, and the stadium erupts with the cheers of a hundred thousand ghosts, a goddess, and Roxy, who looks quite comfortable onstage by this point.

My entire body feels like it's gone through a garbage disposal, but I don't even care, because, oh my actual gosh, we just caught the most powerful sword in the entire world. I'm still in a daze as the others cheer around me.

"Serwa, that was incredible!" screams Gavin.

"Me? I didn't do anything! Did you see Eunju fighting it?"

"Forget me," yells Eunju. "What about Mateo's driving skills! Those lions didn't stand a chance!"

Mateo's so relieved there are actual tears in his eyes, and he's blubbering out something that's more snot than words.

Even Boulder looks proud of us as he transfers from Eunju's shoulder to mine. "I haven't seen fighting like that since I helped Alexander the Great capture Egypt!"

We're all laughing now because we did it. *We did it!* We're so excited no one notices that the Tupperware has started shaking . . .

Or that the sword has cut its way out of it.

Roxy's voice booms over the speakers, "Serwa, look out!"

All I see is a flash of black metal before Eunju tackles me to the ground. Up onstage, Roxy extends a hand toward us, and all the ghosts in the immediate vicinity form a circle around our group. What the— Is she making them do that? How? Their bodies grow even more solid, and when Pointy can't break through their wall, it turns to the only living being left to attack.

Dubu.

"No!" screams Eunju. She claws and screams at the ghosts to let her through, but they won't budge. We can do nothing but watch as the sword flies straight for the Samoyed.

But instead of running away, he rushes toward it, his mouth open wide like he's about to catch a Frisbee, and he—

—swallows it.

24

How to Wander Through the Woods

*"Your eyes can betray you. Your ears can deceive you.
Trust nothing. Believe no one."*

—From the *Nwoma*

EUNJU'S DOG ATE THE Sword of Asaase Yaa.

We all watch in shock as Dubu burps and begins scratching behind his ear like he didn't just ingest one of the most dangerous items in the history of the world. When it becomes clear Dubu isn't about to become a doggy shish kebab right before our eyes, Eunju finally pushes her way through the ghosts and runs over to her pet. She buries her face in his fluffy white neck, openly crying in relief.

A screech cuts through Eunju's sobs.

Immediately I think we're in bigger trouble than ever. Antoa was obviously tasked with watching over the sacred weapon, and we just—

"The dog! All that work and it's the dog who— Oh, this is *too good*. I'm so glad I stuck around to watch this!"

In a flash of golden light, Antoa appears in front of Eunju with a stunned Roxy in tow. The ghosts immediately gather around my cousin, as if awaiting another order. I have no idea how she got them to protect us. As far as I know, neither divine wisdom *nor* black magic gives you the power to control the undead.

Antoa is literally doubled over in laughter, wiping tears from her eyes.

Okaaay . . . This is not the reaction I was expecting.

"You're . . . You're not mad?" I venture.

"Mad? You five have provided me with better entertainment than I've seen in hundreds of years! I should be thanking you."

Boulder pats me on the head. "You hear that, Serwa?" he says. "I told you this mission would pay off."

"What?!" I cry. "Just yesterday you called it, and I quote, 'the worst idea you've ever encountered since you watched King Midas try to scratch his butt'!"

"I recall no such thing."

Fortunately, Antoa pays us no mind. "You know what? I usually don't do this, but I think you deserve a reward."

A tiny glass vial full of gold liquid appears in her palm, and she hands it to Roxy. "One vial of pure divine wisdom, redeemable at any time and any place, without having to summon me or any other god or use any Adinkra. That'll do whatever you need it to do, but only once, so choose wisely. And to top it off, I'll even protect the dog, too." She twirls a finger, and Dubu glows gold for a second before going back to his normal white. "There. That'll ensure your pooch suffers no ill side effects due to his unusual treat. Man, I can't wait to see my mom FREAK when she discovers her prized sword is now inside a *dog*."

Oh Nyame, that is not a conversation I am looking forward to.

"Why are you helping us?" I ask suspiciously. Maybe I shouldn't question a goddess, but something isn't adding up here. She has no reason to get involved in this.

The goddess sees my fingers reaching for Nokware, which I had picked up and put back on my wrist in its bracelet form.

She rolls her eyes. "Please. As if that toothpick could do anything to me. Relax, little Slayer—if I wanted to harm you, you'd be in ribbons already. I just wanted to personally meet the humans my mother sent on a quest for the first time in centuries." She looks directly at me with those too-bright, starlike eyes all the gods share. "When you've been alive as long as I have, you encounter all sorts of people—good people, bad people, mostly somewhere-in-between people—but in all that time, I've never met anyone like you, Serwa. That alone makes it worth seeing what you're capable of."

Me? What's so special about me?

I'm about to ask the goddess what she means when she says, "Whoops! It seems I'm late for my weekly limbo tournament with the mmoatia." She gives a sly wink to Boulder, who gets visibly flustered. "Buggers are little, but I'm very flexible." Her bass guitar poofs into a pair of all-black horn-rimmed sunglasses, and the goddess slips them on with a grin. "See you around, kids! And remember, if you ever have any enemies in need of smiting, dismembering, or plain old-fashioned maiming, you know who to call!"

Antoa vanishes, and Boulder climbs into my backpack muttering, "I'm too old for this. I need a nap."

"What was that about?" mutters Eunju.

I just shake my head. *Gods.*

After Antoa disappears, the ghosts disperse, though a few linger around Roxy, maybe hoping to get a selfie with her. I turn to check on Gavin and Mateo . . .

But they're gone.

I spin in a circle. The entire resort is gone. All around me is nothing but dead, blackened trees.

I'm in the destroyed forest we sailed by earlier.

Akwaaba, Oseiwa, the voice from before whispers, welcoming me in Twi.

I pull out Nokware and slip into a defensive stance.

Trying to hide the panic in my voice, I call out, "Actually, my name is Serwa. My parents preferred that form of the name to the traditional one."

I swear the forest laughs—not like a human does with their mouth, but in a way that shudders through my skin. *Names are meaningless when you're as old as I am.*

"A-and how old are you?"

Older than the oldest thing you've ever known and ever will. Older than bones. Older than time.

Something brushes my cheek. I swing my sword, hitting nothing but air.

Little Serwa . . . doesn't even know what she is. Doesn't even know what she can do . . .

"Who are you?" I scream. My magic is sparking inside me— somehow, it knows this place and I don't understand why. I don't get what's going on.

But if the forest has the answers, it's not sharing them. The voice laughs again, the sound crawling across my spine.

The forest is no place for little girls who don't know their own story.

A touch on my other cheek.

I swing.

I miss.

Whatever this thing is, it's toying with me, and that makes me so angry my vision goes red. The Big Feeling churns in my stomach again, and I just want to open my mouth and let all the hot lava pour out, allow it to run freely until it destroys this creature that knows more about me than I know about myself.

Now I realize why this place seems familiar—the feeling I get here is the same one I get in my dreams of the dark void. The two places must be one and the same.

Good, Serwa. Let it all out. Let me *out,* the voice purrs, and the power swells inside me, rising like a tide. It's beneath my skin now, burning, about to—

"Serwa? Are you okay?" asks Roxy.

I blink, and I'm suddenly I'm in the concert arena again. The others are looking at me with freaked-out expressions.

"I— What happened?"

"You tell us. It looked like you were going to say something, then you just . . . spaced."

None of them saw the forest. None of them heard the voice. I almost tell them what happened, but then I don't want them to worry. "It's nothing," I say, shaking my head. "I'm just tired."

I quickly pull out the yellow seed and bury it under the grass so I don't have to answer any more questions. We all let out a sigh of relief as the vine elevator sprouts to life again, this time with a button that points up.

"Is it kind of weird that I'm going to miss this place?" asks Gavin as we all pile inside. "It actually wasn't that bad, aside from the fact we almost died several times."

Mateo shudders as he squeezes water out of his sweater. "Speak for yourself. I'm g-g-gonna have lion-filled nightmares for weeks."

"Better than having to pick up metal dog poop," complains Eunju, though she's lovingly scratching Dubu behind the ears.

"Sorry, no autographs!" Roxy yells to her new ghost super-fans, who all float away sadly.

I step one foot in the elevator and freeze, feeling that touch on my cheek again.

"Serwa," calls Roxy, and I snap out of the memory to see her reaching toward me. "Come on, let's go home."

Home. For the first time when I hear that word I don't think of my parents and the lake house but of Sunny Oak Towers and my little air mattress, of the art room and Sweetieville and training with the four people in front of me.

"Yeah . . . let's go home," I say, and I turn my back on the underworld to grab my cousin's hand.

25

How to Save a Dog

"A god's whims are to be obeyed, never questioned.
Grave fates await those who dare defy them."

—From the *Nwoma*

TIME PASSES DIFFERENTLY IN the magical world.
It felt like we were in Asamando forever, but when the
elevator deposits us back in Eunju's living room, it's only
Saturday evening. We could all go back to our respective
houses now, our mission completed, but we'd told our
families we'd be gone till Sunday night. Besides, none of
us are ready to face Asaase Yaa's wrath just yet.

"Well, guess we better go," says Roxy.

The four of us who don't live here awkwardly begin
packing our stuff. Eunju watches us for a few seconds
before nervously blurting out, "You know, you guys
don't *have* to leave. My parents won't be back until
tomorrow. . . ."

What follows is my first foray into a time-honored
tradition of normal kid culture: the sleepover.

We camp out in Eunju's ridiculously oversize theater
room because she discovered that Gavin and Mateo
haven't seen Battlestar Dimensions either and she
refuses to let that stand. Eunju makes us all watch the
special extended director's cut of the first movie (with
actor commentary!). Mateo and I keep asking questions
through the whole thing, while Gavin and Roxy talk

about the mural. Eunju acts like she hates all of it, but she's laughing more than I've ever seen her laugh.

Then Roxy demands to know everyone's birthday so she can do our birth charts. Everyone agrees that I am a classic Leo-Virgo cusp, which I hope is a good thing, since I have absolutely no idea what any of those words mean. When the group learns that my birthday was exactly a week ago, Gavin declares that it's illegal to let such an occasion go by without any baked goods. So we all migrate to the kitchen to whip up a cake from scratch. (And by that I mean Mateo whips up a cake from scratch while the rest of us take turns licking the spatula and making unreasonable demands about the amount of frosting he should use.)

Eunju manages to dig up some paper party hats and a number six–shaped candle, and Roxy leads the whole group in a rousing rendition of "Happy Birthday" (the Stevie Wonder version, not the boring usual version), in which everyone but her is both off-beat *and* off-key.

We spend the rest of the evening kicking each other's butts in *Super Smash Brothers* while Dubu snores away on the couch and Boulder shouts unhelpful advice about the best way to suck a flying fox into a magic portal.

When I wake up in the morning, I don't remember exactly when everyone fell asleep. All I know is it is before dawn, and the entire room is quiet and dark yet also warm and cozy.

I carefully slide Roxy's phone out of her pocket and snap a pic of Eunju sleeping with her head on an equally passed out Gavin's shoulder, because I know that's going to make great blackmail one day. I tuck a blanket around Mateo, who is still covered in flour, and think about how different this birthday celebration was from my last one with my parents.

There wasn't anything super fancy about the night. It had

none of the magic that has defined my life for the past twelve years and counting.

But it was the best. And I wouldn't change a second of it.

I spy Boulder rifling through one of the cabinets while everyone sleeps. Guess those old mmoatia instincts toward thievery and trickery die hard.

"Thank you for your help today, even though I know you didn't want us going on this mission at all," I tell him, startling him into dropping the Nintendo Switch controller he was attempting to pilfer.

The mmoatia scoffs. "Don't thank me. I was only doing my duty to your father. If anything happened to you, I would never hear the end of it."

I frown. "Why do you always do that? Act like you don't care when anyone tries to get close to you?"

Boulder bristles, and for a second I think he might shut me down. But then he says, "I have been alive for thousands of years, Serwa, and in that time I have known millions of humans. All varied in age, creed, and race, yet one thing remains the same: I outlived every single one. At this point it is . . . easier to not get closer than I have to."

My breath catches in my lungs. I knew Boulder had other partners before my dad, but it never fully hit me that he's watched each one die, whether in battle or from natural causes. That must be so lonely, even for an immortal spirit.

"I understand," I say, and the mmoatia blinks in surprise that for once I didn't try to fight him. "Thank you all the same. Good night, Boulder. And if you're going to take anything, go for one of the utensils."

Boulder lets out a small smile. "Noted. Good night, Serwa."

I settle into a reclining chair and to try to steal a bit more sleep while I can. Come sunrise, we'll have Asaase Yaa to deal with, and something tells me we're all going to need to be wide-awake for that. . . .

"SO, YOU MEAN TO tell me that my sword—the same sword that has defeated thousands upon thousands of enemies and faced down some of the strongest warriors the world has ever seen—is inside that *dog*?"

Asaase Yaa stares at us like we're trying to convince her the sky is actually made of fruit punch. And you know what? I don't blame her. It's now late Sunday morning and the GCC and I have summoned her once more in Sweetieville. Even though I had hours to think about how to explain to the goddess what happened in Asamando, the truth still sounds more bonkers than any lie I could invent.

However, we couldn't it put off forever. I fight the urge to grasp my pendant and instead wave my hand toward Dubu, who is currently rubbing his butt in circles all over Candy Cane Commons. "Your weapon is inside that dog," I repeat. "Check for yourself if you'd like."

Soft green light pools in Asaase Yaa's palm, and Dubu lifts into the air to float in front of her. She waves her hand in front of his snout, and the same light starts glowing from his stomach. Her eyes widen.

"You're telling the truth. This creature has truly ingested my sword."

We all brace ourselves, ready to be smitten, or turned into flowers, or whatever other punishment the goddess deems fit. But instead of anger, there comes laughter.

"The dog—! He really—!" Asaase Yaa doubles over with her arms around her middle, and she guffaws so hard that all of Sweetieville shakes. The world itself responds to her mirth—the trees around us grow taller, and flowering vines poke through the cracks in the cement. By the time she calms down, Sweetieville looks less like an abandoned horror show and more like a flower garden.

The six of us stare at her in wonder. Making a goddess laugh has to be better than making her cry, right?

Asaase Yaa straightens up, wiping tears from her eyes. "A deal is a deal, even if your method of delivery was rather unorthodox. In exchange for bringing me my sword, I will now grant you the divine wisdom you seek. Line up before me, children."

I step back with Boulder in my arms as the other four fall into place before the goddess. She raises her hands, then pauses as her face lights up with an idea.

"You five have reminded me of why I loved humanity in the first place—the courage and ingenuity you display in the face of even the strongest obstacles. Therefore, I will grant each of you not only the divine wisdom you requested, but a unique blessing as well."

The GCCers look at me with a mixture of eagerness, wariness, excitement, and confusion on their faces. I give them all encouraging nods, though I'm clueless about what the goddess is referring to.

The scent of lilacs fills the air as Gavin comes forward, and Asaase Yaa places a glowing hand against his forehead.

"In you, I see the courage and tenacity born of surviving great trauma. Yet you are also flexible and fluid, finding reason to laugh like a babbling brook every day. I bless you with the power of the water that twists the rivers and flows into the ocean. May that which is already within you spring forth and bloom forevermore."

On my shoulder, Boulder lets out a sharp gasp. "No one has received an elemental blessing from the gods in decades," he whispers.

Wow, I guess the goddess *really* wanted that sword back.

Asaase Yaa still looks human, but her voice has transcended, becoming the sound of leaves rustling, of a forest teeming with life. Golden light flows from her palm into Gavin until it swirls beneath his skin in a rippling current. He stands statue still, but his eyes are wide, his mouth open in a soft O of surprise.

When she pulls away, a sea blue wristband, like the kind athletes wear, appears on his right arm. The asaase ye duru Adinkra glows in gold thread on the fabric.

Mateo visibly squirms when Asaase Yaa puts her hand on his forehead next.

"In you, beneath a layer of fear, I see a kind heart that searches for the best qualities in those determined to display only the worst. You blow away the shadows, fill the dark spaces with hope. I bless you with the power of the wind that grants breath to life. May that which is already within you spring forth and bloom forevermore." He lets out a soft whimper as the golden light glows into him, too, but slowly he relaxes and stands up straighter to match Gavin beside him. His wristband is sunny yellow, though it bears the same symbol.

Next is Eunju, who flinches a little when the goddess touches her. "Ah, there is so much anger in you, little one. But behind it is a fierce loyalty and the soul of a warrior—yours to claim if only you are brave enough to reach for it. I bless you with the power of the fire that races through volcanoes and illuminates the night. May that which is already within you spring forth and bloom forevermore."

Eunju startles like she's been shocked when her red wristband appears. Her eyes spark bright with something I caught a glimpse of when she battled Pointy, and my chest feels ready to burst with pride. This must be how parents feel at graduation. Gods, I should've taken a video of this.

When she gets to Roxy, Asaase Yaa pauses. I swear a line appears between her eyebrows, though it's gone so quickly I might have imagined it.

"And you, dear child of my day, have gifts still to uncover. But in you I see a nurturer who puts others first. I bless you with the power of the earth that nourishes all the flora that grows within it and the fauna that live upon it. May that which is already within you spring forth and bloom forevermore."

Roxy actually vibrates with joy as her patron goddess's magic floods through her veins and her forest green wristband materializes on her arm. Suddenly I wonder what Asaase Yaa would say if she looked deep inside me, too. Would she think I was ready to take the Initiation Test and help protect the Midnight Drum? After all, I did succeed in evading Amokye—twice. And I got us in and out of the underworld, even with that spooky dead forest calling to me. Speaking of that . . . would Asaase Yaa be able to sense the Big Feeling inside me that seems to be getting stronger by the day?

But the goddess has nothing to give me, because I was born with my powers, so I just watch as my friends receive theirs. When it's all over, the divine light fades, and, minus the wristbands, the GCCers look exactly like they did before.

The goddess pulls a pair of horn-rimmed sunglasses—bright green as opposed to her daughter's black ones—out of thin air and puts them on. "This has been absolutely lovely, but I have much to do today, starting with a photoshoot in an overgrown orchid field north of St. Mary's. If there is nothing else you need, I'll be going now. Come, fuzzy canine." Asaase Yaa crooks a finger, and a startled Dubu zips through the air toward her.

Horror floods Eunju's face. "No! You can't take him!"

She rushes for Dubu, but the goddess lifts him out of her reach. "The whole point of this mission was for you to retrieve the sword for me," says Asaase Yaa. "Now that I finally have it back, I'm not going to leave it with a bunch of children just because it currently resides within this creature."

Eunju looks broken at the thought of losing Dubu, and I can't stomach the thought of her going back to that cold, tense house of hers without him. Boulder must feel me stiffen, because he hisses up at me, "What did I tell you about bargaining with a god?"

Ignoring him, I turn to Asaase Yaa. "But surely you have far more important things to worry about than one mangy dog?"

Mateo is the first to realize what I'm trying to do, and quickly jumps in. "You are clearly the most p-p-powerful of the gods, and you already have enough on your p-p-plate. Let us take care of him for you. That way you won't have to worry about a creature so far b-b-beneath you."

The goddess narrows her eyes, and I can't tell if we've just made things better or worse.

"Plus, you're already so busy creating content for your wonderful channel," Gavin adds. "Why split your energy when you don't have to?"

Asaase Yaa practically puffs up from his compliment. "Being a globally successful influencer *does* take an enormous amount of my time. . . ."

Roxy seals the deal by looking down at her feet, every bit the traditional humble Ghanaian girl. "All we want is to serve you as best we can, Mother Earth. It would be the greatest honor of our lives to handle this task for you."

Okay, now she's laying it on a bit thick if you ask me.

The goddess eyes us each suspiciously, then sighs. "Fine, you may keep the creature! But I reserve the right to call on him at any time."

Eunju lets out a strangled cry of relief, and the rest of us all grin. For once, a deity's massive ego actually came in handy.

Asaase Yaa takes one last sweeping glance, not so much at us or Sweetieville, but at the vast forest that stretches beyond. "Take care of yourselves, and more importantly, this land, little ones. It has been through so much pain and heartache already."

That piques my interest, bringing to mind everything Auntie Latricia told me about Harristown Manor and the dark history of Rocky Gorge. "Did something happen here a long time ago? Something that affected the rules of magic in this town?"

There's a long silence before Asaase Yaa says, "The land always knows. Only when you are ready to listen will you hear."

With that uber-cryptic message, the goddess vanishes, leaving both Dubu and the scent of lilacs behind.

Eunju throws her arms around her dog's neck. "Thank you guys so, so much," she sniffs. "Without Dubu I'd . . . I just froze."

"Don't worry about it," says Gavin.

"What are friends for, right?" adds Mateo, giving Dubu a pat on the head.

We all pause at that. This is the first time any one of us has used the word *friends* to describe us. After our trip to Asamando and my impromptu birthday party last night, it doesn't chafe like before.

"Yeah . . . that's what friends are for," I echo. I clap my hands before anyone suggests we start hugging it out. "But okay, the day isn't getting any longer. We still have an adze to defeat. Right, Boulder?"

"This is still an awful idea, and personally, I think we'd be better off returning to Eunju's to finish off that cake."

Moving right along. "We need to figure out exactly how your blessings from Asaase Yaa are going to help us," I say to my Slayers-in-training. "Do you feel any different?"

The other four shake their heads. Gavin starts pinching his wristband and then his own cheeks. "Maybe our powers only activate when we're in danger?" he guesses. "Quick, Eunju— punch me in the face!"

Eunju balks. "I'm not going to punch you in the face!"

"Why not? You're always threatening to! We need to test if I can still feel pain."

"Slayers can still feel p—" I begin, but I don't get it out fast enough to stop Eunju from ramming her fist into Gavin's chin. He crumples to the ground with a groan.

"Okay, that idea was stupid. Nobody else test that idea," he moans as Eunju guiltily helps him back to his feet.

"Maybe it's like Sailor Moon, and we have to say a special phrase to transform?" offers Roxy.

Boulder shakes his head. "In all my years, I've never heard of a Slayer needing to chant or transform to access an elemental blessing. The wristbands should work as permanent Adinkra, giving you the ability to harness a specific element via divine wisdom as long as you're wearing them."

I turn to Mateo, but he has his head bent back in the universal expression of someone trying to hold back a sneeze.

"M-maybe it's—it's—ACHOO!"

Mateo's sneeze blasts all of us off our feet. He flies thirty feet backward, creating a boy-shaped hole in the worm-eaten wooden wall of Marshmallow Mountain. I'm the first one up, and I race through the cloud of dust to pull him out of the rubble.

"I think my p-power's here," he says, still dazed, his yellow wristband lighting up against his arm.

No force on earth can stop the grin that's spreading across my face.

All right, *now* we're talking.

26

How to Fight Like a Slayer

"A good battle is like a dance. Know your particular rhythm as a fighter, for each person's is as different as each star in the sky."

—From the *Nwoma*

WE DECIDE TO TEST Eunju's new abilities first, because she's the most battle-adept person in the group (behind me, of course). I put her up against Veterinarian Barbie, and the rest of us—including Dubu—stand off to the side while Eunju and her opponent circle each other on the commons. Eunju's got a practice sword in her hand—it's clearly her preferred choice of weapon, and after seeing her performance against Pointy, I can't imagine anything better to fit her brutal fighting style.

"Remember, timing and distance are key!" I yell out, hoping my voice doesn't betray my nerves. This moment will decide if everything I've—*we've*—been through over the past week has been worth it.

Boulder holds up the iPad, making sure Eunju sees the timer. "Start on my count. Three. Two. One—"

Eunju leaps before Boulder even says go. The jump sends her hurtling toward the doll, the divine wisdom in her body amplifying her movements like it does for my parents and me. She goes straight for a forward thrust, but Veterinarian Barbie meets her with a middle block, then pushes her off-balance with a diagonal cut. Eunju stumbles back, her right side wide open, and VB takes advantage of her moment of weakness to swing a horizontal swipe straight for Eunju's chest. My stomach sinks. Oh gods, she's still not ready for real battle.

But right as the sword is about to make contact, Eunju's divine wisdom–enhanced instincts kick in. She leaps back and uses her momentum to deliver an upper kick to the doll's chin. It would be a dirty move in a tournament, but battling an adze isn't about fighting fair. It's about fighting to survive.

The kick sends Veterinarian Barbie's head spinning one hundred and eighty degrees. You'd think the fact the doll can now look at her own butt would slow her down, but she only stumbles for an instant before she's back on the offensive. Eunju meets her in the middle, their blades locked in an intricate dance of strike, parry, feint, and strike.

Mateo, Roxy, and I all hold our breaths while Gavin watches the fight with his eyebrows drawn together. "Come on, Eunju, come on," he mutters so softly I don't think he even realizes he's talking out loud.

And then something in the battle shifts. Eunju's wristband goes bright, and she drags her practice sword against the ground like she's striking a match. The air around us grows warmer, and fire sparks to life along the metal of her blade. With a cry, Eunju sweeps in close and slices her flaming weapon vertically down the doll's head. It cuts clean through Veterinarian Barbie's body, her two halves falling away in perfect symmetry.

Panting, Eunju straightens up. Sweat slicks her black bangs to her forehead. "Time!" she calls to Boulder.

He stops the timer. "Three minutes, forty-six point two seconds!"

She turns to the four of us, who are all staring with our mouths open. "How'd I do?"

I stammer, "Um . . . that was—"

"WICKED COOL!" screams Roxy, and a flush spreads across Eunju's face as Mateo, Roxy, and Gavin fawn over her and the fire sword.

Gavin practically shoves everyone out of the way to be the one who fights next. I hand him the staff, and he nods gratefully before sauntering onto the commons and pulling his blue twists into a short ponytail. "Okay, flaming swords are aight, but wait till you see this," he says, rolling his shoulders.

Since Veterinarian Barbie is out of commission, he's up against the graduation doll. Even after Boulder announces the official start of the duel, the two foes continue to circle, each waiting for the other to make the first move.

Gavin's patience wins out, and Graduation Barbie finally moves within his range. It quickly becomes clear that while Eunju's divine wisdom amplified her already impressive strength, Gavin's increased his speed. He's behind the doll in the blink of an eye, twirling his staff in a double-handed spin followed by a cross strike. He skips out of the way of GB's staff, keeping his footwork light and bouncy just like my mom would tell him to do if she were here.

But though Gavin's combos fly almost faster than we can see, he makes the mistake of underestimating his opponent's reach. He lets Graduation Barbie get too close, and there isn't enough space for him to block before she sweeps his legs out from under him. He goes down hard, rolling onto his side to avoid a strike to the face. Eunju's grip tightens around the hilt of her sword, like she's ready to jump in there and help him, but she doesn't. She knows he has to do this on his own.

Graduation Barbie disarms Gavin quickly, and he can't retrieve his weapon with the barrage of strikes she rains down on him. Snarling, he grabs her staff with one hand when it comes toward his face and then thrusts his other in her direction with his wristband throwing blue light. Water shoots from the ground in a plume that engulfs Graduation Barbie, giving Gavin a chance to get up and away from her clutches. The water recedes, leaving behind cuffs of ice around the doll's ankles. While she struggles to free herself, Gavin picks up his staff and strikes forward with it, stopping only an inch from his opponent's throat. A clear winning blow.

"Time, Boulder!" he yells.

"Four minutes, fifteen seconds!" the mmoatia yells back.

Gavin whoops. He bounds over to Eunju, his staff balanced on his shoulders. "So, how'd I do?" he asks in a singsong voice.

She sniffs and looks away. "It was all right," she says haughtily, and the rest of us share affectionate eye rolls.

Mateo loses the rock paper scissors game to Roxy, so he's up next. He moves toward one of the swords, but I stop him. "Between Eunju, Gavin, and me, we have enough people focused on close-combat weapons. We could use some long-range defense." I hold up the bow and arrow set I used during my demonstration on our first day of training. "Why don't you try archery? I've been watching you, and I think you'd be great at it."

Mateo blinks at me, and I realize too late how that must have sounded. Heat rushing to my face, I shove the quiver at him. "Not that I've been watching *you* specifically. I watch everyone—but not like a stalker or anything! I mean, just get out there!"

Since Mateo is fighting with a bow, Pilot Barbie knows that

the secret to overwhelming him will be staying within close range at all times. As soon as Boulder yells *go*, the doll rushes into his orbit, and Mateo wisely leaps back. His wristband glows and his wind blessing kicks in, launching him high into the air. From there, he uses the vantage point to fire two arrows in quick succession.

One hits Pilot Barbie in the chest, and the other goes into her leg, but that isn't enough to slow her down. Mateo is forced to land, having not mastered his blessing enough to remain airborne for long. Pilot Barbie is waiting for him, and he doesn't have time to catch his breath before her sword is slashing toward him in a forward strike. He uses both hands to raise his bow in a block, then kicks her legs out from under her. However, Pilot Barbie pulls him down with her, and they go rolling through the grass as dirt, rocks, and sticks go flying into the air.

From there, Mateo relies on a lot of hand-to-hand combat, causing more debris to dislodge around him. Those of us on the sidelines look at each other with concern. Why isn't he using his magic?

"Uh hey, Mateo, buddy, you know you can do the wind thing, right?" Gavin calls out.

After pushing Pilot Barbie away with an uppercut to the chin, Mateo backs up and points skyward.

We all crane our necks to see the rocks, branches, dirt, and other debris that Mateo intentionally kicked up in his scuffle floating above Pilot Barbie's head.

Mateo clenches his fist, and it all comes raining down on her like a hundred tiny missiles. The doll goes down, buried beneath the earth weaponized via the sky, and doesn't come back up.

His time? Four minutes, eight seconds.

"Not bad," I say, punching him in the shoulder when he goes by, which earns me the sight of his ears going red.

We're out of Barbies by the time it's Roxy's turn, so she's up against her bright yellow teddy bear, Mr. Pretty. I spread out the weapons before her, and she gravitates toward the spear. I lift an eyebrow. "Getting real traditional, huh, Aba?" I tease, using her day name.

She shrugs as she tests the spear's weight. "Somebody needs to rep the motherland."

Mateo, Gavin, Eunju, and I all hold our breath as Roxy shifts into a defensive stance in front of Mr. Pretty. Her eyes narrow, then widen.

Roxy straightens up, drops her spear, then stands stock-still with her eyes closed and cheeks puffed out like she's concentrating real hard.

"What is she d-d-doing?" Mateo wonders aloud.

"She looks like she's taking a poop," snorts Eunju.

"Hey, Roxy, you taking a poop?" calls Gavin.

My cousin's eyes fly open with annoyance. "I was *trying* to see if I could connect to the ghosts in Asamando, but clearly I can't. How about this instead?"

Roxy closes her eyes once more and lifts up her hands, her wristband pulsing with green light. A tremor courses through the earth, and flowering vines explode from beneath the commons to wrap around Mr. Pretty. The teddy bear struggles to break free, but Roxy's magic is merciless. The flora winds itself around every limb until there is nothing but a giant green ball of vines and rainbow petals where the toy once stood.

Roxy bounces on her feet. "Does this count?" she asks excitedly.

We all stare at the floral cocoon that was once Mr. Pretty.

"Y-yeah," I say with a gulp. "It counts."

That's the last time I'll ever underestimate flower power.

THE ELEMENTAL BLESSINGS HELP everyone a lot, but there are still the finer points of combat and magic they can only learn from someone with experience in both. I help them all hone their techniques until sundown, which was when we all promised our respective families we'd be back from our sleepover. By the end of the day everyone is sweaty and dusty, but they're looking a little less like a bunch of randos I plucked off the street and more like the highly trained Slayers I need them to be.

As the others pack to leave, I turn to Boulder, who has been taking notes on the iPad to track everyone's progress. "What do you think?" I whisper.

The mmoatia huffs, his lips twitching up only a fraction, which is basically the Boulder equivalent of breaking into a huge grin. "I think that perhaps this plan of yours might not fail after all and that you are a better teacher than we first thought."

That tiny bit of praise feels better than all the divine wisdom in the world.

27

How to Get Caught

*"One can do everything right and
still have their plans go awry."*

—From the *Nwoma*

THE GCCERS SPEND THE next three days honing
their new abilities under my supervision. During school
hours, in those rare times when we're not distracted
by classwork or planning the mural, we keep our eyes
peeled for the adze. In the evenings, I teach them all I
know about fighting, magic, and everything in between.

Gradually, each one begins to get their respective
power under control. The first time Gavin manages to
turn a bowl of water from liquid to mist to ice, we all
cheer. We cheer even louder when Mateo uses his new
wind-enhanced senses to hit dead center on a target
while blindfolded. Eunju continues to fight just like she
does everything else—headfirst and forcefully, not stopping or slowing for anyone or anything. She's woven
fire into her technique, so when she's on the battlefield
she's basically a living inferno. More than anyone, the
way she fights reminds me of my mom, which is the
best compliment anyone could receive ever.

And Roxy. Though she decides to keep the spear for symbolic reasons, she's still more comfortable using her plant magic and Adinkra to fight. It only takes her two days to memorize the one hundred and ten base Adinkra that Slayers use, and by the end of the third, she's making up spell combos I never even thought of. She even got the idea of drawing Adinkra onto clear stickers so we always have some with us in case we're ever again in a situation where we can't draw anything, like when we fought Pointy.

If I'm being honest, she's . . . better at the Adinkra than I am. Not that I'm jealous or anything. So what if it took her less than a month to master something I still haven't in more than a decade of training? It's fine. It's cool.

Really.

However, though our training progress is going amazingly, our *figure out who at our school is a bloodsucking nightmare creature* progress has hit a snag. And by snag, I mean the trail has gone ice-cold. The adze hasn't shown itself since it attacked us while we were picking up trash, and I can't find any evidence that it has destroyed anything since the generator fire. None of the wards I drew around the grounds has been triggered, though I secretly doubted they'd work when the ones at my lake house didn't, either.

I've been watching both Mrs. Dean, because she's super shady, and Mr. Riley, because he's basically walking vampire bait. Nothing. It feels like we're in a cat-and-mouse game with the adze now, but I'm not sure which side is the cat and which is the mouse. For all we know our vampire has already left the town to find its next meal. But something—Slayer's intuition, maybe, or paranoia, or a mix of both—tells me it's hunting us just as much as we're hunting it.

Now it's Thursday, exactly two weeks since Boahinmaa destroyed my house and one day before Back-to-School Night.

The school has completely transformed for the event, with work crews coming in this week to hang streamers from the ceiling and glittering white paper lanterns from the windows. Every space has been polished to a T, and even Mr. Riley has managed some semblance of order from that chaos he calls an art room.

In homeroom and first period, I try to come up with a plan to lure the vampire out of hiding. All I want to do is brainstorm with Eunju and Mateo, since we all share a cluster, but I can't risk it with Ashley right there, too. Besides, even though Eunju is a lot nicer to me at school now, she still gets aloof whenever her best friend is around. I'm not going to force her to choose between Ashley or the GCC, but I wish it didn't have to be a choice.

The bell rings, but before anyone can leave for their next class, Mrs. Dean calls out, "Where is my paperweight?"

When no one responds, she motions for Mateo to close the door. We all give each other nervous looks as she says, "My glass bird paperweight, the one that usually sits on my desk. I know it was here when I arrived this morning, and this is my first class of the day. If the person who took it does not come forward right now, the entire class will face disciplinary action."

Shouts of protest ring through the room, and still no one confesses. I slump back in my seat with a groan as Mrs. Dean starts going from desk to desk demanding that each person empty their backpack for her. Honestly, who would even steal a paperweight, anyway? A rock would do the job just as well.

A flash of reflected light from beneath my desk catches my eye. I reach down and my stomach drops about eight thousand miles when I feel something poking out of the front pocket of my backpack. Something cold and hard and definitely bird shaped.

Mrs. Dean's paperweight is in my bag.

I snatch my hand back, hoping no one noticed. How did it

get there? And when? If only Boulder was here—he would've alerted me the moment it happened. But ever since our adze search hit a stall, he's started hanging out in my locker to see if he can catch any hint of the vampire while the rest of us are in class.

Across the table, Ashley gives me a sweet smile that anyone who doesn't know her might think is nice. "Something wrong, Serwa?"

"Nothing," I snap, even though everything is wrong. I'm already on thin ice at this school after the food fight and the cheating accusation. Another strike and they'll expel me for real.

"You sure? You look kind of tense."

I clamp my lips shut, refusing to let her goad me into saying something I know I'll regret.

Mateo opens his mouth like he's about to come to my defense, but Eunju beats him to it.

"Lay off her, Ash. Serwa wouldn't do something like that," she snaps.

The words themselves aren't harsh, but her tone very much is. Ashley's astonishment is hilarious—I'm willing to bet my good crossbow this is the first time Eunju has ever pushed back at her about anything, and Ashley literally does not know how to react. Eunju nods once at me before fiddling with her wristband. Luckily, when it's not glowing, it's indistinguishable from a non-magic accessory. I nod back with gratitude, then return my attention to the fact that it very much looks like I stole this stupid thing.

There's only one option: I've got to get rid of the bird. But just as I grab a marker to draw a concealment spell around the paperweight, Mrs. Dean pops up behind me.

"Open your bag, Sarah," she says, and with those four words, I know it's all over.

Heat rising to my face, I put down the marker and hand her my backpack.

BY THIS POINT, IT feels like I've seen Principal Hashimoto more often than some of my actual teachers. She's staring at me sternly as Mrs. Dean describes how I've been causing problems in her classroom since the day I arrived. When Mrs. Dean finally finishes her rant about my uncooperative, disruptive, and combative nature, the principal asks, "And what do you have to say for yourself, Ms. Boateng?"

That y'all have way bigger problems than me to worry about, like the literal vampire roaming your halls! I want to scream, but there's no use. I bet even if they saw the adze for themselves, they still wouldn't believe me. Mrs. Dean and Principal Hashimoto already have an idea about who I am and what I'm like, and nothing I say or do could ever change their minds. To them, I'll always be nothing more than a problem that needs solving.

"I didn't do it," I choke out, hating how small my voice feels.

"Did you see anyone come near your bag?"

I shake my head.

Principal Hashimoto sighs. "I don't like meting out punishment without solid proof, but it is concerning that this is your third incident report in less than two weeks. Here at Rocky Gorge Middle School, we pride ourselves on our values of high achievement and distinguished behavior. So far, you have not been living up to them."

Tears burn at the back of my eyes. How is it that I can face down entire teams of monsters without even flinching, but her words cut deeper than Asaase Yaa's sword?

She continues. "Because we can't rule out the possibility that another student put the paperweight in the bag to try to frame you, I will reduce your punishment from an expulsion to a suspension."

Mrs. Dean puckers her lips. "Surely you can do more than that?"

"I'm afraid I can't, not without solid, indisputable proof that she took your item."

"Will the suspension at least extend to extracurricular activities, including Back-to-School Night?"

"Yes, it will extend to Back-to-School Night as well."

Back-to-School Night? Why does she care so much about me missing that, of all things?

I call on every scrap of courage inside me to say, "Principal Hashimoto, with all due respect, I feel like I'm being unfairly targeted."

Even though I was speaking to the principal, Mrs. Dean lets out an offended gasp.

"Are you accusing me of being racist?" she shrieks. I didn't say that, but the fact that's what she heard speaks volumes. "Never in my life . . . I have been a tireless champion of diversity and creating opportunities for minorities. I chose Mr. Alvarez as our classroom monitor! How dare you call me racist?!"

"Please relax, Alma. No one here is questioning your commitment to diversity."

You can practically see the steam coming out of Mrs. Dean's ears. I have to bite the inside of my cheek to keep from spitting at her. Mateo might be one of the nicest people I know, but I'm pretty sure even he wouldn't be okay with her using him as a shield, as if being nice to one person of color erases any bad thing you do to another.

Frustration flares up within me, as does the Big Feeling. "This isn't fair!" I cry, banging my fist on the principal's desk.

A hole splinters in the desk where my hand makes contact with the wood. All three of us flinch back in horror. What the—? Was that magic? But I didn't even draw an Adinkra!

"I—I didn't mean to—!" I stammer, but the damage is done. With that one action, my fate is sealed, and my suspension is extended into next week.

Principal Hashimoto finally lets us go, and then it's just me and Mrs. Dean alone in the front office waiting for Auntie Latricia to come pick me up. I don't know where the front office lady went—restroom, maybe—but without her there, the air is downright frosty. I inch toward one of the chairs to sit down, but Mrs. Dean moves in front of me before I can.

"You can play innocent all you want, Sarah," she hisses, "but I know what you really are."

Suddenly it feels like all the oxygen's been sucked out of the room. She knows I'm a Slayer? How?

Mrs. Dean steps forward until my back is against the wall, leaving me nowhere to go. She's so close I can count each of the gray hairs sprouting out of her wrinkly nose.

"You think you can just show up at this school and behave however you want. But we have rules here. And order. Traditions that someone like you can't break."

There's no window in the door to Principal Hashimoto's office, and the front-desk lady still isn't back. No one's here to witness Mrs. Dean looming over me like a vulture.

"This will be your third and final warning, Sarah. Fall in line or see what happens when I am truly angered."

I want to fight back. I want to do something, anything, but I'm frozen in place as Mrs. Dean swoops off to her next class.

The front office lady returns to find me shaking in my seat, and she gives me a sympathetic look. She probably thinks I'm just nervous because of my upcoming suspension. A dark, inky pressure builds in my chest, and not even rubbing the back of my ear can make it go away.

Mrs. Dean knows. She *knows*.

I'm still sitting there in shock waiting for Auntie Latricia when Mr. Riley enters the front office. He flashes the secretary a cheery smile. "Morning, Penny. Hope you and the kids are doing well. Timmy just started fifth grade, right? They grow so fast!" He gestures toward me. "I heard about the . . . incident this morning with Serwa. You know that initiative I've been doing with her and a few other students, the Good Citizens Committee? Serwa has left a few belongings at the mural site she needs to pick up before she leaves the premises."

What in the name of Nyame is he talking about? All my stuff (and Boulder) is currently in my locker.

But Miss Penny buys his story, and minutes later I'm behind the school, walking toward the mural. It's 80 percent done now, and honestly looking really cool. With Mr. Riley's help, the other four GCCers have transformed their ideas into vibrant designs, their hearts laid bare through art.

Mateo drew the beach he grew up on in California, complete with a crashing surf and bustling tourists, while Gavin painted a portrait of two men who must be his foster dads. Eunju's section is a simple collage of symbols that make up her life—Dubu, the spaceship from Battlestar Dimensions, the South Korean flag, and lines of code that are meant to represent her parents' work. And Roxy went full abstract, blooming shapes and bright splashes of color that you only realize after a second look are flowers growing out of a skull.

At first, each section seems so different from the others that there's no way it should make one coherent image. But further inspection reveals the way each piece feeds into the next—Gavin's colors repeat in Roxy's, and the boardwalk in Mateo's section effortlessly folds into Eunju's collage.

It's a little chaotic and a whole lot messy, but somehow, it works.

Kind of like us.

The bare 20 percent is, of course, my section, which we were planning to tackle today during sixth period. But now the mural will never get finished in time for Back-to-School Night, and it's all my fault because the Powers That Be have dictated there's no place for me in this school after all.

As I stare at the unfinished mural, the Big Feeling returns with a vengeance. It drowns me from the inside out, and suddenly the world is too big and too loud. A choked sob escapes my lips, and now I'm running. I'm running, and I don't know where I'm going. I don't even care that this is basically guaranteed to make my suspension even worse. I can't be here anymore. I can't do this.

My legs carry me away from the wall and back into the forest where Bullseye attacked my friends and me on the second day of school. I don't stop until I'm deep in the woods near the stream. There I double over, hands on my knees and tears running down my face. My arm throbs with a cut from one of the branches I crashed through during my mad dash.

Mrs. Dean was right—I've caused nothing but trouble for everyone since the day I arrived. I'm the reason the mural isn't going to get finished in time for Back-to-School Night, and the reason Aunt Latricia is going to have to take precious time off she can't afford to lose in order to pick me up early.

I haven't even caught the adze at our school yet. I've failed the number one, most important job of being a Slayer. No wonder my parents left me behind and refuse to let me take the Initiation Test. I'm not like them and never will be.

And the Big Feeling. No matter how hard I try to fight it, it's always lurking beneath my skin, destroying every inch of progress I try to make. It churns inside me now, and if it could speak, I'm sure it'd be saying the same phrase over and over again.

Not good enough. Not good enough. Not good enough.

If my parents were here, they'd tell me to lift my head up. Maybe recite a line from the *Nwoma* about how a Slayer never, ever gives in to despair.

But they're not here and I'm not a Slayer. Not really.

So there, with no one but the trees and the stream and the sky to hear, I let out every emotion I've been holding in since Boahinmaa's attack.

And I cry.

And cry.

And cry.

IT FEELS LIKE I'VE been sobbing in the woods behind the school for hours, but it can't have been more than ten minutes. I need to head back to the front office before they assume I came out here to set a fire or whatever other delinquent activity they're convinced I do.

Just like I suspected, there was nothing of mine by the mural or anywhere near it. But Mr. Riley was very specific about me going behind the school. Why? One theory is he wanted me all alone so he could attack me. . . . No, I know for a fact he's not the adze. But what other reason would he have to interfere with my suspension like this?

I wipe the tears from my face with a dirt-streaked sleeve, steeling myself to return, when I catch sight of the clock tower looming over the trees like a beacon. The same clock tower that stood on the plantation. Everything about the mystery of the adze and the wonky magic in this town keeps coming back to the school— or rather, what the school was more than a century ago.

Something magical happened at Harristown Manor, something that is still affecting this town all these decades later. Auntie Latricia's comments about a witch in her family line, the adze's fascination with the book on Rocky Gorge's history, the fact that there were likely descendants of the Abomofuo among the enslaved population in this town . . . I just know it's all connected, but the *how* refuses to reveal itself. I need answers, but the people who lived this history are long gone, and the ones who should have protected it hid it instead.

The Big Feeling is still roiling in my stomach, but instead of dwelling on that, I focus on the thing that keeps me rooted to the spot—not my divine wisdom but my own stubbornness, which refuses to let me give up when I've come so far. I sweep my eyes around the clearing, once again searching for any clues I've missed.

My gaze lands on the stream. It's hardly more than a trickle, and yet it's flowing, even out here where nobody can see it. As I stare at that tiny sparkle of water, an idea blooms in my mind.

Tano, Bia, Antoa, and so many other gods—all of them draw their power from rivers that people worship in Ghana.

And what's a stream? A very small river.

I crouch beside the water and draw a single Adinkra with my finger in the mud—a bird with its neck twisted so that its head faces its back. Sankofa, the Adinkra of remembrance. I press my palms flat against the earth, hands glowing with divine wisdom as I search for . . . I don't know what, honestly. Something alive, some presence in this water watching over everything that's happened in this town.

All I get is dirt under my fingernails. I'm starting to feel more than a little silly, but I can't give up yet. I draw forth every good memory I've made in this town and push those feelings into my palms.

I think about walking with Mateo under a starry sky while the rest of the town slept.

I think about the pride I felt when Gavin overcame his fear of sharp objects to help capture Asaase Yaa's sword.

I think about how Eunju's eyes lit up when she talked about her favorite movies, giving me the first glimpse of the girl she tries so hard to hide from the world.

I think about how Auntie Latricia and Roxy have been reaching out to me from the day I arrived, standing by my side before I even realized I needed the support.

I think about myself. All the things I've done since coming to Rocky Gorge and still want to do.

And that's when I sense it—a fluttering heartbeat that tells me this place is alive, just like my ancestors must have felt the first time they prayed to their rivers.

Asaase Yaa's words return to me: *The land always knows. Only when you are ready to listen will you hear.*

"Please," I ask with the same reverence I used when I called on Asaase Yaa. "I'm ready to listen."

The land breathes beneath my fingers, and I breathe along with it. Just like that, the river answers my plea, and I find myself deep inside a memory.

28

How to Learn the Truth

*"It is only through remembering the past that
one knows how to head for the future."*

—From the *Nwoma*

I'M IN ROCKY GORGE, yet I'm not. This is the town
as it was back in the 1800s, and though the trees are the
same, the air itself feels different—lighter and crisper, as
if in my time it had grown heavy over the years from
all the secrets it had to hide. I'm standing next to the
stream behind the school, except it's not a stream anymore—it is (was?) a mighty river, winding through the
trees in powerful, white-foamed rapids that shake the
ground beneath my feet.

The sky is so bright that at first I think it's daytime,
but wait. . . . That's not sunlight. That's fire—flames
burning against a nighttime sky. Thick plumes of smoke
waft my way, and my lungs constrict instinctively even
before I can smell it.

It takes a few seconds of orienting myself before I
realize I'm not alone. A Black man maybe a decade or
so older than my dad paces on the riverbank about a
dozen feet away. He's covered in sweat and grime and

has an old-timey musket strapped to his back over his worn shirt and pants.

George Riley, the magic of the memory whispers into my head. That surname . . . I'm looking at Mr. Riley's ancestor.

George's frightened expression brightens when a second person runs into the clearing from the direction of the clock tower. She's Black, too, and surprisingly, she has her own rifle, which I know was rare for a woman back then. Judging from the way her hands grip the stock and barrel, she knows how to use it.

Agnes James, the magic whispers. *James* is Auntie Latricia's surname. This woman is Roxy's ancestor. Of all the people the river could have showed me, why these two?

George's face falls when Agnes shares the news that a militia of more than one hundred white men has been spotted at the outskirts of town. Any minute now, the army will reach the manor.

At the last word, I look up. The river brought me to the night of the Harristown Manor uprising that Auntie Latricia told me about, the one she claimed her own ancestor fought in. She said it shut down the plantation, but right here, right now, the rebels are backed into a corner with no way out.

George lets out a strangled cry that cuts straight through my chest, his body looking like it's crumpling into itself as hope leaves him. The terror in his eyes is palpable—if they lose tonight, they will die painful deaths. They'll be made examples of to discourage any other enslaved people with thoughts of rebellion. They came so far, fought so hard, for nothing.

Agnes steps forward, bright purple energy rolling off her in waves even as her hands shake around her gun.

I stifle a gasp—black magic.

Roxy's ancestor was an obayifo.

But this isn't the kind of black magic I've seen the adze or even Boahinmaa use. It's similar, like how navy and cerulean are both shades of blue yet are different from each other. But this black magic has been separated from the source for so long that it's evolved into something else.

Something new.

And power is rolling off George Riley, too, though his is bright and golden—divine wisdom. Mr. Riley's family was descended from a Slayer, but just like with Agnes, George's power has deviated in an unrecognizable way.

It shouldn't be possible, but it's true.

An obayifo and a Slayer, working together to save the only home they've ever known.

And thanks to the magic of the river, I not only see what happened but also feel Agnes's and George's emotions as if they were my own. I sense their despair when they realize, for all their magic, neither of them can take on a hundred men by themselves. Tears well in my eyes at their sorrow that they've doomed not only themselves but their respective children with their futile dream of freedom.

Then Agnes gets an idea. Though she's not sure why, she's learned over the years that her magic is always strongest next to a body of water. On their own they can only do so much, but together . . .

She leads George into the river, which starts to swirl and glow from the combined light of their powers. They want to defeat the militia, yes, but more importantly, they want to defend the people they love, make it so no one can come in and harm them ever again.

Everything I know about magic tells me their spell shouldn't work. George has no Adinkra to channel his divine wisdom.

Agnes doesn't need Adinkra, but her black magic should be too chaotic to be used in a constructive way.

But as they stand there, hand in hand, the rapids swirling around their waists, the water grows brighter. They don't need any Adinkra because the river itself acts as a conduit for their magic, melding their hopes and power together until it's a single blinding source with no beginning and no end that reaches to the far corners of the town.

My veins buzz with energy as their magic reverberates through the ground toward the manor, the site of the approaching battle. Agnes's magic targets the militia, calling upon the souls of the ancestors to drag down their wagons and horses and paralyze their weapons. George's magic bolsters the uprising's exhausted fighters, granting them temporary Slayer-level strength that allows them to fight the weakened militia even with less numbers. Though we can't see the battle from where we are, we can hear it, and through the magic of the river, all three of us feel the moment when the tide turns to the rebels' favor.

Even though I knew ahead of time that the uprising was destined to succeed, I can't help crying out in joy. They did it! They really did it.

But it's not enough. Yes, the rebels defended themselves this time, but there's hundreds—no, thousands more enemies where these came from, with the power and resources to destroy the entire town. George and Agnes won this night, but if they want their descendants to survive the war, they need a magic that'll extend far past this one battle.

Agnes is thinking of her sons, and George is thinking of his daughter, when the spell shifts. This time, instead of channeling their magic toward fighting, they focus on protection. They imagine a great cocoon surrounding all of Harristown, shielding the inhabitants—their own bloodlines in particular—from all those who'd wish them harm. Agnes and George had worked so hard to keep their respective powers secret, just like every generation before them had. They need to create a safe haven for the magic—a place where it could be secured until the time came when it had to be summoned once more.

The spell to defeat the militia shook the town, but this one feels like it shakes the world. The air around us seems to shatter and re-form in the exact same instant, the ward of protection growing to encompass the river, the forest, the entire town. The feeling I've experienced since I arrived in Rocky Gorge washes over me stronger than ever—a sense that the world here is serene and plain, that there's no reason to suspect something hiding beneath the surface. This is a veil of secrecy meant to protect rather than shun.

But this second spell pushes both George and Agnes to the edges of their magic. They're so bright, like twin gods, but the river has taken everything from them and it's still not enough. I cry out a warning, but they can't hear me. And even if they could, I know they wouldn't stop.

The obayifo and the Slayer share a single smile, both of them content in the knowledge that they did all they could to give their respective families a chance to thrive in a world where they were never meant to.

And then their bodies slip under the water as the river claims them both, and the memory quietly fades away.

29

How to Know Where You're From

"Never forget that you are all who came before you."

—From the *Nwoma*

WHEN I RETURN TO the present day, I'm on my hands and knees beside the stream, and I'm not alone. Mr. Riley is kneeling next to me.

A knowing smile stretches across his face. "I take it you saw my great-great-grandpa George, huh?"

Tears run down my cheeks. "They died," I cough out, my voice cracking on the words. "Agnes and George, they died protecting the town. I—I saw it. I *felt* it."

Mr. Riley nods, his eyes filling with sadness. He pulls a paint-stained handkerchief out of his pocket and hands it to me, then waits until I've wiped my face and calmed down a bit before he speaks again. "I remember how distraught I was when my father told me the truth about our family's powers. My own ancestor died protecting Rocky Gorge, yet the current residents won't even honor the history of this land. Too many of them want to bury the stories of the people who were enslaved on it."

"So you've had divine wisdom all along?" I ask.

Instead of answering, he gestures toward the scratch on my arm. "That looks like it hurts. May I help?"

I nod hesitantly, wondering what he's going to do. He gingerly wraps his hands around my forearm. His tattoos begin to glow, and my pain immediately begins to ease as his magic flows into me. Soon the skin on my arm is as smooth and as brown as it's always been.

I gape up at him. "But I thought only mmoatia could use healing magic!"

He shakes his head. "It's likely my family's powers began as divine wisdom—in the way you understand it—from one of our ancestors back in Africa. But when our ancestor was brought here, the magic morphed into what we needed to survive in this new environment. You saw how my grandpa George could imbue others with power. For me, it has manifested as healing. It's just like I told you on the first day of school—I rarely stay injured for long."

"Didn't you say you were from down South?"

"My mother is from South Carolina, but my father's family has lived here in Rocky Gorge since the 1700s. It's through him that I inherited the role of the Keeper, the one who ensures that the history of the null zone isn't forgotten."

The null zone. That must be the name of the spell over Rocky Gorge that prevents anyone from detecting magic within its borders. All this time I thought it was some weird magical anomaly, when it was really a sanctuary.

"So, if you still have your ancestral powers, does that mean Roxy . . . ?"

Mr. Riley nods. "The James line has always had a strong connection to the dead. However, the power within them went dormant a few generations ago. The Keepers decided that, unless it surfaces again, we shouldn't bother them. Secretly, though, I've been hoping your cousin might manifest it one day on her own."

My mind flies back to the concert in Asamando and how the ghosts literally raced to follow Roxy's command. That's what Asaase Yaa must have meant about my cousin having her own power even before she received her blessing.

"But if you knew all about magic, why haven't you stopped the adze?" I demand. "It bit you!"

"No magic user can be detected within the null zone, regardless of the kind of magic performed," says Mr. Riley. "This was meant to protect those who lived here, first after the Harristown Manor uprising and again when the town became a stop on the Underground Railroad."

He sighs. "It also means that, though I suspected the string of accidents at school were caused by black magic, I couldn't be sure until I caught the person in the act. Even then, I don't have the power to remove an adze from its host. All I can do is monitor and try to mitigate the damage whenever possible."

I almost ask him if he's ever considered contacting the Abomofuo, but I don't, because I already know the answer. Everything about the null zone goes against their rules of divine wisdom and black magic staying separate. If the Abomofuo ever learned the truth about this place, they would either dismantle the null zone or take it over for their own purposes.

My hands touch the soil beneath me, taking in all that has happened here. In less than a day, everything I thought I knew about how magic works has been flipped upside down. But instead of throwing me off, the knowledge anchors me. There's so much more to the world than I ever imagined, and I want to know everything about it.

"Why didn't you show me all this when I first arrived?" I ask.

If I'd known all this from the start, I would've approached the adze hunt very differently. Mr. Riley and I might've even caught it by now if we'd worked together.

"I didn't know if I could trust you," he says bluntly. "You arrive, and suddenly strange things start happening all over the school. At first I thought . . . Honestly, I was worried you were sent here to take apart the null zone. But after what's happened these last few days, I know I was wrong. Someone who wanted to destroy the power hiding in this town wouldn't be working so hard to protect it."

Mr. Riley extends a hand toward me. "Stand, Serwa. And thank you for all you've done trying to protect what my ancestors built."

I stare at his outstretched palm, my shame from before rearing its ugly head once more. But Mr. Riley is smiling like I've personally saved his life. It doesn't change the fact I've messed up once . . . twice . . . Okay, like a million times. But it does make me feel like my screwups aren't the most important thing about me.

I might've failed to catch the adze up until now, but the battle isn't over yet. George and Agnes didn't give up. They fought until the very end with everything they had.

And I will, too.

With one last look at the stream and all the secrets swirling within its waters, I take Mr. Riley's hand and rise to my feet.

***

WHEN WE EXIT THE forest, I see the clock tower and the school grounds in a new light. It's no longer just the place where I've been trapped for eight hours a day for the last two weeks. It's the center of everything that the ancestors of this town died to protect, a haven for everyone within, though they don't realize it.

My eyes fall on the mural, and for the first time, I don't feel panicky when I look at the blank section where my art should be. Images of all the places I've been and the people I've loved flash across my mind. Together, they form a chain—not one of bondage like what George and Agnes fought against, but one of connection, bridging me to everyone who came before and everyone who will come after. George and Agnes might not be my direct ancestors, but I'm tied to them now, too, through the sacrifice that made it possible for me to be in this town at all.

I am from everyone who has ever loved me. I am from those who fought for me centuries before I was ever born. And now that I have this knowledge, it's my turn to fight for them, too.

Memories of everything that has happened since the first day of school come roaring back—Mr. Riley passing out, the attack in the woods, Mrs. Dean's weird hatred of me. The pieces clink together one by one until it suddenly hits me why Mrs. Dean did what she did today.

And, most importantly, what I need to do to solve our vampire problem once and for all.

30

How to Hatch a Plan

"Check your plan a dozen times, and then a dozen more, and then a third dozen before you even think to act."

—From the *Nwoma*

"THE ADZE HAS POSSESSED Mrs. Dean, and she's going to make her move tomorrow during Back-to-School Night," I declare. The others look up from their milkshakes in alarm.

It's evening now, and school has been out for several hours. Auntie Latricia was way calmer about my suspension than I'd expected, and I spent the rest of the day after she picked me up reading magazines in the break room of Rocky Gorge General Hospital while she finished up her shift. Then we stopped by Auntie Francesca's store so we could pick up the ingredients needed to make a traditional Ghanaian meal of waakye, shito, fried tilapia with mako, and bofrot with powdered sugar. Roxy joined us in the kitchen when she got home from school, and the three of us had so much fun putting it all together that for a little while, things actually felt normal.

But I haven't forgotten the revelation I had back at

the river, which is why I've called this after-dinner meeting with the GCC. Though Auntie Latricia believed me when I told her that the suspension was unfair, she's still not about to let me wander off into the woods right now. So we're back at the playground—sorry, the *tot lot*—with the silence wards up, just like the first time we met outside school. The air hums with everyone's combined magic, and we're currently going to town on the milkshakes Mateo brought from the café.

"What makes you say th-that?" he asks, a spoonful of cookies and cream halfway to his mouth.

"This morning in the principal's office, Mrs. Dean was super weird about the event. Like, she made it very clear that even if they didn't suspend me, they shouldn't let me go to it," I explain. "Think about it. Back-to-School Night is one of the only times parents, students, and teachers are on the grounds at the same time. With all those people around, it won't be hard to feast on a few victims and make it look like an accident. It's practically an all-you-can-eat buffet for an adze."

Roxy nods, her own spoon dangling from her lips. "And the school is so far from the hospital that it'll take a while for anyone to get there if something bad happens."

"Bingo. Which is exactly why we're not going to let anything bad happen. Mrs. Dean thinks she's won by getting me out of the picture, but she doesn't know about the four of you."

I take in Eunju sitting cross-legged on her jacket, her favorite practice sword strapped to her hip; Gavin lying in the grass, a water bubble dancing across the fingers of the hand that's not holding his shake; Mateo looking up at me expectantly, anxiety plain on his face though he refuses to give in to it; and Roxy, her expression determined, like if the adze were here right now, she'd be the first to take a swing at it.

Before I left school today, Mr. Riley made me promise not to do anything rash about the vampire without alerting him first. I hate to break my word only a few hours later, but if he knew what I wanted to do, he'd try to stop us. I can't afford that risk.

"Mrs. Dean thinks she's setting a trap for us and all our families," I continue, "but we're going to beat her at her own game and trap *her* on Back-to-School Night instead. We're not going to let her take control of the null zone."

"What's a null zone?" Eunju asks. Shooting a quick glance at Roxy, I quickly explain everything I learned about magic in this town, the Riley and James families, and the reason the adze came here to begin with.

By the time I'm done, Mateo, Gavin, and Eunju are all wide-eyed with awe, but I only have eyes for a surprisingly blank-faced Roxy. "I know it's a lot to take in," I say slowly, "but it's all—"

"Bull!" she screams. It's the first time I've ever heard her curse or yell, and the shock of it makes me flinch. "It's all bull! You're telling me all this time my family's had magic powers and no one said anything?!"

Whoa. I don't know what reaction I expected, but it wasn't this. "I don't understand. Why aren't you excited?"

"I'd be pretty stoked to find out one of my ancestors was a witch," Gavin chimes in.

Roxy stares at us as if we've all lost our minds. "If my family's so powerful, why did we have to sell our house and move into that tiny apartment to afford my dad's legal fees? Why does my mom have to break her back working twenty-four seven at a job that doesn't pay her what she deserves? If my family's so powerful, why was I powerless to stop those officers when they came to take my dad away?!"

Roxy is full-on shouting now, and it's only thanks to the Adinkra I drew that the entire complex can't hear her breaking down.

"You wanna know the big secret? Here it is: Long before I was born, my dad came to the US and overstayed his visa. There was nothing for him back in Ghana, so he paid an American woman to marry him in order to get citizenship. He got it, and they divorced before my dad met my mom, but the woman kept demanding more and more money each year for keeping her silence. And he paid it, until a few years ago, when he couldn't afford it anymore."

A green card marriage. Everyone in the immigrant community knows about them, but they're kept hush-hush—no one wants to risk saying anything that could incriminate a loved one. My heart breaks for Roxy as I start to predict the turn this story is about to take.

"When the woman stopped getting her payments, she reported my dad to the authorities. The statute of limitations only protected her, so even though both of them broke the law, he was the one who faced the consequences. But now you're saying this whole time I could've summoned ghosts to scare the lady into not snitching or to stop the officers from taking him away?"

I'd heard about people who take advantage of the undocumented, knowing full well that immigrants can't fight the exploitation without making things worse. I'm filled with rage at this woman whose name I don't even know.

But all the anger in the world isn't going to bring Roxy's dad back.

My cousin lets out a shaky laugh. "What's the point of having all this power if you can't use it when it really counts?"

The laugh breaks into whimper. Now Roxy is crying right there in the middle of the tot lot. "It's not fair," she heaves out between sobs. "It's just not fair."

I take a step toward my cousin with the intention of comforting her, but someone else gets there first. Eunju—who I've never seen hug anyone or anything but her dog—wraps her arms around Roxy and pulls her in tight.

"I'm so sorry," says Eunju, her voice thick with tears. "For everything. All of it."

Her tone makes it clear she's apologizing for more than just what happened to Uncle Patrick. Roxy stiffens at first, but then returns the hug as she presses her face into Eunju's shoulder. When they pull apart, an understanding passes between them. I don't think it'll fix everything, but it's a start.

Roxy sniffs, then turns to me, Mateo, and Gavin. "Sorry for freaking out on you guys like that."

"You have n-n-nothing to apologize for," says Mateo as Gavin nods along. "You're right. It's n-not fair."

"Thank you," she says with another sniff, "for not judging him."

"We would never do that," I reassure her.

"Most people do. All they hear is 'deported,' and suddenly it's like he isn't a person at all."

"That's because most people are jerks."

My parents and I have struggled so hard to adjust in America, even with all the right papers and forms and privileges. I never want to hear any opinion about what immigrants do to survive in this country from people who don't know what it takes to pick up your entire life and go somewhere where you're resented.

I put my hand on Roxy's shoulder. "I'm sorry about what

happened to your dad. But you're not powerless. You've never been. And you couldn't help him, but it's not too late to save other people who need you. I think that's the real power, even more than the magic—no matter how bad things get, you always have another chance."

Roxy looks up at me, and a determination just like her ancestor's flashes in her eyes. "Let's get this vampire," she says.

My chest swells with pride. I wait a minute for the air to clear, then open my backpack and say into it, "Boulder, can you bring out the map of the school?" He crawls out, yawning, and hands me the rolled-up blueprints, which I spread on the ground.

I try to suppress a grin. This is the most exciting part of any hunt—that moment when your ideas turn into action.

"As soon as Mrs. Dean senses trouble, she'll slip back into her firefly form, which makes her indestructible and almost impossible to catch. But if we can trap her in an enclosed space, she'll be forced to return to her more vulnerable human form. We can remove the adze in her then."

Mateo gnaws his bottom lip. "You're sure it's Mrs. D-Dean? I had her last year, too, and, and she's never b-b-been that b-b-bad."

Gavin snorts. "That's how people like her always play it." His voice goes high in a bad imitation of the teacher as he waves his straw around. "'Oh, woe is me, how can I be racist when I'm nice to the Latino kid with the stutter?'"

Mateo's face falls. "Is th-th-that all I am to you?" he asks softly. "Th-the Latino k-k-kid with the st-stutter?"

The rest of us squirm awkwardly as Gavin cringes with remorse. "Oh no, I didn't—sorry. I was speaking for her, not me. But I shouldn't have said that."

Mateo still looks hurt, so I jump in, "I think what Gavin was trying to say is that a lot of times people will use being nice to one person of color as a shield to get away with being awful to others. I know you want to see the best in everyone, but you don't deserve to be used like that."

Roxy nods. "And no offense to you or Eunju, really, but you two aren't Black. There's stuff people say and do to me, Serwa, and Gavin that they'd never say or do to you guys."

Mateo and Eunju nod slowly, and I appreciate that they're sitting with Roxy's words rather than rushing to argue. It's an awkward conversation, and not nearly as fun as talking about magic or battle strategy, but I'm glad we're having it. If you can't get real with your friends, are you really friends at all?

I tap the gym with my finger. "We're going to split up. Roxy, Gavin, you two will cause a distraction that gets everyone as far from the gym as possible. Mateo, Eunju, you're in charge of securing the gym office. For this to work, every door, window, even the vents need to be covered. There can't be a single crack for the adze to escape through."

"But where will you be?" asks Gavin, and now my nerves start kicking in.

I take a deep breath. "I'm the bait. I'll lure Mrs. Dean into the gym and keep her distracted until you all get everyone to safety and we can face her together."

The movies make it seem like a hero going up against a villain all by themselves is this supercool, amazing thing. But right now, the thought of being alone with an adze makes me want to throw up. Every Slayer is trained to fight one-on-one if needed, but even my mom doesn't like to go into direct confrontation without someone guarding her back.

But we don't have a choice. Boulder confirms this by adding, "Serwa ran the plan by me on the way over here, and I agree it is your best chance of neutralizing the adze with minimal witnesses . . . or casualties."

"Are you sure you'll be all right?" Eunju asks me, and I force my face into the *I've totally got this* leader expression my friends need from me right now.

"Of course I will. Don't forget, I've been fighting adze longer than you four have known how to read."

That smooths the worried looks from their faces. We spend the next hour fleshing out where everyone needs to be and when. Once we all know our roles backward and forward, Roxy leans back against the riding elephant and sighs. The grass around her visibly wilts at her sorrow. "Don't get me wrong, I'm glad we're finally going to catch this thing, but I'm a little sad that this is going to be over soon."

We all know what *this* means—all the time we've been spending together, the late nights and early mornings spent pushing one another to be the best Slayers possible. When we started training, I had no idea I'd get so used to being around these four. Now that the end is near, the thought of only bumping into them in the halls bums me out more than I thought it would.

Surprisingly, Eunju speaks up. "It doesn't have to be the end if we don't want it to be."

It's so unlike her usual tough-girl image that we all stare. Gavin pokes her in the shoulder. "You getting soft on us, Kim?"

Eunju goes bright red. "N-no! I just meant . . . who's to say there aren't more adze lurking in the town, or some other monsters we haven't even heard of? Even after we deal with Mrs. Dean, we should keep training, just to protect ourselves."

Now Roxy pushes up on Eunju's other side. "Oh my gosh, admit it. You *like* hanging out with us, don't you?"

"That's not—!"

"Eunju likes us! Eunju likes us!" Roxy and Gavin start singing in unison, and at this point Eunju is redder than a tomato. Mateo and I join in, and I wish we could stay like this forever, just the five of us ready to face down whatever the world tries to throw our way.

But a glare from Boulder slams me back to reality with one crucial fact I let myself forget: There is no *after* for this group, because as soon as we have the adze under control, I'll have to wipe their memories for their own safety.

That means no more training sessions at Sweetieville. No more talking strategy during sixth period, no more impromptu birthday parties like the normal kid I've never been. They're not even gone yet, but suddenly I miss my friends so strongly my voice cracks as I say, "A-all right. Hands in, everybody."

We stack our hands on top of one another's. "Okay, on three, 'Let's get this bug,'" I say. "One, two—"

"Wait, do you mean on three itself, or after three?" Gavin cuts in.

"Literally everyone does after three!"

"I don't!" exclaims Roxy.

"Neither d-d-do I!" Mateo chimes in.

Eunju pulls a face. "Why would you—?"

"Let's get this bug!" I yell, and the others join in at different times, and it's all completely wrong, and somehow, it's absolutely perfect.

31

How to Catch an Adze

*"When the moment to strike comes,
take it—no matter the cost."*

—From the *Nwoma*

LIKE MOST THINGS IN Rocky Gorge, Back-to-School Night is super extra for no good reason. It's only six p.m. on Friday, and already the parking lot is full of fancy cars. The parents act like they're on the red carpet when they walk up the front steps, and they stroll through the halls oohing and ahhing at all the student art and dioramas on display as the lights from the decorations sparkle over their faces. There's something weird about seeing your classmates with their families. It's like you've only ever known them as black-and-white sketches, and now that they're with the people who raised them, they're in full color for the first time.

The only thing missing is the GCC's mural. The staff hung a canvas cloth over the unfinished painting, since that's the kind of school this is—they'd rather cover up something they feel isn't good enough than risk anyone thinking that everything here isn't perfect.

Since I'm still technically (and unfairly) suspended

from school grounds until Monday, I had to sneak in the back way, through delivery doors to the cafeteria's kitchen, where caterers were so busy getting appetizers ready no one noticed me slip through. From there, I used my evasion tactics and knowledge of the school's camera systems to get to the main office unseen.

I burst in on a surprised Principal Hashimoto putting on some lipstick.

"Serwa! I thought I told you—"

That's all she could get out before I jabbed a pressure point on her neck with my thumb. Her lipstick tube fell from her hand, and her knees buckled as she passed out. Fortunately, I was there to catch her and ease her down to the floor.

"Sorry, nothing personal," I whispered as I dragged her limp body behind her desk. I propped her up against the wall and drew a deep sleep plus mind wipe combo on her. "When you wake up, this will all be over, and you won't remember a thing."

Next I opened the door to the security room to find a single security guard seated in front of the computer watching attendees arrive. He frowned when I entered. "This room is off-limits to—"

I used the same techniques to knock him out cold. Then I rolled him in his wheeled chair out of the way.

As I squint into the screen now, Boulder hops up onto the desk with the iPad, and we watch Back-to-School Night getting underway. Just like on the night of my stealth mission, the feeds show all the common areas of the school. We can see parents milling in and out of the media center, and kids excitedly dragging their siblings through the halls to show them their work on display. I even make out Mrs. Dean standing in front of her classroom greeting people as they come in. If I could, I'd reach through the screen and snatch the adze out of her right now.

I search the grid of videos for my friends. Mateo's sweater and Eunju's braid are easy enough to make out as they secure the gym office, both having escaped their families for a few minutes to put wards in place to seal off the room's exits. I don't see Roxy or Gavin, which is how I know they're in position, too—her in the girls' restroom at one end of the school, him in the cafeteria bathroom at the other end.

"Does this ever get less nerve-racking?" I whisper to Boulder. I put on a pretty good show for the others, but honestly, I'm terrified. We only have one chance to pull this off, and if we get it wrong, we're going to have an extremely angry adze on our hands. There are hundreds of people here for tonight's event, and all their lives depend on us not screwing this up. Only we can protect what the ancestors of this town fought so hard to create.

My anxiety must show on my face because Boulder reaches up and touches my cheek, like he sometimes used to do with Dad. He seems just as surprised as I am by the gesture.

"I've spent several centuries with the Abomofuo, so I can confirm that the fear you feel before a hunt never gets better," he says. "But you've created a solid plan. Your parents would be proud—I know I am."

I lean into his touch, and for once even the fact that he smells like wet dirt doesn't bother me. "Thanks. And about what you said before about outliving all your human friends . . . I know one day you'll have to say goodbye to my family, but as long as I'm alive, you'll always have me. No matter what."

Boulder blinks at me, his eyes suddenly misty. He turns away with a fake-sounding cough. "Focus on the mission, Serwa," he says gruffly, but I can hear the smile in his voice.

Before I can tease the mmoatia for being a big softie, Mateo's voice crackles through the iPad, which we have set to a running group call for tonight. "G-gym's secure."

I squeeze my pendant for good luck.

Go time.

Boulder clears his throat, and the Adinkra I drew on him begin to glow. When he leans into the intercom mic, it's Principal Hashimoto's voice that says, "Mrs. Dean, you are wanted in the gym. Mrs. Dean, please come to the gym immediately."

On the computer screen, Mrs. Dean looks confused, but she apologizes to the parents she's speaking to and heads for the gym, which Mateo and Eunju have just vacated. As soon as the red double doors close behind her, I whisper into the iPad, "Roxy, Gavin, you're up."

Seconds later, two loud bangs ring through the halls—the sounds of pipes bursting at each end of the school. Though I don't see it happen, it's easy to imagine Gavin increasing the water pressure to the breaking point, and Roxy's calling forth roots to strangle the plumbing until it explodes.

Chaos descends upon Rocky Gorge Middle School. A few of the teachers, Mr. Riley included, begin herding parents and students outside while the evacuation alarm blares. I feel a twinge of guilt watching our teacher scramble along with everyone else, but my gut tells me I was right not to involve him in tonight's plan.

Mrs. Dean runs to the gym exit, but it's already been locked from the outside. There's only one way out of the gym now— via the stage door—and that's where my friends are going to come in at the first sign of trouble.

It won't be long until the emergency trucks get here, so there's not a second to waste. Everyone else has done their part. Now it's all up to me.

I leave Boulder behind as I climb out the main office window and scale the wall to the roof. I race across it with laser focus, the chilly September air biting at my cheeks even though the sun hasn't fully set yet. Once I get to the portion of the roof over the gym, I crouch low, summon Nokware, and cut a hole into the cement big enough for me to fit through. Now I can hear Mrs. Dean's frantic screams.

"Let me out of here!" she yells as she bangs against the locked door. "Help! Someone's still inside!"

I drop down from the rafters soft as a cat. "No one's coming for you, adze," I say in a voice that I hope sounds as powerful as Mom's always does in the middle of a fight.

Mrs. Dean whirls around, and her fear turns into anger. "I should have known you were behind this, Sarah. Unlock this door right now."

"My name is *Serwa*." I point Nokware at her. "And you don't get to tell me what to do anymore."

She lets out a strangled gasp at the sword. "Put that weapon down immediately!" she barks as she steps back in alarm.

"We can do this the easy way, or the hard way. I don't want to hurt you, but I won't hold back if you choose wrong," I warn. With the sword, I motion her to move toward the gym office.

"I have no idea what you're talking about! This isn't funny!"

No sign of any wings or claws yet. Just how long is she going to keep up this innocent act?

Footsteps pound behind me. The others have finally arrived through the stage door, and they join me in a semicircle around Mrs. Dean, their various weapons raised. Her eyes go wide like a bug's and settle on Mateo.

"Don't tell me you're a part of this, too, Mateo, after all I've done for you," she cries, and he flinches. "How could you do this to me?"

Guilt floods his face, but then he shakes his head. He steps a little closer toward me and takes a deep breath. Every word that comes out next is slow and deliberate. "No. You d-don't get to use me as a shield while hurting my friends anymore."

Pride swells in my chest. I nod at Eunju, and she throws a magicked jump rope, which immediately wraps around Mrs. Dean's body and mouth. It doesn't constrict enough to hurt her, only enough to make sure she can't pull her fangs out while we work.

"Help me move her into the gym office," I say.

Gavin wheels out a chair and says, "Please, be seated," as he slides it into the back of her knees. Mrs. Dean's eyes silently plead with us as we scoot her behind the desk piled with netting, field hockey sticks, and a deflated basketball.

"Close the door and get the Tupperware ready," I instruct.

Something about this feels too . . . easy. Adze usually put up more of a fight when cornered like this. But you know what? No need to question it. I'll take easy for once.

I step forward, and the gye nyame symbol I drew on my palm begins to glow. When I press my hand against Mrs. Dean's forehead, the magic flows out of me into her, illuminating us both. Creatures of black magic can't stand direct contact with divine wisdom, so this much straight to her brain should force the adze right out of her body and into the enchanted container we brought. I push everything I have into the symbol as Mrs. Dean stares at me, wide-eyed and frantic.

One second passes.

Two.

Ten.

Sweat drips down my back. I put as much magic as I possibly can into the symbol, but the truth is staring us smack in the face.

I was wrong. Mrs. Dean isn't the adze after all.

32

How to Fall into a Trap

*"There are complications in battle that no amount
of strategy can predict. In those moments,
be ready to fight until the last."*

— From the *Nwoma*

HOW COULD I HAVE been so wrong?

"Serwa?" asks Roxy, and my mouth is frozen, because how can I tell them I just risked all our lives for nothing? Before I can get a word out, the screeching static of the intercom buzzes to life, and high-pitched laughter echoes through the gym.

"Oh, Serwa, you were so, so close." The voice blaring through the speakers is distorted, but I can tell it's someone around our age. "If only you'd watched a little more carefully."

My stomach plummets toward my feet. While we were busy setting up our trap for Mrs. Dean, the adze was setting its own trap for us.

And now it's in the front office. Where I left Boulder, the security guard, and Principal Hashimoto behind, thinking they'd be safe.

Mateo and Roxy both flinch as the intercom screeches to life again. "Your little plan might have actually worked . . . if you'd picked the right target," the vampire says with a chuckle. "Luckily for me, you didn't. I haven't eaten this well in years."

Eunju bares her teeth, fire sparking along the sharp edge of her sword. Gavin glances anxiously toward the gym's exit doors. I know he's thinking about everyone who's outside on the blacktop. Fear claws through my stomach, and my vision goes blurry from nausea. We thought we'd evacuated them for their protection, but all we did was herd them for the adze.

My fault. This is all my fault.

Mr. Riley, our classmates, their families—are they dead? Are they bleeding out on the asphalt right now?

Bile rises in the back of my throat—no, I need to calm down! The adze wants us to panic and slip up so catching us will be even easier. Think about this rationally, Serwa. It's only been a few minutes since the evacuation—even the fastest adze couldn't bite all those people in that time. And even if it did, a single bite wouldn't drain enough blood to kill them. It might knock them unconscious, but prolonged exposure to black magic is what really harms an adze's victim. The people on the blacktop are still alive, I'm sure, but they're in grave danger if we don't act fast.

Mrs. Dean begins to shimmy in her chair, trying to escape her bindings. I quickly pinch the pressure point in her neck and she's out in seconds. Then I draw the deep sleep/mind wipe Adinkra combo on her forehead with a marker. Hopefully it's not a permanent one, but I don't have time to double-check.

"Come on, guys," I say. "We'll leave her in here."

We exit the office, locking the door behind us, and on its window I draw four hearts joined together like a clover—nyame dua, a protective ward. Mrs. Dean might not be my favorite person, but I still don't want her to be a casualty in whatever's about to go down.

"What do we do? What's going on?" asks Gavin as Bullseye laughs and laughs over the intercom. He and the other three look to me for guidance. I tighten my grip on Nokware, heart blocking my throat, and force down my terror to try to look at the situation as logically as my parents would.

Adze are naturally evasive. If Bullseye had wanted to escape, it could have easily hopped into a new host while we were preoccupied with Mrs. Dean. The trail would've gone cold, and we would've been sitting ducks for its next assault.

But it went all the way to the front office and got on the intercom just to taunt us—to taunt *me* specifically. It doesn't want to escape—it *wants* me to come find it. I'm thinking it either has a plan for taking us down on the way, or it's confident it has the strength to deal with us if we make it.

This is a trap.

And the only way out is through.

"We head to the front office and confront Bullseye there," I say, my voice projecting a sureness I don't feel.

Roxy lets out a sound of distress. "But it can watch us through the cameras," she says. "It could pick us off one by one before we even get there."

"It could," I admit. I try not to let myself think about Boulder, small and helpless in the adze's clutches. I'm going to get him out of there. I'm going to get us all out of here. "But the fact it's inside with us means it's not out on the blacktop with everyone else. It wants a fight, and we're going to give it one."

Mateo is trembling, and even Gavin looks like he might vomit. Every second we spend dallying is one that helps

Bullseye, but I need my team at their absolute best if we want any hope of surviving this.

"I know you're terrified. I am, too. Even Slayers with years of training under their belt can freeze up before a fight." I look each one of them in the eye, hoping to pass on a bit of the strength my parents have given me. "But you all captured the Sword of Asaase Yaa. You are the first people in decades to receive blessings from the goddess. I *know* you can do it. I need you to know it, too."

Eunju and Roxy look at each other nervously, while Gavin's hands shake around his staff.

To my surprise, it's Mateo who steps forward first. He nocks an arrow into his bow, and wind whips around the gym as determination fills his eyes. "Lead th-the way," he says.

We fall into formation with me at the front, Gavin, Eunju, and Roxy in the middle, and Mateo bringing up the rear. I press my ear against the gym's interior door. There's no sound coming from the corridor on the other side, which only heightens my nerves. Silence means that somewhere, a predator is waiting.

Here we go, I mouth to the others. Holding Nokware up in a front guard stance, I shove the door open with my foot, and we all burst through to see what the adze has waiting for us.

33

How to Survive a Hunt

"When in the heat of battle, trust your sword."

—From the *Nwoma*

THE HALLWAY IS COMPLETELY empty. Bright green-and-blue streamers—the RGMS school colors— lie in tatters on the ground, along with ripped posters and broken plates. The remains of a celebration turned frantic evacuation. The gym isn't far from the cafeteria, so our shoes squelch through growing puddles from the pipe Gavin burst.

"This hallway is covered by the security system," I mutter to the others, all the while checking above, behind, and side to side for any threat. "From here on out, assume the adze can see every move we make and—"

A skittering sound from above, like a cat running across a hardwood floor, cuts me off. The blood rushes through my ears—I know that noise.

"Fall back!" I yell. "Take cover!"

But not fast enough. One of the ceiling tiles shifts to the side and something drops straight onto my head.

Tiny, razor-sharp claws sink into my face, and I manage to yank the creature off with the hand that isn't holding Nokware just in time for another to land on me.

Another drops from the ceiling.

And then ten more.

And then a whole swarm.

"What are these things?" screams Eunju as she bats one of the creatures away with her sword, only for two more of them to grab her braid and yank her backward.

"Bonsam!" I scream.

They range in size from as small as an apple to about as large as a football, with leathery gray skin and batlike wings the color of wet cement. The little monsters aren't particularly strong, but you have to watch out for their iron fangs and the talons on each hand and foot. Like mmoatia, bonsam usually live in forests, where they use their hooked feet to hang from branches before they drop onto unsuspecting prey. But there are at least a hundred shrieking all around us, trying to rip my friends and me to shreds. Just how many black magic creatures did Bullseye rally while I was so busy being wrong about Mrs. Dean?

I pull my collar up over my nose to protect my face as best I can and use the broad side of Nokware to bash away the bonsam attacking Eunju. She's holding back her fire, likely not wanting to burn any of us in such a small space. Gavin's taken advantage of the water sloshing around the hallway to shoot tiny ice missiles at each one of the nasty things, but it seems like for each one he destroys, two more appear to take its place.

Roxy is at the biggest disadvantage as we're too far from the outside for her earth powers to help much, and she still hasn't been able to unlock her ancestors' ghost magic again. She calls forth some shriveled roots through cracks in the tiled floor, but the bonsam easily fly out of their reach. Half a dozen of the monsters grab her spearhead, and soon they're dragging her up toward the ceiling while she holds on for dear life.

We slash and hack and thrash, but there are too many and they're too fast. The swarm circles around me, scratching at the exposed part of my face and yanking at my braids like they're trying to rip them out of my head. Tears of pain blur my vision. No way. We can't go down here, not like this—

Suddenly the bonsam attacking me fly backward, as if pushed away by an invisible hand. Their screeches intensify as a whirling cyclone appears in the middle of the hallway and sucks them all up vacuum-style. Mateo kneels atop one of the lockers, face tight in concentration as his magic fights to keep the cyclone alive. One bonsam manages to break through the maelstrom and only gets a few feet before Mateo's arrow hits it and it explodes into a puff of dust.

"You all g-go ahead! I've got th-this!" he yells over his shoulder.

"But you're going to run out of arrows!" I protest.

In response, he twitches a finger, and one of his fallen arrows zooms from the ground to hit another bonsam struggling to escape the twister. Everything in me screams to not leave him behind, but his wind powers are more useful here than the rest of us combined. I yell at the others to keep moving, and we let Mateo cover our backs as we rush farther down the hallway.

We're halfway across the school when the intercom buzzes on again. This time the vampire doesn't even say anything, just laughs and laughs. I still can't tell who it is, but at this point, I don't care. Regardless, they're going down.

There's a hallway that goes straight past the sixth-grade

classrooms to the front office, but I don't want to risk another attack in tight quarters. Instead, I take us around the long way to the route that cuts through the media center.

When we reach the corner that'll bring us to it, heavy breathing rumbles through the air. I motion for everyone to stop and peek my head around the wall to see a hulking figure at least twice the size of a pro football player hanging upside down between two book stacks. Long iron fangs extend past its bottom lip, and its skin is a waxy bubblegum pink, clashing horribly with its stringy, shoulder-length crimson hair.

"A sasabonsam," I whisper to the other three. I spoke as quietly as I could, but one of the monster's furred, pointed ears immediately swivels toward the sound. We all freeze, not even daring to breathe.

A tense second passes. Another.

The sasabonsam's ear flicks back to its original position. We all let out silent sighs of relief.

Roxy pulls her phone from her pocket and quickly types something in her notes app: *All of us go in @ once?*

After the obayifo and the adze, the sasabonsam are the creatures that give the Abomofuo the most trouble. There are two varieties—the vampire kind and the ogre kind. It looks like we've got a vampire on our hands, and even my parents would have a hard time getting past that thing without a scrape or two.

I nod, but Eunju shakes her head and gestures for Roxy to hand her the phone. *Too risky,* she types. *You all go. I stay*

"What? No!" I protest, then slap my hand over my mouth. The sasabonsam shudders and sniffs, but luckily my little outburst didn't wake it.

You can't fight it alone, I type.

Now Gavin shakes his head before pointing toward himself,

then Eunju, then the monster. His meaning is clear—they'll distract the sasabonsam while Roxy and I head to the office.

A determined glance passes between them, and it's clear nothing I say or type will convince them that this is the world's most bonkers idea.

You've protected us. Now let us protect you, Eunju types.

She tosses Roxy's phone back to her, and before I can physically stop them, she and Gavin dash straight into the media center.

"Hey, Shrek called, he wants his ugly back!" Eunju screams, immediately snapping the sasabonsam out of its stupor.

I doubt a monster of black magic even knows what Shrek is, but he doesn't seem very happy about the comparison. With a rumbling roar, the sasabonsam launches himself hook feetfirst at Gavin and Eunju, who break formation at the last second and run in opposite directions. The monster crashes into one of the bookshelves, then pivots to chase Gavin. But Eunju presses her palm flat against one of the stacks, and flames devour the books. She rams her body into the bookshelf, toppling it onto the creature.

The smell of burning pink flesh fills the air as the sasabonsam struggles to dislodge itself from the burning books. The fire begins to spread, but Gavin spreads his arms wide, and the sprinklers above the media center burst open to douse the flames. Now equal parts burned and waterlogged, the sasabonsam struggles to its feet, where it meets Eunju and Gavin fighting in tandem, staff and sword moving in perfect rhythm in spite of—or maybe because of—their constant bickering.

It seems like they might have the upper hand, but then the sasabonsam grabs Gavin by the ankle and tosses him into Eunju. They go flying, and it's only Eunju quickly summoning a wall of fire around them that keeps the sasabonsam from tearing at them again.

I don't even realize how long I've been staring until Roxy tugs on my arm. "Now's our chance!" she whispers. Sure enough, the sasabonsam's back is now to the hallway leading to the front office. There's nothing else I can do for Eunju or Gavin right now—I have to trust all the training and their own magic will be enough.

With one last reluctant glance their way, Roxy and I charge toward the front office.

There are no creepy crawlies running around the lobby, which immediately puts me on edge. The door to the front office is ajar and flowing from it is the same unnatural cold I felt that first day I saw the adze. My teeth chattering, I step defensively in front of Roxy. "Follow my lead," I whisper, and even though she looks like she might pass out, she nods with her spear held high.

Our breath creates clouds as we nudge the main door open and enter the front office. The door to Principal Hashimoto's office is open, and through it we can see the adze leaning back in its seat with its feet up on the desk.

"There you are, Serwa," says Ashley. Her lip curls back, revealing blood dripping down her fangs, and her normally blue eyes burning molten gold. Principal Hashimoto is still slumped over where I left her, two bite marks in the side of her neck. "Took you long enough."

34

How to Fight Your Friend

"Once possessed, there is no way to reason with someone hosting an adze. Do not waste precious time trying."

—From the *Nwoma*

ASHLEY . . . It was Ashley all along.

Suddenly, all the snide comments, the way she was so interested in me from the day I arrived, my unease around her, make perfect sense.

She's Bullseye's host, and I had no idea.

My vision goes red. I'm about to lunge for the adze with no plan, just pure anger, when she lifts Boulder by the neck.

"One wrong move, and I'll pop your little friend here like a grape," warns the vampire.

Boulder squirms in her grasp, blood dribbling down his neck, too. Ashley shakes him like a baby doll. "I've never been a fan of mmoatia blood. Far too nutty for my taste."

"Let him go," I spit. My hand shakes around the hilt of Nokware, but I can't get any closer or try drawing any Adinkra without risking Boulder's life.

"How about this? I'll give you something you want in exchange for something I want. Hand over the Midnight Drum, and I'll let your hairy little pet go."

Something inside me tightens at the mention of the drum, and I swear I feel the same touch on my cheek I felt back in Asamando. "I have no idea where the drum is."

"But your parents do," says the adze. "And your safety might be one of the few things they'd be willing to trade that information for."

My heart blocks my throat as Bullseye's meaning hits me. It wants to take me hostage and use me as bait. I don't know which thought is scarier—that my parents might give up the drum to save me . . .

Or that they might not.

"Why are you even here?" I'm stalling now. Maybe if I keep Bullseye talking, it'll give me enough time to figure a way out of this. "Why would you choose a random middle school girl as your host?"

"Surely you've noticed by now black magic is impossible to detect within the limits of Rocky Gorge?"

It's Ashley's voice, but the words don't match her sunny face. She's all dressed up in a pink dress with a tulle skirt for tonight, too. But she didn't choose that outfit—the vampire did. The real Ashley is somewhere deep inside the smirking monster in front of me.

Bullseye continues, "That's why Boahinmaa stationed me here a year ago—to see if I could figure out how the zone was formed. She wants to re-create it to disguise our forces from the likes of you and your meddling society."

Bullseye has been here for a year . . . which is exactly when Ashley's stepbrother got sick and she began shunning Roxy.

Roxy must have pieced together the timeline as well, because she snarls, "You took advantage of Ashley's grief to possess her."

The adze lets out a mean laugh, and Boulder whimpers as Ashley's pink nails tighten around him. "It was so easy, too. Usually, a host puts up a fight when you first enter their mind, but hers was so addled by sorrow that I established control immediately. And, thanks to her stepmother being a teacher here, no one questioned why I was around school after hours as I conducted my research."

The adze talks about the null zone as if it's still a mystery to be solved. Good—it hasn't learned the truth of how black magic and divine wisdom were combined to protect this place. And if I have anything to say about it, it never will.

"Why did you attack Mr. Riley? And us, outside?" I ask.

"An adze's gotta eat sometimes," Bullseye says, batting Ashley's eyelashes with feigned innocence. "My focus was meant to be just the null zone, but once your oblivious parents dropped you into this town, my objective shifted to capturing their daughter."

I've never seen Roxy angrier than she looks right now. For all the fraught history between her and Ashley, they were best friends once. A bond like that doesn't just disappear.

I look over at Boulder, who seems so small in the adze's grip. It would take only a few bites for the vampire to devour him whole. "If I give myself up, will you let him go?"

Ashley nods. "In fact, I'll leave this school and never bother another person in it again."

"No, Serwa—!" Boulder begins to scream, but Ashley squeezes him tighter to cut him off. I can practically hear his bones grinding from here, and I suddenly wish I hadn't been so mean to him about his smell or tendency to hog the remote.

Boulder might be a cranky old coot, but he's *my* cranky old coot. I can't lose any more family members than I already have.

I have to give myself up. There's no other choice here. Plus, there's the small consolation that the adze won't kill me right away, at least not until it gets what it wants from my parents.

Just as I open my mouth to agree, Roxy steps in front of me and says to Ashley, "Remember that time your mom took us to the pool back in third grade?"

"What are you doing?" I whisper to her, but she ignores me and keeps talking.

"You had just finished your swimming lessons, and you were so excited to dive into the deep end for the first time."

I get what Roxy is trying to do now, but it's not going to work. One of the first things they teach a Slayer is that once an adze has taken control of somebody, unless it leaves willingly, no force but magic can get it out. Roxy can reminisce all she wants, but the Ashley she made all those memories with isn't here right now.

"But when you got to the top of the diving board, you looked down at the water and got too scared to jump," says Roxy, her voice hoarse. "You stood there for nearly an hour, held up the whole line, until I climbed up and we jumped off together. Do you remember that, Ash?"

The adze cocks its head to the side. "I don't care about your preadolescent musings. The clock is ticking, Serwa. Which are you going to protect—the Midnight Drum, or your mmoatia?"

"Roxy, get back here," I order, but she's already gotten halfway between me and the adze. If it loses its patience and attacks her, I won't be able to help.

"Do you remember that year I was failing math and you came to my place every day after school to tutor me until I caught up?" continues Roxy, taking another step toward the adze. "Or when your brother was first diagnosed, and I stayed up with you on the phone until four a.m. while you cried? I know we're not friends anymore, but we were once. And I know somewhere deep down that means something to you. To both of us."

Roxy is so close now she could reach out and touch the adze. The vampire hasn't tried to attack her, but it hasn't pulled away, either.

"Remember our old band name? The one we said we would start that YouTube channel with?"

And then something happens that I've never seen or even heard of—the golden glow in the adze's eyes fades, and when it speaks, it's Ashley's voice that says, "The dynamic duo, Rocky and Ash."

It's only a half-second change, but that's all the time Roxy needs. As the adze falters, Roxy slams her shoulder into its belly, knocking it off-balance. Then Roxy grabs Boulder from its grasp before jumping behind the front office desk.

The adze lets out an inhuman screech and lunges after her, only to find itself trapped inside a glowing wooden cage that Roxy summoned by smashing an eban sticker on top of the desk. Claws form at the tips of Ashley's hands, and the vampire slashes at the bars with them. The cage ripples under the assault but holds fast.

Now that Roxy and Boulder are safe, nothing stops me from charging full speed at the adze. I plunge Nokware through the bars toward its neck, but the vampire blocks it with an open palm. The golden glow is back in its eyes, and if anger were fire, its glare would burn me to ash.

"Boahinmaa wants you alive," it snarls, "but she never said you had to have all your limbs."

The adze's face twists into itself, compound bug eyes bursting through Ashley's skin, dripping fangs shredding her lip, and the sharp, curled antennae that earned it the nickname Bullseye sprouting from her forehead. Roxy's cage was big enough for a human child, but Bullseye is more than double Ashley's size, and the force of its transformation shatters the wood to bits. I cover my eyes with my arm to protect them from splinters. When I can see again, before me is a giant insect monster where a girl once stood.

"Look out!" Roxy and Boulder cry as Bullseye lunges for me. I try to dive out of the way, but it manages to get its claws around my wrist. The adze lifts me like I weigh nothing and tosses me through the front office window. I crash onto a patio outside the building, and there's no time to be dazed, because the vampire is flying straight toward me on iridescent wings.

When this all started, I was terrified to go one-on-one against an adze. But that was before I watched everyone else in the GCC risk their lives for me. Before I watched Boulder almost die just to keep us safe. Every one of my friends is giving their all in this fight.

Now it's my turn.

I swing and duck and dodge and strike with a speed even I didn't know I had. But the adze matches me blow for blow, and even though I know it won't kill me yet, each swipe is meant to do serious harm. The tugging, syrupy feeling inside me is burning hot, like fire might come out of my hands if I let go of my sword.

One serious disadvantage I have is that I don't want to kill the vampire while it's still possessing Ashley. I just want to immobilize it so I can get it out of her head. *Then* I'll deal with the bug.

Instead of stabbing Bullseye, I slash it superficially across the chest. It lets out a roar as golden blood flies everywhere. Then it picks me up with its talons and we go up, up, up until we are level with the clock face in the tower. The vampire's wings whir louder and faster than helicopter blades, and the force of their wind wrenches Nokware from my hand. The adze snarls in my face as my sword plummets uselessly to the grass below.

"Boahinmaa will have the Midnight Drum. And when she does, the mother will return," the adze hisses.

The mother. That has to be Nana Bekoe. This fight isn't just me against Bullseye—if I lose, Boahinmaa and her forces will be that much closer to freeing the most dangerous obayifo who has ever walked this earth. They'll use the null zone to hide their next assault against countless innocent people, sullying every-thing George and Agnes fought for.

But I'm up here without a weapon. I have nothing to draw an Adinkra with, and, unlike my friends, I don't have an ele-mental blessing. Once the adze takes me away, there's nothing to stop it from coming back to finish off the GCC and everyone else in town.

Thinking about the adze hurting me makes my body go numb. But thinking about it hurting Roxy or Gavin or Mateo or Eunju sets something on fire in my chest. That swirling molten lava feeling bubbles up inside me, and this time there's no way to stop it.

No—I don't *want* to stop it.

With my entire body humming like I've been struck by light-ning, I open my mouth.

And I scream.

35

How to Scream

"A Slayer either wins or dies. There is no in-between."

—From the *Nwoma*

MY SCREAM TEARS THROUGH the night like a thousand thunderclaps booming together at the same time. The force of it shatters every single one of the windows that have earned Rocky Gorge Middle School the title of Most Modern Building in Town. Bullseye and I fall in a shower of golden blood and glass, and it's only sheer luck that I land in one of the bushes instead of on my neck. Even as I haul myself to my feet, the strange power under my skin is still lighting me up like a firework.

My scream forced the adze back into its human form, and it crawls on the grass as I walk toward it. From the light flickering around its body, I can tell it's trying to slip into firefly mode and escape, but the scream disoriented it too much to do so.

"What are you?" it moans. Ashley's eyes are wide with the same fear the adze's victims must have felt when it pounced on them.

The Adinkra in my palm lights up as my anger rises for all the people the vampire terrorized and all the relationships it destroyed.

"I'm the girl who just kicked your butt."

With that, I slam my hand against Ashley's forehead.

Mom always said that this was the most dangerous part of any hunt—not the fangs or the black magic, but this moment when you remove the parasite from the host's head. One wrong move can leave their brain looking like spaghetti, and I don't want to do more damage to Ashley's mind than the adze already has.

At first I don't feel anything but black magic and a raging need for blood, but then I sense something else—a line in her mind dividing one part from the rest. This is the place where the adze ends and Ashley begins. I press on that line, making it wider and wider until the two sections are completely separate.

When I pull back my hand, a tiny firefly, hardly bigger than my pinky nail, glows in the center of my palm.

It's hard to imagine something so harmless-looking causing so much trouble. Part of me wants to step on it, but instead I put it in the magically altered Ziploc bag I shoved in my pocket before the hunt. It'll probably get squished in there, but luckily for it and unfortunately for us, that won't kill it when it's in bug form.

Now that the adze has been neutralized, Ashley's face is clearing like she's waking from a dream that lasted months. "Serwa?" she asks. I'm surprised she recognizes me. That means she must have been vaguely conscious through her possession, which is a terrifying thought.

Without saying anything, I hit the pressure point on her neck and she's out. There will be time for questions later. Right now, nothing matters more than finding my friends, even if it means throwing myself back into a nest of bonsam and sasabonsam.

I take one step toward the school when several people come running out of it.

"Serwa!" my friends all yell.

I didn't cry when Boahinmaa destroyed my house. I didn't cry when my parents abandoned me to go hunt for her. But seeing my friends running toward me, battered and bruised but alive, makes the tears rush out. We crash into each other in what might be the world's worst group hug, and now I'm blubbering so hard I'm not sure they can even hear me.

"I thought you were all . . . that you weren't going to make it out!" I say between the snot and the tears. I take in Gavin's and Eunju's waterlogged grins, Mateo's scratched up face and glasses, and a tearful Roxy with Boulder in her hands.

They're safe. Thank the gods, they're safe.

"We were all fighting and suddenly we felt this *boom*, and then all the monsters just fled," explains Eunju, grinning wider than I've ever seen her grin. "Whatever you did out here, it worked. We did it!"

And that's when it really hits me—we *did* do it. And somehow that feels less important than the fact we did it together.

Gavin glances over my shoulder. "Oh man, what happened out here?"

Now that the high of surviving is wearing off, it's clear that we are in some deep doo-doo right now. The school is completely wrecked, there's golden blood and shattered glass shining under the streetlights, and even with our magic it's going to take forever to get this all cleaned up. And we haven't even checked out the blacktop yet.

Someone walks around the corner of the school, and I feel

like a proud mama duck when everyone quickly slips into their defensive stances. But it's just Mr. Riley.

"There's a perfectly logical explanation for all of this, I swear," I blurt out at his shock.

"What did you *do*?" he snaps, and wow, anger really does not suit the man. "You could've compromised the null zone! You could've been *killed*!"

I hold up the Ziploc bag. "But we caught the adze!" I say weakly.

Mr. Riley stares at the firefly, then pulls his hand down his face with a groan. "Well, this is certainly a Back-to-School Night for the books. Let me see your wounds."

Since Boulder is still recovering from his altercation with Bullseye, Mr. Riley tends to our luckily minor injuries.

Then we all get to work on reuniting kids with parents. Everyone on the blacktop is dazed, having been temporarily frozen by the wave of black magic that washed over them. The few people Bullseye managed to bite before setting its trap for us are woozy, but they'll live.

But the entire time, my mind is replaying my scream and Mr. Riley's question.

What the heck *did* I do?

36

How to Wash Vampire Goo
Out of Your Hair

"It is important to rest and recuperate after every battle.
A burned-out Slayer is more likely to become
a dead Slayer."

—From the *Nwoma*

THE FREAK DUAL WATER and gas leak that happened at Rocky Gorge Middle School on Back-to-School Night is all the local news can talk about for days.

That's the false story Mr. Riley gave the police and emergency services when they finally arrived. Everyone was forced to leave the premises immediately after that, and now, on Sunday night, we're all awaiting the verdict about whether or not officials will deem the school structurally sound enough for us to return tomorrow.

I've seen the rest of the GCC once since the battle against Bullseye, and that was yesterday afternoon, when we met up to discuss what we should do with the vampire. Mateo and Eunju both voted to flush it down the toilet, while Gavin and Roxy wanted to mail it out of town. But Boulder warned that, since we can't contact the Abomofuo to hand Bullseye over to them, we shouldn't lose sight of it, because then there'd be no guarantee it wouldn't escape and immediately come back to kill us all. So, for the time being, Bullseye remains in the Ziploc bag, inside a locked briefcase, beneath a giant pile of sweaters in the back of Roxy's closet. It's far from a maximum-security prison, but it's all we've got till my parents return.

Thinking about my parents makes my chest grow tight, and I'm lucky Roxy is on her bed working on her scrapbook so she can't see me tearing up on the air mattress. The smell of rubber cement is making me a little dizzy, but not enough to get up and open the window.

I should be ecstatic right now. We caught the adze! We protected the town and the null zone! But my excitement can't break through the haze of dread curling through my body. The others asked how I managed to turn the tide of the battle at the last second and defeat Bullseye, but I can't tell them the truth: that I didn't use any divine wisdom at all. And, in fact, there is no Adinkra combination that could do what I did. Divine wisdom constructs. It creates. What I did back there was so destructive that it had to be . . .

Black magic. I used black magic to defeat the adze.

I don't want to believe it. It feels wrong to even think it, but it's the only explanation that makes sense. I can use black magic, and it's the sole reason my friends and I didn't die Friday night.

All these years I've been pushing down that Big Feeling inside me, thinking it was just my emotions. But ever since I came to this town, it has reached a point where I can't ignore it anymore.

And my parents . . . What would they do if they knew I was the very kind of monster they've spent their whole lives trying to destroy?

Unless I'm like George and Agnes and Mr. Riley, and I have a variant magic ability . . . No, if I did, my parents would, too, right? I've never received a direct blessing from a god like my friends have. What I did had to be black magic.

I don't realize I'm shaking until Roxy comes over and lies beside me on the air mattress.

"It's all right," she says as she rubs circles on my back. "We're safe now. No one knows what really happened. And now that we don't have the adze to worry about, we have all the time in the world to prepare for any retaliation from Boahinmaa."

Boulder gives me a judgy look from his nest in the closet. I know exactly what he's thinking—now that we've caught the adze, it's time for me to wipe my friends' memories just like I promised I would.

I know Boulder is annoyed, but I just . . . I haven't been able to do it. I can't erase the only people aside from my parents who have ever truly accepted me.

Roxy's hand moves from my back to my braids. "How long have you had these in?"

"Almost two months." It's so wild to think that the last time I had my hair done I had my parents, a home, no friends, and no black magic to worry about.

"Then it's time to take them out. Here, I'll help you. Let's have a wash day."

I don't have the energy for wash day, but Roxy isn't taking no for an answer. I let her wrap an old towel around my shoulders and settle me on the floor. She sits on the couch behind me so she can hack off the braids a few inches below where my natural hair meets the braiding hair. Then she begins undoing what's left of the box braids.

"Did you know there's a lady up in Minnesota who swears

that she married Bigfoot and that he left her to run off with her yoga instructor?" she asks.

I begin undoing one of the braids, too, my fingers moving on autopilot from all the times I used to do this with my mom. "I didn't."

"It was all the cryptid-hunting community could talk about for days! They sent a whole team and everything to check it out, but it turned out her ex-husband was just, like, mad hairy. And we thought Boulder was bad."

I let out a real laugh for the first time since our battle with the adze. Even without turning around I can feel her grinning at me as she separates out the braiding hair from my head and tosses the chunks into a plastic bag. "Oh, and do you know right here in Maryland we have our own cryptid? It's called the snallygaster, and they say it's half bird, half reptile. . . ."

I have no idea how Roxy does it, but by the time we've removed the last of the braids, I feel better than I have in forever. She even helps me wash my hair, too, and while it's deep conditioning we make our dinner of chicken nuggets, mac and cheese, and half an ice cream cake Auntie Latricia had stashed in the back of the freezer. We plop down on the couch with our cake and try to figure out which show to binge for the rest of the evening.

"What are you grinning about over there?" I ask when I catch her smiling to herself while I scroll through Netflix.

She scrunches her nose. "Nothing, it's just . . . with my dad in Ghana and my mom working all the time, it's nice to have someone around here at night again. It feels like having a sister." Roxy blinks, then quickly stutters, "I–I mean, it's obviously not the same thing, and I know you have your own family and stuff—"

"I get it." And I really do. I love Mom and Dad more than anything, but I never realized how great it is living with someone your own age. "My mom says that back home, because people traditionally live with their whole extended family, there really isn't a difference between your cousins and your siblings. So, in a way, that makes us sisters."

"Even though we're not related by blood?"

"Of course. Family is family."

It's probably the most embarrassing thing I've ever said, but Roxy's smile makes it all worth it.

We're both quiet for a long, long time before Roxy finally says, "What's going to happen to Ashley now that she's free from the adze?"

"Physically, she'll be fine," I reassure her. "There shouldn't be any permanent marks on her. Mentally . . . that's harder to say." I hate the way Roxy's face falls, but I can't lie about this. "The hosts don't remember the adze specifically, but they do feel a sense of loss for a chunk of their life they'll never get back. Some handle that grief well, and others . . . don't."

It's too early to see which category Ashley is going to fall into yet. For her own sake, I hope it's the former.

"Are you going to try to be her friend again?" I ask.

Roxy bites her lip. "When Ashley stopped speaking to me, it felt like the world ended. We'd been best friends since kindergarten. We did everything together. And then one day she just decided I wasn't good enough for her anymore. I don't think anyone's ever made me feel as bad about myself as she has this last year. For a long time, I would have given up literally anything just to be her friend again."

My cousin leans back, the spoon sticking out of her mouth as she stares up at the ceiling, deep in thought. "But you know what? I don't feel that way anymore. I have new friends now, ones who don't pretend to like me only to talk trash behind my back. And I know some of that was the adze's doing, but it doesn't change the fact that the cracks were starting to show between me and Ashley long before the vampire arrived. So, no. Maybe we'll be friends again one day, but for now, I'm good."

I don't know what to say. *I'm proud of you* doesn't begin to cover it. "I still can't believe I was so focused on Mrs. Dean that I missed all the warning signs for Ashley."

Roxy lifts one shoulder. "I can. Mrs. Dean is the worst. Mateo says last year she wished him a happy Cinco de Mayo because she knew 'how important that holiday is to your people.' His family's from Guatemala, not Mexico, but even if she knew the difference, I don't think she'd care."

I pull a face. "Maybe there's some black magic in her somewhere and we just didn't see it. Why else would she be so awful?"

"Nah, some people don't need a vampire playing around in their head to get them to do bad things. They just want to treat others however they like. And the only way to win against them is to live your life the way you want to, because nothing makes them madder than knowing they can't get to you."

I blink in surprise. The girl sitting next to me now is so different from the one I met when I first got to this town.

And I've changed, too. All the GCC members have.

Roxy catches me looking at her and grins. "You know, Serwa, I'm really glad you came to Rocky Gorge."

I grin back. "So am I."

And weirdly enough, I mean it.

I'm still going to have to erase the GCCers' memories—there's no getting around that. I should steal their wristbands too, now that I think about it. But even if Roxy doesn't remember what we've been through these last few weeks, I'm still going to be living with her and my aunt. If we got this close once, we can do it again. Same with Eunju, Gavin, and Mateo. I'll befriend them as many times as it takes if it means I don't have to lose them.

Whatever the Big Feeling is, I'll defeat it. Who knows, maybe I'll even pick up a mortal hobby like swimming or crocheting or something boring like that. My parents were right—even the Initiation Test can wait a year or two. My time in Rocky Gorge is what matters now.

Soon it's time to wash the deep conditioner out of my hair. I'm bent over the kitchen sink, water running down my face and ears, when Roxy says, "Whoa, your parents let you get a tattoo?"

My parents letting me get a tattoo? Hahahahaha—no. They most certainly did not. "What are you talking about?"

"Right here, there's some kind of symbol behind your right ear. It looks like an Adinkra, but I don't recognize it."

An Adinkra tattoo behind my ear? What in the . . . ? "Can you take a picture of it?"

Roxy does so with her phone, and we huddle over it, my curls still dripping everywhere.

Just like she said, right on the spot where my ear meets my head is an Adinkra about the size of my thumbnail. It's similar to sankofa, the symbol of remembrance, but it's been . . . corrupted somehow. The lines are thin and jagged, drawn in an ink so red it almost looks like blood.

"You recognize it?" asks Roxy.

I shake my head, trying to hide how badly this is freaking me out. This whole time I've had an Adinkra tattooed on me and I never knew. Whoever did it clearly never expected me to find it, because how many people can look behind their own ear?

All the times my parents have done my hair . . . They must have seen it, and yet they never said anything. Why not?

Boulder's asleep in his little nest in the closet, but I wake him up, shove Roxy's phone in his face, and ask, "What do you know about this?"

I've grown up with Boulder, which is how I can tell he's lying when he says, "It's a birthmark. You've had it since you were a baby."

"No, it's not. It's an Adinkra. Which one is it? And who put it on me? Was it my parents?"

"It is a birthmark," he repeats. "Nothing more, nothing less."

Suddenly I want to scream at him, but I can't risk destroying the apartment the way I destroyed the school.

Boulder's face gets all sad, and he sighs. "Serwa, please trust that everything I do, everything your parents have done, is to protect you. I know you want answers, but just . . . not yet. You have to wait a little longer. Please."

That's easy to say when you're not the one walking around feeling like there's a nuclear power plant inside your stomach. But I let it drop, because it's clear Boulder isn't going to tell me anything else, not without my parents here.

And honestly, I don't know if I'd believe anything he said anyway.

The tattoo reveal pretty much ruins our chill night in. Long after Roxy has gone to bed, I'm still lying there thinking about the mark. I keep touching the spot—it doesn't feel any different than the rest of the skin back there, not raised like a scar or anything. Without Roxy, I never would have found it. Is this why I always feel a desire to rub behind my ear when I get overwhelmed?

I thought catching the adze would be the end of all our problems, but it seems like there are more secrets than any of us realized hiding in the shadows. Every time I close my eyes, the adze's words bounce around my mind like a Ping-Pong ball.

What are you?

If you had asked me even a month ago, I would have said the daughter of Edmund and Delilah Boateng. A Slayer-in-training. A darn good Mario Kart player. But now . . . I don't know. I just don't know.

Suddenly it's too hot in here. The walls push in, threatening to trap me inside. The tugging—the black magic—inside me is back, and if I stay in this room another second, I might throw up, or scream, or worse.

The roof. I'll go up to the roof where it's calm and cool, and if I explode, I won't hurt anybody except myself and a bunch of sleepy pigeons.

I throw my windbreaker over my pajamas, double-check that Roxy and Boulder are still asleep, and lift the window.

And that's when I see Boahinmaa standing on the sidewalk smiling up at me, looking just as beautiful as she did the day she almost killed my whole family.

37

How to Interview a Vampire

"Trust no witch."

—From the *Nwoma*

SOMETHING WEIRD HAPPENS TO the suburbs after midnight. The streetlights never go off, but nobody is outside, making the entire area look like an abandoned carnival funhouse version of itself. Right now, there's no one but the stars and the moths watching as Boahinmaa and I stare each other down across the tot lot.

I don't know why I came downstairs when she gestured toward the playground. A smart person would have woken up Roxy or Boulder. A smart Slayer would already have her sword pointed at the witch's neck. But I'm not feeling smart right now. I don't know how I'm feeling, honestly, but it's definitely not smart.

Boahinmaa says something to me in a language that sounds a lot like Twi, but I can't understand it. When I don't respond, she shakes her head and says in English, "Wow. Akosua didn't even teach her daughter Ga. Her own father's language."

"Are you here to get revenge for Bullseye?" I spit.

The obayifo lifts a perfectly threaded eyebrow. "Who in the world is Bullseye?"

All I want is to summon Nokware and take this woman down once and for all, but what chance do I have against her? My parents just barely survived a battle with her when they were fighting side by side.

But, unlike that day at the lake house, Boahinmaa doesn't look out for blood tonight. Straight black hair cascades over her shoulders, parted neatly to the side. Gold jewelry winks at her ears, wrists, and throat, and her fitted red jacket, matching tapered pants, and high heels look like they came straight off a Hollywood set.

My hand flinches toward my bracelet when she starts moving, but she steps past me to take a seat on the swings. "I came all this way to talk to you, of course."

"I have nothing to say to you."

"Is that so?" She runs a manicured nail down one of the wooden beams on the swing set. Dark rot bubbles up beneath her touch. "In that case, perhaps I'll pay a visit to your little friend's café. I'm sure the health inspector would love to get a call about black mold in the kitchen."

My heart feels like it's going to beat straight out of my chest. Boahinmaa knows about Mateo. If she knows about him, she probably knows about every other member of the GCC. All of them and their families have targets on their backs, and it's all my fault.

"You leave the Alvarezes alone!"

The black magic rises inside me again, and Boahinmaa smiles. "Answer a few of my questions, and I'll be happy to. I don't wish to stay here too long. This null zone is strategically useful, but it's making my magic feel strange."

Everything about this basically has IT'S A TRAP written on it in big red letters, but I take a seat on the swing next to her anyway.

"If you're here for the Midnight Drum, you're wasting your time. I don't know where it is," I say.

"Of course you don't. The Abomofuo might be a joke of an institution, but even they wouldn't leave information like that in the hands of a twelve-year-old," she replies. "But I'm not here about the drum, either. I just wanted to talk to you about what happened at the school the other day. That was one of the most impressive displays of black magic I've ever heard of. I know obayifo three times your age who could not do what you did."

Boahinmaa says this like it's a good thing, like I didn't cause so much damage that they might shut down school next week. Even thinking about the amount of destruction I caused makes me want to throw up. "I'm glad you enjoyed it, because I'm never using those powers ever again."

The witch starts swinging on the swing, and she looks so out of place here with her fancy clothes I almost want to laugh. "You not using your magic is like a flower deciding not to turn to the sun—you can try all you want to stop it, but it's still going to happen."

"It won't. It's dangerous and evil, and I don't want it."

Boahinmaa stops swinging and stares at me with a cold look in her eyes. "Our magic is not evil."

"Black magic destroys everything it touches."

She lets out a snort. "Ah yes, the old Abomofuo teachings. Divine wisdom creates, and therefore it is good. Black magic destroys, and therefore it is bad. No room for nuance or gray areas."

Her eyes glow red when she turns to me, and I can see the tips of her fangs when she says, "A fire clearing a forest so new growth may thrive is destruction. Cancer cells multiplying to poison their host is creation. Creation and destruction may be opposites, but neither is inherently good or bad."

Hold on. That can't be right. What she's saying goes against everything I've ever been taught. If black magic isn't evil, then . . .

"But what about the adze?" I argue. "Taking over someone's mind, forcing them to drink human blood, and spreading misfortune sounds pretty evil to me."

"The adze cannot help being born adze any more than a lion can help being born a lion. By that logic, humans are evil for eating cows."

"That's not the same thing!"

"Is it not?"

No, it's not, even though I can't explain why. I suddenly wish Gavin were here. He's the debate master, not me.

Boahinmaa continues, "There was a time when my sister understood that the world cannot be separated into easy binaries. But it seems she failed to teach this to her daughter."

Sister? What is this lady even talking about, who is her sis—

Oh.

Oh.

Boahinmaa's eyes go wide with a new expression— surprise. "She didn't tell you," she says, her tone unreadable. "Your mother really didn't tell you that I'm her sister."

And now it's impossible to miss that she and my mom have the same strong chin and thick lips. They both have that fire in the eyes like they're just waiting for a reason to fight the entire world. I didn't notice it before, or maybe I didn't *want* to notice it, but now the truth is staring me smack in the face:

Boahinmaa is my aunt.

I sputter out several sounds that aren't words before I can finally say, "But if you're sisters, then that means my mom is—"

"An obayifo. Surely you must have noticed that your mother isn't like other people, even other Slayers?"

I have. Even when I was little, I knew that my mom was stronger and faster than every other member of the Abomofuo. But I always thought that was because she trained so much harder than everybody else, not because she was the type of monster she always fought.

She's an obayifo. She's a witch.

And I am, too.

It feels like someone has pulled the entire world out from under my feet and I'm spinning, spinning through the air with no end in sight. The black magic rises again, and I double over, clutching my stomach as I try to force it back down.

Moving faster than I can see, Boahinmaa is at my side. "Somebody—most likely your parents—put a seal on you to keep your black magic dormant, but it's growing too strong to be contained. Unless that seal is removed, your magic will keep coming out in fits and bursts you cannot control." Purple light swirls around her palm as she reaches for my ear. "Say the word, and I can break it for good."

"Don't touch me!" I smack her hand away and fall backward onto the gravel. I pretend the black magic is a piece of paper I can fold over and over again until it's a tiny square that can't hurt me or anyone else. Once I'm in control, I say, "You're a liar. You tried to kill my entire family. You killed my grandma! Why should I believe anything you say?"

Boahinmaa stares at me for a second before holding her hand straight out, palm up. "If you don't believe what I say, then believe your magic. Look through my memories and see the truth for yourself."

I don't want to use Adinkra on this woman. I don't want to spend another second with her. But this is the closest I've gotten to getting any answers about what I actually am. If I don't do this, what's going to happen to me? To my friends?

Boahinmaa wiggles her fingers. "I will only make this offer once, Serwa."

Before I can convince myself that this is a bad idea, I pull a marker from my windbreaker. On her palm I draw sankofa, just like I did when I asked the river behind the school to reveal the truth of Rocky Gorge.

Divine wisdom flows out of me into the Adinkra, and brilliant golden light fills the tot lot as the magic drags me from the present day into my aunt's memories.

38

How to Look Back

"To forget the past is to forget who you are."

—From the *Nwoma*

I OPEN MY EYES on a street I don't know but that knows me. *Osu*, the magic whispers in my ear. A neighborhood in Accra near the ocean.

Accra, the capital of Ghana, and my mom's hometown.

It's almost nighttime, and the air is full of the sights and sounds of a bustling summer evening. Highlife music blares somewhere in the distance above the chaotic honking of car horns, and my stomach rumbles at the scent of the plantains on a street hawker's cart. This is my home—my ancestral home. The country I haven't been in since I was five.

Two girls run into an alleyway, the older one close to my age, the younger one maybe eight or nine. Their oversize shirts are yellowed and baggy. The bigger one is barefoot, while the younger one wears shoes that are clearly too small for her feet.

"We're going to get in trouble!" whines the youngest.

341

Boahinmaa, the magic tells me, and it's almost impossible to imagine the filthy, terrified little girl in front of me as the deadly, terrifying obayifo I know.

"Only if you keep looking like we're doing something wrong!" snaps the older one, and I don't need the magic to identify her, because I would know that voice anywhere in the world, across space and time.

The lanky girl with the hardened glint in her eyes is my mom.

They watch their target, the plantain hawker on the side of the road crouched over his little stand. When the man turns his attention away from his goods, Mom nods at her sister. "Okay, go!"

Boahinmaa runs in front of the street hawker, only to pretend to trip right in front of his cart and immediately burst into tears. As the merchant helps her to her feet, Mom presses a hand against the ground. A bolt of black magic zips from her fingers across the dirt and destroys the back half of the man's cart.

Plantains and nuts go flying everywhere. In the chaos, Boahinmaa is able to stuff several handfuls of food down her shirt before running away. The hawker yells something at them both that I don't understand, but honestly, the energy of adults upset with troublemaking kids is the same all over the world. I'm still staring at the sisters' intertwined hands as they run off laughing when the memory shifts.

Now we're in a house so tiny it makes even Roxy's apartment look like a mansion. The walls are the kind of brown you can tell was once white, and the only light comes from a single flickering lightbulb in the middle of the ceiling. Mom and Boahinmaa sit on the ground, the plantains on a chipped plate on an upside-down box between them.

"If we're careful, this could last us several days," Mom says hopefully.

Boahinmaa sniffs and rubs at her eyes with a dirty sleeve. "I don't want to eat plantains and nuts anymore. I want chicken and rice and salad." A pair of fangs pop out over her quivering bottom lip, and I startle. "I want to hunt."

"You know it's not safe for us to hunt while Mother is gone," Mom says. Fangs appear in her mouth, too, and she rubs her tongue over them.

Seeing a young version of my mom with fangs reminds me of something my dad told me early on in my training. *Just like there are different kinds of people, there are different kinds of obayifo,* he said. *Some are vampiric, others aren't. But all are masters of black magic.*

Boahinmaa and my mother are both the vampiric kind of obayifo. But I've never seen fangs in her mouth—or in mine, for that matter. Is . . . Is the seal blocking that, too? If I break it, will I need to start drinking blood to survive?

In a few tiny bites, the girls' food is gone. Boahinmaa starts to cry, and for a second it looks like Mom might, too, before she scoots over and wraps her sister in her arms.

"One day we're going to have a big house. We can eat all the chicken and rice and salad we want. And when we don't feel like eating human food, we can hunt until we've had our fill. And . . . And it'll be by the water so we can swim whenever we want, and it'll be painted pink!"

"I like blue better," Boahinmaa says with a sniff.

Mom rubs the tears from her sister's face with her hand, just like she always used to do for me. "Then I'll paint it blue just for you, Effi."

Her words hit me like a punch to the gut. *Our* house was by the water. Our house was painted blue.

"You promise?" Boahinmaa (Effi?) asks, and Mom extends her finger for a pinkie swear.

"I promise. I'll always be here for you."

Someone bangs the thin door open. Mom immediately jumps in front of her sister, fangs bared and black magic swirling in her hands.

An older woman charges into the room, and both girls' faces immediately light up. "Mother!" they exclaim in unison.

A shiver runs down my spine. This is Nana Bekoe, famed general of the black magic forces that nearly took out the Abomofuo during the Third Great War. The most dangerous obayifo who has ever lived.

My grandmother.

Nana Bekoe doesn't look nearly as terrifying as I expected, though her green fitted Ankara-print blouse is far nicer than her daughters' clothes. She's round-faced, like Boahinmaa, but has the same nose and chin as Mom and me. She could pass for any random Ghanaian woman if it wasn't for the way shadows inch toward her, betraying her danger with every step.

"They're coming. Hurry!"

The last word is barely out of her mouth when several members of the Abomofuo burst through the door with swords, spears, and bows raised. There's half a dozen of them, but I only recognize two: the middle-aged woman in combat gear leading the operation and the teenage boy loading a crossbow beside her.

Grandma Awurama and her son, Kwabena, who will one day be my father.

Dad's eyes meet Mom's and . . . it's hatred. Pure, unfiltered hatred on both sides. The memory tells me this is their first meeting, and from the tense energy crackling in the air, it's about to end in bloodshed.

"Don't bother trying to fight, Nana Bekoe," my dad's mother warns my mom's mother. Grandma Awurama was described to me as nothing but kind and loving, but the steel in her voice makes me shiver, even though there's no way she can hurt me in this memory. "You must face the Okomfo for the crimes your black magic cells committed in Takoradi."

Nana Bekoe barks out a laugh. "Since when is it a crime to feed your people? Or are we so lowly in your eyes we do not deserve even that?"

"It's a crime when your feeding leaves people injured and under an adze's thrall." Grandma Awurama lifts her akrafena. "Come with us quietly. Let us not spill blood in front of the children."

Up until now, Mom has been standing in front of Effi looking like she'll rip off the head of anyone who takes a step toward her sister. But then Nana Bekoe nods her way, and Mom's demeanor shifts. In an instant she switches into attack mode and charges for the Abomofuo.

I knew my mom was a good fighter—the best fighter—but seeing her now, with her black magic at full power, I realize she's been holding back my entire life. Her eyes glow crimson and her magic is like a hurricane, unrestrained by the Slayers' Adinkra rules. She disarms the first man who rushes her, bashing him in the temple with the hilt of his own sword, then whirling around to strike the man behind him.

One of the women hits Mom in the side with her spear, and with a howl of rage, Mom lets out a roiling blast of black magic that engulfs her attacker and another Slayer caught in the cross fire. In less than a minute, four Slayers lie in crumpled heaps on the ground—they're not dead, but they won't be getting up anytime soon. Blood drips down Mom's hands as she pivots beneath Grandma Awurama's sword and swings her claws toward the older woman's gut.

Only to be intercepted by Dad, who blocks her with the leather guards around his forearms. They swing and slash for each other, not in a training spar but a real, to-the-death battle that fills me with the deep, primal terror all children feel when their parents are in danger. I'm living proof that they will both survive this night and eventually join the same side. But right now, all I see are two enemies fighting to the death.

Grandma Awurama and Dad are so busy trying to take down Mom that no one notices Nana Bekoe slap her hand against the wall. Cracks of black magic spread up through the structure, and there's barely time for Mom to grab Effi and run before the house collapses.

The memory shifts to what looks like an abandoned construction site. Time has passed, and all that's left of Nana Bekoe's house in the distance is a plume of smoke. It's raining now, and the blood on Mom's body is washing off to mix in the mud below. The obayifo general paces angrily through the rain while her two daughters shiver in it.

"How did they even find me?" Nana Bekoe mutters. "I bet it was that Kwaku. He must have sold out my location—"

"How could you destroy our house while we were still in it?" explodes Mom, ignoring the warning look Effi throws at her. "Now where are we supposed to sleep?"

I hear the sound of flesh hitting flesh before I actually see Nana Bekoe's hand move. Mom falls to her knees with her cheek swelling. Effi kneels beside her with a shocked cry.

"And what was that sorry excuse for fighting back there?" my grandmother screams. "You should have been able to handle them all easily, but you've been slacking on your training, haven't you? Pathetic. Simply pathetic."

Mom's eyes line with tears, but she lowers her head. All the fire she showed earlier is gone. "I'm sorry, Mother," she whispers. "I'll be better next time."

Nana Bekoe lets out a scoff and turns away. "I need to reconvene with our allies in Takoradi immediately. Stay here, and don't cause any trouble while I'm gone. I'll come for you when you're needed."

The leader of the black magic forces vanishes, leaving her daughters alone in the rain. The two sisters curl around each other as they lean against a half-finished wall. Effi holds her arms tightly around my mother's waist, like she's the only good thing she's ever had.

"Big blue house," Effi whispers again and again. Just those three words. "Big blue house. Big blue house."

Just like with the memory of Rocky Gorge, the magic once again lets me feel the emotions of the subject—this time Effi's. Her sadness and terror permeate the magic, bringing tears to my own eyes. My mom had told me that she grew up poor, but never in a million years would I have guessed . . .

And I still don't understand how Mom and Effi went from being the world's closest sisters to almost ripping out each other's throats.

The magic shifts again. This time Nana Bekoe and her daughters are standing in front of a restaurant in the heart of Accra, the smells of roasted meat and frying fish thick in the air. Mom is older now, maybe in her late teens, and Effi is about my age. Nana Bekoe walks around my mother in a circle, inspecting her like one might a new car.

"My allies and I have worked hard to get you into this year's crop of Abomofuo's recruits so you can pass us information from the inside. Do you understand how much is at stake with this mission?"

"Yes, Mother."

"Don't you dare let me down."

"I won't, Mother."

There is no joy on my mom's face—just a steely desire to fulfill her mission no matter what.

Nana Bekoe tilts my mother's chin up with a single finger. "I raised you to be the sword that could turn the tide of this war. Be my warrior, Akosua."

"I will, Mother."

My grandmother grips Mom's shoulder once. I guess that's her version of a goodbye. Effi's goodbye hug is way more sentimental, and as Akosua's arms wrap around her sister's waist, the first hint of emotion in this memory passes over her face.

"I'll come back for you, Effi," she promises. "Remember the big blue house."

And then my mother disappears to destroy her enemies from the inside.

39

How to Make a Mistake

*"Strike with intention. One wrong move can be
the difference between life and death."*

—From the *Nwoma*

BOAHINMAA'S ADULT VOICE RINGS through my
ears as the memory fades to gray.

*At first, Akosua sent us weekly status reports from the
Abomofuo Compound. Her spying began to shift the war in our
favor.* My aunt's voice is in my head. It rattles through
my bones. *But then we went weeks without hearing from her.
Weeks turned into months. None of the bonsam or black magic
mmoatia our mother sent to the Compound could get through
the wards to find out what had happened to her. Eventually,
our mother wrote her off as a failure and began training me to
take over her role as the lead fighter of her forces.*

A memory flickers by of a now-teenage Effi running
through a makeshift obstacle course in a forest while
Nana Bekoe yells commands at her. Effi gets through
each obstacle with sleek precision and speed, until she
stumbles on the last rock climb down and crashes to the
ground. As she struggles to get up, Nana Bekoe walks
over and slams her face back into the mud.

"Not good enough!" the witch screams as her daughter struggles to breathe around the dirt filling her mouth. "Akosua finished this course in half that time when she was your age!"

The memory shifts again. This time, the girl goes through every obstacle without faltering. Little Effi, who had dreamed of chicken and rice, is now a warrior capable of taking down Slayers all on her own.

Boahinmaa's adult voice booms in my head again. *But even though everyone else gave up on my sister, I never did. I was so sure she would come back to us—come back for* me*—that I risked everything to go find her. I searched all over Ghana until I found one of your Middle Men and lured him in with my spell. Once I was done feeding on him, I had an adze possess him so he could get me into the Compound. I knew my mother wouldn't help me, because she'd already written Akosua off, so I went by myself.*

The world around me morphs into the orange and white walls of the Compound. I watch as a teenage Effi literally walks right into the Abomofuo stronghold on the arm of the Middle Man that one of her adze has possessed. Her terror at being in this place that has harmed so many of her kind is outweighed by her determination to either find her sister alive or make those who killed her suffer for it.

Her surprise is my own when she finally finds Mom alone in one of the dozens of training rooms, working through a sword combo I know well. She isn't just alive—she's practically glowing, looking happier and healthier than Effi has ever seen her. The sisters stare at one another, the joyous reunion the younger one imagined slipping away.

"Effi! What are you doing here?" Mom exclaims, eyes flicking nervously between her sister and the door at the other side of the room.

"I'm here to rescue you, of course!" replies Effi. "Come on, let's go."

Effi tries to pull her sister out of the room, but Mom won't budge. "I can't go back to our mother," she chokes out. "I—I won't."

"What are you even saying? Have they brainwashed you?"

"No! Listen to me. They'll let you stay if you're willing to seal your powers."

Effi recoils. "Seal my powers? Is that what they did to you? You gave up a part of yourself to become their pet after all they've done to our kind?"

"It's not like—!"

The far door opens with a creak. Dad and Grandma Awurama enter the training room. I can tell that something shifted during Mom's time at the Compound, because the way Dad smiles at her now is a world apart from the murderous glare he gave her when they met. It's how he's smiled at her my whole life, like she makes his world better just by being in it.

The smile fades when he sees Effi. "Akosua, who is this?" he asks, not recognizing the scared little girl in the witch standing before him now.

Mom's mouth opens and closes with no answer, unable to explain to her new family the presence of a member of the one she left behind.

I feel the exact moment Effi's heart breaks in two when Mom yanks her arm out of her sister's grip. "She's no one. No one at all."

I know my mother well enough to guess her thought process in that moment: deny any connection to Effi so that no one in the Compound realizes what she is and hurts her because of it. But my aunt doesn't see that.

Effi had already been broken by the fear that her sister had died. But the truth—that her sister abandoned her to join their enemies—utterly destroys her. She isn't even thinking when she lets her magic free, a plume of pure chaos rushing through the room toward Grandma Awurama and Dad.

"We've been infiltrated by an obayifo!" cries my grandmother as she dodges the first attack. "Sound the alarms!"

The battle that follows is bloody and brutal, with my mom and her sister at the center of it. Effi holds her own against several of the Slayers, even Grandma Awurama, who fights like a warrior goddess from a folktale.

Eventually, my grandmother and Effi end up on the roof of the Compound's main hall. Effi is exhausted, having used so much of her magic to sneak into the Compound in the first place. Grandma Awurama stands over her, sword ready to strike. In all the pictures I've seen, my dad's mother is always smiling or laughing, but there is nothing kind in the expression she gives my aunt—only the cold, steely gaze of a Slayer ready to finish off her foe.

Effi and I realize the truth at the same moment: My grandmother is going to kill her.

Effi's gaze frantically searches for help until it lands on my mom, who has just scrambled onto the roof with my dad, both of them covered head to toe with blood and bruises.

"Akosua, help me!" Effi screams. "Help me, sister, please!"

Mom's eyes go wide. They go from Effi to my grandma, then back again.

She sees the choice before her—save her sister or save the woman who's become the mother she never had.

She hesitates.

And the betrayal Effi feels at that moment hurts more than a thousand swords to the heart ever could.

Grandma Awurama brings down her akrafena, and in that same instant, the last tiny flare of Effi's magic sparks to life. The corner of the roof they're on crumbles away beneath their feet. Mom surges forward, screaming at the top of her lungs, but Dad pulls her away to safety.

Effi survives the fall.

My grandmother doesn't.

The memory shifts again, past the chaos of the Compound trying to regroup from the surprise attack, past my father grieving the loss of his mother.

As for Effi, she literally crawls away from the wreckage, hauling her broken, bleeding body inch by painful inch forward. Her anger is a living creature, alive and roaring through my body.

I watch as she sheds her old name. The girl who snuck into the Compound had been a naive little fool. The obayifo who came out was something new. Someone with revenge in her heart where her sister used to be.

I watch as Effi dies and Boahinmaa is born.

TEARS ARE STREAMING DOWN my face when we return to the present and the reality of the tot lot. After the bright, vibrant colors of Accra, Sunny Oak Towers and the surrounding neighborhood feel so dull and gray, like broken dollhouse versions of a city.

"You're lying!" I say. "That wasn't my mom! She would never do that!" But I know that the magic would never lie. Everything I just saw was 100 percent true.

My mother is an obayifo. The daughter of one of the most powerful ones who ever existed.

And Mom chose to turn her back on her people, on her own family, to become someone who hunts them down.

"Perhaps Akosua chose to hide the truth from you because she was ashamed of her past, that she herself is one of the creatures she now considers so beneath her. I don't know," says Boahinmaa. "She can paint me the villain of your family's story all she wants, but that doesn't change the fact your mother hurt me long before I ever hurt her."

My aunt gently helps me to my feet. Pure power radiates off her every movement—if Effi is in there anywhere, she's been long buried beneath magic and rage. "Your parents chose to seal your black magic because the Abomofuo feared it might be dangerous. They want to control you. But women like you and me, like your mother and grandmother, have always been viewed as dangerous in this world. Our skin color, our cultures are considered dangerous to a system that thrives when we hate those things about ourselves."

The black magic in me hums in agreement with her words.

"But *dangerous* is just another word for powerful," she continues. "You think you're strong now? You wouldn't believe the things you could do, who you could become, with that seal gone. I can break it for you, if you'd like."

I sniff, wiping the tears from my face. "Why would you do that for me?" What would Boahinmaa have to gain from me coming into my magic?

"Consider it the first in a series of belated birthday gifts from your favorite aunt."

She steps away and dusts an invisible piece of lint off her jacket. "But of course, it's your call. I would never force you to do anything with your magic or your body without your permission. Unfortunately, I cannot say the same for my sister." She turns from me. "Good night, Serwa. I hope you have a pleasant rest of your weekend."

And then she's gone, the faintest glimmer of gold dust on the swing seat the only sign she was ever here at all.

40

How Not to Hold a Family Reunion

"When one mission ends, another begins."

—From the *Nwoma*

BOAHINMAA'S VOICE—MY AUNT'S VOICE—
rings through my head long after she's gone.

Your mother hurt me long before I ever hurt her.

They want to control you.

You wouldn't believe the things you could do, who you could become, with that seal gone.

I keep running my fingers over the mark behind my ear, as if touching it might give me the answers to exactly what would happen to me once it was removed.

Part of me wants to break the seal and let the full force of my power finally come out. Part of me wishes I could go back to never knowing it existed.

I want to believe that my parents put it on me for my own good, but they've lied to me about so much. They've lied to me about EVERYTHING. If I can't trust them to tell me what I really am, how can I trust that I'm actually better off with the seal than without it?

"Hello, Earth to Serwa, can you hear me?"

I snap my head up to look at Eunju, who is waving her hand in my face. Today is Monday, our first day back since they cleaned up the damage from Back-to-School Night. Everything feels normal enough. During math class we had a sub instead of Mrs. Dean, who Principal Hashimoto told us will be taking "an extended leave of absence due to extenuating circumstances." Mrs. Dean should have no memories of or injuries from what happened to her in the gym, but I guess our confrontation left some kind of impact on her regardless.

I know I should feel bad for her, but I don't. She was horrible to me and my friends. But is that the black magic in me talking? Does not feeling sorry for her make me a bad person?

"Sorry, I was just thinking," I say to Eunju, which is the truth. Right now we're in the cafeteria, which feels almost disgustingly normal after everything that's happened these past few days. Eunju shifts awkwardly from foot to foot, turning her lunch box over in her hands while Roxy comes to join us.

"Right. Well, anyway . . . with Ashley gone, I was wondering if . . ." Eunju's eyes land on the empty table where she and Ashley usually sat for lunch. Eunju FaceTimed with her over the weekend, so we know she's fine, but something tells me it's going to be a while before she's ready to come back to school.

"You want to sit with us in the art room?" I finish for her. Eunju nods, face tomato red.

You know, after all she's done to Roxy it would serve her right for me to turn her down. But that's not my call to make. I raise an eyebrow in silent question to my cousin, who just today decided to come to the art room for the first time.

Roxy thinks it over for all of a second before offering Eunju her arm. "The more the merrier. But you have to sit in Gavin's burp blast zone."

And that's how the five of us find ourselves all willingly in the art room at the same time together, Mr. Riley grinning to himself at his desk like he knew this would happen all along. For a few minutes all I do is watch Mateo go over math problems with Roxy while Gavin and Eunju engage in a heated argument over which of their favorite anime characters would win in a fight. These are my friends, and just chilling with them is so normal yet I love it so much.

All of this will go away the second the others learn what I really am.

"S-Serwa?" Mateo nudges my shoulder. "You all right?"

"Y-yeah! Never better!" I lie.

Now everyone is looking at me, and I can feel the black magic churning. "What's wrong?" asks Gavin.

"If something's bothering you, let us know. We can help," Roxy adds.

But they can't help me, not with this. And they've already done enough. They don't need to get involved in my identity crisis, too.

"Let's talk more later," I say. From behind the teacher's desk, Mr. Riley gives me a sympathetic nod. I wonder how much of his Keeper knowledge extends into the realm of vampire witches.

My friends stare at me, clearly wanting to push more but not knowing how. I stare back, and we legit might have stayed that way until the end of class had the loudspeaker not crackled to life.

"Serwa Boateng, please come to the front office. Serwa Boateng, to the front office."

In the name of Nyame's bunched-up undies, what *now*? A million possibilities run through my head, none of them ending well for me.

But none of the millions of possibilities comes close to reality, which is Mom and Dad sitting in Principal Hashimoto's office like it's something they do every day.

I freeze in the doorway, my mind suddenly going blank. No way. There's no way they're here.

But the smiles on their faces are exactly like I remember. "Serwa!" cries Dad. The dimple in his left cheek appears when he smiles, and it's so familiar that my body is moving before my mind can catch up. I throw myself into his arms and he smells just like always, like fresh laundry and pine cologne, and I guess crying is just a thing I do now, because I'm blubbering all over his shirt.

"What's going on? Why are you here?" I ask when I calm down enough to speak again.

"Our business trip ended early," explains Mom, the lie flowing easily. She's got her twists up in a bun and is wearing the tortoiseshell glasses she puts on when she is too tired for contacts. "We flew out first thing to come see you."

They sign me out of school for the day, and in the car they explain everything that has happened since I last saw them.

"We followed Boahinmaa's trail for weeks, trying to figure out exactly how she got through our wards," Dad explains, and it's so amazing that I'm listening to one of his never-ending stories that I almost start crying again. Boulder sits in his lap while Mom drives. The mmoatia stares up at him in awe, and he keeps poking my dad as if he can't believe he's actually here in the flesh. "The trail went cold for a little while, but then we received an anonymous tip about an adze sighting in a suburb south of Chicago."

"From there, it was your standard catch-and-retrieval mission," Mom jumps in. "It took us a little while to infiltrate her lair, but yesterday we caught her."

Wait . . . Hold up. "You caught Boahinmaa?"

"Yes, yesterday morning. She's been in Abomofuo custody ever since."

But there's no way they caught Boahinmaa yesterday morning; I spoke to her last night. Was the figure I met some sort of illusion? No, I touched her hand when I looked into her memories. That was really her at the tot lot last night.

Then who in the name of Asaase Yaa did my parents capture yesterday?

"Is something the matter?" asks Dad, glancing at me in the rearview mirror.

I force my face into the excited expression I should have upon hearing this news. "I just can't believe she's really gone."

"Neither can I," says Mom. There's no hint of affection in her voice, no trace of the girl who promised her sister a big blue house by the water. "But she is. And she can't hurt us anymore."

I want to tell her she's wrong, that whoever they captured in Chicago isn't the real Boahinmaa. But if I say that, then I'll have to explain everything else I learned yesterday. And I'm not ready to talk about that yet—about the seal, about our family history, about Mom leaving her own sister to die. I'm not ready for this happy reunion I've dreamed of for so long to be over.

Dad takes us to IHOP for a celebratory Defeated a Vampire and Reunited the Family Breakfast. IHOP used to be my favorite restaurant in the whole world, but this French toast can't hold a candle to Miss Gloria's. Now, sitting in this booth, all I can think about is how Mateo would scan the menu for recipes to try and how Eunju, Roxy, and Gavin would argue over whether we should split the mozzarella sticks or chicken strips. I haven't even been in Rocky Gorge that long, but it feels like my life was an empty canvas before I came here and now every corner is filled with my friends.

The friends who have no idea what I really am or what I can do.

I must be sulking into my eggs, because Mom nudges my foot under the table. "Don't look so down, Serwa!" she says. "It's over! We've won!"

"But . . . what happens now?" I ask. It takes all my control not to touch the seal behind my ear. Is Mom's seal in that spot, too? How suspicious would it look if I tried to get a peek at it?

"Boahinmaa's fate is up to the Okomfo and the gods now. As for us, we've already been handed our next assignment. After we eat, we'll stop by the apartment to pack up your things and then head for the airport for our flight to San Francisco."

"We're leaving Rocky Gorge?" I squeak out. "But what about school?"

"You'll go back to homeschooling like we did before."

"But what about Auntie Latricia? She's going to freak if she gets back from work and I'm not there!"

"We already called her and explained the situation. She's a little sad that she won't be here to see us off, but you can always FaceTime her and Roxy to say goodbye."

I can't keep the shock off my face. Mom frowns. "You knew from the start that your stay here was temporary. I thought you'd be excited for things to go back to normal."

I should be excited. Not that long ago, I would've traded every single thing I owned if it meant never having to hear the name Rocky Gorge ever again. But that was before I actually got to know this place. That was before I had friends—actual friends—for the first time in my life. Now the thought of losing all this hurts just as much as losing the lake house did.

My throat closes up, so all I can do is nod.

But this is the way it's always been. My parents go places—I follow.

I'm fighting back tears all the way to the parking lot, but when Dad unlocks the car, I can't make myself get in.

If I get into that car, there will be no more late-night training sessions with the GCC. No more impromptu sleepovers, no more joking with the others about what Mr. Riley might look like if he grew a mustache.

No more Roxy. No more Eunju. No more Gavin. No more Mateo.

Just me and that empty-canvas life again.

"How do you know Boahinmaa?" I ask Mom, suddenly unable to keep everything inside.

Mom blinks. "Why do you ask?"

"It's just, back at the lake house, she spoke like she knew you. Did you know each other when you were younger?"

Tell me the truth, I silently beg. *Tell me the truth about what we are, what she was to you, and I'll tell you everything.*

She stares at me, an unreadable expression on her face.

Then she shakes her head. "I only know her from the battlefield. Nowhere else."

The world goes quiet except for a single word buzzing in my ears, over and over and over again:

Liar. Liar. Liar.

"Stop lying to me," I mumble.

"What?"

"I SAID, STOP LYING TO ME!"

You never, ever, E V E R raise your voice to Ghanaian parents. It's the fastest way to get your butt whooped straight to Asamando. But if the black magic inside me was a firecracker during Back-to-School Night, it's a volcano now, and nothing on earth can stop it from erupting over the three of us.

"I know everything! I know you're really an obayifo! I know Boahinmaa is your sister! And I know all about the seal you put on me!"

Mom and Dad both look like I just punched them in the gut. Part of me is still hoping against hope they'll tell me I'm wrong.

But they won't, because they can't.

"You lied to me!" I scream, not even caring that people in the parking lot are starting to stare. "All my life you've been lying! You sealed me up without ever planning to tell me! And my whole life you made me think black magic was the enemy, when you and I are the very things you taught me to hate!"

The magic pulses and swirls in me, begging to be let out, to do something that matches the anger coursing through my veins.

Dad takes a step forward, his hand extended in front of him like he's trying to placate a rabid dog. "Calm down, Serwa. Let's go somewhere and we can . . . we can talk about this."

"I don't want to go somewhere and talk about this! I want answers, and I want them now!"

Purple tendrils of black magic swirl around my hands, and my mom's hand instantly flies toward a ring she uses as a backup to Nokware.

Because my mom is scared. She's scared of *me*.

And that flinch, that movement shatters the tiny amount of control I still have left.

Before anyone else can say or do anything, I gather all the magic I can into my palm.

I touch the back of my ear.

And I break the seal.

41

How to Cause a Blackout

"Be careful who you put your faith in. Many paths once chosen cannot be untaken."

—From the *Nwoma*

IT'S LIKE ALL MY life I've been asleep, and now, for the first time, I'm truly awake.

Every single color, every single sound is magnified a thousandfold. I don't see the blue of the sky but the million little rainbow colors of light that humans see as blue. I don't hear so much as feel the blood pulsing through my parents' bodies as they realize what I've just done.

Alive. I feel *alive*.

"Serwa!" they cry, but they'd have better luck calling to a hurricane.

Mom runs toward me, but on instinct, I slam a shield of pure black magic between us. She summons her akrafena and begins hacking away at it.

"Serwa, listen to me!" she yells.

But I listened to her my whole life, and what did it get me?

Nothing but lies.

After several blows, her sword cuts through my shield, but that's enough time for me to draw Nokware.

Our weapons meet, and the *clang* rings through the entire parking lot. We fly like twin stars in what is not a training exercise this time but an actual battle with real weapons. Before, I could barely keep up with my mom's pace, but with the black magic—my magic—amplifying all my senses, I match her blow for blow. At one point I start to get the upper hand, only for my dad to jump in, daggers in both hands. Now I'm keeping them both at bay, whirling so fast anyone watching us probably just sees three brown-and-black blurs racing across the asphalt.

"Serwa, please!" Mom screams. "Let's talk about this!"

"Why, so you can lie to me some more?" I scream back.

Even as they try to subdue me, both she and my father are pulling their blows. Something about that only makes me angrier, muddling the shrieking thoughts coursing through my head. I thrust out a hand, and a wave of black magic sends a fissure in the parking lot snaking toward Mom. Dad jumps in front of her, shielding her from any damage, but his foot gets caught in the buckling asphalt and he falls. Mom screams his name, but before she can check on him, I throw myself at her.

Our weapons meet again, and a *crack* fills the air as Nokware shatters from the impact. We both go flying back, Mom hitting someone's van and me slamming into the IHOP sign so hard it tilts sideways. I'm back on my feet first, the golden hilt of Nokware still in my hand even though the blade is destroyed.

The truth literally lies in pieces at my feet.

People are all around us now, some filming on their phones, some calling 9-1-1, others just cheering. They think this is a show, that my life falling apart is some sort of stunt.

My pulse thumps louder and louder in my ears. *Monster!* the crowd must be whispering. *MONSTER!* they're screaming.

They're coming for me. They're going to kill me. Just like they tried to kill my aunt.

No. NO!

Adinkra require direction and precision, but black magic simply flows. The earth itself screams as a wave of power explodes from me, blanketing the entire area in a purple-black haze. Phones shatter in people's hands, the IHOP sign sparks and pops, and the traffic light at the street corner flashes several different colors before going dead. I spread my arms and the magic extends past what I can see until I can feel it curling around the very edges of town. Sirens start wailing, and shouts of alarm ring all over Rocky Gorge.

A blackout. I've caused a citywide blackout.

And through it all, the new shield I've put around me never fades, no matter how hard my parents attack it. They're screaming again, but I can't hear them over the sound of the magic roaring through my ears.

Mom finally claws her way through the shield. She lunges for me, but in an instant I become magic and energy, reappearing behind her. She lunges again, and I disappear again, this time stumbling at the other end of the parking lot. What the— I can teleport? I don't know, and I don't care. No time to think— I use the power to carry me far away from the scene of the crime and all the lies.

Teleport. Run. Teleport. Run.

Like this, I escape my parents, hurtling through the streets of Rocky Gorge.

The town looks like something out of an apocalypse movie.

My magic burst the fire hydrants, so water floods the streets, and the flashing lights of ambulances, fire engines, and police cars bathe the buildings.

Nobody knows what's happening and nothing is working, and this is my fault, this is all my fault. I did this, and—

I crash into someone who grabs me by the shoulders. "Serwa! What happened? Are you okay?" It's Auntie Francesca, the lady who runs the Ghanaian grocery store.

And now that I'm no longer running for my life, I feel it for the first time:

The hunger.

I've never wanted anything more than I want the blood I hear pulsing through her veins. My eyes fall to the soft skin of her neck, and my two front canines expand into fangs that poke past my bottom lip. Even though I'm shorter than Auntie Francesca, I overpower her easily, pinning her to the ground with one hand, my teeth inches from that sweet, sweet blood—

I catch my reflection in the older woman's glasses. The Serwa looking back at me is one I don't recognize, with fangs sharper than razors and eyes crimson and bright.

No! What am I doing? I recoil, my fangs retracting into my gums. I can hear my parents shouting behind me, less than a minute away from catching up, and I look down at Auntie Francesca's terrified face again.

I almost—I almost bit her. . . . No. I have to . . . I have to get out of here. I can't . . .

"Serwa!" screams Dad, but I summon the black magic with a single thought in my head: *Away.*

And just like a perfectly trained dog, my magic listens, whisking me away from the chaos I unleashed.

MY MAGIC DROPPED ME off in Sweetieville, the one place in town where my parents won't think to look for me and where I can't hurt anybody else. I'm sitting at the top of Marshmallow Mountain with my head between my knees trying to figure out what the heck just happened.

I broke the seal. I broke the seal and destroyed the town. I broke the seal and destroyed the town and hurt my dad and broke Nokware. I did this. No one else. Me.

Even now, the magic is still spinning inside me, just waiting for a command to go do its thing. I can't believe not even a full day has passed since I spoke to Boahinmaa, and now everything is horrible and it's all my fault.

I have to go back and face them. But if I do, Mom and Dad will take me to the Abomofuo, and then what? Will they kill me? Experiment on me to figure out how I'm able to use both divine wisdom and black magic at the same time without a seal?

No, I can't go back. Not like this.

But I can't hide out in this abandoned amusement park forever. My stomach is rumbling for both real food and blood, neither of which I have out here. I extend my fangs again and run my tongue over them. They're so sharp—I bet if I really wanted to, I could use them as scissors.

The image of me slicing through sheets of loose-leaf paper with my teeth is so funny that I begin to laugh hysterically, and then the laughter turns into tears and the tears into sobs. And now I'm just crying on top of an abandoned concrete mountain shaped like an ice cream sundae because my life is a joke.

I'm crying so hard that my heightened senses almost

miss the sound of several footsteps coming toward me.

"Serwa!" calls Gavin. I let out a small cry of relief at the sight of him and my other friends running onto Candy Cane Commons. Thank the gods, they weren't hurt during the blackout! I jump down from the mountain to join them, but that's when the smell of fresh blood hits me again, and the craving for it cracks through my body like lightning.

"Are you all right?" Roxy asks. "They let everyone out early because of the blackout, but when I went home you weren't there. Did something happen?"

She tries to reach for me, but I recoil back with my hand clamped tight over my nose and mouth. A line appears between her eyebrows. Gods, how do I even begin to explain the confrontation with my parents? "Yeah, I'm—"

Eunju frowns. "What's going on with your eyes?"

Nyame help me, I was so excited to see my friends that I forgot all about my glowing eye problem.

"I—um, I can explain—" I mumble, pressing my hand harder against my mouth in a futile attempt to fight the craving that is growing stronger by the second.

They step closer, and the blood scent overwhelms me so much it's hard to think about anything else.

"Y'all . . . how do we know this is really Serwa?" asks Gavin, and shock ripples through the group. Their wristbands begin to glow as their magic sparks to life alongside their suspicion. "How do we know this isn't an adze? Bullseye could've escaped and possessed her."

"I'm not an adze!" I cry, but to be fair, the fangs protruding from my mouth aren't really helping my case. The four of them close in on me, and the blood craving is so strong now I'm shaking.

"Serwa?" says Mateo, his voice pleading even as his hand

reaches for the wristwatch we enchanted to turn into his bow. "Say something. P-p-prove it's really you."

I can't. There's nothing I can say or do that can explain away the eyes or the blackout or the fangs. And if my friends get any closer, I don't think I can stop myself from hurting them in a way no amount of magic could ever fix.

All at once, I know what I have to do.

The others all cry out as my magic lifts them into the air, pinning their arms to their sides so they can't use their weapons or draw any Adinkra.

"What are you doing?" screams Eunju.

I give myself one last look at their faces—the faces of the only friends I've ever made and likely ever will.

"Something I should have done a long time ago."

And with that, my magic reaches into their minds to erase their memories.

Every joke we shared. Every battle we won. The big moments and the small—I take every single one. Now if the Abomofuo or anyone else come looking for me, all these kids will be able to tell them is that I'm Roxy's cousin who lived with her for a few weeks and never talked to anyone. And they won't even be lying, because their memories will reflect the fake truth. No one at school will ever be able to dispute it, either, because we rarely interacted there outside of the GCC meetings.

When there isn't any bit of me left in my friends' minds besides what someone might think about any random classmate, I turn around and I run. I don't know where I'm going or why.

I just run and run and run.

And then, suddenly, Boahinmaa is there, golden and beautiful, her arms outstretched. I throw myself into them and sob as she strokes my hair.

"I know," she whispers. That's all she says—those two words over and over again—as she picks me up and carries me away from the nightmare I created. The screech of sirens and screams of terror from the town fade away, and on instinct I burrow closer to my aunt. The black magic rolling off her once scared me so much, but now it's my only anchor in a world spiraling out of control.

One single fact cuts through my confusion and fear: I can't go back. My parents will never forgive me for attacking them like that. The Okomfo will never let me be a Slayer now that I've broken my seal.

Once again, the life I knew has been ripped from under my feet. But this time, I don't have friends to help me build a new one. All I have is myself, a power I don't understand, and an aunt I'm not sure I trust.

"Where are we going?" I ask between the tears. Boahinmaa strokes my hair, and it feels so much like how Mom used to that I almost start crying again.

"Home."

Author's Note

I WISH I COULD say I based Serwa Boateng on myself, but honestly? She is way, way, waaaaaaaay cooler than I was at twelve years old. While she spends seventh grade fighting vampires, I spent most of mine writing fanfic on DeviantArt.

But one thing we both have in common is being immigrants from Ghana. I wrote this book for anyone who relates to the feeling of straddling two worlds yet never fully belonging in either. When I felt most disconnected from my culture, I turned to stories of Anansi, Nyame, and all the other myths to remind myself that I was part of something bigger than I could ever imagine.

Ghana is a country comprised of more than a hundred tribes, each with their own unique histories and customs. While there are some overlaps among the various peoples, trying to say there is One Ghanaian Culture™ is like trying to argue there is one color of M&M—fundamentally untrue and, even if it wasn't, how boring would that be?

Serwa Boateng's Guide to Vampire Hunting draws mostly from the folklore and customs of the Akan ethnic group, of which the Ashanti and the Kwahu (my mom's tribe!) are both a part, among many others. But the adze is a creature from Ewe folklore (my maternal grandmother's tribe), and even the Adinkra themselves were created by the Bono people of a region now split between Ivory Coast and Ghana before the symbols were adopted by other groups. Not only that, but so many primary sources on the original history of our land were decimated during colonization, and much of what remained was warped by outsiders' colonial lenses.

All this is to say that some things in this story might be different from, or flat-out contradict, other depictions of the same concepts. If that sounds confusing, then congrats! You're learning the same lesson Serwa does—that the world rarely fits into neat little categories, no matter how badly we want it to.

While I tried to be as accurate as possible, what's fantasy without a little, well, fantasy? For example, Amokye, the old woman who guards the river between life and death, is a real folkloric figure. However, there's no record of her sending giant water lions after troublemaking children (. . . as far as we know, anyway). Think of this novel not as a textbook on Ghanaian folklore, but as a *remix* incorporating the old and new to create something recognizable yet all its own.

But that's how these stories have existed for as long as anyone can remember, from back when my ancestors told these myths to one another around the light of roaring fires to keep the night at bay. These are living, breathing tales that change juuuuust a bit with each telling, yet remain true to the spirit of the source. It is one of the greatest honors of my life to add my own to this ever-growing canon.

From the bottom of my heart, thank you for joining Serwa and me on this journey. Best of luck to you, Slayers. Now, if you'll excuse me, I have some fanfic to write.

Glossary

Aba (ah-buh) the Fante version of the day name of a girl born on a Thursday. Like Roxy!

Abomofuo (ah-boh-moh-FWO) *hunters* in Twi. An organization dedicated to defending the world from the forces of black magic. Comprised of Slayers (like me!), Middle Men, and Okomfo.

abosom (ah-BOH-sohm) the godly children of Nyame and Asaase Yaa, tasked to watch over the earth. Tend to be tied to physical locations, like rivers and lakes, though there are exceptions. Have enough intra-family drama to put the Kardashians to shame. Singular: **obosom** (oh-BOH-sohm)

Accra (ah-KRAH) the capital of Ghana

Acheampomaa (ah-chih-ahm-po-MAH-ah) a Ghanaian's girl's name and my middle name. Literally no one but my parents calls me that though, and only when I've messed up, like, really bad.

Adinkra (eh-dihn-KRAH) Akan symbols used to convey complex messages. Often tied to proverbs.

adze (ah-DJEH) a vampire that can transform into a firefly and possess the human mind. Bad news.

Akan (ah-KAHN) one of the largest ethnic groups in Ghana. In fact, they've lived in the region since long before it ever WAS Ghana! Comprised of lots of different subgroups.

Akosua (ah-koh-soo-YAH) Akan-given name for a female child born on a Sunday. Like my mom!

akrafena (ah-krah-fih-NAH) a traditional Ashanti sword that often has a black blade and a gold hilt. Often has Adinkra carved into it. Try not to touch the pointy end because it hurts—a lot. Just . . . trust me on this one.

akwaaba (ah-KWAH-ah-bah) *welcome* in Twi

akwadaa boni (ah-kwah-DAAH boh-NIH) *troublesome child* in Twi. Often used as a term of endearment. (*Most* of the time . . .)

Amankwah (ah-mahn-KWAH) a Ghanaian surname belonging to lots of perfectly nice people, and, unfortunately, my ETERNAL NEMESIS DECLAN

Amokye (ah-moh-CHIH) the old woman who guards the river at the boundary between life and death. In dire need of a vacation. Preeeetty sure she hates me.

Anansi (ah-nahn-SEE) an Akan folkloric figure sometimes depicted as a man, sometimes depicted as a spider, always depicted as a pain in the butt. Though he wasn't traditionally worshipped as a god, he has weaseled his way into the role over the centuries, much to the irritation of his actually divine siblings. Last I heard he was hanging with some kid from Chicago. . . .

Antoa Nyamaa (ahn-toh-AH nyah-MAH-ah) goddess of justice and retribution and one of the most powerful members of the pantheon. She can play a *wicked* bass solo, though!

Asaase Yaa (ah-SAH-ah-say yah) goddess of the earth and wife of Nyame. Her sacred day is Thursday. These days she seems to be more interested in upping her follower count than all that hippie-dippie forest stuff, though.

Asaman (ah-SAH-mahn) *ghost* in Twi

Asamando (ah-SAH-man-do) the realm of ghosts, aka the underworld. Home to the spirits of the ancestors and also some pretty great parties. Fun place to visit—as long as you're okay with never coming back.

Awurama (ah-woo-rah-MAH) literally means Lady Ama. A variation of the Akan day name Ama, given to a female child born on a Saturday. Like my dad's mother!

ayie (eh-yee-AY) a traditional Akan funeral. In the old times, used to last a whole week. Can actually be pretty upbeat. Remember those dancing Ghanaian pallbearers who went viral? That's what an ayie is like.

Bekoe (beh-koh-ee) a Ghanaian name comprised of *be* (came) and *koe* (to fight), so loosely translating to Fighter or Warrior. Often given to a child born during wartime, which might explain why Nana Bekoe is the way she is. . . .

Bia (bee-YUH) god of the bush and twin brother of Tano. Usually chill, until someone brings up that time his twin screwed him over. Then he gets *intense*.

Boahinmaa (bo-ah-hin-MAH-AH) a Ghanaian girl's name meaning *She who has left her people*

Boateng (bo-ah-TING) an Akan surname coming from the Twi words *boa* (help) and *tene* (to straighten/make upright), so it loosely translates to *helper*. There's lots of Boatengs running around Ghana, but I highly doubt I'm related to them all.

bofrot (BOH-froat) a West African dessert of fried dough rolled into balls and sometimes powdered with sugar. Also called buffloaf. I once ate thirteen in a single sitting. . . . World's most delicious mistake.

bonsam (bohn-SAHM) creatures of black magic with hooks for feet. They hang in trees waiting to drop down on unsuspecting victims.

day name a name given to an Akan child based on the day of the week on which they're born. There's lots of variations among the different tribes. However, not everyone goes by their day name.

djembe (djehm-BAY) **drum** a drum from West Africa made of a wooden body and an animal-skin head. Playing one well is a very impressive skill that I very much do not have.

Ɛ (eh) a vowel in the Akan alphabet. Pronounced similar to the first syllable in *elephant*.

Effi (eh-FEE) a Ghanaian girl's name

Fante (fahn-TEE) one of the subgroups of the Akan people, mainly located in the central and coastal regions of Ghana. My uncle Patrick and cousin Roxy come from this tribe!

Ga (gah) an ethnic group of Ghana, Togo, and Benin

Ghana (GAH-nuh) a West African nation sandwiched between Ivory Coast and Togo. It was once known as the British colony Gold Coast. Though they share the same name, the current country Ghana and the ancient empire Ghana were in two different locations!

Gollywood (GOH-lee-wood) a nickname for the film industry in Ghana. Imagine your favorite soap opera cranked up to a million. Their films are a lot like that. It's amazing.

-hene (heh-neh) a suffix added to a title to indicate leadership. Okomfohene = Leader of the Okomfo. Asantehene = Chief of the Ashanti people. You get the idea.

honam (hoh-NAHM) a person's body

jollof (joh-LOHF) a West African dish of rice cooked in a tomato stew, often garnished with meat, vegetables, and/or seafood. It is an indisputable fact that the Ghanaian version is the best kind. No, YOU'RE biased!!!

kente (kehn-TAY) a Ghanaian textile cloth woven with silk and cotton. It can be done in lots of different colors, but the orange, black, and green combo is the most famous. Traditionally it was only worn by royalty; nowadays anyone can wear it. (And look good while doing it, too!)

Kumasi (kooh-mah-SIH) second-largest city in Ghana and former capital of the Ashanti Empire. Literally means "Under the Kum Tree." Birthplace to lots of cool people, including some author who wrote a YA book about two teens trying to kill each other.

Kwabena (kwah-BEH-nah) Akan day name for a male child born on a Tuesday. Like my dad!

Kwaku (kway-KOO) an Akan day name for a boy born on a Wednesday. Fun fact, this is actually Anansi's first name!

Kwasi Benefo (kway-SEE beh-neh-FOH) a folkloric figure famous for being the only human to have ever entered Asamando and lived to tell the tale. His first name, Kwasi, is the Akan day name for a boy born on a Sunday. You'd think after his first couple of wives died he would've given up, but that's a romantic for you.

mako (meh-KOH) a hot-pepper sauce made with tomatoes, onion, and peppers. VERY! SPICY!!!

medaase (meh-DA-ah-si) *thank you* in Twi

medaase paa (meh-DA-ah-si pah) *thank you very much* in Twi

mmoatia (moh-AY-tee-UH) forest spirits specializing in healing magic. All Slayers are partnered with one upon passing their Initiation Test. They come in three kinds: red, black, and white. One singular mmoatia is technically an **aboatia**, but people use the terms interchangeably these days. All are extremely old and strangely obsessed with reality TV.

Nana (nah-NUH) a term given to a distinguished figure or elder, like a chief, priest, or god. Can also be a given name, like Nana Bekoe.

nokware (noh-KWAH-rih) *truth* in Twi. Something, apparently, *some* members of my family aren't very good at . . .

Nsamanfo (en-SAH-mahn-foh) the ancestors. They live down in Asamando, where I assume they're having the time of their afterlives.

Nsiah (en-see-AH) a Ghanaian name meaning sixth-born.

nwoma (en-WOH-muh) *book* in Twi. The *Nwoma* is a book containing all the wisdom passed down from the Abomofuo of old. When kids misbehave, they are forced to write sentences from it.

Nyame (nyah-MIH) most powerful god in the Akan pantheon. Also known as Onyame and Onyankopon, among other names. Created the world. Represented by the Adinkra gye nyame. Lives in the sky and never answers anyone's texts, much to his wife's and kids' chagrin.

Ɔ (OH) a vowel in the Akan alphabet. Pronunced similarly to the first syllable in *umbrella*.

obayifo (oh-bay-YEE-foh) a witch who controls black magic. Literally translates to *child snatcher*. Some suck human blood, others don't. VERY BAD NEWS.

obeah (oh-bay-YUH) a system of spiritual practices from the West Indies. There are theories that they derive from the Akan belief in the obayifo, though there is debate among scholars on the main origin.

Okomfo (oh-kohm-FOH) traditional priests working in service to the gods. They run the Abomofuo, overseeing the network of Middle Men, and the training and selection of all Slayers. Probably the grumpiest group of old people you'll ever meet.

Okomfohene (oh-kohm-FOH-heh-neh) leader of the Okomfo

okra (awh-KRAH) a soul. Not to be confused with the food, though the latter is delicious.

Oseiwa (oh-seh-WAH) female form of the name Osei and the traditional form of the name Serwa. Means *noble one*. I might be biased, but I like my spelling better.

Osu (oh-SOO) a neighborhood in Accra that borders the Atlantic Ocean

sasabonsam (sah-sah-bohn-SAHM) bigger, uglier cousin of the bonsam. Known for being bright pink.

Serwa (sehr-WAH) an alternate form of the name Oseiwa, which itself is the female form of the name Osei, meaning *noble one*. Not to be confused with the English name Sarah, *Mrs. Dean*.

shito (shih-taw) a hot pepper sauce made with dried fish and prawns. It is VERY. SPICY. You have been warned!

sunsum (soon-soom) a person's breath of life, spirit, or shadow. Also called **honhom** in some dialects.

Takoradi (tah-koh-rah-DEE) one half of the twin cities of Sekondi-Takoradi in southwestern Ghana

Tano (tah-NOH) god of war and the twin brother of Bia. Will do anything—and I mean *anything*—to win a fight. Kind of a jerk, but in an entertaining way.

Tegare (teh-gah-RIH) god of hunters and the patron deity of the Abomofuo. Probably the most reasonable of all the abosom (which isn't saying much, since their idea of "reason" is very different from ours).

Twi (chwee) a dialect of the Akan language spoken by millions of people in Ghana and around the world. Not to be confused with the first syllable in *Twitter* or *Twilight*. (Though the latter is my favorite vampire movie, and I'm not ashamed to admit it!)

waakye (wah-ah-CHEH) a Ghanaian dish made of rice and black-eyed beans boiled in sorghum leaves. Really good with eggs and shito!

Yeni aseda (yeh-NEE ah-sih-DAH) an idiom meaning *There are no thanks between u*s. Aka *No need to thank me.* Say this after paying for someone's lunch if you want them to love you forever.

Adinkra Dictionary

abode santann (ah-boh-dih-YEH sahn-TAHN)
- The all-seeing eye
- Symbol of the Abomofuo

adwo (ah-DJOH)
- Symbol of serenity and peace
- Used to calm down a target

akoben (ah-koh-BEHN)
- The war horn
- Used as a summons/call to action

akofena (ah-koh-feh-NUH)
- Swords of war
- Courage and authority
- Also literal swords

asaase ye duru (ah-SAH-ah-say yeh droo)
- Literally *The Earth has weight*
- Symbol of providence and Asaase Yaa, aka Mother Earth

asawa (as-SAH-wah)
- The sweet berry
- Symbol of sweetness and pleasure
- Used to create a pleasant, euphoric sensation

denkyem (DEHN-chehm)

- The crocodile
- Symbol of adaptability and cleverness
- Used to make something switch forms

dwennimmen (djwahn-nih-MAYN)

- The ram's horn
- Represents strength, humility, and concealment
- Used to hide/deflect attention from something

eban (eh-BAHN)

- Fence
- Creates barriers

epa (eh-PAH)

- The handcuffs
- Represent bondage, law and order, and slavery
- Creates a chain

gye nyame (jih nyah-MIH)

- Literally means *except Nyame*
- Symbol of Nyame
- From the proverb: "Abodee santan yi firi tete; obi nte ase a onim n'ahyase, na obi ntena ase nkosi n'awie, gye Nyame." = "This Great Panorama of creation dates back to time immemorial; no one lives who saw its beginning and no one will live to see its end, except Nyame."

hwe mu dua (shweh moo doo-YAH)

- The measuring stick
- Symbol of quality, perfection, and excellence
- Used to improve an object's innate qualities

hye wo nhye (sheh woh en-SHEH)

- Symbol of permanence and endurance
- Used to make a spell's effect permanent

mframadan (em-frahm-ah-DAHN)

- Wind house
- Symbolizes fortitude and security
- Used to strengthen an object

mpatapo (em-PAH-tah-POH)

- The reconciliation knot
- Symbolizes reconciliation, pacification, and peace
- Used to freeze/paralyze/repress a target

nkonsonkonson (en-kohn-SOHN-kohn-SOHN)

- The chain link
- Symbol of unity and brotherhood
- Used to forge connections

nkyimu (en-chih-MOO)

- Symbol of precision
- Used to increase an object's accuracy

nkyinkyin (en-CHEEN-cheen)

- Symbol of toughness and resilience
- Twisting
- Used to make a target sturdier

nsoromma (en-soh-roh-MAH)

- The star
- Symbol of faith
- Used to create light

nyame dua (nyah-MIH doo-YAH)

- Symbol of Nyame's protection
- Used as a protective ward to repel black magic

sankofa (sahn-koh-FAH)

- The bird with its head facing toward the past
- Symbol of remembrance
- Used to draw forth memories

sesa wo suban (say-SAH woh-soo-BAHN)

- Symbol of transformation, rebirth, and renewal
- Used to transform something from one state to another

Acknowledgments

YOU'D THINK BY THE time you release your fourth book, writing acknowledgments would be easier. But nope, it's as nerve-racking as ever! Still, I'm going to do my best to thank every person who helped bring *Serwa Boateng's Guide to Vampire Hunting* to life.

First, thanks to my agent, Quressa Robinson, for not laughing in my face when I said I had an idea for a young girl who hunted treasure and fought vampires. As soon as we dropped the treasure part, this became an actually good idea! Thank you to everyone at Nelson Literary Agency for all the work you do in championing authors.

Thank you to Rick Riordan, not just for picking my story to be a part of your imprint, but for writing Percy Jackson so that ten-year-old me could pick it up and fall in love with stories of modern-day kids full of adventure and mythology. Thank you to Stephanie Lurie and Ashley Fields for the editorial vision that pushed this story to the next level. Thank you to everyone in copyediting, design, production, sales, marketing, publicity, and every other department at Disney Hyperion who helped bring the book to life. You're all honorary Slayers now!

Thank you to all the scholars, historians, researchers, and regular people I spoke to in the process of researching Ghanaian histories and cultures. Special thanks to Simon Charwey for sharing your studies of Adinkra as both a design and a living language, and the late Aaron Mobley for compiling the Adinkra dictionary that I used as my primary reference for pronunciations and meanings. And thank you to Prof Dr. Adams Bodomo for a thorough analysis of the book's cultural accuracy and appropriateness.

An author is nothing without her village. Thank you to Deborah Falaye, Swati Teerdhala, June CL Tan, Deeba Zargarpur, Brittney Morris, Leah Johnson, Tracy Deonn, Tanvi Berwah, Crystal Seitz, Chelsea Beam, Namina Forna, Kwame Mbalia, and every other author friend who has sprinted with me/ encouraged me/commiserated with me at four a.m. during the process of wrangling this book into working order. You know who you are!

Thank you to my non-writer friends for listening to me spout conspiracy theories about vampires twenty-four seven. I'd like to think if any of you were being mind-controlled by vampires, I'd notice right away, but no promises there.

Last but not least, thank you to my family for always indulging me when I wanted to hear one more story. This is your tale as much as it is Serwa's. Wo nsa akyi beye wo de a ente se wo nsa yam.

COMING NEXT:

SERWA BOATENG'S
GUIDE TO
WITCHCRAFT AND MAYHEM